Small Favour

Small Favour

A novel of
the Dresden Files

Jim Butcher

www.orbitbooks.net

ORBIT

First published in Great Britain in 2008 by Orbit

A CIP catalogue record for this book is available from the British Library.

ISBN 978-1-84149-696-2

Typeset in Garamond 3 by
Palimpsest Book Production Limited, Grangemouth, Stirlingshire
Printed and bound in the UK by CPI Mackays, Chatham, ME5 8TD

Orbit
An imprint of
Little, Brown Book Group
100 Victoria Embankment
London EC4Y 0DY

An Hachette Livre UK Company
www.hachettelivre.co.uk

www.orbitbooks.net

For the forum-going fans at jim-butcher.com. I'm pretty sure your bosses would be upset if they saw your posting stats, guys, but I won't tell if you won't.

Acknowledgements

Many folks deserve thanks as usual, particularly my family, who has to put up with my insanity during deadline crunches; my agent, Jenn, who has to make excuses to my editor when I'm late; and my editor, Anne, who in turn has to make excuses for me to her bosses; plus the Beta Asylum, who have the ongoing task of pointing out warts on my babies. The lunatics.

This time I have to add new folks to the list – the local and visiting players at NERO Central, who were good enough to step around me during various roleplay and combat actions, while I finished off the last few chapters of *Small Favour* in the corner of the tavern.

1

Winter came early that year; it should have been a tip-off.

A snowball soared through the evening air and smacked into my apprentice's mouth. Since she was muttering a mantra-style chant when it hit her, she wound up with a mouthful of frozen cheer – which may or may not have been more startling for her than for most people, given how many metallic piercings were suddenly in direct contact with the snow.

Molly Carpenter sputtered, spitting snow, and a round of hooting laughter went up from the children gathered around her. Tall, blond, and athletic, dressed in jeans and a heavy winter coat, she looked natural in the snowy setting, her cheeks and nose turning red with the cold.

'Concentration, Molly!' I called. I carefully kept any laughter I might have wanted to indulge in from my voice. 'You've got to concentrate! Again!'

The children, her younger brothers and sisters, immediately began packing fresh ammunition to hurl at her. The backyard of the Carpenter house was already thoroughly chewed up from an evening of winter warfare, and two low 'fortress' walls faced each other across ten yards of open lawn. Molly stood between them, shivering, and gave me an impatient look.

'This can't possibly be real training,' she said, her voice quavering with cold. 'You're just doing this for your own sick amusement, Harry.'

I beamed at her and accepted a freshly made snowball from little Hope, who had apparently appointed herself my squire. I thanked the small girl gravely, and bounced the snowball on my palm a few times. 'Nonsense,' I said. 'This is wonderful practice. Did you think you were going to start off bouncing bullets?'

Molly gave me an exasperated look. Then she took a deep breath, bowed her head again, and lifted her left hand, her fingers spread wide. She began muttering again, and I felt the subtle shift of energies moving as she began drawing magic up around her in an almost solid barrier, a shield that rose between her and the incipient missile storm.

'Ready!' I called out. 'Aim!'

Every single person there, including myself, threw before I got to the end of *aim*, and snowballs sped through the air, flung by children ranging from the eldest, Daniel, who was seventeen, down to the youngest, little Harry, who wasn't yet big enough to have much of a throwing arm, but who didn't let that stop him from making the largest snowball he could lift.

Snowballs pelted my apprentice's shield, and it stopped the first two, the frozen missiles exploding into puffs of fresh powder. The rest of them, though, went right on through Molly's defenses, and she was splattered with several pounds of snow. Little Harry ran up to her and threw last, with both hands, and shrieked merry triumph as his bread-loaf-sized snowball splattered all over Molly's stomach.

'Fire!' I barked belatedly.

Molly fell onto her butt in the snow, sputtered some more, and burst out in a long belly laugh. Harry and Hope, the youngest of the children, promptly jumped on top of her, and from there the lesson in defensive magic devolved into the Carpenter children's long-standing tradition of attempting to shovel as much snow as possible down the necks of one another's coats. I grinned and stood there watching them, and a moment later found the children's mother standing beside me.

Molly took after Charity Carpenter, who had passed her coloring and build on to her daughter. Charity and I haven't always seen eye-to-eye – well, in point of fact, we've hardly ever seen eye-to-eye – but tonight she was smiling at the children's antics.

'Good evening, Mister Dresden,' she murmured.

'Charity,' I replied amiably. 'This happen a lot?'

'Almost always, during the first real snowfall of the year,' she said. 'Generally, though, it's closer to Christmas than Halloween.'

I watched the children romping. Though Molly was growing quickly, in a number of senses, she reverted to childhood easily enough here, and it did me good to see it.

I sensed Charity's unusually intense regard and glanced at her, lifting an eyebrow in question.

'You never had a snowball fight with family,' she said quietly, 'did you?'

I shook my head and turned my attention back to the kids. 'No family to have the fight with,' I said. 'Sometimes the kids would try, at school, but the teachers wouldn't let it happen. And a lot of times the other kids did it to be mean, instead of to have fun. That changes things.'

Charity nodded, and also looked back at the kids. 'My daughter. How is her training progressing?'

'Well, I think,' I said. 'Her talents don't lie anywhere close to the same areas mine do. And she's never going to be much of a combat wizard.'

Charity frowned. 'Why do you say that? Do you think she isn't strong enough?'

'Strength has nothing to do with it. But her greatest talents make her unsuited for it in some ways.'

'I don't understand.'

'Well, she's good with subtle things. Delicate things. Her ability at handling fine, sensitive magic is outstanding, and increasing all the time. But that same sensitivity means that she has problems handling the psychic stresses of real combat. It also makes the gross physical stuff a real challenge for her.'

'Like stopping snowballs?' Charity asked.

'Snowballs are good practice,' I said. 'Nothing gets hurt but her pride.'

Charity nodded, frowning. 'But you didn't learn with snowballs, did you.'

The memory of my first shielding lesson under Justin DuMorne wasn't a particularly sentimental one. 'Baseballs.'

'Merciful God,' Charity said, shaking her head. 'How old were you?'

'Thirteen.' I shrugged a shoulder. 'Pain's a good motivator. I learned fast.'

'But you aren't trying to teach my daughter the same way,' Charity said.

'There's no rush,' I said.

The noise from the children stopped, dropping to furtive whispers, and I winked at Charity. She glanced from the children to me, amusement evident in her face. Not five seconds later Molly shouted, 'Now!' and multiple snowballs came zipping toward me.

I lifted my left hand, focusing my will, my magic, and drew it into the shape of a broad, flat disk in front of me. It wasn't a good enough shield to stop bullets, or even well-thrown baseballs, but for snowballs it was just fine. They shattered to powder on my shield, revealing it in little flashes of pale blue light as a circular plane of force centered on the outspread fingers of my extended left hand.

The children laughed as they cried out their disapproval. I shouted, 'Hah!' and lifted a triumphant fist.

Then Charity, standing behind me, dumped a double handful of snow down the neck of my coat.

I yelped as the cold ate my spinal cord, jumped up out of my tracks, and danced around trying to shake the snow out from under my clothes. The children cheered their mother on and began flinging snowballs at more or less random targets, and in all the excitement and frivolity I didn't realize that we were under attack until the lights went out.

The entire block plunged into darkness – the floodlights illuminating the Carpenters' backyard, house lights in every nearby home, and the streetlights were all abruptly extinguished. Eerie, ambient werelight reflected from the snow. Shadows suddenly yawned where there had been none before, and the scent of something midway between a skunk and a barrel of rotting eggs assaulted my nostrils.

I yanked my blasting rod out of its holder on the inside of my coat and said to Charity, 'Get them inside.'

'Emergency,' Charity said in a far calmer voice than I had managed. 'Everyone into the safe room, just like in practice.'

The children had just begun to move when three creatures I had never seen before came bounding through the snow. Time slowed as the adrenaline hit my system, and it felt like I had half an hour to study them.

They weren't terribly tall, maybe five-foot-six, but they were layered with white fur and muscle. Each had a head that was almost goatlike, but the horns atop them curled around to the front like a bull's rather than arching back. Their legs were reverse-jointed and ended in hooves, and they moved in a series of single-legged leaps more than running. They got better air than a Chicago Bull, too, which meant I was dealing with something with supernatural strength.

Though, thinking about it, I couldn't actually remember the last time I'd dealt with something that *didn't* have supernatural strength, which is one of the drawbacks of the wizard business. I mean, some things are stronger than others, sure, but it wouldn't much matter to my skull if a paranormal bruiser could bench-press a locomotive or if he was merely buff enough to juggle refrigerators.

I trained the tip of my blasting rod on the lead whatsit, and then a bunch of snow fell from above in my peripheral vision, landing on the ground beside me with a soft thump.

I threw myself into a forward dive, rolled over one shoulder, and came to my feet already moving laterally. I was just in time to avoid the rush of a fourth whatsit, which had knocked the snow loose just before it dropped down onto me from the tree house Michael had built for his kids. It let out a hissing, bubbling snarl.

I didn't have time to waste with this backstabbing twit. So I raised the rod as its tip burst into scarlet flame, unleashed my will, and snarled, '*Fuego!*'

A wrist-thick lance of pure flame leapt from the blasting rod and seared the creature's upper body to blackened meat. The excess heat melted snow all around it and sent up a billow of scalding steam. Judging by the tackle hanging between the thing's legs as the steam burst up from the snow, it probably inflicted as much pain as the actual fire.

The whatsit went down, and I had to hope that it wasn't bright enough to play possum: The Carpenter children were screaming.

I whirled around, readying the rod again, and didn't have a clear shot. One of the white-furred creatures was running hard after Daniel, Molly's oldest brother. He'd begun to fill out, and he ran with his fingers locked on the back of the coats of little Harry and Hope, the youngest children, carrying them like luggage.

He gained the door with the creature not ten feet behind him, its wicked-looking horns lowered as it charged. Daniel went through the door and kicked it shut with his foot, never slowing down, and the creature slammed into it head-on.

I hadn't realized that Michael had installed all-steel, wood-paneled security doors on his home, just as I had on mine. The creature probably would have pulverized a wooden door. Instead it slammed its head into the steel door, horns leading the way, and drove a foot-deep dent into it.

And then it lurched away, letting out a burbling shriek of pain. Smoke rose from its horns, and it staggered back, swatting at them with its three-fingered, clawed hands. There weren't many things that reacted to the touch of steel like that.

The other two whatsits had divided their attention. One was pursuing Charity, who was carrying little Amanda and running like hell for the workshop Michael had converted from a free-standing garage. The other was charging Molly, who had pushed Alicia and Matthew behind her.

There wasn't time enough to help both groups, and even less to waste over the moral dilemma of a difficult choice.

I turned the rod on the beastie chasing Charity and let it have it. The blast hit it in the small of its back and knocked it from its hooves. It flew sideways, slamming into the wall of the workshop, and Charity dashed through the door with her daughter.

I turned my blasting rod back to the other creature, but I already knew that I wouldn't be in time. The creature lowered its horns and closed on Molly and her siblings before I could line up for another shot.

'Molly!' I screamed.

My apprentice seized Alicia's and Matthew's hands, gasped out a word, and all three of them abruptly vanished.

The creature's charge carried it past the space they'd been in, though something I couldn't see struck its hoof and sent it staggering. It wheeled around at full speed, kicking up snow as it did, and I felt a sudden, fierce surge of exaltation and pride. The grasshopper might not be able to put up a decent shield, but she could do veils like they were going out of style, and she'd kept her focus and her wits about her.

The creature slowed, head sweeping, and then it saw the snow being disturbed by invisible feet, moving toward the house. It bawled out another unworldly cry and went after them, and I didn't dare risk another blast of flame – not with the Carpenters' house in the line of fire. So instead I lifted my right hand, triggered one of the triple-layered rings on it with my will, and sent a burst of raw force at the whatsit.

The unseen energy struck it in the knees, throwing its legs out from under it with such strength that its head slammed into the snow. The disturbance in the snow rushed around toward the front door of the house. Molly must have realized that the deformation of the security door would make it difficult, if not impossible, to open, and once again I felt fierce approval.

But it faded rather rapidly when the whatsit that had been playing possum behind me slammed into the small of my back like a sulfur-and-rotten-egg-driven locomotive.

The horns hit hard and it hurt like hell, but the defensive magic on my long black leather duster kept them from impaling me. The impact knocked the wind out of me, snapped my head back sharply, and flung me to the snow. Everything got confusing for a second, and then I realized that it was standing over me, ripping at the back of my neck with its claws. I hunched my shoulders and rolled, only to be kicked in the nose by a cloven hoof, and an utterly gratuitous amount of pain came with a side order of whirling stars.

I kept trying to get away, but my motions were sluggish, and the whatsit was faster than me.

Charity stepped out of the workshop with a steel-hafted ball-peen hammer in her left hand, and a heavy-duty contractor's nail gun in her right.

She lifted the nail gun from ten feet away and started pulling the trigger as she walked forward. It made *phut-phut-phut* sounds, and the already seared whatsit started screaming in pain. It leapt up wildly, twisting in agonized gyrations in midair, and fell to the snow, thrashing. I saw heavy nails sticking up out of its back, and the smoking wounds were bleeding green-white fire.

It tried to run, but I managed to kick its hooves out from under it before it could regain its footing.

Charity whirled the hammer in a vertical stroke, letting out a sharp cry as she did, and the steel head of the tool smashed open the whatsit's skull. The wound erupted with greyish matter and more green-white fire, and the creature twitched once before it went still, its body being consumed by the eerie flame.

I stood up, blasting rod still in hand, and found the remaining beasties wounded but mobile, their yellow, rectangular-pupiled eyes glaring in hate and hunger.

I ditched the blasting rod and picked up a steel-headed snow shovel that had been left lying next to one of the children's snow forts. Charity raised her nail gun, and we began walking toward them.

Whatever these things were, they didn't have the stomach for a fight against mortals armed with cold steel. They shuddered as if they had been a single being, then turned and bounded away into the night.

I stood there, panting and peering around me. I had to spit

blood out of my mouth every few breaths. My nose felt like someone had superglued a couple of live coals to it. Little silver wires of pain ran all through my neck, from the whiplash of getting hit from behind, and the small of my back felt like one enormous bruise.

'Are you all right?' Charity asked.

'Faeries,' I muttered. 'Why did it have to be faeries?'

2

'Well,' Charity said, 'it's broken.'

'You think?' I asked. The light touch of her fingers on my nose was less than pleasant, but I didn't twitch or make any sounds of discomfort while she examined me. It's a guy thing.

'At least it isn't out of place,' Michael said, knocking snow off of his boots. 'Getting it set back is the sort of thing you don't mind forgetting.'

'Find anything?' I asked him.

The big man nodded his head and set a sheathed broadsword in a corner against the wall. Michael was only a couple of inches shorter than me, and a lot more muscular. He had dark hair and a short beard, both of them peppered with silver, and wore blue jeans, work boots, and a blue-and-white flannel shirt. 'That corpse is still there. It's mostly a burned mess, but it didn't dissolve.'

'Yeah,' I said. 'Faeries aren't wholly beings of the spirit world. They leave corpses behind.'

Michael grunted. 'Other than that there were footprints, but that's about it. No sign that these goat-things were still around.' He glanced into the dining room, where the Carpenter children were gathered at the table, talking excitedly and munching the pizza their father had been out picking up when the attack occurred. 'The neighbors think the light show must have come from a blown transformer.'

'That's as good an excuse as any,' I said.

'I thank God no one was hurt,' he said. For him it wasn't just an expression. He meant it literally. It came of being a devout Catholic, and maybe from toting around a holy sword with one of the nails from the Crucifixion wrought into the blade. He shook himself and gave me a short smile. 'And you, of course, Harry.'

'Thank Daniel, Molly, and Charity,' I said. 'I just kept our visitors busy. Your family's who got the little ones to safety. And Charity did all the actual smiting.'

Michael's eyebrows went up, and he turned his gaze on his wife. 'Did she now?'

Charity's cheeks turned pink. She briskly swept up the various tissues and cloths I'd bloodied, and carried them out of the room to be burned in the lit fireplace in the living room. In my business, you don't ever want samples of your blood, your hair, or your fingernail clippings lying around for someone else to find. I gave Michael the rundown of the fight while she was gone.

'My nail gun?' he asked, grinning, as Charity came back into the kitchen. 'How did you know it was a faerie?'

'I didn't,' she said. 'I just grabbed what was at hand.'

'We got lucky,' I said.

Michael arched an eyebrow at me.

I scowled at him. 'Not every good thing that happens is divine intervention, Michael.'

'True,' Michael said, 'but I prefer to give Him the credit unless I have a good reason to believe otherwise. It seems more polite than the other way around.'

Charity came to stand at her husband's side. Though they were both smiling and speaking lightly about the attack, I noticed that they were holding hands very tightly, and Charity's eyes kept drifting over toward the children, as if to reassure herself that they were still there and safe.

I suddenly felt like an intruder.

'Well,' I said, rising, 'looks like I've got a new project.'

Michael nodded. 'Do you know the motive for the attack?'

'That's the project,' I said. I pulled my duster on, wincing as the motion made me move my stiffening neck. 'I think they were after me. The attack on the kids was a diversion to give the one in the tree a shot at my back.'

'Are you sure about that?' Charity asked quietly.

'No,' I admitted. 'It's possible that they're holding a grudge about that business at Arctis Tor.'

Charity's eyes narrowed and went steely. Arctis Tor was the heart of the Winter Court, the fortress and sanctum sanctorum of Queen Mab herself. Some nasty customers from Winter had stolen Molly, and Charity and I, with a little help, had stormed the tower and taken Molly back by main force. The whole mess had been noisy as hell, and we'd pissed off an entire nation of wicked fae in the process of making it.

'Keep your eyes open, just in case,' I told her. 'And let Molly know that I'd like her to stay here for the time being.'

Michael quirked an eyebrow at me. 'You think she needs our protection?'

'No,' I said. 'I think you might need hers.'

Michael blinked. Charity frowned quietly, but did not dispute me.

I nodded to both of them and left. Molly wasn't rebelling against everything I told her to do purely upon reflex these days, but fait accompli remained the best way of avoiding arguments with her.

I shut the door to the Carpenter household behind me, cutting off the scent of hot pizza and the sound of loudly animated children's voices, raucous after the excitement.

The November night was silent. And very cold.

I fought off an urge to shiver and hurried to my car, a beat-up old Volkswagen Beetle that had originally been powder blue, but was now a mix of red, blue, green, white, yellow, and now primer grey on the new hood my mechanic had scrounged up. Some anonymous joker who had seen too many Disney movies had spray-painted the number 53 inside a circle on the hood, but the car's name was the Blue Beetle, and it was going to stay that way.

I sat looking at the warm golden light coming from the house for a moment.

Then I coaxed the Beetle to life and headed for home.

3

'And you're sure they were faeries?' Bob the skull asked.

I scowled. 'How many other things get their blood set on fire when it touches iron and steel, Bob? Yes, I think I know a faerie when I get my nose broken by one.'

I was down in my lab, which was accessed by means of a trapdoor in my basement apartment's living room and a folding wooden stepladder. It's a concrete box of a room, deep enough under the rest of the boardinghouse I live in to be perpetually cool. In the summer that's nice. Come winter, not so much.

The lab consisted of a wooden table running down the center of the room, and was surrounded on three sides by tables and workbenches against the outer wall of the room, leaving a narrow walkway around the table. The workbenches were littered with the tools of the trade, and I'd installed those white wire shelving units you can get pretty cheap at Wal-Mart on the walls above the benches, creating more storage space. The shelves were covered with an enormous variety of containers, from a lead-lined box to burlap bags, from Tupperware to a leather pouch made from the genital sac of, I kid you not, an actual African lion.

It was a gift. Don't ask.

Candles burned around the room, giving it light and twinkling off the pewter miniature buildings on the center table, a scale model of the city of Chicago. I'd brought down a single writing desk for Molly – all the room I had to spare – and her own notebooks and slowly accumulating collection of gear managed to stay neatly organized despite the tiny space.

'Well, it looks like someone is holding Arctis Tor against you,' Bob said. The skull, its eye sockets glowing with orange flickers of light like candles you couldn't quite see, sat on its own shelf on the uncluttered wall. Half a dozen paperback romance novels littered the shelf around it, and a seventh had fallen from the shelf and now lay on the floor, obscuring a portion of the silver summoning circle I'd installed there. 'Faeries don't ever forget a grudge, boss.'

I shook my head at the skull, scooped up the fallen book, and put it back on the shelf. 'You ever heard of anything like these guys?'

'My knowledge of the faerie realms is mostly limited to the Winter end of things,' Bob said. 'These guys don't sound like anything I've run into.'

'Then why would they be holding the fight at Arctis Tor against me, Bob?' I asked. 'Hell, we weren't even the ones who really assaulted Winter's capital. We just walked in on the after-math and picked a fight with some of Winter's errand boys who had swiped Molly.'

'Maybe some of the Winter Sidhe hired out the vengeance gig as contract labor. These could have been Wyldfae, you know. There's a lot more Wyld than anything else. They *could* have been satyrs.' His eyelights brightened. 'Did you see any nymphs? If there are satyrs, there's bound to be a nymph or two somewhere close.'

'No, Bob.'

'Are you sure? Naked girl, drop-dead gorgeous, old enough to know better and young enough not to care?'

'I'd have remembered that if I'd seen it,' I said.

'Feh,' Bob said, his eyelights dwindling in disappointment. 'You can't do anything right, Harry.'

I rubbed my hand against the back of my neck. It didn't make it hurt any less, but it gave me something to do. 'I've seen these goat guys, or read about them before,' I said. 'Or at least something close to them. Where did I put those texts on the near reaches of the Nevernever?'

'North wall, green plastic box under the workbench,' Bob provided immediately.

'Thanks,' I said. I dragged out the heavy plastic storage box. It was filled with books, most of them leather-bound, hand-written treatises on various supernatural topics. Except for one book that was a compilation of 'Calvin and Hobbes' comic strips. How had that gotten in there?

I picked up several of the books, carried them to the part of the table that was modeled as Lake Michigan, and set them down. Then I pulled up my stool and started flipping through them.

'How was the trip to Dallas?' Bob asked.

'Hmmm? Oh, fine, fine. Someone was being stalked by a Black Dog.' I glanced up at the map of the United States hanging on the wall beneath Bob's shelf on a thick piece of poster board. I absently plucked a green thumbtack from the board and poked it into Dallas, Texas, where it joined more than a dozen other green pins and a very few red ones, where the false alarms had been. 'They contacted me through the Paranet, and I showed them how to give Fido the bum's rush out of town.'

'This support network thing you and Elaine have going is really smart,' Bob said. 'Teach the minnows how to gang up when a big fish shows up to eat them.'

'I prefer to think of it as teaching sparrows to band together and chase off hawks,' I said, returning to my seat.

'Either way, it means less exposure to danger and less work for you in the long run. Constructive cowardice. Very crafty. I approve.' His voice turned wistful. 'I hear that they have some of the best strip clubs in the world in Dallas, Harry.'

I gave Bob a hard look. 'If you're not going to help me, at least don't distract me.'

'Oh,' Bob said. 'Check.' The romance I'd put back on the shelf quivered for a second and then flipped over and opened to the first page. The skull turned toward the book, the orange light from its eyes falling over the pages.

I went through one old text. Then two. Then three. Hell's bells, I knew I'd seen or read something in one of these.

'Rip her dress off!' Bob shouted.

Bob the skull takes paperback romances very seriously. The next page turned so quickly that he tore the paper a little. Bob is even harder on books than I am.

'That's what I'm talking about!' Bob hollered as more pages turned.

'They couldn't have been satyrs,' I mumbled out loud, trying to draw my thoughts into order. My nose hurt like hell and my neck hurt like someplace in the same zip code. That kind of pain wears you down fast, even when you're a wizard who learned his basics while being violently bombarded with baseballs. 'Satyrs have human faces. These things didn't.'

'Weregoats?' Bob suggested. He flipped another page and kept reading. Bob is a spirit of intellect, and he multitasks better than, well, pretty much anybody. 'Or maybe goatweres.'

I stopped for a moment and gave the skull an exasperated look. 'I can't believe I just heard that word.'

'What?' Bob asked brightly. 'Weregoats?'

'Weregoats. I'm fairly sure I could have led a perfectly rich and satisfying life even if I hadn't heard that word or enjoyed the mental images it conjures.'

Bob chortled. 'Stars and stones, you're easy, Harry.'

'Weregoats,' I muttered, and went back to reading. After finishing the fifth book, I went back for another armload. Bob shouted at his book, cheering during what were apparently the love scenes and heckling most of the rest, as if the characters had all been live performers on a stage.

Which would probably tell me something important about Bob, if I were an astute sort of person. After all, Bob himself was, essentially, a spiritual creature created from the energy of thought. The characters within a book were, from a certain point of view, identical on some fundamental level – there weren't any images of them, no physical tangibility whatsoever. They were pictures in the reader's head, constructs of imagination and ideas, given shape by the writer's work and skill and the reader's imagination. Parents, of a sort.

Did Bob, as he read his books and imagined their events,

regard those constructed beings as . . . siblings, of some sort? Peers? Children? Could a being like Bob develop some kind of acquired taste for a family? It was entirely possible. It might explain his constant fascination with fictional subject matter dealing with the origins of a mortal family.

Then again, he might regard the characters in the same way some men do those inflatable sex dolls. I was pretty sure I didn't want to know.

Good thing I'm not astute.

I found our attackers on the eighth book, about halfway through, complete with notes and sketches.

'Holy crap,' I muttered, sitting up straight.

'Find 'em?' Bob asked.

'Yeah,' I said, and held up the book so he could see the sketch. It was a better match for our goatish attackers than most police sketches of perpetrators. 'If the book is right, I just got jumped by gruffs.'

Bob's romance novel dropped to the surface of the shelf. He made a choking sound. 'Um. Did you say gruffs?'

I scowled at him and he began to giggle. The skull rattled against the shelf.

'Gruffs?' He tittered.

'What?' I said, offended.

'As in "The Three Billy Goats Gruff"?' The skull howled with laughter. 'You just got your ass handed to you by a *nursery tale?*'

'I wouldn't say they handed me my ass,' I said.

Bob was nearly strangling on his laughter, and given that he had no lungs it seemed gratuitous somehow. 'That's because you can't see yourself,' he choked out. 'Your nose is all swollen up and you've got two black eyes. You look like a raccoon. Holding a dislocated ass.'

'You didn't see these things in action,' I said. 'They were strong, and pretty smart. And there were four of them.'

'Just like the Four Horsemen!' he said. 'Only with petting zoos!'

I scowled some more. 'Fine, fine,' I said. 'I'm glad I can amuse you.'

'Oh, absolutely,' Bob said, his voice bubbling with mirth. ' "Help me, help me! It's the Billy Goats Gruff!" '

I glared. 'You're missing the point, Bob.'

'It can't be as funny as what has come through,' he said. 'I'll bet every Sidhe in Winter is giggling about it.'

'Bet they're not,' I said. 'That's the point. The gruffs work for Summer. They're some of Queen Titania's enforcers.'

Bob's laughter died abruptly. 'Oh.'

I nodded. 'After that business at Arctis Tor, I could understand if someone from Winter had come after me. I never figured to do this kind of business with Summer.'

'Well,' Bob pointed out, 'you did kind of give Queen Titania's daughter the death of a thousand cuts.'

I grunted. 'Yeah. But why send hitters now? She could have done it years ago.'

'That's faeries for you,' Bob said. 'Logic isn't exactly their strong suit.'

I grunted. 'Life should be so simple.' I thumped my finger on the book, thinking. 'There's more to this. I'm sure of it.'

'How high are they in the Summer hierarchy?' Bob asked.

'They're up there,' I said. 'As a group, anyway. They've got a reputation for killing trolls. Probably where the nursery tale comes from.'

'Troll killers,' Bob said. 'Trolls. Like Mab's personal guard, whose pieces you found scattered all over Arctis Tor?'

'Exactly,' I said. 'But what I did there ticked off Winter, not Summer.'

'I've always admired your ability to be unilaterally irritating.'

I shook my head. 'No. I must have done something there that hurt Summer somehow.' I frowned. 'Or helped Winter. Bob, do you know—'

The phone started ringing. I had run a long extension cord from the outlet in my bedroom down to the lab, after Molly had nearly broken her neck rushing up the stepladder to answer a call. The old windup clock on one shelf told me that it was after midnight. Nobody calls me that late unless it's something bad.

'Hold that thought,' I told Bob.

'It's me,' Murphy said when I answered. 'I need you.'

'Why, Sergeant, I'm touched,' I said. 'You've admitted the truth at last. Cue sweeping romantic theme music.'

'I'm serious,' she said. Something in her voice sounded tired, strained.

'Where?' I asked her.

She gave me the address and we hung up.

I barely ever got work from Chicago PD anymore, and between that and my frequent trips to other cities as part of my duties as a Warden, I hadn't been making diddly as an investigator. My stipend as a Warden of the White Council kept me from bankruptcy, but my bank account had bled slowly down to the point where I had to be really careful to avoid bouncing checks.

I needed the work.

'That was Murphy,' I said, 'making a duty call.'

'This late at night, what else could it be?' Bob agreed. 'Watch your back extra careful, boss.'

'Why do you say that?' I said, shrugging into my coat.

'I don't know if you're up on your nursery tales,' Bob said, 'but if you'll remember, the Billy Goats Gruff had a whole succession of brothers.'

'Yeah,' I said. 'Each of them bigger and meaner than the last.'

I headed out to meet Murphy.

Weregoats. Jesus.

4

I was standing there watching the fire with everyone else when the beat cop brought Murphy over to me.

'It's about time,' she said, her voice tense. She lifted the police tape and beckoned me. I had already clipped my little laminated consultant's ID to my duster's lapel. 'What took you so long?'

'There's a foot of snow on the ground and it doesn't show signs of stopping,' I replied.

She glanced up at me. Karrin Murphy is a wee little thing, and the heavy winter coat she wore only made her look smaller. The large, fluffy snowflakes still falling clung to her golden hair and glittered on her eyelashes, turning her eyes glacial blue. 'Your toy car got stuck in a drift, huh? What happened to your face?'

I glanced around at all the normals. 'I was in a snowball fight.'

Murphy grunted. 'I guess you lost.'

'You should have seen the other guy.'

We were standing in front of a small five-story apartment building, and something had blown it to hell.

The front facing of the building was just gone, as if some unimaginably huge ax had sliced straight down it. You could see the floors and interiors of empty apartments, when you could get a glimpse of them through the pall of dust and smoke and thick falling snow. Fires burned in the building, insubstantial behind the haze of flame and winter. Rubble had washed out into the street, damaging the buildings on the other side, and the police had everyone cordoned off at least a block away. Broken glass and steel and brick lay everywhere. The air was acrid, thick with the stench of burning materials never meant to feed a fire.

Despite the weather, a couple of hundred people had gathered at the police cordons. Some enterprising soul was selling hot coffee from a big thermos, and I hadn't been too proud to cough up a dollar for a foam cup of java, powdered creamer, and a packet of sugar.

'Lots of fire trucks,' I noted. 'But only one ambulance. And the crew is drinking coffee while everyone else shivers in the cold.' I sipped at my cup. 'The bastards.'

'Building wasn't occupied,' Murphy said. 'Being renovated, actually.'

'No one got hurt,' I said. 'That's a plus.'

Murphy gave me a cryptic look. 'You willing to work off the books? Per diem?'

I sipped coffee to cover up a wince. I far prefer a two-day minimum. 'I guess the city isn't coughing up much money for consultants, huh?'

'SI's been pooling the coffee money, in case we needed your take on something.'

This time I didn't bother to hide the wince. Taking money from the city government was one thing. Taking money from the cops in SI was another.

Special Investigations was the CPD's version of a pool filter. Things that slipped through the areas of interest of the other departments got dumped on SI. Lots of times those things included the cruddy work no one else wanted to do, so SI wound up investigating everything from apparent rains of toads to dogfighting rackets to reports of El Chupacabra molesting neighborhood pets from its lair in a local sewer. It was a crappy job, no pun intended, and as a result SI was regarded by the city as a kind of asylum for incompetents. They weren't, but the inmates of SI generally did share a couple of traits – intelligence enough to ask questions when something didn't make sense, and an inexcusable lack of ability when it came to navigating the murky waters of office politics.

When Sergeant Murphy had been Lieutenant Murphy, she'd been in charge of SI. She'd been busted for vanishing during twenty-four particularly critical hours of an investigation. It wasn't like she could tell her superiors that she was off storming a frozen fortress in the near reaches of the Nevernever, now, could she? Now her old partner, Lieutenant John Stallings, was in charge of SI, and he was running the place on a strained, frayed, often knotted shoestring of a budget.

Hence the lack of gainful employment for Chicago's only professional wizard.

I couldn't take their money. It wasn't like they were rolling in it. But at the same time, they had their pride. I couldn't take that, either.

'Per diem?' I told her. 'Hell, my bank account is thinner than a tobacco lobbyist's moral justification. I'll go hourly.'

Murphy glowered up at me for a moment, then gave me a grudging nod of thanks. Proud doesn't always outweigh practical.

'So what's the scoop?' I asked. 'Arson?'

She shrugged. 'Explosion of some kind. Maybe an accident. Maybe not.'

I snorted. 'Yeah, because you call me in on maybe-accidents all the time.'

'Come on.' Murphy pulled a dust mask from her coat pocket and put it on.

I took out a bandanna and tied it around my nose and mouth. All I needed was a ten-gallon hat and some spurs to complete the image. Stick 'em up, pahdner.

She glanced back at me, her face hard to read under the dust mask, and led me to the building adjacent to the ruined apartment. Murphy's partner was waiting for us.

Rawlins was a blocky man in his fifties, comfortably overweight, and looked about as soft as a Brinks truck. He'd grown in a beard frosted with grey, a sharp contrast against his dark skin, and he wore a weather-beaten old winter coat over his off-the-rack suit.

'Dresden,' he said easily. 'Good to see you.'

I shook his hand. 'How's the foot?'

'It aches when I'm about to get asked to leave,' he said soberly. 'Ow.'

'It's better if you've got deniability,' Murphy said, folding her arms in what an astute observer might have characterized as a tone of stubborn argument. 'You've got a family to feed.'

Rawlins sighed. 'Yeah, yeah. I'll be out by the street.' He nodded to me and walked off. He'd recovered from being shot in the foot pretty well, and wasn't limping. Good for him. Good for me, too. I'd been the one to get him into that mess.

'Deniability?' I asked Murphy.

'There hasn't been anything specific,' Murphy said, 'but people up the line from SI have made it very clear that you are persona non grata.'

That stung a bit, and my voice turned a shade more brittle than I had intended. 'Oh, obviously. The way I keep helping CPD with things they couldn't handle themselves is just inexcusable.'

'I know,' Murphy said.

'I'm lucky they haven't charged me with gross competence and contributing to social order and had me locked away.'

She waved a tired, dismissive hand. 'It's always something. That's the way organizations are.'

'Except that when the country club gets a bug up its nose and decides that someone is out, nobody dies as a result,' I said, and added, 'mostly.'

Murphy glared at me. 'What do you want me to do about it, Harry? I called in every chip I'd ever collected just to keep my fucking job. There's no chance at all of me making command again, much less moving up to a position where I could effect real change within the department.'

I clenched my jaw and felt a flush rising up my neck. She hadn't said it, but she'd lost her command and any bright future for her career because she'd been covering my back. 'Murph—'

'No,' she said, her tone calmer and steadier than it might have been. 'I'd really like to know, Dresden. I've paid you out of my own pocket when the city wouldn't spend it. The rest of

SI throws in all the money they can spare into the kitty to be able to pay you when we really need you. You think maybe I should moonlight at a burger joint to pay your fees?'

'Hell's bells, Murph,' I said. 'It isn't about the money. It's never been about the money.'

She shrugged. 'So what are you bitching about?'

I thought about it for a second and said, 'You shouldn't have to tap-dance around the demands of all the ladder climbers to do your job.'

'No,' she said, her tone frank. 'Not in a reasonable world. But if you haven't noticed, that world must be in a different area code. And it seems to me that you've had to end-run your superiors once or twice.'

'Bah,' I said. 'And touché.'

She smiled faintly. 'It sucks, but that's what we've got. You done whining?'

'Hell with it,' I said. 'Let's work.'

Murphy jerked her head at the rubble-choked alley between the damaged building and its neighbor, and we started down it, climbing over fallen brick and timber where necessary.

We'd gone about three feet before the stench of sulfur and acrid brimstone seared my nostrils, sharp even through the smell of the gutted apartment building. There's only one thing that smells like that.

'Crap,' I muttered.

'I thought it smelled familiar,' Murphy said. 'Like back at the fortress.' She glanced at me. 'And . . . the other times I've smelled it.'

I pretended not to notice her glance. 'Yeah. It's Hellfire,' I said.

'There's more,' Murphy said quietly. 'Come on.'

We pressed on down the alley until we passed the edge of the wrecked portion of the gutted building. One step, there was nothing but wreckage. The next, the brick wall of the building reasserted itself. The demarcation between structure and havoc was a rough, jagged line stretching up into the dust and the snow and the smoke – all except for a portion of wall perhaps five feet off the ground.

There, instead of a broken line of shattered brick and twisted rebar, a perfectly smooth semicircle bit into the wall.

I leaned closer, frowning. The scent of Hellfire grew stronger, and I realized that something had *melted* its way through the brick wall – a shaft of energy like a giant drill bit. It had to have been almost unimaginably hot to vaporize brick and concrete and steel, leaving the rim of the area it had touched melted to smooth glass, though half of the basketball-sized circle was missing, carried away by the collapsing wall.

Any natural source of heat like that would have sent out a thermal bloom that would have scoured the alley I was standing in, leaving it blackened and sere. But the alley was littered with the usual city detritus, where it wasn't choked with rubble, and several hours' worth of snow had piled up there as well.

'Talk to me,' Murphy said quietly.

'No normal fire is this contained,' I said.

'What do you mean?'

I gestured vaguely with my hands. 'Fire generated with magic is still *fire*, Murph. I mean, sure, you can call up tremendous heat and energy, but once it gets to you it *behaves* like heat. It still does business with the laws of thermodynamics.'

'So we're talking mojo,' Murphy said.

'Well, technically mojo isn't—'

She sighed. 'Are we dealing with magic or not?'

As if the scent of Hellfire weren't enough to give it away. 'Yeah.'

Murphy nodded. 'You call up fire all the time,' she said. 'I've seen it do a lot of things that didn't look like normal fire.'

'Oh, sure,' I said, holding my hand over the surface of the flame-bored bricks. They were still warm. 'But if you want to control it once you call it up, it takes additional energy to focus the fire into a desired course. Controlling the energy is usually as much effort as the fire itself, if not more.'

'Could you do something like this?' she asked, gesturing at the building.

Once upon a time she would have inflected that question a whole lot differently, and I'd have gotten nervous about whether the hands in her pockets were holding a gun and handcuffs. But that had been a long time ago. Of course, back then I probably wouldn't have given her a straight answer either, like I would now.

'Not a chance in hell,' I said quietly, and not entirely metaphorically. 'I'm pretty sure I couldn't call up this much energy in the first place. And even if I could, I wouldn't have anything left to control it with.' I closed my eyes for a moment, trying to feel any lingering traces of power around the area, but the destruction and subsequent drift of dust and snow and smoke had obscured any coherent patterns that might have given me hints about how the working had been accomplished.

I did, however, notice something else. The surface of the cut was not perpendicular to the wall of the building. It went in at an angle. I frowned and squinted back behind me, trying to line it up with the wall of the building on the other side of the alley.

Murphy knew me well enough to see I'd noticed something, and I knew her well enough to see her sudden interest make furrows between her eyebrows as she forced herself to be quiet and let me work.

I got up and went to the far side of the alley. A light coating of snow and dust had coated the wall.

'Watch your eyes,' I murmured, squinting my own to slits. Then I raised my right hand, called up my will, and murmured, '*Ventas reductas.*'

The wind I called up wasn't the usual burst I commonly used. It was far more toned-down than that, and it poured steadily from my outstretched hand. All the work I was doing with Molly had allowed me to rethink a lot of my basic evocations, the fast and dirty magic that wizards used in desperate and violent situations. I'd been trying to teach the spell to Molly, but she didn't have the raw strength I had, and it would have practically knocked her unconscious to call up a heavy blast of air. I'd modified my teaching, just to get her comfortable with using a bit of air magic, and we'd accidentally developed a passable impersonation of an electric blow-dryer.

I used the dryer spell to gently brush away dust and snow from the wall. It took me about a minute and a half, and when I was finished I caught another scent under the brimstone stench and said, 'Double crap.'

Murphy stepped forward with her flashlight and shone it on the wall.

The sigil had been painted on the wall in something thick and brown that smelled like blood. At first I thought it was a pentacle, but I saw the differences immediately.

'Harry,' Murphy said quietly. 'Is it human?'

'Most likely,' I said. 'Mortal blood is the strongest ink you can use for symbols like this in high-energy spells. I don't think anything else could have contained the amounts of energy it would have taken to blow up this building.'

'It's a pentacle, right?' Murphy asked. 'Like the one you wear.'

I shook my head. 'Different.'

'How so?' Her mouth twitched at one corner. 'Other than the blood, I mean.'

'A pentacle is a symbol of order,' I said quietly. 'Five points, five sides. It represents the forces of air, earth, water, fire, and spirit. It's contained within a circle, the points touching the outer ring. It represents the forces of magic bound within human control. Power balanced with restraint.' I gestured at the symbol. 'See here? The points of the star fall far outside the ring.'

She frowned. 'What does it mean?'

'I have no idea,' I said.

'Gosh,' she said. 'You're worth the money.'

'Ha-ha. Look, even if I'd seen this symbol before, it could mean different things to different people. The Hindus and the Nazis have very different ideas about the swastika, for example.'

'Can you make a guess?'

I shrugged. 'Off the top of my head? This looks uncomfortably like a combination of the pentacle and the anarchy symbol. Magic unrestrained.'

'Anarchist wizards?' Murphy asked.

'It's just a guess,' I said. My gut told me it was a good one, though, and I got the impression that Murphy had the same feeling.

'What's the symbol for?' Murphy asked. 'What is it meant to do?'

'Reflect power,' I said. 'My guess is that the energy that drove through the building was reflected from this sigil, which means . . .' I kayaked down a logic cascade as I spoke. 'Which means that the energy had to come *in* from somewhere else first.' I turned around slowly, trying to judge the angles. 'The incoming beam must have gone right through the collapsed part of the building and—'

'Beam?'

I pointed at the semicircular hole in the ruined wall. 'Yeah. Heat energy, a whole lot of it.'

She studied the hole. 'It doesn't look like it would be big enough to take down the building.'

'It isn't,' I said. 'Not in an explosion, anyway. This just drilled a hole. Might have started a fire as it went, but it couldn't have sheared off the front of the building like that.'

Murphy frowned, tilting her head. 'Then what did?'

'Working on it,' I mumbled. I judged the angles as best I could and took off down the alley. The firemen were still hard at work on the building, and we had to walk over several hoses as we emerged into the street at the back of the apartment building. I crossed the street and walked down the length of the building there, my hand raised, senses questing for any residual magic. I didn't find any, but I did smell Hellfire again, and a couple of feet later I found another not-pentacle, identical to the first, also hidden under a light dusting of snow.

I kept going clockwise around the ruined building. I found two more symbols on the undamaged building on its next side, and one more across the street from the front of the ruined apartments, and then I completed the circle, arriving back at our original reflective symbol.

Five reflection points, which had guided a truly freaking frightening amount of energy through the building, forming one single, enormous shape as they did.

'It's a pentagram,' I said quietly.

Murphy frowned. 'What?'

I touched the round, smooth bore mark on the destroyed building's wall. 'The beam of energy that ripped through the building right here was one of five sides of a pentagram. A five-pointed star.'

Murphy regarded me blankly.

I reached into my pocket and pulled out a piece of chalk. 'Okay, look. Everyone learns to draw this in grade school, right?' I quickly sketched out a star on a clear bit of brick wall – five strokes of the chalk, forming five points. 'Right?'

'Right,' Murphy said. 'You get them from the teacher when you get an A.'

'Another example of symbols having disparate meanings,' I said. 'But look here, in the middle.' I filled in the closed shape in the center of the star. 'That's a pentagon shape, see? The center of the pentagram. That's where you contain whatever it is you're trying to contain.'

'What do you mean, contain?'

'A pentagram like this one is a symbol of power,' I said. 'It's got a lot of uses, depending on how you employ it. But most often you use it to isolate or contain an entity.'

'You mean like summoning a demon,' Murphy said.

'Sure,' I said. 'But you can use it to trap other things too, if you do it right. Remember the circle of power at Harley MacFinn's place? Five candles formed the pentagram on that one.'

Murphy shuddered. 'I remember. But it wasn't this big.'

'No,' I admitted. 'And the bigger you make it, the more juice it takes to keep it going. I've never, ever heard of one that would take this much energy to activate.'

I drew little X shapes at the points of the star and drew the chalk from one to the next, thickening the lines of the example pentagram. 'Get it? The beam streamed from one reflector to the next, melting holes through the building as it went. The reflectors formed the beam into one huge pentagram at ground level, more or less.'

Murphy frowned and squinted at the simple diagram. 'The center of that shape couldn't have covered the whole building.'

'No,' I said. 'I'd need a good map to be sure, but I think the center of the pentagram must have been about twenty feet back from the front door. Which is why only the front half of the building collapsed.'

'The explosion came from inside this pentagon thing? Magical TNT?'

I shrugged. 'The explosion came from inside the pentagram's center, but not necessarily *from* the pentagram. I mean, it could have been a normal device of some kind.'

'Square in the middle of the giant, scary pentagram?' Murphy asked.

'Maybe,' I said, nodding. 'It depends on what the pentagram was being employed for. And to know that, I'd have to know which way was its north.' I circled the topmost point of the chalk pentacle. 'The direction of the first line, I mean.'

'Does it make a difference?'

'Yeah,' I said. 'Most everybody draws those stars just like I did. Bottom left to the topmost point as the first stroke. That's how you draw it when you want to defend something, ward something away from a location, or banish a spiritual entity.'

'So this could have been a banishing spell?' Murphy asked.

'It's possible. But you can do a lot of other things with it, if you draw it differently.'

'Like build a cage for things,' Murphy said.

'Yeah.' I frowned, troubled. 'Or open a doorway for something.'

'Which, judging by your face, would be bad.'

'I . . .' I shook my head. I didn't even want to know what kind of terror would need a pentagram that huge in order to squeeze into our world. 'I think if something sized to fit this pentagram had come through it, there would probably be more than one building on fire.'

'Oh,' Murphy said quietly.

'Look, until I know what the pentagram's purpose was, all I can do is speculate. And there's something else weird here, too.'

'What's that?'

'There's not a trace of residual magic, and there should be. Hell, with this much power being tossed around, the whole area should practically be glowing. It isn't.'

Murphy nodded slowly. 'You're saying they wiped their prints.'

I grimaced. 'Exactly, and I have no idea how to do it. Hell's bells, I didn't know it was *possible*.'

I sipped at my coffee in the silence and pretended the shiver that went down my spine was from the cold. I passed the cup to Murphy, who took a sip from the opposite side and passed it back to me.

'So,' she said, 'we're left with questions. What is a major-league supernatural hitter doing placing a huge pentagram under an empty apartment building? What was his goal in creating it?'

'And why blow up the building afterward?' I frowned and thought of an even better question. 'Why *this* building?' I turned to Murphy. 'Who owns it?'

'Lake Michigan Ventures,' Murphy replied, 'a subsidiary of Mitigation Unlimited, whose CEO is—'

'Triple crap,' I spat. 'Gentleman Johnnie Marcone.'

5

I tried to collect some of the blood in the reflective symbols and use it in a tracking spell to follow it back to its original owner, but it was a bust. Either the blood was already too dry to use or else the person who had donated it was dead. I had a bad feeling it wasn't the winter air that made the spell fail.

Typical. Nothing was ever simple when Marcone was involved.

Gentleman Johnnie Marcone was the robber baron of the streets of Chicago, and the undisputed lord of its criminal underworld. Though he'd long been under legal siege, the bastions of paperwork defended by legions of lawyers had never been conquered, and his power base had grown steadily and quietly. They probably could have tried harder to take him down, but the heartless fact of the matter was that Marcone's management style was a better alternative than most. He'd put the *civil* back in *civil offender*, harshly cutting down on violence against civilians and law enforcement alike. It didn't make his business any less ugly, just tidier, but it could have been worse, as far as the city's authorities were concerned.

Of course, the authorities didn't know that it *was* worse. Marcone had begun expanding his power base into the supernatural world as well, signing on to the Unseelie Accords as a freeholding lord. It made him, in the eyes of the authorities of the supernatural world, a kind of small, neutral state, a recognizable power, and I had no doubt that he'd begun using that new power to do what he always did – create more of the same.

All of which had been made possible by Harry Dresden. And the truly galling thing about the entire situation was that it had been the least evil of the options that had been available to me at the time.

I looked up from the circle I'd chalked on the concrete beneath a sheltered overhang in the alley and shook my head. 'Sorry. Can't get anything. Maybe the blood is too dry. Maybe the donor is dead.'

Murphy nodded. 'I'll keep an eye on the morgues, then.'

I broke the circle with a swipe of my hand and rose from my knees.

'Can I ask you something?' Murphy said.

'Sure.'

'Why don't you ever use pentagrams? All I ever see you draw is circles.'

I shrugged. 'PR mostly. Run around making lots of five-pointed stars in this country and people start screaming about Satan. Including the satanists. I've got enough problems. If I need a pentagram, I usually just imagine it.'

'You can do that?'

'Magic's in your head, mostly. Building an image in your mind and holding it there. Theoretically you could do everything without any chalk or symbols or anything else.'

'Then why don't you?'

'Because it's a pointlessly difficult effort for identical results.' I squinted up at the still-falling snow. 'You're a cop. I need a doughnut.'

She snorted as we left the alley. 'Stereotype much, Dresden?'

'Cops do a lot of running around in their cars, and they don't always get to control their hours, Murph. Lots of times they can't leave a crime scene to hit a drive-through. So they need food that can sit in a car for hours and hours without tasting foul or giving them food poisoning. Doughnuts are good for that.'

'So are granola bars.'

'Is Rawlins a masochist, too?'

Murphy casually bumped her shoulder against my arm when I was between steps, making me wobble, and I grinned. We emerged onto the mostly empty street. The firemen had been wrapping up their job when I arrived, and every truck but one had departed. Once the flames were out the show was over, and there were no rubberneckers anymore. Only a few cops were in sight, most of them in their cars.

'So what happened to your face?' Murphy asked.

I told her.

She concealed a smile. ' "The Three Billy Goats Gruff"?'

'Hey. They're tough, all right? They kill trolls.'

'I saw you do that once. How hard could it be?'

I found myself grinning. 'I had a little help.'

Murphy matched my smile. 'One more short joke and I'm taking a kneecap.'

'Murphy,' I chided, 'petty violence is beneath you. Which is saying something.'

'Keep it up, wise guy. I'm always going to be taller than you once you're lying unconscious on the ground.'

'You're right. That was a low blow. I'll try to rise above it.'

She showed me a clenched fist. 'Pow, Dresden. Right to the moon.'

We reached Murphy's car. Rawlins was in the passenger seat, pretending to snore. He wasn't the sort to just fall asleep.

'So, Summer made a run at you,' Murphy said. 'You think the attack on Marcone's building is connected with that?'

'I lost my faith in coincidence,' I said.

'Get in,' she said. 'I'll give you a ride home.'

I shook my head. 'There might be something I can do here, but I need to be alone. And I need a doughnut.'

Murphy arched a delicate dark-gold eyebrow. 'Ooooooo-kay.'

'Get your mind out of the gutter and give me the damned doughnut.'

Murphy shook her head and got in her car. She tossed me a sack from Dunkin' Donuts that was sitting on Rawlins's side of the dashboard.

'Hey!' Rawlins protested without opening his eyes.

'For a good cause,' I told him, nodding my thanks to Murphy. 'Call you when I know something.'

She frowned at my nose. 'You sure you want to be alone?'

I winked one of my blackened eyes at her. 'Some things a wizard has to do for himself,' I said.

Rawlins swallowed a titter.

I get no respect.

They drove off and left me in the silently falling snow in the still hours before dawn. There were still a couple of fire crews and uniform cops there, the latter blocking off the street, though the former weren't actively firefighting. The building was out, and coated in a layer of ice – but I guess there always could have been something hidden in the walls and ready to pop out again. I overheard one of them telling another that the road crew that was supposed to clean the rubble out of the street was helping a city plow truck stuck in the snow, and would be there when they could.

I trudged to about a block away, found an alley not choked, and went in with my doughnut. I debated for a moment what approach I would take. My relationship with this particular source had changed over the years, after all. Reason indicated that sticking with long-standing procedure was my best bet. Instinct told me that reason had disappointed me more than once, and that it wasn't thinking in the long term anyway.

Over the years, my instincts and I have gotten cozy.

So, instead of bothering with a simple bait-and-snare, I braced my feet, held out my right hand palm up, placed the doughnut upon it like an offering, and murmured a Name.

Names, capital N, have power. If you know something's Name, you automatically have a conduit with which you can reach out and touch it, a way to home in on it with magic. Sometimes that can be a really bad idea. Speak the Name of a big, bad spiritual entity and you might be able to touch it, sure – but it can touch *you* right back, and the big boys tend to do it a lot harder than any mortal. It's worth as much as your soul to speak the Name of beings like that.

But the Nevernever is a big place, and not to mix metaphors, but there are plenty of fish in that sea. There are literally count-less beings of far less metaphysical significance, and it really isn't terribly difficult to get one of them to do your bidding by invoking its Name.

(People have Names, too. Sort of. Mortals have this nasty habit of constantly reassessing their personal identity, their values, their beliefs, and it makes it a far more slippery business to use a mortal's Name against them.)

I know a few Names. I invoked this one as lightly and gently as I could in an effort to be polite.

It didn't take me long, maybe a dozen repetitions of the Name before the entity it summoned appeared. A basketball-sized globe of blue light dived out of the snow overhead and hurtled down the alley toward my face.

I stood steady as it came on. Even with relatively minor summonings, you never let them see you flinch.

The globe snapped to an instant halt about a foot away from the doughnut, and I could just make out the luminous shape of the tiny humanoid figure within. Tiny, but not nearly so tiny as the last time I had seen him. Hell's bells, he must have been twice as tall as the last time we'd spoken.

'Toot-toot,' I said, nodding to the pixie.

Toot snapped to attention, piping, 'My lord!' The pixie looked like an athletically slender youth, dressed in armor made of discarded trash. His helmet had been made from the cap to a three-liter bottle of Coca-Cola, and tufts of his fine lavender hair drifted all around its rim. He wore a breastplate made from what looked like a carefully reshaped bottle of Pepto-Bismol, and carried a box knife sheathed in orange plastic on a rubber-band strap over one shoulder. Rough lettering on the box knife's case, written in what looked like black nail polish, proclaimed, *Pizza or Death!* A long nail, its base carefully wrapped in layers of athletic adhesive tape, was sheathed in the hexagonal plastic casing of a ballpoint pen at his side. He must have lifted the boots from a Ken doll, or maybe a vintage GI Joe.

'You've grown,' I said, bemused.

'Yes, my lord,' Toot-toot barked.

I arched an eyebrow. 'Is that the box knife I gave you?'

'Yes, my lord!' he shrilled. 'This is my box knife! There are many who like it, but this one is mine!' Toot's words were crisply precise, and I realized that he was imitating the drill sergeant from *Full Metal Jacket*. I throttled the sudden smile trying to fight its way onto my face. It looked like he was taking it seriously, and I didn't want to crush his tiny feelings.

What the hell. I could play along. 'At ease, soldier.'

'My lord!' he said. He saluted by slapping the heel of his hand against his forehead and then buzzed a quick circle around the doughnut, staring at it intently. 'That,' he declared, in a voice much more like his usual one, 'is a doughnut. Is it *my* doughnut, Harry?'

'It could be,' I said. 'I'm offering it as payment.'

Toot shrugged disinterestedly, but the pixie's dragonfly wings buzzed in excitement. 'For what?'

'Information,' I said. I jerked my head at the fallen building. 'There was a seriously large sigil-working done in and around that building several hours ago. I need to know anything the Little Folk know about what happened.' A little flattery never hurt. 'And when I need information from the Little Folk, you're the best there is, Toot.'

His Pepto-armored chest swelled up a bit with pride. 'Many of my people are beholden to you for freeing them from the pale hunters, Harry. Some of them have joined the Za-Lord's Guard.'

'Pizza Lord' was the title some of the Little Folk had bestowed upon me – largely because I provided them with a weekly bribe of pizza. Most don't know it, even in my circles, but the Little Folk are everywhere, and they see a lot more than anyone expects. My policy of mozzarella-driven goodwill had secured the affections of a lot of the locals. When I'd demanded that a sometime ally of mine set free several score of the Folk who had been captured, I'd risen even higher in their collective estimation.

Even so, 'Za-Lord's Guard' was a new one on me.

'I have a guard?' I asked.

Toot threw out his chest. 'Of course! Who do you think keeps the Dread Beast Mister from killing the brownies when they come to clean up your apartment? We do! Who lays low the mice and rats and ugly big spiders who might crawl into your bed and nibble on your toes? We do! Fear not, Za-Lord! Neither the foulest of rats nor the cleverest of insects shall disturb your home while we draw breath!'

I hadn't realized that in addition to the cleaning service, I'd acquired an exterminator too. Handy as hell, though, now that I thought about it. There were things in my lab that wouldn't react well to becoming rodent nest material.

'Outstanding,' I told him. 'But do you want the doughnut or not?'

Toot-toot didn't even answer. He just shot off down the alleyway like a runaway paper lantern, but so quickly that he left falling snow drifting in contrail spirals in his wake.

Typically speaking, faeries get things done in a hurry – when they want to, at any rate. Even so, I'd barely had time to hum through 'When You Wish Upon a Star' before Toot-toot returned. The edges of the sphere of light around him had changed color, flushing into an agitated scarlet.

'Run!' Toot-toot piped as he streaked down the alley. 'Run, my lord!'

I blinked. Of all the things I'd imagined hearing from the little fae on his return, that had not been on my list.

'Run!' he shrilled, whirling in panicked circles around my head.

My brain was still processing. 'What about the doughnut?' I asked, like an idiot.

Toot-toot zipped over to me, set his shoulders against my forehead and pushed for all he was worth. He was stronger than he looked. I had to take a step back or be overbalanced. 'Forget the doughnut!' he shouted. 'Run, my lord!'

Forget the doughnut?

That, more than anything, jarred me into motion. Toot-toot was not the sort to give in to panic. For that matter, the little fae had always seemed to be . . . not ignorant so much as *innocent* of the realization of danger. He'd always been oblivious to danger in the past, when there was mortal food on the line.

In the silence of the snowy evening I heard a sound coming from the far end of the alley. Footsteps, quiet and slow.

A quivering, fearful little voice in my head told me to listen to Toot, and I felt my heart speed up as I turned and ran in the direction he'd indicated.

I cleared the alley and turned left, slogging through the deepening snow. There was a police station only two or three blocks from here. There would be lights and people there, and it would probably serve as a deterrent to whatever was after me. Toot flew beside me, just over my shoulder, and he'd produced a little plastic sports whistle. He blew on it in a sharp rhythm, and through the falling snow I dimly saw half a dozen spheres of light of various colors, all smaller than Toot's, appear out of the night and begin to parallel our course.

I ran for another block, then two, and as I did I became increasingly certain that something was following in my wake. It was a disturbing sensation, a kind of crawly tingle on the back of my neck, and I was sure that I had attracted the attention of something truly terrible. Mounting levels of fear followed that realization, and I ran for all I was worth.

I turned right and spotted the police station house, its exterior lighting a promise of safety, its lamps girded with haloes in the falling snow.

Then the wind came up and the whole world turned frozen and white. I couldn't see anything, not my own feet as I struggled through the snow, and not the hand I tried holding up in front of my face. I slipped and went down, and then bounced back to my feet in a panic, certain that if my pursuer caught me on the ground, I would never stand again.

I slammed a shoulder into a light pole and staggered back from it. I couldn't tell which way I was facing in the whiteout. Had I accidentally stumbled into the street? There would probably be no cars moving in this mess, but if one was, even slowly,

I'd never see it in time to get out of the way. I wouldn't be able to hear a car horn either.

The snow was coming so thick now that I had trouble breathing. I picked a direction that seemed as if it would take me to the police station and hurried on. Within a few steps I found a building with one outstretched hand. I used it to guide me, leaning one hand against the solid wall. That worked fine for twenty feet or so, and then the wall vanished, and I stumbled sideways into an alley.

The howling wind went silent, and the sudden stillness around me was a shock to my senses. I pushed myself to my hands and knees and looked behind me. On the street the blinding curtain of snow still swirled, thick and white and impenetrable, beginning as suddenly as a wall. In the alley the snow was barely an inch deep, and except for a distant moan of wind it was silent.

At that instant I realized that the silence was not an empty one.

I wasn't alone.

The glittering snow on the alley floor blended seamlessly into a sparkling white gown, tinted here and there with streaks of frozen blue or glacial green. I lifted my eyes.

She wore the gown with inhuman elegance, its rippling fabric draping with feminine perfection, her body a perfect balance of curves and planes, beauty and strength. The gown was cut low, and left her shoulders and arms bare. Her skin made the snow seem a bit sallow by comparison. Glittering colors flickered at her wrists, her throat, and upon her fingers, always changing, cycling through deep blue and green and violet iridescence. Her fingernails glittered with the same impossibly shifting hues.

Upon her head was a circlet of ice, elegant and intricate, as if it had been formed from a single crystalline snowflake. Her hair was long, past her hips, long and silken and white, blending into the gown and the snow. Her lips – her gorgeous, sensual lips – were the color of frozen raspberries.

She was a vision of beauty, the kind that has inspired artists for centuries, immortal beauty that is rarely imagined, much less actually seen. Beauty like hers should have struck me sense-less with joy. It should have made me weep and give thanks to the Almighty that I had been allowed to look upon it. It should have stopped my breath and made my heart lurch with delight.

It didn't.

It terrified me.

It terrified me because I could also see her eyes. They were wide, feline eyes, vertically slitted like a cat's. They shifted color in time with her gems – or, more likely, the gems changed color in time with her *eyes*. And though they, too, were beautiful beyond the bounds of mortality, they were cold eyes, inhuman eyes, filled with intelligence and desire, but empty of compassion or pity.

I knew those eyes. I knew *her*.

If fear hadn't taken the strength from my limbs, I would have run.

A second form appeared from the darkness behind her and hovered in the shadows at her side like an attendant. It resem-bled the outline of a cat – if any domestic cat ever grew so large. I couldn't see the color of its fur, but its green-gold eyes reflected the cold blue light, luminous and eerie.

'And well should you bow, mortal,' mewled the feline shape. Its voice was damned eerie, throbbing in strange cadences while producing human sound from an inhuman throat. 'Bow before Mab, the Queen of Air and Darkness. Bow before the monarch of the Unseelie fae, the Winter Court of the Sidhe.'

6

I gritted my teeth and tried to summon up a salvo of snark. It wouldn't come. I was just too scared – and with good reason.

Think of every fairy-tale villainess you've ever heard of. Think of the wicked witches, the evil queens, the mad enchantresses. Think of the alluring sirens, the hungry ogresses, the savage she-beasts. Think of them and remember that somewhere, sometime, they've all been real.

Mab gave them *lessons*.

Hell, I wouldn't be surprised if she'd set up some sort of certification process, just to make sure they were all up to snuff.

Mab was the ruler of fully half of the realm of Faerie, those areas of the Nevernever, the spirit world, closest to our own, and she was universally respected and feared. I'd seen her, seen her in the merciless clarity of my wizard's Sight, and I knew – not just suspected, but *knew* – exactly what kind of creature she was.

Fucking terrifying, that's what. So terrifying that I couldn't summon up a single wiseass comment, and that just doesn't happen to me.

I couldn't talk, but I could move. I pushed myself to my feet. I shook with the cold and the fear, but faced the Faerie Queen and lifted my chin. Once I'd done that, proved that I knew where my backbone was, I was able to use it as a reference point to find my larynx. My voice came out coarse, rough with apprehension. 'What do you want with me?'

Mab's mouth quivered at the corners, turning up into the tiniest of smiles. The feline voice spoke again as Mab tilted her head. 'I want you to do me a favor.'

I frowned at her, and then at the dimly seen feline shape behind her. 'Is that Grimalkin back there?'

The feline shape's eyes gleamed. 'Indeed,' Grimalkin said. 'The servitor behind me bears that name.'

I blinked for a second, confusion stealing some of the thunder from my terror. 'The servitor behind you? There's no one behind you, Grimalkin.'

Mab's expression flickered with annoyance, her lips compressing into a thin line. When Grimalkin spoke, his voice bore the same expression. 'The servitor is my voice for the time being, wizard. And nothing more.'

'Ah,' I said. I glanced between the two of them, and my curiosity took the opportunity to sucker punch terror while confusion had it distracted. I felt my hands stop shaking. 'Why would the Queen of Air and Darkness need an interpreter?'

Mab lifted her chin slightly, a gesture of pride, and another small smile quirked her mouth. 'You are already in my debt,' the eerie, surrogate voice said for her. 'An you wish an answer to that question, you would incur more obligation yet. I do not believe in charity.'

'There's a shock,' I muttered under my breath. Whew. My banter gland had not gone necrotic. 'But you missed the point of the question, I think. Why would *Mab* need such a thing? She's an immortal, a demigod.'

Mab opened her mouth as Grimalkin said, 'Ah. I perceive. You doubt my identity.' She let her head drift back a bit, mouth open, and an eerie little laugh drifted up from her servitor. 'Just as you did in our first meeting.'

I frowned. That was correct. When Mab first walked into my office in mortal guise years ago, I noticed that something was off and subsequently discovered who she really was. As far as I knew, no one else had been privy to that meeting.

'Perhaps you'd care to reminisce over old times,' mewled the eerie voice. Mab winked at me.

Crap. She'd done that the last time I'd bumped into her. And once again, no one else knew anything about it. I'd been indulging in wishful thinking, hoping she was fake. She was the real Mab.

Mab showed me her teeth. 'Three favors you owed me,' Mab said — sort of. 'Two yet remain. I am here to create an opportunity for you to remove one of them from our accounting.'

'Uh-huh,' I said. 'How are you going to do that?'

Her smile widened, showing me her delicately pointed canines. 'I am going to help you.'

Yeah.

This couldn't be good.

I tried to keep my voice steady and calm. 'What do you mean?'

'Behold.' Mab gestured with her right hand, and the layer of snow on the ground stirred and moved until it had risen into a sculpture of a building, about eighteen inches high. It was like watching a sand castle melt in reverse.

I thought I recognized the building. 'Is that . . . ?'

'The building the lady knight asked you to examine,' confirmed Mab's surrogate voice. It's amazing what you can get used to if your daily allowance of bizarre is high enough. 'As it was before the working that rent it asunder.'

Other shapes began to form from the snow. Rather disconcertingly detailed shapes of cars rolled smoothly by beside the building, typical Chicago traffic — until one of them, an expensive town car, turned down the alley beside the building, the one I'd walked down not an hour before. I had to take a couple of steps to follow it as it came to a halt and stopped. The snow car's doors opened, and human shapes the size of the old *Star Wars* action figures came hurrying out of the vehicle.

I recognized them. The first was a flat-top, no-neck bruiser named Hendricks, Marcone's personal bodyguard and enforcer. His mother was a Kodiak bear; his father was an Abrams tank, and after he got out of the car, he reached back into it and came out with a light machine gun that he carried in one hand.

While Hendricks was doing that, a woman got out of the other side of the car. Gard was tall, six feet or so, though Hendricks made her look petite. She wore a smart business suit with a long trench coat, and as I watched she opened the car's trunk and removed a broadsword and an all-metal shield maybe two feet across. She passed her hand over the surface of the shield, and then quickly covered it with a section of cloth that had apparently been cut to fit it.

Both of them moved in a tense, precise, professionally concerned cadence.

The third man out of the car was Marcone himself, a man of medium height and build, wearing a suit that cost more than my car, and he looked as relaxed and calm as he always did. Marcone was criminal scum, but I'll give the rat his due – he's got balls that drag the ground when he walks.

Marcone's head whipped around abruptly, back down the alley the way they'd just come, though neither Hendricks nor Gard reacted with a similar motion. He produced a gun with such speed that it almost seemed magical, and little puffs of frost blazed out from the muzzle of the snow-sculpted weapon.

Hendricks reacted immediately, turning to bring that monster weapon to bear, and tiny motes of blue light flashed down the alley, representing tracer fire. Gard put her shield and her body between Marcone and whatever was at the end of the alley. They hurried into a side door of the building, one that had been destroyed in the collapse. Hendricks followed, still spraying bursts of fire down the alley. He, too, vanished into the building.

'Hell's bells,' I breathed. 'Marcone was *inside?*'

Mab flicked her hand in a slashing gesture, and the top two-thirds of the little snow building disintegrated under a miniature arctic gale. I was left with a cutaway image of the building's interior. Marcone and his bodyguards moved through the place like rats through a maze. They sprinted down a flight of stairs. At the bottom Marcone stabbed at some kind of keypad with short, sharp, precise motions and then looked up.

Heavy sheets of what looked like steel fell into place at the top and bottom of the stairs simultaneously, and I could all but hear the ominous *boom!* as they settled into place. Gard reached up and touched the center of the near door, and there was a flash of light bright enough to leave little spots in my vision. Then they hurried down a short hallway to another keypad and repeated the process. More doors, more flashes of light.

'Locking himself in . . .' I muttered, frowning. Then I got it. 'Wards. Blast doors. It's a panic room. He built a panic room.'

Grimalkin made a low, lazy yowling sound that I took for a murmur of agreement.

My own apartment was set up with a similar set of protections, which I could invoke if absolutely necessary – though, granted, my setup was a little more Merlin and a little less Bond. But I had to wonder what the hell had rattled Marcone enough to send him scurrying for a deep hole.

Then Gard's head snapped up, looking directly at where Mab currently stood, as if the little snow sculpture could somehow see the titanic form of the Winter Queen looking down upon her. Gard reached into her suit pocket, drew out what looked like a slender wooden box, the kind that really high-end pen sets come in sometimes, and took a small, rectangular plaque of some kind from the box. She lifted it, facing Mab again, and snapped the little plaque in her fingers.

The entire snow sculpture collapsed on itself and was gone.

'They saw the hidden camera,' I muttered.

'Within her limits, the Chooser is resourceful and clever,' Mab replied. 'The Baron was wise to acquire her services.'

I glanced up at Mab. 'What happened?'

'All Sight was clouded for several moments. Then this.'

At another gesture the building re-formed – but this time little clouds of frost simulated thick smoke roiling all around it, obscuring many details. The whole image, in fact, looked hazier, grainier, as if Mab had chosen to form it out of snowflakes a few sizes too large to illustrate details.

Even so, I recognized Marcone when he came stumbling out the front door of the building. Several forms hurried out behind him. They surrounded him. A plain van appeared out of the night, and the unknown figures cast him through its open doors. Then they entered and were gone.

As the van pulled away, the building shuddered and collapsed in on itself, sliding down into the wreckage and ruin I'd seen.

'I have chosen you to be my Emissary,' Mab said to me. 'You will repay me a favor owed. You will find the Baron.'

'The hell I will,' I said before my brain had time to weigh in on the sentiment.

Mab let out a low, throaty laugh. 'You will, wizard child. An you wish to survive, you have no choice.'

Anger flared in my chest and shoved my brain aside on its way to my mouth. 'That wasn't our deal,' I snapped. 'Our bargain stipulated that I would choose which favors to repay and that you would not coerce me.'

Mab's frozen-berry lips lifted in a silent snarl, and the world turned into a curtain of white agony that centered on my eyes. Nothing had *ever* hurt so much. I fell down, but I wasn't lucky enough to hit my head and knock myself unconscious. I couldn't move. I couldn't breathe. I couldn't scream.

Then there was something cold beside me. And something very soft and very cold touched my ear. I recognized the sensation, from the far side of the pain. Lips. Mab's lips. The Queen of Air and Darkness placed a gentle row of kisses down the outside ridge of my ear, then sucked the lobe into her mouth and bit down quite gently.

In the other ear I heard Grimalkin's voice speaking in a low, tense, hungry whisper. 'Mortal brute. Whatever your past, whatever your future, know this: I am Mab, and I keep my bargains. Question my given word again, ape, and I will finish freezing the water in your eyes.'

The pain receded to something merely torturous, and I clenched my teeth down hard over a scream. I could move again. I flinched away from her, scrambling until my back hit a wall. I covered my eyes with my hands and felt some of my frozen eyelashes snap.

I sat there for a minute, struggling to control the pain, and my vision gradually faded from white to a deep red, and then to black. I opened my eyes. I could barely focus them. I felt a wetness on my face, touched it with a finger. There was blood in my tears.

'I have not coerced you, nor dispatched any agent of mine to do so,' Mab continued, as if the break in the conversation had never happened. 'Nonetheless, if you wish to survive, you will serve me. I assure you that Summer's agents will not rest until you are dead.'

I stared at her for a second, still half-dazed from the pain and once again deeply, sincerely, and wisely frightened. 'This is another point of contention between you and Titania.'

'When one Court moves, the other perforce moves with it,' Mab said.

I croaked, 'Titania wants Marcone dead?'

'Put simply,' she replied. 'And her Emissary will continue to seek your death. Only by finding and saving the Baron's life will you preserve your own.' She paused. 'Unless . . .'

'Unless?'

'Unless you should agree to take up the mantle of the Winter Knight,' Mab said, smiling. 'I should be forced to choose another Emissary if you did, and your involvement in this matter could end.' Her eyelids lowered, sleepily sensual, and her surrogate voice turned liquid, heady, an audible caress. 'As my Knight you would know power and pleasure that few mortals have tasted.'

The Winter Knight. The mortal champion of the Winter Court. The previous guy who had that job was, when last I knew, still crucified upon a frozen tree within bonds of ice, tortured to the point of death and then made whole, only to begin the process again. He'd lost his sanity somewhere in one of the cycles. He wasn't a real nice guy when I knew him, but no human being should have to suffer like that.

'No,' I said. 'I don't want to end up like Lloyd Slate.'

'He suffers for your decision,' she said. 'He remains alive until you take up the mantle. Accept my offer, wizard child. Give him release. Preserve your life. Taste of power like none you have known.' Her eyes seemed to grow larger, becoming almost luminous, and her not-voice was a narcotic, a promise. 'There is much I can teach you.'

A decent person would have rejected her offer out of hand.

I'm not always one of those.

I could offer you some excuses, if you like. I could tell you that I was an orphan by the time I was six. I could tell you that the foster father who eventually raised me subjected me to more forms of psychological and physical abuse than you could shake a stick at. I could tell you that I'd been held in unjust suspicion for my entire adult life by the White Council, whose principles and ideals I'd done my best to uphold. Or maybe I could say that I'd seen too many good people get hurt, or that I'd looked upon a lot of nasty things with my indelible wizard's Sight. I could tell you that I'd been caught and abused by the creatures of the night myself, and that I hadn't ever really gotten over it. I could tell you that I hadn't gotten laid in a really long time.

And all of those things would be true.

But the fact of the matter is that there's simply a part of me that isn't so nice. There's a part of me that gets off on laying waste to my enemies with my power, that gets tired of taking undeserved abuse. There's this little voice inside my head that sometimes wants to throw the rules away, stop trying to be responsible, and just *take* what I want.

And for a minute, I wondered what it might be like to accept Mab's offer. Life among the Sidhe would be . . . intense. In every sense a mortal could imagine. What would it be like to live in a house? Hell, probably a *big* house, if not a freaking castle. Money. Hot showers every day. Every meal a feast. I'd be able to afford whatever clothes I wanted, whatever cars I wanted. Maybe I could do some traveling, see places I'd always wanted to see. Hawaii. Italy. Australia. I could learn to sail, like I always wanted.

Women, oh, yeah. Hot and cold running girls. Inhumanly beautiful, sensuous creatures like the one before me. The Winter Knight had status and power, and those are even more of an aphrodisiac to the fae than they are to us mortals.

I could have . . . almost anything.

All it would cost me was my soul.

And no, I'm not talking about anything magical or meta-physical. I'm talking about the core of my identity, about what makes Harry Dresden who and what he is. If I lost those things, the things that define me, then what would be left?

Just a heap of bodily processes – and regret.

I knew that. But all the same, the touch of Mab's chilled lips on my ear lingered on, sending slow, pleasant ripples of sensation through me when I breathed. It was enough to make me hesitate.

'No, Mab,' I said finally. 'I don't want the job.'

She studied my face with calm, heavy eyes. 'Liar,' she said quietly. 'You want it. I can see it in you.'

I gritted my teeth. 'The part of me that wants it doesn't get a vote,' I said. 'I'm not going to take the job. Period.'

She tilted her head to one side and stared at me. 'One day, wizard, you will kneel at my feet and ask me to bestow the mantle upon you.'

'But not today.'

'No,' Mab said. 'Today you repay me a favor. Just as I said you would.'

I didn't want to think too hard about that, and I didn't want to openly agree with her, either. So instead I nodded at the patch of ground where the sculptures had been. 'Who took Marcone?'

'I do not know. That is one reason I chose you, Emissary. You have a gift for finding what is lost.'

'If you want me to do this for you, I'm going to need to ask you some questions,' I said.

Mab glanced up, as if consulting the stars through the still-falling snow. 'Time, time, time. Will there never be an end to it?' She shook her head. 'Wizard child, the hour has nearly passed. I have duties upon which to attend – as do you. You should rise and leave this place immediately.'

'Why?' I asked warily. I got to my feet.

'Because when your little retainer warned you of danger, wizard child, he was not referring to me.'

On the street outside the alley, the gale-force wind and the white wall of blowing snow both died away. On the other side of the street, two men in long coats and big Stetson hats stood facing the alley. I felt the sudden weight of their attention, and got the impression that they had been surprised to see me.

I whirled to speak to Mab – only to find her gone. Grimalkin, too, both of them vanished without a trace or a whisper of power to betray it.

I turned back to the street in time to see the two figures step off the sidewalk and begin moving toward me with long strides. They were both tall, nearly my own height, and thickly built. The snowfall hadn't lightened, and the street was a smooth pane of unbroken snow.

They were leaving cloven footprints on it.

'Crap,' I spat, and fled back down the narrow, featureless alley.

7

At this sign of retreat, the two men threw back their heads and let out shrill, bleating cries. Their hats fell off when they did, revealing the goatlike features and curling horns of gruffs. But they were bigger than the first attack team – bigger, stronger, and faster.

And as they closed the distance on me, I noticed something else.

Both of them had produced submachine guns from beneath their coats.

'Oh, come on,' I complained as I ran. 'That's just not fair.'

They started shooting at me, which was bad news. Wizard or not, a bullet through the head will splatter my brains just as randomly as the next guy's. The *really* bad news was that they weren't just spraying bullets everywhere. Even with an automatic weapon, it isn't easy to hit a moving target, and the old 'spray and pray' method of fire relied upon blind luck disguised as the law of averages: Shoot enough bullets and eventually you have to hit something. Do your shooting like that and sometimes you'll hit the target, and sometimes you won't.

But the gruffs shot like professionals. They fired in short, burping little bursts, aimed fire, even if it suffered from the fact that they were moving while they did it.

I felt something hit my back, just to the left of my spine, an impact that felt somewhat like getting slugged in the back by someone with a single knuckle extended. It was a sharp, unpleasant sensation, and the way my balance wavered was more due to the fact that it surprised and frightened me than to the actual force it imparted. I kept running, ducking my head down as far as I could, hunching up my shoulders. The defensive magics woven into my coat could evidently stop whatever rounds the gruffs were using, but that didn't mean an unlucky ricochet couldn't bounce some lead into me from the front or sides, around the coat – and getting shot in the lower legs, ankles, or feet would probably kill me as certainly as one through the head. It would just take a little more effort on the gruffs' part to make it stick.

It's hard to think when someone's trying to kill you. We human beings aren't wired to be rational and creative when we know our lives are in danger of a swift and violent end. The body has definite ideas of which survival strategies it prefers to embrace, and those are generally limited to 'rip threat to pieces' or 'run like hell.' No thinking need be involved, as far as our instincts are concerned.

Our instincts were a long time in the making, though, and the threats that can come after us now have outpaced them. You can't outrun a bullet, and you don't go hand-to-hand with a gunman unless you're certain you are about to die anyway. Speed and mindless aggression weren't going to keep me alive. I needed to figure a way out.

I felt another bullet hit the lower part of my coat. It caught spell-strengthened leather and tugged it forward, just the way a thrown rock might have done. Admittedly, though, the rock wouldn't have made that angry-hornet buzzing noise as it struck. I dumped a garbage can over behind me, hoping it might trip up the gruffs for a second and buy me a little time.

Hey, *you* try coming up with a cogent, rational course of action when you're running down a frozen alley with genuine fairy-tale creatures chasing you, spitting bullets at your back. It's way harder than it looks.

I didn't dare turn to face them. I could have raised a shield to stop the gunfire, but once I had stopped moving, I figured odds were fantastic that one of them would just hop over me like a Kung Fu Theater extra, and they'd come at me from two directions at once.

In fact, if I were them, and had tracked me to that alley . . .

The chattering gunfire from behind me ceased, and I realized what was happening.

I raised my staff as I neared the far end of the alley, pointed it ahead of me, and screamed, '*Forzare!*'

My timing wasn't perfect. The unseen force I released from the end of the staff rushed out ahead of me, an invisible battering ram. It struck the third gruff just as the fae-thug stepped around the corner, a massive oak cudgel readied in his hands. The blast didn't hit him squarely. It would have thrown him a goodly ways if it had. Instead it caught the right side of his body, ripping the cudgel away from him and sending the gruff into a drunken, spinning stagger.

I don't know much about goats, but I do know a little about horses, having taken care of my second mentor Ebenezar McCoy's riding horses on his little farm in Missouri. Their feet are awfully vulnerable, especially considering how much weight they're putting on such a relatively small area. Any one of a hundred little things can go wrong. One of them is the possibility that some of the surprisingly frail little bones just above the back of the hoof could be fractured or broken. A pastern or fetlock injury like that can lame a horse for weeks, even permanently.

So as I passed the staggered gruff, I swung my heavy staff like a baseball bat, aiming at the back of one of his hooves. I felt the impact in my hands and heard a sharp crack. The gruff let out a high-pitched and utterly bestial scream of surprise and pain, and tumbled to the snow. I all but flew on by, lengthening my stride, crossing the street and heading for the nearest corner, before his buddies could get a clear shot at me.

When you drive game, you'd damn well better be sure that the one you're driving the prey toward is ready and able to handle it.

I ducked around the next corner maybe half a second before the guns behind me coughed and burped again, chewing chips of brick from the wall. There was a steel door on the side of the building, an exit-only door with no handle on the outside. I couldn't stay ahead of the gruffs for long. I took a chance, stopped, and pressed my hand against the door, hoping like hell it had a push-bar opening mechanism and not a dead bolt.

Something went right. I felt the bar on the other side, reached out with my will and another murmur, 'Forzare,' and directed the force against the other side of the door. It popped open. I went through and pulled it shut behind me.

The building was dark, silent, and almost uncomfortably warm in contrast with the night outside. I leaned my head against the metal door for a second, panting. 'Good door,' I wheezed. 'Nice door. Nice, locked, hostile-to-faeries door.'

My ear was in contact with the door, and it was the only reason I heard the movement immediately on its other side. Snow crunched quietly.

I froze in place.

I heard a scraping sound, and a snorted breath that sounded like something you'd hear from a horse. Then nothing.

It took me maybe three seconds to realize that the gruff on the other side of the door was doing the same thing I was: listening to see if he could hear who was on the other side.

It couldn't have been more than six inches away.

And I was standing there in complete darkness. If something went wrong and the gruff came in after me, I could forget running. I couldn't see the floor, the walls, or any obstacles that might trip me up. Like stairs. Or a mound of rusty razor blades.

I froze, not daring to move. Metal door or not, if the gruff had the right submachine gun and the right kind of ammunition, he could riddle me with holes right through the steel. There was no telling what other weapons he might be packing, either. I'd once seen a sobering demonstration of how to skewer someone on a sword from the other side of a metal door, and it hadn't been pretty.

So I stood very still and tried to think quietly.

It was about then that I remembered one of those movies with the maniac in the ghost mask, where one of the kids in the opening segment leans against a bathroom stall, listening exactly the same way I was. The killer, in the neighboring stall, rams a knife into the victim's ear.

It was a panic-inducing thought, and suddenly I had to fight the urge to bolt. My ear began to itch furiously. If I hadn't known that the gruffs were *trying* to flush me out like a rabbit from his briar patch, I might not have managed to keep my cool. It was a near thing, but I did it.

A week and a half went by before I heard another exhalation from a larger-than-human chest, and a pair of quick, light crunches of cloven hooves on snow.

I pushed away from the door as silently as I could, trembling with adrenaline, fatigue, and cold. I had to think ahead of these assholes if I wanted to get out in one piece. Inky, Binky, and Pinky knew I'd come in here, and they weren't about to give up the chase. Right now one of them was watching the door I'd come in to make sure I didn't backtrack. The other two were circling the building, looking for a way in.

I was pretty sure I didn't want to be hanging around when they found it.

I drew off the pentacle amulet I wore around my neck, murmured, and made a tiny effort of will. The amulet began to glow with gentle blue light.

I stood in a utility corridor of some kind. Bare concrete floor met unpainted drywall. There were a couple of doors on the right side of the hall, and another one at the far end. I checked them out. The first door opened into a room containing several commercial-grade heating and air-conditioning units, all hooked up to a ductwork octopus. No help there.

The next room was padlocked shut. I felt a little bad for doing it, but I lifted my staff, took a moment to close my eyes and concentrate, and then sent another pulse of energy down the rune-carved length of wood, this time focused into a blade of pure force. It sliced through the hasp and bit into the heavy wood of the door behind it. The lock fell to the floor, its cleanly severed steel glowing dull orange at the edges.

The room beyond was probably the workshop of the building's handyman. It wasn't large, but it was neatly organized. It held a woodworking bench, tools, and various supplies – lightbulbs, air filters for the units next door, replacement parts for doors, sinks, and toilets. I availed myself of a few things and dropped my last two twenties onto the workbench by way of apology. Then I stalked back out into the hallway and continued into the building.

The next door was locked, too. I jimmied it open with the crowbar I'd taken from the tool room. It made some noise.

A deep-throated bawl of animal sound came from the far side of the metal door. Something slammed against it, but not hard enough to bring it down, and the sound was followed by an immediate yowl of pain. I bared my teeth in a grin.

The far side of the door opened onto the lobby of an office building, very sparse. A light was blinking on a panel with a keypad on it, next to the door I'd just forced open. Apparently I had triggered the building's security system. That was fine by me. The nearest police station was only a little more than a block from here, and the lights and the appearance of mortal police officers would probably make the gruffs fade and wait for a better moment to settle my hash.

But wait. If the building had a security system, I had to have tripped it when I came in the side door, and that had been a couple of minutes ago. Why hadn't the cops shown up already?

The weather, most likely. Travel would be slow. Lines would be down, causing all kinds of power and communication problems. There would be traffic accidents everywhere there was traffic, and in the wake of all the manpower diverted to Marcone's wrecked building, the station would be overloaded with work, even this late at night. It might take several minutes longer than usual for the police to respond.

A shadow moved outside the building's front door, and one of the gruffs appeared there.

I didn't have minutes.

I was moving before I had consciously recognized the fact, running for the elevators. The steel security gate inside the door would prevent the gruff from crashing through the glass to come at me, but that didn't stop the gruff from lifting its submachine gun and opening up on me.

The gun sounded like heavy canvas ripping, only a thousand times louder. The window shattered and glass flew everywhere. Some of the bullets struck the security gate, throwing off sparks, most of them shattering, a couple bouncing wildly around the lobby. The rest came at me.

I had my left hand stretched out toward the gruff as I ran, and my will was focused on the bracelet on my wrist. Made of a braid of many metals, the chain of the bracelet was hung with multiple charms in the shape of medieval shields. The power of my will rushed into the bracelet, focused by the enchantments I'd laid upon it when I had prepared it. My will coalesced into a concave dome of barely visible blue energy between me and the gruff, and bullets slammed against it, shattering in bursts of light that rippled over the surface of the energy shield like tiny waves in a still pond.

All three of the elevator doors stood open, and I rushed into the nearest and rapidly hit the buttons for every floor up to the top of the building. Then I leapt out, repeated the process in the second elevator, and then jumped into the third and headed straight for the top. No sense in making it easy for the gruffs to follow me up, and even a moment's delay might buy me the time I needed.

The elevator doors closed – then buzzed and sprang open again.

'Oh, come on!' I shouted, and hit the close-door button hard enough to hurt my thumb.

I growled and watched as the elevator twitched closed again, and then once more sprang open, a sad little *ding* emerging from a half-functioning bell. I was jabbing the button like a lunatic when the gruffs demonstrated their opinion of mortal security systems.

Sure, the touch of metal was anathema to the beings of Faerie. Sure, they couldn't hammer their way through a metal door or bash through a heavy metal gate.

Brick walls, on the other hand, presented fewer problems.

There was a thunder crack of sound, and the wall beside the front door exploded inward. I don't mean it fell in. It literally exploded as the momentum of a superhumanly powerful being struck the wall from the far side and shattered it. Bits of brick flew like bullets. A ceramic pot holding a plastic plant shattered. Several pieces zipped into the elevator and bounced around inside of it. A cloud of brick dust billowed through the lobby.

The gruff who had just one-upped the Big Bad Wolf bulled its way through the cloud, curling ram's horns first. It staggered a step or two, shaking its head, then focused on me and let out another bleating howl.

'Augh!' I screamed at the elevator, jabbing the button. 'Close, close, close!'

It did. The car began rising just as the stunned gruff brought his weapon to bear and opened up. Bullets ripped through the relatively flimsy metal of the elevator's door, but my shield bracelet was ready and none of them found their target – who let out a howling, adrenaline-drunken laugh of defiance as the elevator rose.

What they say is true: There's nothing as exhilarating as being shot at and missed. When the shooter happens to be a fairy-tale hit man, it just adds to the zest.

Fourteen floors later I emerged into a darkened hallway and, guided by the light of my upraised amulet, I found the door to the roof. It was an exterior door with a heavy dead bolt, and there was no way that the crowbar was going to get it open.

I took a step back, lifted my staff, and focused my will on the door. Once upon a time I would have just let fly with my will and blasted it right out of its frame, a fairly exhausting bit of spellcraft. Instead I pointed the end of the staff at the bottommost hinge on this side and barked, '*Forzare!*'

A blade of unseen energy, like that I had used on the padlock, severed the hinge with a miniature crack of thunder. I did it for the middle and lower hinges too, then used the crowbar to pry the heavy door out of its setting and hurried out onto the roof.

There was a lot of wind up this high, even though the night was fairly calm. The towers of the city could funnel even a mild breeze into a virtual gale, and tonight this rooftop was on the receiving end. The wind ripped my coat out to one side, and I had to lean against it. At least there wasn't much snow – except where a portion of architecture created a lee against the wind. There it was piled deep.

It took me a second to orient. When you're fourteen floors up, it gives you an alien perspective of streets and buildings that might otherwise be familiar. I figured out which side of the building I'd come in on and hurried to it, searching for the escape route I'd spotted on the way in.

It wasn't the fire escapes, which decorated two sides of the building in a weathered steel framework. Those things are noisy as hell, and the gruffs would be watching them. Instead I leaned out over the edge and looked at the niche in the brick wall. It ran the entire vertical length of the building, a groove about three feet wide and two feet deep. There was one on either side of each corner of the building, probably there for the aesthetic value, rising like a three-walled chimney from the ground to the roof.

My breath went a little short. Fourteen floors is a *much* longer way down than it is up, especially when you aren't using things like elevators and fire escapes. Especially when I noted the frost and ice forming on the building's exterior.

I took a moment to debate the sanity of this plan. I'd cut the odds in my favor, assuming there were only three gruffs after me this time. One would have to watch the elevators. Another would have to watch the fire escape. That left only one to actively pursue me. I didn't know how fast the gruff would get to the roof, but I had no doubt that he'd manage it in short order.

The idea of simply pushing the gruff off the roof with a blast of power had a certain appeal, but I decided against it. A fourteen-story drop might just piss the gruff off – and it would absolutely confirm my location. Better to slip away and leave them wondering if I was still hiding in the building.

So I climbed out onto the ledge amidst gusting winds. My nose and fingers went numb almost immediately. I tried to ignore them as I lowered my legs into the groove in the wall and braced my feet against the bricks on either side. Then, my heart pounding madly, I shifted my hips and wriggled a bit, until the outward pressure of my legs against the bricks was the only thing that kept me from kissing sidewalk. Once my arms were low enough, I was able to spread them and plant my forearms against the bricks as well, assisting my legs.

I cannot possibly explain to you how frightened I was, staring down. The swirling snow kept me from seeing the ground at times. Once I started there would be no going back. One slip, one miscalculation, one inconveniently placed patch of ice, and I would be able to add 'pancake' to my impersonation repertoire.

I pushed hard with my arms and let my legs loosen. I slid them down a few inches and tightened them again, until they supported my weight once more. Then I loosened my arms and slid down a few inches before stopping, tightening my arms again and repeating the process.

I started climbing down, shifting my legs and arms in turn, five or six inches at a time, moving down the brick groove inchworm style. I made it about ten feet before an image invaded my mind: a gruff, aiming his gun down at me from a couple of feet away and casually popping several rounds through the top of my head.

I started climbing faster, my stomach turning with reaction to the height and the fear. I heard myself making desperate little grunting sounds. The wind howled, blowing snow into my eyes. Frost formed on my eyelashes. My coat did little to protect me from the wind swirling the length of my body, and I started shaking uncontrollably.

I lost the staff when I was about fifty feet up. It tumbled from my numbing fingers, and I held my breath. The rattle of its impact could attract the gruffs' attention and ruin the whole purpose of taking the madman route off the building.

But the solid length of oak fell into a drift of snow and

vanished silently into the white powder. I labored to emulate it, only less quickly.

I didn't slip until I was ten feet up. I managed to take the fall well, mostly because I landed in the same snowdrift that had received my staff. I struggled up out of the freezing white, and almost went back down when my staff tangled in my legs. I took it up in mostly nerveless hands and staggered out of the drift.

A sphere of light whipped past the other end of the alley, then reappeared and shot toward me.

Toot-toot's face was unusually sober, even grim. He zipped up to me and held a finger to his lips. I nodded at him and mouthed, *I need to know how to get out.*

Toot's sphere of light bobbed once in acknowledgment and then sped away. I looked up. Other balls of glowing light darted about the skies, flickers that you would barely even notice if you didn't know what to look for. I took a precaution while I waited.

As before, I didn't wait long. Toot returned a moment later and beckoned me. He took the lead and I followed him. I was getting colder. The fall into the drift had covered me in a light layer of snow, which had then melted. Wet clothes are exactly the worst thing to be wearing in that kind of weather. I had to keep moving. Hypothermia isn't as dramatic a death as being ripped apart by bullets, but it'll get the job done.

When I got to the far end of the alley, I heard another bleating cry from a gruff, drifting on the moaning wind, softened by the falling snow. I glanced back and just barely saw motion as a gruff descended the side of the building the same way I had — though much more swiftly.

A second later there was an agonized, inhuman scream as the gruff got to the bottom and discovered that the snow had hidden the box of nails that I had stolen from the tool room and spread liberally over the ground. The screams went on for several seconds. One of the nails must have pierced the gruff's hoof, and as tired and cold as I was, I still had energy enough to grin. That one wasn't going to be dancing in elf circles anytime soon.

I'd lamed two of them, and figured it would be enough to make them back off the chase, at least for the moment. But you never can tell. I wasted no time in following Toot through back alleys and away from the chosen emissaries of Summer. Around me the little glowing Christmas balls of light, the Za-Lord's Guard, darted back and forth, a wary ring of sentinels spread in a perimeter that moved as I did.

Several blocks away I found an all-night grocery store and staggered in out of the cold. The clerk glared at me until I hobbled over, clumsily dug change out of my pockets, and left it next to the cash register before shuffling to the coffee counter. At that point the clerk evidently decided that he wouldn't have to get out the shotgun or whatever he had behind the counter, and went back to staring out the window.

There were a few other shoppers there, and I saw a police car crunch through the snow on the street outside, probably responding to the alarm at the building. Nice and public. Probably safe. I was so cold I could barely fill up the cup. The coffee, which burned my tongue a little, was absolutely delicious, even served black. I guzzled the hot drink and felt sensation begin returning to my body.

I stood there for a moment with my eyes closed and finished the coffee. Then I crushed the paper cup and tossed it into the trash.

Someone had snatched John Marcone, and I had to find him and protect him. I had a feeling that Murphy wasn't going to be thrilled with the circumstances around this one. Hell's bells, *I* wasn't happy with it. But that really wasn't what was bothering me.

What *really* worried me was that Mab had been involved.

What was the deal with having Grimalkin along to do her talking for her? Aside from making her seem even more extremely disturbing than usual, I mean. Oh, sure, Mab may have seemed fairly straightforward, but there was a lot more going on than she was saying.

For example: Mab had said that Summer's hit men were after

me because Mab had chosen me to be her Emissary. But for that to be true, she had to have done it hours ago, at least a little while before the first crew of gruffs had attacked me at the Carpenter place.

And *that* had happened several hours *before* the bad guys grabbed Marcone.

Someone was running a game, all right. Someone was keeping secrets.

I had a bad feeling that if I didn't find out who, why, and how, Mab would toss me into the trash like a used paper cup.

Right after she crushed me, of course.

8

A wide-axled, full-of-itself, military-wannabe truck crunched through the snowy streets and came to a halt outside the little grocery store. The lights glared in through the doors. I squinted at it. After a minute the Hummer's horn blared in two short beeps.

'Oh, you've got to be kidding me,' I muttered. I hobbled to the door and out to the truck, which blended seamlessly with the background and the foreground, and with most of the air.

The driver-side window rolled down and revealed a young man whom fathers of teenage daughters would shoot on sight. He had pale skin and deep grey eyes. His dark, slightly curly hair was long enough to declare casual rebellion, and tousled to careless perfection. He wore a black leather jacket and a white shirt, both of them more expensive than any two pieces of furniture at my apartment. In marked contrast, there was a scarf inexpertly crocheted from thick white yarn around his neck, under the collar of the jacket. He faced straight ahead, so that I saw only his profile, but I felt confident that he was smirking on the other side of his face, too.

'Thomas,' I said. 'A lesser man than me would hate you.'

He grinned. 'There's someone lesser than *you*?' He rolled his eyes to me on the last word, to deadpan the delivery, and his face froze in an expression of absolute neutrality. He stayed that way for a few seconds. 'Empty night, Harry. You look like . . .'

'Ten miles of bad road?'

He forced a smile onto his mouth, but that was as far as it went. 'I was going to go with "a raccoon."'

'Gee. Thanks.'

'Get in.'

He took the monorail to the other side of the Hummer's cab to unlock the passenger-side door. I showed up eventually, and noticed every little ache in my body on the way – especially the throbbing burn centered on my broken nose. I tossed my staff into the back of *Das Truck*, half expecting an echoing clatter when it landed. I got in, shut the door, and put on my seat belt while Thomas got the truck moving. He peered carefully into the heavy snow, presumably looking for some runty little sedans he could drive over for fun.

'That's gotta hurt,' he said after a moment.

'Only when I exhale,' I said testily. 'What took you so long?'

'Well, you know how much I love getting called in the middle of the night to drive through snow and ice to play chauffeur for grumpy low-life investigators. The anticipation slowed me down.'

I grunted in what might have been construed as an apologetic manner by someone who knew me.

Thomas did. 'What's up?'

I told him everything.

Thomas is my half brother, my only family. I'm allowed.

He listened.

'And then,' I concluded, 'I went for a ride in a monster truck.'

Thomas's mouth twitched up in a quick smile. 'It *is* kinda butch, isn't it.'

I squinted around the truck. 'Do TV shows start an hour later in the backseat than they do up here?'

'Who cares?' Thomas said. 'It's got TiVo.'

'Good,' I said. 'It might be a little while before I return you to your regularly scheduled programming.'

Thomas let out a theatrical sigh. 'Why me?'

'Because if I want to find Marcone, the best place to start is with his people. If word gets out that he's gone missing, there's no telling how some of them might react when I come snooping around. So you've got my back.'

'What if I don't *want* your back?'

'Cope,' I said heartlessly. 'You're family.'

'You've got me there,' he admitted. 'But I wonder if you've thought this through very thoroughly.'

'I try to make thinking an ongoing process.'

Thomas shook his head. 'Look, you know I don't try to tell you your business.'

'Except tonight, apparently,' I said.

'Marcone is a grown-up,' Thomas said. 'He signed on to the Accords willingly. He knew what he was going to be letting himself in for.'

'And?' I said.

'And it's a jungle out there,' Thomas said. He squinted through the thick snow. 'Metaphorically speaking.'

I grunted. 'He made his bed, and I should let him lie in it?'

'Something like that,' Thomas said. 'And don't forget that Murphy and the police aren't going to be thrilled with a "Save the Kingpin" campaign.'

'I know,' I said, 'and I'd love to stand back and see what happens. But this isn't about Marcone anymore.'

'Then what is it about?'

'Mab skinning me alive if I don't give her what she wants.'

'Come on, Harry,' Thomas said. 'You can't really think that Mab's motives and plans are that direct, that cut-and-dried.' He adjusted the setting of the Hummer's wipers. 'She wants Marcone for a reason. You might not be doing him any favors by saving him on Mab's behalf.'

I scowled out at the night.

He held up a hand, ticking off fingers. 'And that's assuming that, one, he's alive at all right now. Two, that you can find him. Three, that you can get him out alive. And four, that the opposition doesn't cripple or kill you.'

'What's your point?' I asked.

'That you're playing against a stacked deck, and that you have no idea if Mab is going to be there to cover your bets when the bad guys call.' He shook his head. 'It would be smarter for you to skip town. Go someplace warm for a few weeks.'

'Mab might take that kinda personal,' I said.

'Mab's a businesswoman,' Thomas said. 'Creepy and weird, but she's cold, too. Calculating. As long as you still represent a potential recruit to her, I doubt she'd elect to depreciate your value prematurely.'

'Depreciate. I like that. You might be right – unless, to return to the original metaphor, Mab isn't playing with a full deck. Which the evidence of recent years seems to imply with increasing frequency.' I nodded out the window. 'And I've got a feeling that I'd have had even more trouble with the gruffs I've seen so far if we weren't in the middle of a freaking blizzard. If I waltz off to Miami or somewhere warm, I'll be putting myself that much nearer to the agents of Summer – who are also planning my murder.'

Thomas frowned and said nothing.

'I could run, but I couldn't hide,' I said. 'Better to face it here, on my home ground, while I'm still relatively rested' – I let out a huge and genuine yawn – 'instead of waiting for faerie goons from one Court or the other to, ah, depreciate me by surprise after I've been on the run for a few weeks.'

'What about the Council?' Thomas demanded. 'You've been wearing the grey cloak for how long, now? And you've fought for them how many times?'

I shook my head. 'Right now the Council is still stretched to the limit. We might not be in open battle with the Red Court at the moment, but the Council and the Wardens have got years of catch-up work to do.' I felt my jaw tighten. 'Lot of warlocks have come up in the past few years. The Wardens are working overtime to get them under control.'

'You mean kill them,' Thomas said.

'I mean kill them. Most of them teenagers, man.' I shook my head. 'Luccio knows my feelings on the matter. She refuses to assign any of it to me. Which means that other Wardens are forced to pick up the slack. I'm not going to add to their work-load by dragging them into this mess.'

'You don't seem to mind adding to mine,' Thomas noted.

I snorted. 'That's because I respect them.'

'So long as we have that clear,' he said.

We drove past a city snowplow. It had foundered in a deep drift, like some kind of metallic Ice Age beast trapped in a tar pit. I watched it with bemusement as Thomas's truck crunched slowly, steadily on by.

'By the way,' he asked, 'where do you want to go?'

'First things first,' I said. 'I need food.'

'You need sleep.'

'Tick-tock. Food will do for now.' I pointed. 'There, an IHOP.'

He hauled the big truck into a slow, steady turn. 'Then what?'

'I ask people impertinent questions,' I said. 'Hopefully turning up pertinent answers.'

'Assuming someone doesn't kill you while you do.'

'That's why I'm bringing my very own vampire bodyguard.'

Thomas parked across three spaces in the tiny, otherwise unoccupied lot of an International House of Pancakes.

'I like the scarf,' I said. I leaned over and inhaled through my nose as best I could. It stung, but I detected a faint whiff of vanilla and strawberries. 'She make it for you?'

Thomas nodded without saying anything. The leather-gloved fingers of one hand traced over the soft, simple yarn. He looked quietly sad. I felt bad for mentioning Justine, my brother's lost lover. Then I understood why he wore the gloves: If she'd made it for him, a token of her love, he didn't dare touch it with his skin. It would sear him like a hot skillet. So he kept it close enough for him to smell her touch upon it, but he didn't dare let it brush against him.

Every time I think my romantic life is a wasteland, I look at my brother and see how much worse it could be.

Thomas shook his head and killed the engine and we sat for a moment in silence.

So I clearly heard a deep male voice outside the truck say, 'Don't either of you move.' There was the distinct *click-clack* of a shotgun's pump working. 'Or I will kill you.'

9

When there's a gun pointed at you, you've got two options: Either you move, fast and unexpectedly, and hope that you get lucky, or you freeze and try to talk your way clear. Given that I had really limited room in which to attempt to dodge or run, I went with option B: I held still.

'I don't suppose,' I asked hopefully, 'that this is the full military model?'

'It has individually heated seats and a six-disk CD changer,' Thomas said.

I scowled. 'Uh-huh. Those are way cooler than silly features like armor and bulletproof glass.'

'Hey,' Thomas said, 'it's not my fault you have special needs.'

'Harry,' said the man with the shotgun, 'hold up your right hand, please.'

I arched an eyebrow at that. Typically the vocabulary of thugs holding guns to your head ran a little light on courtesy phrases like *please*.

'You want me to kill him?' Thomas murmured, barely audible.

I twitched my head in a tiny negative motion. Then I lifted up my right hand, fingers spread.

'Turn it around,' said the man outside. 'Let me see the inside of your wrist.'

I did.

'Oh, thank God,' breathed the voice.

I'd finally placed it. I turned my head to one side and said through the glass, 'Hey, there, Fix. Is that a shotgun you're holding to my head, or are you just glad to see me?'

Fix was a young, slender man of medium height. His hair was silver-white and very fine, and though no one would ever accuse him of beauty, there was a confidence and surety in his plain features that gave them a certain appeal. He was a far cry from the nervous, scrawny kid I'd first met several years ago.

He wore jeans and a green silk shirt – nothing more. He obviously should have been freezing, and he just as obviously wasn't. The thickly falling snowflakes weren't striking him. Every single one seemed to find its way to the ground around him somehow. He held a pump-action shotgun with a long barrel against his shoulder, and wore a sword on a belt at his hip.

'Harry,' he said, his voice steady. His tone wasn't hostile. 'Can we have a polite talk?'

'We probably could have,' I said, 'if you hadn't started off by pointing a gun at my head.'

'A necessary precaution,' he said. 'I needed to be sure you hadn't taken Mab's offer.'

'And become the new Winter Knight?' I asked. 'You could have asked me, Fix.'

'If you'd become Mab's creature,' Fix said, 'you would have lied. It would have changed you. Made you an extension of her will. I couldn't trust you.'

'You're the Summer Knight,' I replied. 'So I can't help but wonder if that wouldn't make you just as controlled and untrustworthy. Summer's not all that happy with me right now, apparently. Maybe you're just an extension of Summer's will.'

Fix stared at me down the barrel of the shotgun. Then he lowered it abruptly and said, 'Touché.'

Thomas produced from nowhere a semiautomatic pistol scaled to fit his truck, and had it trained on Fix's head before the other man had finished speaking the second syllable of the word.

Fix's eyes widened. 'Holy crap.'

I sighed and took the gun gently from Thomas's grip. 'Now, now. Let's not give him the wrong idea about the nature of this conversation.'

Fix let out a slow breath. 'Thank you, Harry. I—'

I pointed the gun at Fix's head, and he froze with his mouth partly open.

'Lose the shotgun,' I told him. I made no effort to sound friendly.

His mouth closed and his lips pressed into a thin line, but he obeyed.

'Step back,' I said.

He did it.

I got out of the car, carefully keeping the gun trained on his head. I recovered the shotgun and passed it back to Thomas. Then I faced the silver-haired Summer Knight in dead silence while the snow fell.

'Fix,' I said quietly, after a moment had passed. 'I know you've been spending a lot of time in the supernatural circles lately. I know that plain old things like guns don't seem like a significant threat, in some ways. I know that you probably meant it as a message, that you weren't coming after me with everything you could bring to bear, and that I was supposed to consider it a token of moderation.' I squinted down the sight of Thomas's gun. 'But you crossed a line. You pointed a gun at my head. Friends don't do that.'

More silence and snowfall.

'Point another weapon at me,' I said quietly, 'and you'd damned well better pull the trigger. Do you understand me?'

Fix's eyes narrowed. He nodded once.

I let him look down the gun's barrel for a few more seconds and then lowered it. 'It's cold,' I said. 'What do you want?'

'I came here to warn you, Harry,' Fix said. 'I know Mab has chosen you to act as her Emissary. You don't know what you're getting into. I came to tell you to stand clear of it.'

'Or what?'

'Or you're going to get hurt,' Fix said quietly. He sounded tired. 'Maybe killed. And there's going to be collateral damage along the way.' He held up a hand and continued, hurriedly, 'Please understand. I'm not threatening you, Harry. I'm just telling you about consequences.'

'I'd have an easier time believing that if you hadn't opened the conversation by threatening to kill me,' I said.

'The last Summer Knight was murdered by his Winter counterpart,' Fix replied. 'In fact, that's how most of them die. If you'd taken service with Mab, I wouldn't stand a chance in a fair fight against you, and we both know it. I did what I had to in order to warn you and still protect myself.'

'Oh,' I said. 'It was a *precautionary* shotgun aimed at my skull. That makes it different.'

'Dammit, Dresden,' Fix said. 'What do I have to do to get you to listen to me?'

'Behave in a vaguely trustworthy fashion,' I said. 'For instance, next time you know that Summer's hitters are about to make a run at me, maybe you could call me on a telephone and give me a little heads-up.'

Fix grimaced. His face twisted into an expression of effort. When he spoke his jaws stayed locked together, but I could, with difficulty, understand the words. 'Wanted to.'

'Oh,' I said. A big chunk of my anger evaporated. It was probably just as well. Fix wasn't the one who deserved to be on the receiving end of it. 'I can't back off.'

He drew in a breath and nodded as if in comprehension. 'Mab's got a handle on you.'

'For now.'

He gave me a rather bleak smile. 'She isn't the sort to let go of anyone she wants to keep.'

'And I'm not the sort who gets kept,' I replied.

'Maybe not,' Fix said, but he sounded dubious. 'Are you sure you won't reconsider?'

'We're going to have to agree to disagree.'

'Jesus,' Fix said, looking away. 'I don't want to square off against you, Dresden.'

'Then don't.'

He stared quietly at me, his expression serious. 'I can't back off, either. I like you, Harry. But I can't make you any promises.'

'We're playing for opposite teams,' I said. 'Nothing personal. But we'll do what we have to do.'

Fix nodded.

We didn't speak for almost a minute.

Then I laid the shotgun down in the snow, nodded, and got back into Thomas's truck. I gave the huge automatic back to my brother. Fix made no move toward the shotgun.

'Harry,' he said, as the truck started to pull out. His mouth twitched a few times before he blurted, 'Remember the leaf Lily gave you.'

I frowned at him, but nodded.

Thomas got the truck moving again and started driving. Windshield wipers squeaked. Snow crunched beneath tires, a steady white noise.

'Okay,' Thomas said. 'What was that all about? Guy's supposed to be a friend, and he screwed you over. I thought you were going to pistol-whip him for a minute. Then you start getting all teary-eyed.'

'Metaphorically speaking,' I said tiredly.

'You know what I mean.'

'He's under a geas, Thomas.'

Thomas frowned. 'Lily's got him in a brain-lock?'

'I doubt she'd do that to Fix. They go back.'

'Who, then?'

'My money is on Titania, the Summer Queen. If she told him to keep his mouth shut and not to help me, he wouldn't get a choice in the matter. Probably why he showed up armed and tried to intimidate me. He wouldn't be able to speak to me outright, but if he's delivering a threat in order to further Titania's plans, it might let him get around the geas.'

'Seems pretty thin to me. You believe him?'

'Titania's done it to him before. And she doesn't really like me.'

'You kill someone's daughter, that happens,' he said.

I shrugged wearily, tired to my bones. The combination of pain, cold, and multiple bursts of adrenaline had worn me down a lot more than I had realized. I couldn't stop another yawn.

'What was he talking about as we pulled out?'

'Oh,' I mumbled. 'After that mess at Arctis Tor, Lily gave

me a silver pin in the shape of an oak leaf. It makes me an Esquire of Summer. Supposedly I can use it to whistle up help from Titania's Court. It's their way of balancing the scales for what we did.'

'Never a bad thing to be owed a favor,' Thomas agreed. 'You got it on you?'

'Yeah,' I said. It was, in fact, in a little ring box within the inner coat of my duster. I got it out and showed it to Thomas.

He whistled. 'Gorgeous work.'

'The Sidhe know pretty,' I agreed.

'Maybe you can use it and get them to back off.'

I snorted. 'It's never that simple. Titania could decide that the best way to help me would be to break my back, paralyze me from the waist down, and dump me into a hospital bed so her gruffs won't have to kill me.'

Thomas grunted. 'Then why would Fix mention it?'

'Maybe he was compelled to,' I said. 'Maybe Titania's hoping I'll call for help and she'll have a chance to squash me personally. Or maybe . . .'

I let my voice trail off for a moment, while I kicked my punch-drunk brain in the stomach until it threw up an idea.

'Or maybe,' I said, 'because he wanted to warn me about it. The gruffs have found me twice now, and they haven't been physically tailing or tracking me. Neither location was one of my regular hangouts. And how did Fix find me just now, in the middle of a blizzard? He sure as hell didn't coincidentally pick a random IHOP.'

Thomas's eyes widened in realization. 'It's a tracking device.'

I scowled at the beautiful little silver leaf and said, not without a certain amount of grudging admiration, 'Titania. That conniving bitch.'

'Damn,' Thomas said. 'I feel a little bad for pointing a gun at the shrimp, now.'

'I probably would, too,' I said, 'if I wasn't so weirded out by the fact that Fix is starting to be as crabwise and squirrelly as the rest of the Sidhe.'

Thomas grunted. 'Better get rid of that thing before more of them show up.'

He hit the control that lowered the passenger window. It coughed and rattled a little before it jerked into motion, instead of smoothly gliding down. Wizards and technology don't get along so well. To high-tech equipment I am the living avatar of Murphy's Law: The longer I stayed in Thomas's shiny new oil tanker, the more all the things that *could* go wrong, *would* go wrong.

I lifted the leaf to chuck it out, but something made me hesitate. 'No,' I murmured.

Thomas blinked. 'No?'

'No,' I said with more certainty, closing my hand around the treacherous silver leaf. 'I've got a better idea.'

10

I finished the spell that I thought would keep the gruffs busy and climbed wearily out of my lab to find Thomas sitting by the fireplace. My big grey dog, Mouse, lay beside him, his fur reflecting highlights of reddened silver in the firelight, watching Thomas's work with interest.

My brother sat cross-legged on the floor, with my gun lying disassembled on a soft leather cloth upon the hearth. He frowned in concentration as he cleaned the pieces of the weapon with a brush, a soft cloth, and a small bottle of oil.

Mister, my hyperthyroid tomcat, bounded over the minute I opened the trapdoor to the lab, and hurried down the folding staircase into the subbasement.

'Go get 'em, tiger,' I muttered after him by way of encouragement. 'Make them run their little hooves off.'

I left the door open, heaved myself to the couch, and collapsed. Mouse's tail thumped the floor gently.

'You all right?' Thomas asked.

'Tired,' I said. 'Big spell.'

'Uh-huh,' he said, working industriously on the weapon's barrel. 'What building did you burn down?'

'Your apartment, if you don't lay off the wiseass commentary,' I said. 'Give me a minute and we'll get moving.'

Thomas gave me a sidelong, calculating look. 'I needed another minute or two anyway. When's the last time you cleaned this thing?'

'Uh. Who's the president now?'

Thomas clucked his teeth in disapproval and returned to the gun. 'Let me know when you're ready.'

'Just give me a minute to catch my breath,' I said.

When I woke up there was dim light coming from my mostly buried basement windows, and my neck felt like the bones had been welded together by a badly trained contractor. The various beatings I'd received the night before had formed a corporation and were attempting a hostile takeover of my nervous system. I groaned and looked around.

Thomas was sitting with his back against the wall beside the fireplace, as relaxed and patient as any tiger. His gun, mine, and the bent-bladed kukri knife he'd favored lately lay close at hand.

Down in my lab something clattered to the floor from one of the shelves or tables. I heard Mister's paws scampering over the metal surface of the center table.

'What are you grinning at?' my brother asked.

'Mister,' I said.

'He's been knocking around down there all morning,' Thomas said. 'I was going to go round him up before he broke something, but the skull told me to leave him alone.'

'Yeah,' I said. I creaked to my feet and shuffled to my little alcove with delusions of kitchenhood. I got out the bottle of aspirin and downed them with a glass of water. 'For your own safety. Mister gets upset when someone gets between him and his packet of catnip.'

I shuffled over to the lab and peered down. Sure enough, the little cloth bag containing catnip and the silver oak leaf pin still hung from the extra-large rubber band I'd snipped and fixed to the ceiling directly over Little Chicago. As I watched, Mister hopped up onto a worktable, then bounded into the air to bat at the cloth bag. He dragged it down to the table with him, claws hooked in the fabric, and landed on the model of Lincoln Park. My cat rubbed his face ecstatically against the bag for a moment, then released it and batted playfully at it as the rubber band sent it rebounding back and forth near him.

Then he seemed to realize he was being watched. He turned his face up to me, meowed smugly, flicked the stub of his tail jauntily, and hopped to the floor.

'Bob?' I called. 'Is the spell still working?'

'Aye, Cap'n!' Bob said. 'Arrrrr!'

'What's with that?' Thomas murmured from right beside me.

I twitched hard enough to take me up off the floor, and glared at him. 'Would you stop doing that?'

He nodded, his expression serious, but I could see the corners of his mouth quivering with the effort not to smile. 'Right. Forgot.'

I growled and called him something unkind, yet accurate. 'He wouldn't stop begging me to take him to see that pirate movie. So I took him with me the last time I went to the drive-in down in Aurora, and he got into it. It's been dying down, but if he calls me "matey" one more time I'll snap.'

'That's interesting,' Thomas said, 'but that's not what I was asking about.'

'Oh, right,' I said. I pointed at the catnip bag. 'The leaf's in there.'

'Isn't that just going to draw Summer's goons here?'

I let out a nasty laugh. 'No. They can't see it through the wards around the lab.'

'Then why the big rubber band?'

'I linked Summer's beacon spell to the matrix around Little Chicago. Every time the leaf gets within a foot of the model, my spell transfers the beacon's signal to the corresponding location in the city.'

Thomas narrowed his eyes in thought, and then suddenly grinned in understanding as Mister pounced on the catnip again, this time landing near the Field Museum. 'If they're following that beacon, they'll be running all over town.'

'In two and a half feet of snow,' I confirmed, grinning.

'You're sadistic.'

'Thank you,' I said solemnly.

'Won't they figure it out?'

'Sooner or later,' I admitted, 'but it should buy us a little time to work with. 'Scuse me.'

I shambled to the door and put on my coat.

'Where to first?' Thomas asked.

'Nowhere just yet. Sit tight.' I grabbed my square-headed snow shovel from the popcorn tin by the door, where it usually resided with my staff, sword cane, and the epically static magic sword, *Fidelacchius*. Mouse followed me out. It was a job of work to get the door open, and more than a little snow spilled over the threshold. I started with shoveling the stairs and worked my way up, a grave digger in reverse.

Once that was done, I shoveled the little sidewalk, the front porch of the boardinghouse, and the exterior stairs running up to the Willoughbys' apartment on the second floor. Then I dug a path to the nest of mailboxes by the curb. It took me less time than I thought it would. There was a lot of snow, but it hadn't formed any layers of ice, and it was basically a question of tossing powder out of the way. Mouse kept watch, and I tried not to throw snow into his face.

We returned to my apartment, and I slung the shovel's handle back down into the popcorn tin.

Thomas frowned at me. 'You had to shovel the walk? Harry . . . somehow I'm under the impression that you aren't feeling the urgency here.'

'In the first place,' I said, 'I'm not terribly well motivated to bend over backward to save John Marcone's Armani-clad ass. I wouldn't lose much sleep over him. In the second place, my neighbors are elderly, and if someone doesn't clean up the walks they'll be stuck here. In the third place, I've got to do whatever I can to make sure I'm on my landlady's good side. Mrs. Spunkelcrief is almost deaf, but it's sort of hard to hide it when assassin demons or gangs of zombies kick down the door. She's willing to forgive me the occasional wild party because I do things like shovel the walk.'

'It's easier to replace an apartment than your ass,' Thomas said.

I shrugged. 'I was so stiff and sore from yesterday that I had to do something to get my muscles loosened up and moving. The time was going to be gone either way. Might as well take care of my neighbors.' I grimaced. 'Besides . . .'

'You feel bad that your landlady's building sometimes gets

busted up because you live in it,' Thomas said. He shook his head and snorted. 'Typical.'

'Well, yeah. But that's not it.'

He frowned at me, listening.

I struggled to find the right words. 'There are a lot of things I can't control. I don't know what's going to happen in the next few days. I don't know what I'm going to face, what kind of choices I'm going to have to make. I can't predict it. I can't control it. It's too big.' I nodded at my shovel. 'But that, I can predict. I know that if I pick up that shovel and clear the snow from the walkways, it's going to make my neighbors safer and happier.' I glanced at him and shrugged. 'It's worthwhile to me. Give me a minute to shower.'

He regarded me for a second and then nodded. 'Oh,' he said, with the tiniest of smiles. He mimed a sniff and a faint grimace. 'I'll wait. Gladly.'

I cleaned up. We were on the way out the door when the phone rang.

'Harry,' Murphy said. 'What the hell is going on out there?'

'Why?' I asked. 'What the hell *is* going on out there?'

'We've had at least two dozen . . . well, I suppose the correct term is "sightings." Everything from Bigfoot to mysterious balls of light. Naturally it's all getting shunted to SI.'

I started to answer her, then paused. Marcone and the outfit were involved. While they didn't have anywhere near the influence in civic affairs that they might have wanted, Marcone had always had sources of information inside the police department – sources his subordinates could, presumably, access as well. It would be best to exercise some caution.

'You calling from the station?' I asked her.

'Yeah.'

'We should talk,' I said.

Murphy might not want to admit that anyone she worked with could be providing information to the outfit, but she wasn't the sort to stop believing the truth just because she didn't like it. 'I see,' she said. 'Where?'

'McAnally's,' I said. I checked a clock. 'Three hours?'

'See you there.'

I hung up and started for the door again. Mouse followed close at my heels, but I turned and nudged him gently back with my leg. 'Not this time, boy,' I told him. 'The bad guys have a lot of manpower, access to skilled magic, and I need a safe place to come home to. If you're here there's no way anyone is going to sneak in and leave me a present that goes boom.'

Mouse huffed out a breath in a sigh, but sat down.

'Keep an eye on Mister, all right? If he starts getting sick, take the catnip away.'

My dog gave the door to the lab a dubious glance.

'Oh, give me a break,' I said. 'You're seven times as big as he is.'

Mouse looked none too confident.

Thomas blinked at me, and then at the dog. 'Can he understand you?'

'When it suits him,' I grumped. 'He's smarter than a lot of people I know.'

Thomas took a moment to absorb that, and then faced Mouse a little uncertainly. 'Uh, okay, look. What I said about Harry earlier? I wasn't serious, okay? It was totally a joke.'

Mouse flicked his ears and turned his nose away from Thomas with great nobility.

'What?' I asked, looking between them. 'What did you say?'

'I'll warm up the car,' Thomas said, and retreated to the frozen grey outdoors.

'This is my *home*,' I complained to no one in particular. 'Why do people keep making jokes at my expense in my own freaking *home*?'

Mouse declined to comment.

I locked up behind me, magically and materially, and scaled Mount Hummer to sit in the passenger seat. The morning was cold and getting colder, especially since I was fresh from the shower, but the seat was rather pleasantly warm. There was no way I'd admit to Thomas that the luxury feature was superior to armored glass, but gosh, it was cozy.

'Right,' Thomas said. 'Where are we headed?'

'To where they treat me like royalty,' I said.

'We're going to Burger King?'

I rubbed the heel of my hand against my forehead and spelled *fratricide* in a subvocal mutter, but I had to spell out *temporary insanity* and *justifiable homicide*, too, before I calmed down enough to speak politely. 'Just take a left and drive. Please.'

'Well,' Thomas said, grinning, 'since you said "please."'

11

Executive Priority Health was arguably the most exclusive gym in town. Located in downtown Chicago, the business took up the entire second floor of what used to be one of the grand old hotel buildings. Now it had office buildings on the upper levels and a miniature shopping center on the first floor.

Not just anyone could take the private elevator to the second floor. One had to be a member of the health club, and membership was tightly controlled and extremely expensive. Only the wealthiest and most influential men had a membership card.

Oh, and me.

The magnetic stripe on the back of the card didn't work when I swiped it through the card reader. No surprise there. I'd had it in my wallet for several months, and I doubt the magnetic signature stored on the card had lasted more than a couple of days. I hit the intercom button on the console.

'Executive Priority,' said a cheerful young woman's voice. 'This is Billie, and how may I serve you?'

Thomas glanced at me and arched an eyebrow, mouthing the words, *Serve you?*

'You'll see,' I muttered to him. I addressed the intercom. 'My card seems to have stopped working. Harry Dresden and guest, please.'

'One moment, sir,' Billie said. She was back within a few seconds. 'I apologize for the problem with your membership card, sir. I'm opening the elevator for you now.'

True to her word, the elevator opened, and Thomas and I got in.

It opened onto the main area of Executive Priority.

'You're kidding me,' Thomas said. 'Since when do *you* go to the gym?'

It looked pretty typically gymlike from here. Lots and lots of exercise machines and weight benches and dumbbells and mirrors; static bikes and treadmills stood in neatly dressed ranks. They'd paid some madman who thought he was a decorator a lot of money to make the place look hip and unique. Maybe it's my lack of fashion sense talking, but I thought they should have held out for one of those gorillas who has learned to paint. The results would have been of similar quality, and they could have paid in fresh produce.

Here and there men, mostly white, mostly over forty, suffered through a variety of physical activities. Beside each and every one of them was a personal trainer coaching, supporting, helping.

The trainers were all women, none of them older than their late twenties. They all wore ridiculously brief jogging shorts so tight that it had to be some kind of minor miracle that allowed the blood to keep flowing through the girls' legs. They all wore T-shirts with the gym's logo printed on them, also tight – and every single woman there had the kind of body that made her outfit look fantastic. No gym in the world had *that* many gorgeous girls in its employ.

'Ah,' Thomas said after a moment of looking around. 'This isn't a typical health club, is it?'

'Welcome to the most health-conscious brothel in the history of mankind,' I told him.

Thomas whistled quietly through his teeth, surveying the place. 'I'd heard that the Velvet Room had been retooled. This is it?'

'Yeah,' I said.

A brown-haired girl jiggled over to us, her mouth spread in a beauty-contest smile, and for a second I thought her shirt was about to explode under the tension. Bright gold lettering over her left breast read, BILLIE.

'Hello, Mister Dresden,' she chirped. She bobbed her head to

Thomas. 'Sir. Welcome to Executive Priority. Can I get you a drink before your workout? May I take your coats?'

I held up a hand. 'Thanks, Billie, but no. I'm not here for the exercise.'

Her smile stayed locked in place, pretty and meaningless, and she tilted her head to one side.

'I'm here to speak to Ms. Demeter,' I said.

'I'm sorry, sir,' Billie said. 'She isn't in.'

The girl was a confection for the eyes, and I felt sure that the other four senses would feel just as well fed after a bit of indulgence, but she wasn't a good liar. 'Yeah, she is,' I said. 'Tell her Harry Dresden is here.'

'I'm sorry, sir,' she said again, like a machine stuck on repeat. 'Ms. Demeter is not in the building.'

I gave her my toothiest smile. 'You're kind of new here, eh, Billie?'

The smile flickered, then stabilized again.

'Thomas.' I sighed. 'Give her a visual?'

My brother looked around, then went over to a nearby rack of steel dumbbells and picked up the largest set there, one in each hand. With about as much effort as I'd use to bundle twigs, he twisted the steel bars around each other, forming an asymmetric X shape. He held it up to make sure Billie saw it, and then dropped it at her feet. The weights landed with a forceful thump, and Billie flinched when they did.

'You should see the kinds of things he can bend and break,' I said. 'Expensive exercise machines, expensive furniture, expensive clients. I don't know how hard he could throw some of this stuff around, but I'd be lying if I told you that I wasn't kinda curious.' I leaned down a little closer and said, 'Billie, maybe you should kick this one up the line. I'd hate them to dock your pay to replace all the broken things.'

'I'll be right back, sir,' Billie said in a squeaky whisper, and scurried away.

'Subtle,' Thomas noted.

I shrugged. 'It saves time.'

'How'd you get a membership to a place like this?'

'It's Marcone's place. He thinks I'm less likely to trash it if I'm dazzled by friendly boobs.'

'Can't say I blame him,' Thomas admitted. His eyes locked on one particular girl who was currently at a table, filling out paperwork. She froze in place, and then looked up, very slowly. Her lips parted as she stared at Thomas, and her dark eyes widened. She started breathing faster, and then shook herself and hurriedly looked down again, pretending to read her paperwork.

My brother closed his eyes slowly and then turned his head away from the girl with the kind of steady, deliberate motion one uses to shut a heavy door. When he blinked his eyes open again, their color had shifted from deep grey to a pale grey-white, almost silver.

'You okay?' I asked him quietly.

'Mmmm,' he murmured. 'Sorry. Got distracted. There's . . . a kind of energy here.'

Which I probably should have thought of, dammit. This building was home to constant, regular acts of lust and desire. Those kinds of activities left a sort of psychic imprint around them, a vibe Thomas must have picked up on.

Vampires like my brother take not blood, but life-energy from their victims. Showing off his supernatural strength might have simplified things for us, but it also cost Thomas some of that energy, the same way an afternoon of hiking might leave you and me particularly hungry.

Usually vampires of the White Court fed during the act of sex. They could induce desire in others, overwhelm their victims with undiluted, primal lust. If he wanted to Thomas could have paralyzed the girl where she stood, stalked over to her, and done whatever he pleased to her. There wouldn't have been anything she could do to stop him. Hell, she would have begged him to do more, and to hurry up about it.

He wouldn't do it. Not anymore, anyway. He'd fought that part of himself for years, and he'd finally found a way to keep

it under control – by feeding in the equivalent of tiny, harm-
less nibbles from the customers in the upper-tier beauty salon
he owned and operated. I gathered that while it did enable him
to remain active and in control of himself, it was nowhere near
as satisfying as acquiring energy the old-fashioned way – in a
stalking seduction culminating in a burst of lust and ecstasy.

I knew that his Hunger, that inhuman portion of his soul
that was driven by naked need, was screaming at him to do
exactly that. If he did, though, it could do the girl serious harm,
even kill her. My brother wasn't like that – but denying his
Hunger wasn't something that came naturally. It was a fight.
And I knew what drove him to it.

'That girl looks a little like Justine,' I commented.

He froze at the name, his expression hardening. By gradual
degrees his eyes darkened to their usual color again. Thomas
shook his head and gave me a wry smile. 'Does she?'

'Enough,' I said. 'You okay?'

'As I ever am,' he said. He didn't actually thank me, but it
was in his voice. I pretended that I hadn't heard it there, which
was what he expected me to do.

It's a guy thing.

Billie came fibrillating back over to us. 'This way, please, sir,'
she said, her smile once again firmly in place. She led us rather
nervously through the gym, passing the hallway that led to the
showers and private 'therapy' rooms in back. The door she led
us through went to a very plain, practical, businesslike hallway,
one you'd find in any office building. She nodded to the last
door in the hall, the corner office, and then retreated quietly.

I ambled up to the door, knocked once, and then opened it
to find Ms. Demeter sitting in her large but practical office
behind her large but practical desk. She was a fit-looking woman
in early middle age, lean, well dressed, and reserved. Her real name
wasn't Demeter, but she preferred the professional sobriquet,
and now wasn't the time to needle her.

'Ms. Demeter,' I said, keeping my tone neutral. 'Good day.'

She finished turning off her laptop, folded it shut, and put it away in a drawer before she looked up and gave me a quiet nod. 'Mister Dresden. What happened to your face?'

'It's always like this,' I said. 'I forgot to put on my makeup today.'

'Ah,' she said. 'Will you have a seat?'

'Thanks,' I said. I sat down across the desk from her. 'I apologize if I've inconvenienced you.'

Her shoulder twitched in a nanoshrug. 'It's nice to know the limitations of those I've appointed my receptionist,' she replied. 'What can I do for you?' Then she lifted her hand. 'Wait. Allow me to rephrase. What can I do to most quickly get rid of you?'

A sensitive guy might have felt a little hurt by that remark. Good thing I'm me. 'I'm looking for Marcone,' I told her.

'Have you called his office?'

I blinked slowly at her once. Then I repeated, 'I'm looking for Marcone.'

'I'm sure you are,' Demeter said, her expression never flickering. 'What does that have to do with me?'

I felt a tight smile strain my lips. 'Ms. D, I can't help but wonder why you instructed your receptionist to tell anyone who asked after you that you weren't in the office.'

'Perhaps I had some paperwork I needed to get done.'

'Or perhaps you know that Marcone is missing, and you're using it as a tactic to stall any of his lieutenants who come nosing around looking to fill the void.'

She stared at me for a moment, her expression giving away nothing. 'I really can't say that I know what you're talking about, Mister Dresden.'

'You sure you don't want to get rid of me?' I asked. 'You want me to stay here and lean on you? I can make it really hard for you to do business, if I'm feeling motivated.'

'I'm sure,' Demeter replied. 'Why would you want to find him?'

I grimaced. 'I have to help him.'

She arched a single, well-plucked eyebrow. 'Have to?'

'It's complicated,' I said.

'And not terribly credible,' she replied. 'I am well aware of your opinions regarding John Marcone. And even assuming that I had any information as to his whereabouts, I'm not sure that I'd wish to make a bad situation worse.'

'How could you do that?' I asked.

'By involving *you*,' she replied. 'You clearly do not have Mr. Marcone's best interests in mind, and your involvement could push his captors into precipitous action. I doubt you'd lose a moment's sleep were he to be killed.'

I would have shot back a witty reply if I hadn't slipped on a banana peel of self-recrimination, having said more or less those exact words not long before.

'But sir!' came Billie's voice in protest from the hall outside.

The doorway darkened behind me, and I turned to find several large men standing there. The foremost of their number was a big guy, late forties, with an ongoing romance with beer, or maybe pasta. He wore his heart on his potbelly. His well-tailored suit mostly hid the gut, and it would have concealed the shoulder rig and sidearm he wore beneath it if he'd made the least effort to avoid exposing it as he moved.

'Demeter,' the big man said. 'I need to speak to you privately.'

'You couldn't afford me, Torelli,' Demeter replied smoothly. 'And I'm in the middle of a business meeting.'

'Get one of your whores to get him off,' Torelli said. 'You and I have to talk.'

She arched an eyebrow at him. 'Regarding?'

'I need a list of your bank accounts, security passwords, and a copy of your records for the last six months.' He scowled, looming over her. Torelli was the kind of guy who was used to getting his way if he loomed and scowled enough. I knew the type. I tried to glance past the goons to see whether Thomas was in the hallway, but could detect no sign of him.

'One wonders if you have been partaking of your product,' Demeter said. 'Why on earth should I provide you with my records, accounts, and funds?'

'Things are going to change around here, whore. Starting

with your attitude.' Torelli glanced at two of the four men behind him and angled his head toward Demeter. The two goons, both of them medium-caliber Chicago bruisers, stepped around Torelli and walked toward her.

I grimaced. I didn't care for Demeter much, personally, but I needed her, and I wouldn't be able to talk her into helping me if she were laid up in intensive care. Besides, she was a girl, and you don't hit girls. You don't let two-bit hired bullies do it, either.

I stood up and turned to face Torelli's men, staff in hand. I gave them my hardest look, which didn't even slow them down. The one on the right threw something at my face, and I had no time to work out what it might be. I ducked, recognized it as a snow-speckled winter glove, and realized that it had been a distraction.

The guy on the left came in on me when I was ducking and kicked a steel-toed work boot at my left knee. I turned my leg and took it on the shin. It hurt like hell, but at least I could still move. I rolled to one side, placing the goon on my left between myself and the goon on the right. He threw a looping right hand at me, and I met his knuckles with my staff. Knuckles crunched. The goon howled.

The other one bulled past his pain-stunned partner and came at me, obviously planning on tackling me to the floor so that all of his buddies could circle up and kick me for a while.

Couldn't have that. So I raised my right hand, clenched in a fist, baring four triple-wire bands, one on each finger. With a thought and a word I released the kinetic energy stored in one of the rings. It hit the goon like a locomotive, slamming him back and to the floor with a very satisfying thud.

I turned and kicked the stunned first goon in *both* shins, *hah*, then placed one of my heels against his hip and shoved him to the floor. He crumpled.

I turned to find myself staring down the barrel of Torelli's gun.

'Not bad, kid,' the would-be kingpin said. 'That judo or something?'

'Something like that.'

'I could use a man of your skills, once my health club finishes' – he gave Demeter a sour glance – 'reprioritizing.'

'You couldn't afford me,' I said.

'I'm going to be able to afford a lot,' he said. 'Name your price.'

'One hundred and fifty-six gajillion dollars,' I said promptly.

He squinted at me, as if trying to decide if I was joking. Or maybe he was just trying to figure out how many zeros I was talking about. 'Think you're cute, huh?'

'I'm freaking adorable,' I said. 'Especially with the raccoon face I've got going here.'

Torelli's features darkened. 'Kid. You just made the last mistake of your life.'

'God,' I said. 'I *wish*.'

Thomas put the barrel of his Desert Eagle against the back of Torelli's head and said in a pleasant voice, 'Lose the iron, nice and slow.'

Torelli stiffened in surprise and wasted no time in complying. He turned his head slightly, looking for his other two goons. I could see a pair of feet lying toes-up in the hallway, but there was no other sign of them.

I stepped up to him and said calmly, 'Take your men and get out. Don't come back.'

He regarded me with dull eyes, then pressed his lips together, nodded once, and began gathering up his men. Thomas picked up Torelli's gun and stuck it down the front of his pants, just like you're not supposed to do. He walked quietly over to stand beside me, his eyes tracking every movement the thugs made.

They departed, half carrying the poor bastard with the broken hand, while the two in the hallway staggered along, barely recovered from being choked unconscious.

Once they were gone I turned to face Demeter. 'Where were we?'

'I was questioning your motives,' she said.

I shook my head. 'Helen. You know who I am. You know

what I do. Yeah, I think Marcone is a twisted son of a bitch who probably deserves to die. But that doesn't mean I'm planning on carrying out the deed.'

She stared at me in silence for ten or fifteen seconds. Then she turned to her desk, drew out a notepad, and wrote something on a piece of paper. She folded it and offered it to me. I reached out for it, but when I tugged she didn't let go.

'Promise me,' she said. 'Give me your word that you'll do everything you can to help him.'

I sighed. Of course.

The words tasted like a rancid pickle coated in salt and vinegar, but I managed to say them. 'I will. You have my word.'

Demeter let go of the paper. I looked at it. An address, nothing more.

'It might help you,' she said. 'It might not.'

'That's more than I had a minute ago,' I said. I nodded to Thomas. 'Let's go.'

'Dresden,' Demeter said as I walked to the door.

I paused.

'Thank you. For handling Torelli. He would have hurt some of my girls tonight.'

I glanced back at her and nodded once.

Then Thomas and I headed for the suburbs.

12

Marcone's business interests were wide and varied. They had to be when you're laundering as much money as he was. He had restaurants, holding companies, import/export businesses, investment firms, financial businesses of every description – and construction companies.

Sunset Point was one of those boils festering on the face of the planet: a subdivision. Located half an hour north of Chicago, it had once been a pleasant little wood of rolling hills around a single tiny river. The trees and hills had all been bulldozed flat, exposing naked earth to the sky. The little river had been choked into a sludgy trough. Underneath the blanket of snow the place looked as smooth and white and sterile as the inside of a new refrigerator.

'Look at this,' I said to Thomas. I gestured at the houses, each of them on a lot that exceeded the building's foundation by the width of a postage stamp. 'People *pay* to live in places like this?'

'You live in the basement of a boardinghouse,' Thomas said.

'I live in a big city, and I rent,' I said. 'Houses like these go for several hundred thousand dollars, if not more. It'll take thirty years to pay them off.'

'They're nice houses,' Thomas said.

'They're nice cages,' I responded. 'No space around them. Nothing alive. Places like this turn a man into a gerbil. He comes home and scurries inside. Then he stays there until he's forced to go back out to the job he has to work so that he can make the mortgage payments on this gerbil habitat.'

'And they're way nicer than your apartment,' Thomas said.

'Totally.'

He brought the Hummer to a crunching halt in the snow, glaring through the windshield. 'Damn snow. I'm only guessing where the streets are at this point.'

'Just don't drive into what's going to be somebody's basement,' I said. 'We passed Twenty-third a minute ago. We must be close.'

'Twenty-third Court, Place, Street, Terrace, or Avenue?' Thomas asked.

'Circle.'

'Damned cul-de-sacs.' He started forward again, driving slowly. 'There,' he said, nodding to the next sign that emerged from the haze. 'That one?'

'Yeah.' Next to the customized street sign was a standard road sign declaring Twenty-fourth Terrace a dead end.

'Damned foreshadowing,' I muttered.

'What's that?'

'Nothing.'

We drove through the murky grey and white of a heavy snowfall, the light luminous, without source, reflected from billions of crystals of ice. The Hummer's engine was a barely audible purr. By comparison the crunch of its tires on snow was a dreadful racket. We rolled past half a dozen model houses, all of them lovely and empty, the snow piling up around windows that gaped like eye sockets in a half-buried skull.

Something wasn't right. I couldn't have told you what, exactly, but I could feel it as plainly as I could feel the carved wood of the staff I gripped in my hands.

We weren't alone.

Thomas felt it too. Moving smoothly, he reached an arm behind the driver's seat and drew forth his sword belt. It bore an old U.S. Cavalry saber he'd carried on a number of dicey occasions, paired up with a more recent toy he'd become fond of, a bent-bladed knife called a kukri, like the one carried by the Ghurkas.

'What is that?' he asked quietly.

I closed my eyes for a moment, reaching out with my arcane

senses, attempting to detect any energies that might be moving in around us. The falling snow muffled my magical perceptions every bit as much as it did my physical senses. 'Not sure,' I said quietly. 'But whatever it is, it's a safe bet it knows we're here.'

'How do you want to play it if the music starts?'

'I've got nothing to prove,' I said. 'I say we run like little girls.'

'Suits me. But don't let Murphy hear you talking like that.'

'Yeah. She gets oversensitive about "little."'

My shoulders tightened with the tension as Thomas drove forward slowly and carefully. He stopped the car beside the last house on the street. It had a finished look to it, the bushes of its landscaping poking up forlornly through the snow. There were curtains in the windows, and the faint marks of tire tracks, not quite full of new snowfall, led up the drive and to the closed garage.

'Someone's behind that third window,' Thomas said quietly. 'I saw them move.'

I hadn't seen anything, but then I wasn't a supernatural predator, complete with a bucketful of preternaturally sharp senses. I nodded to let him know that I'd heard him, and scanned the ground around the house. The snow was untouched. 'We're the first visitors,' I said. 'We're probably making someone nervous.'

'Gunman?'

'Probably,' I said. 'That's what most of Marcone's people are used to. Come on.'

'You don't want me to wait out here?'

I shook my head. 'There's something *else* out here. It might be nothing, but you're a sitting duck in the car. Maybe if you'd gotten the armored version . . .'

'Nag, nag, nag,' Thomas said.

'Let's be calm and friendly,' I said. I opened the door of the Hummer and stepped out into snow that came up over my knees. I made sure not to move too quickly, and kept my hands out in plain sight. On the other side of the Hummer Thomas mirrored me.

'Hello, the house!' I called. 'Anyone home?' My voice had that flat, heavy timbre you can only get when there's a lot of snow, almost like we were standing inside. 'My name is Dresden. I'm here to talk.'

Silence. The snow started soaking through my shoes and my jeans.

Thomas whipped his head around toward the end of the little street, where the subdivision ended and the woods that were next in line for the bulldozers began. He stared intently for a moment.

'It's in the trees,' he reported quietly.

The hair on the back of my neck stood up, and I hoped fervently that whatever was out there, it didn't have a gun. 'I'm not here for trouble!' I called toward the house. I held up two fingers and said, 'Scout's honor.'

This time I saw the curtain twitch, and caught a faint stir of motion behind it. The inner door to the house opened and a man's voice said, 'Come in. Hands where I can see them.'

I nodded at Thomas. He lifted his hand, holding his car key, and pointed it at the Hummer. It clunked and chirped, its doors locking. He came around the car, sword belt hanging over his shoulder, while I broke trail to the front porch, struggling through the snow. I knocked as much of the powder as I could off my lower body, using it as an excuse to give me time to ready my shield bracelet. I didn't particularly want to step through a dark doorway, presenting a shooting-gallery profile to any gunman inside, without taking precautions. When I came in I held my shield before me, silent and invisible.

'Stop there,' growled a man's voice. 'Staff down. Show your hands.'

I leaned my staff against the wall and did so. I'd know those monosyllables anywhere. 'Hi, Hendricks.'

A massive man appeared from the dimness in the next room, holding a police-issue riot gun in hands that made it look like a child's toy. He was built like a bull, and you could apply *thick* and *rocklike* to just about everything in his anatomy, especially if you started with his skull. He came close enough to let me see his close-cropped red hair. 'Dresden. Step aside.'

I did, and the shotgun was trained on my brother. 'You, vampire. Sword down. Fingers laced behind your head.'

Thomas rolled his eyes and complied. 'How come he doesn't have to put his hands behind his head?'

'Wouldn't make any difference with him,' Hendricks replied. Narrow, beady eyes swiveled like gun turrets back to me. 'What do you want?'

I wasn't sure I'd ever heard Hendricks speak a complete sentence, much less string phrases together. It was sort of disconcerting, the way it would be if Mister suddenly developed the capacity to open his own cans of cat food. It took me a second to get over the mental speed bump. 'Uh,' I said. 'I want to . . .'

I realized how lame this was going to sound. I gritted my teeth and said it quickly. 'I want to help your boss.'

There was a clicking sound from the wall, the sound of an audio speaker popping to life. A woman's voice said, 'Send the wizard up.'

Hendricks growled. 'You sure?'

'Do it. The vampire stays downstairs.'

Hendricks grunted and tilted his head to the right. 'Through there and up the stairs, Dresden. Move it.'

'Harry,' Thomas said quietly.

Hendricks brought his shotgun back up and covered Thomas. 'Not you, prettyboy. You stay put. Or both of you get out.'

'It's okay,' I said quietly to my brother. 'I feel better if someone I trust is watching the door anyway. Just in case someone else shows up.' I cast my eyes meaningfully in the direction of the woods where Thomas had said something lurked.

He shook his head. 'Whatever.' Then he leaned back against the wall, casual and relaxed, his hands behind his head as if they were there only to pillow his skull.

I brushed past Hendricks. Without slowing down or looking behind me, I said, 'Careful with that gun. He gets hurt and it's going to be bad for you, Hendricks.'

Hendricks ignored me. I had a feeling it was his strongest conversational ploy.

I went up the stairs, noting a couple of details as I went. First, that the carpet was even cheaper than mine, which made me feel more confident for some obscure reason.

Second, that there were bloodstains on it. A lot of them.

At the top of the stairs I found more bloodstains, including a long smear along one wall. I followed them down to one of three bedrooms on the upper level of the house. I paused and knocked on the door.

'Come in, Dresden,' said a woman's voice.

I came in.

Miss Gard lay in bed. It had been hauled over to the window so that she could see out of it. She had a heavy assault rifle of a design I didn't recognize next to her. The wooden handle of a double-headed battle-ax leaned against the bed, within reach of her hand. Gard was blond, tall, athletic, and while she wasn't precisely beautiful, she was a striking woman, with clean-cut features, icy blue eyes, and an athlete's build.

She was also a mess of blood.

She was soaked in it. So was the bed beneath her. Her shirt was open, revealing a black athletic bra and a long wound that ran the width of her stomach, just below her belly button. Slick grey-red ropy loops protruded slightly from the wound.

My stomach twisted, and I looked away.

'Goodness,' Miss Gard said, her voice quiet and rough, her face pale. 'You'd think you never saw anyone disemboweled before.'

'Just relieved,' I said. I forced myself to face her. 'First time today I've run into someone who looks worse than me.'

She showed me a weary smile for a moment.

'You need a doctor,' I said.

She shook her head. 'No.'

'Yes,' I said. 'You do. I'm surprised you haven't bled to death already. Think of what it would cost Monoc Securities to replace you.'

'They won't need to. I'll be fine. The company has a great health care package.' She picked up a small tube of what looked like heavy-duty modeling glue from the bed at her side. 'This isn't the first time I've had my guts ripped out. It isn't fun, but I'll make it.'

'Damn,' I said, genuinely impressed. 'Are they hiring?'

The question won another faint smile. 'You don't really fit the employee profile.'

'I am tired of being kept down by the man,' I said.

Gard shook her head wearily. 'How did you find us?'

'Demeter,' I said.

She lifted a golden eyebrow. 'I suppose that shouldn't surprise me. Though I've warned him. He's too trusting.'

'Marcone? Is too trusting?' I widened my eyes at her. 'Lady, that pretty much puts you in a paranoiac league of your own.'

'It isn't paranoia – just practical experience. A safe house isn't safe if it isn't secret.' She reached down and pressed bloodied fingers against a loop of gore, gently kneading it back into the wound. She let out a hiss of pain as she did, but she didn't let a little thing like an exposed internal organ get in the way of conversation. 'You threatened her?'

'Uh. Mostly I told her I'd help Marcone.'

She lifted the tube of airplane glue and smeared some of it onto either side of the wound, where she'd pushed her guts back in. She bled a little more. I noted that several inches of the wound had already been closed and sealed together.

'You gave her your word?' Gard asked.

'Uh, yeah, but—' I couldn't take it anymore. 'Look, could you maybe not do that while we talk? It makes it sort of hard for me to focus on the conversation.'

She pressed the edges of the wound together, letting out a breathy curse in a language I didn't know. 'Did you know,' she said, 'that this kind of glue was originally developed as an emergency battlefield suture?'

'Did you know that you're about to find out what I had for breakfast this morning?' I countered.

'I don't know if it's true,' she continued. 'I saw it in a movie. With – dammit – with werewolves.' She exhaled and drew her hands slowly from the wound. Another two or three inches of puckered flesh were now closed together. Gard looked awful, her face grey and lined with pain.

'Why, Dresden? Why are you looking for Marcone?'

'The short version? It's my ass if I don't.'

She squinted at me. 'It's personal?'

'Pretty much. I'll give you my word on it, if you like.'

She shook her head. 'It's not . . . your word that I doubt. That's . . . always been good.' She closed her eyes against the pain and panted for several seconds. 'But I need something from you.'

'What?'

'The White Council,' she rasped. 'I want you to call upon the White Council to recover Marcone.'

I blinked at her. 'Uh. What?'

She grimaced and began packing another couple inches of intestine back into her abdomen. 'The Accords have been breached. A challenge must be lodged. An Emissary summoned. As a Warden' – she gasped for a moment, and then fumbled the glue into place – 'you have the authority to call a challenge.'

Her fingers slipped, and the wound sprang open again. She went white with pain.

'Dammit, Sigrun,' I said, more appalled at her pain than her condition, and moved to help her. 'Get your hands out of the way.' When she did, I managed to close the wound a little more, giving the sharp-smelling glue a chance to bond the flesh closed.

She made an effort to smile at me. 'We . . . we worked well together at the beer festival. You're a professional. I respect that.'

'I'll bet you say that to all the guys who glue your stomach back together.'

'Call the Council,' Gard said. 'Lodge the challenge.'

'I've got a better idea,' I said. 'Tell me where Marcone is, I'll go get him and bring him home, and this will all be over.'

She started pushing the next bit back in, while I waited with the glue. 'It isn't that simple. I don't know where he is.'

I caught on. 'But you do know who took him.'

'Yes. Another signatory of the Accords, just as Marcone is now. I have no authority to challenge their actions. But you do. You may be able to force them into the light, bring the pressure of all the members of the Accords against them.'

'Oh, sure,' I said, laying out more glue. 'The Council just loves it when one of their youngest members drags the entire organization into a fight that isn't their own.'

'You would know, wouldn't you?' Gard rasped. 'It's not as though it would be the first time.'

I held the wound together, waiting on the glue. 'I can't,' I said quietly.

She was breathing too quickly, too hard. I could barely keep the wound closed. 'Whatever you . . . *nggh* . . . say. After all . . . it's your ass on the line.'

I grimaced and withdrew my fingers slowly, making sure the wound stayed closed. We'd gotten the last few inches, and the opening no longer gaped. 'Can't deny that,' I said. Then I squinted at her. 'Who is it?' I asked. 'Which signatory of the Accords swiped Marcone?'

'You've met them once already,' Gard said.

From downstairs Thomas suddenly shouted, 'Harry!'

I whirled toward the door in time for the window, behind me, to explode in a shower of glass. It jounced off my spell-layered leather duster, but I felt a pair of hot stings as bits of glass cut my neck and my ear. I tried to turn and had the impression of something coming at my face. I slapped it aside with my left hand even as I ducked, then hopped awkwardly back from the intruder.

It landed in a crouch upon the bed, digging one foot into the helpless Gard's wounded belly, a creature barely more than the size of a child. It was red and black, vaguely humanoid in shape, but covered in an insect's chitin. Its eyes were too large for its head, multifaceted, and its arms ended in the serrated clamps of a preying mantis. Membranous wings fluttered at its back, a low and maddening buzzing.

And that wasn't the scary part.

Its eyes gleamed with an inner fire, an orange-red glow – and immediately above the first set of eyes another set, this one blazing with sickly green luminescence, blinked and focused independently of the first pair. A sigil of angelic script burned against the chitin of the insect-thing's forehead.

I suddenly wished, very much, that my staff weren't twenty feet away and down a flight of stairs. It might as well have been on the moon, for all the good it was going to do me.

No sooner had that thought come out than the Knight of the Blackened Denarius opened its insectoid maw, let out a brassy wail of rage, and bounded at my face.

13

At one time in my life, a shapeshifted, demonically possessed maniac crashing through a window and trying to rip my face off would have come as an enormous and nasty surprise.

But that time was pretty much in the past.

I'd spent the last several years on the fringes of a supernatural war between the White Council of the wizards and the Vampire Courts. In the most recent years, I'd gotten more directly involved. Wizards who go to a fight without getting their act together tend not to come home. Worse, the people depending on them for protection wind up getting hurt.

The second most important rule of combat wizardry is a simple one: Don't let them touch you.

Whether you're talking about vampires or ogres or some other kind of monstrous nasty, most of them can do hideous things to you if they get close enough to touch – as even a lesser member of the gruff clan had demonstrated on my nose the night before.

The prime rule of combat wizardry is simple too: Be prepared.

Wizards can potentially wield tremendous power against just about anything that might come along – if we're ready to handle it. The problem is that the things that come after us know that too, so the favored tactic is the sudden ambush. Wizards might live a long time, but we aren't rend-proof. You've got to think ahead in order to have enough time to act when the heat is on.

I'd made myself ready and taught young wizards with even less experience than me how to be ready too – for an occasion just such as this.

The coil of steel chain in my coat pocket came out smoothly as I drew it, because I'd practiced the draw thousands of times, and I whipped one end at the mantis-thing's face.

It was faster than me, of course. They usually are. Those two clamps seized the end of the chain. The mantis's jaws clamped down on it, and the creature ripped the chain from my hands with a wrench of its head and upper body, quicker than thought.

That was a positive thing, really. The mantis hadn't had time to notice two important details about the chain: first, that the whole thing was coated in copper.

Second, that a standard electrical plug was attached to the other end.

I flipped my fingers at the nearest wall outlet and barked, '*Galvineus!*'

The plug shot toward the outlet like a striking snake and slammed home.

The lights flickered and went dim. The Denarian hopped abruptly into the air and then came down, thrashing and twitching madly. The electricity had forced the muscles in its jaws and clamps to contract, and it couldn't release the chain. Acrid smoke began to drift up from various points on its carapace.

'Wizard!' Gard gasped. She gripped the wooden handle of her ax and tossed it weakly toward me. I heard shouting and the bellow of a shotgun coming from downstairs. It stayed in the background, unimportant information. Everything that mattered to me was nearly within an arm's length.

The ax bounced and struck against my leg, but my duster prevented it from cutting into me. I picked up the ax – Christ, was it heavy – hauled off, and brought it straight down on the Denarian, as if I'd been splitting cordwood.

The ax crunched home, sinking to the eye somewhere in the Denarian's thorax. The thing's convulsions ripped the weapon out of my hands – and the plug from the wall outlet.

The mantis's head whipped toward me, and it screamed again. It ripped out the ax and came to its feet in the same instant.

'Get clear!' Gard rasped.

I did, diving to the side and going prone.

The wounded woman emptied her assault rifle into the mantis

in two or three seconds of howling thunder, shooting from the hip from about three feet away.

Words cannot convey how messy *that* was. Suffice to say that it would probably cost more to remove the ichor stains than it would to strip and refinish the walls, the floor, and the ceiling.

Gard gasped, and the empty rifle slid from her fingers. She shuddered and pressed her hands to her belly.

I moved to her side and picked her up, trying not to strain her stomach. She was heavy. Not like a sumo wrestler or anything, but she was six feet tall in her bare feet and had more than the usual amount of muscle. She felt at least as heavy as Thomas. I grunted with effort, got her settled, and started for the door.

Gard let out a croaking little whimper, and more blood welled from her injury. Faint pangs of sympathetic pain flickered through my own belly. Her eyes had rolled back in her head. It had taken a lot to beat Gard's apparent pain threshold, but it looked like the visit from the Denarian – and the activity it had forced on her – had done it.

The day just couldn't have gotten any more disturbing.

Until the splattered mass that had been the Denarian started quivering and moving.

'Oh, you have got to be *kidding* me!' I shouted.

Where there had been one big bug thing, now there were thousands of little mantislike creatures. They all began bounding toward the center of the room, piling up into two mounds that gradually began to take on the shape of insectoid legs.

The shotgun downstairs roared again, and running footsteps approached.

'Harry!' Thomas shouted. He appeared at the bottom of the stairs, sword in hand, just as I hurried out the door, still toting Gard.

'We had company up here!' I called. I started down the stairs as quickly and carefully as I could.

'I think there are three more of them down here,' Thomas said, making way for me. He took note of Gard. 'Holy crap.'

A corpse lay on the floor of the entry hall. It was black and furry and big, and I couldn't tell much more about it than that. The top four-fifths of its head were gone and presumably accounted for the mess all over the opposite wall. Its guts were spilled out on either side of its body, steaming in the cold air drifting through the shattered front door. Hendricks crouched in the shadowed living room, covering the entryway with his shotgun.

Something scraped over the floorboards of the ceiling above us.

'What's that?' Thomas asked.

'A giant preying mantis demon, dragging itself over the floor.'

Thomas blinked at me.

'That's just a guess,' I said.

Hendricks growled, 'How is she?'

'Not good,' I said. 'This is a bad spot to be in. No defenses here, not even a threshold to work with. We need to bail.'

'Shouldn't move her,' Hendricks said. 'It could kill her.'

'*Not* moving her will kill her,' I countered. 'Us too.'

Hendricks stared at me, but he didn't argue.

Thomas was already reaching into his pocket. He was tense, his eyes flicking restlessly, maybe in an attempt to track things that he could hear moving around outside. He dug out his key ring and held it with his teeth. Then he took his saber in one hand, that monster Desert Eagle in the other, and started humming 'Froggy Went A-Courting' under his breath.

Gard had slowly grown limp, and her head lolled bonelessly. I was having trouble keeping her steady. 'Hendricks,' I said, nodding at Gard.

Without a word he set the shotgun aside and took the woman from me. I saw his eyes as he did, touched with worry and fear – and not for himself. He took her very gently, something I would never have imagined him doing, and growled, 'How do I know you won't leave us behind? Let them rip us apart while you run?'

'You don't,' I said curtly, picking up my staff. 'Stay if you want. These things will kill you both; I guarantee it. Or you take a chance with us. Your call.'

Hendricks glared at me for a moment, but when he glanced down at the unconscious woman in his arms, the rocky scowl faded. He nodded once.

'Harry?' Thomas asked. 'How do you want to do this?'

'We head straight for your oil tanker,' I said. 'Shortest route between two points and all.'

'They'll have the door covered,' Thomas said.

'I hope so.'

'Okay,' he said, rolling his eyes. 'As long as there's a plan.'

Footsteps crossed the floor above us, and paused at the top of the stairs.

Thomas's gun swiveled toward the stairs. I didn't turn. I covered the doorway.

A voice like out-of-tune violin strings stroked by a rotting cobra hide drifted down the stairs. 'Wizard.'

'I hear you,' I said.

'This situation might be resolved without further conflict. Are you willing to parley?'

'Why not,' I answered. I didn't turn away from the door.

'Have I your word of safe passage?'

'You do.'

'Then you have mine,' the voice answered.

'Whatever,' I said. I lowered my voice to an almost subvocal whisper I was sure only Thomas could hear. 'Watch them. They'll try something the second they get a chance.'

'Why give them the opportunity?' Thomas murmured.

'Because we might find out something important by talking. It's harder to question corpses. Switch with me.'

We traded places, and I kept my staff pointed at the stairs as the mantis-thing came down them. It crouched on the topmost step it could occupy while still maintaining visual contact with the entry hall. It looked none the worse for wear for being blown to hamburger by Gard's rifle.

It crouched, the motion eerie and alien, and tilted its head almost entirely to the horizontal, first one way, then the other, as it looked at us. Then its stomach heaved. For a second I thought it was throwing up, as a yellow-and-pink mucus began to emerge from its mouth. After a second, though, it lifted its clamplike claws and gripped its head, then peeled it back and away from the mucus, the motion disturbingly akin to someone donning a too-small turtleneck sweater. A human face emerged from the mucus and gunk, while the split carapace of the head flopped about on its chest and upper back.

The Denarian looked like she was about fifteen years old, except for her hair, which was silvery grey, short, and plastered to her skull. She had huge and gorgeous green eyes, a heart-shaped face, and a delicate, pointy chin. Her skin was pale and clear, her cheekbones high, her features lovely and symmetrical. The second set of green eyes and the sigil of angelic script still glowed faintly on her forehead.

She smiled slowly. 'I wasn't expecting the chain. I thought fire and force were your weapons of choice.'

'You were standing on top of someone I knew,' I said. 'I didn't feel like burning her or blasting her through the wall.'

'Foolish,' the girl murmured.

'I'm still here.'

'But so am I.'

'You have five seconds to get to the fucking point,' I said. 'I'm not going to let you stall while your buddies get into position.'

Mantis Girl narrowed her eyes. The eyes on her forehead narrowed as well. *Très* creepy. She nodded at Hendricks and Gard. 'My business is with them. Not you, O Warden of the White Council. Give them to me. You may leave in peace. Once they are dead, I will gather my compatriots and we will depart the city without harm to any innocents.'

I grunted. 'What if I need them alive?'

'If you wish, I can wait until you have interrogated them.'

'Yeah, that's what I want: you, standing around behind my back.'

She lifted a talon. 'I give you my solemn word. No harm will come to you or your companion.'

'Tempting,' I said.

'Shall I add in material reward as well?' Mantis Girl asked. 'I'll pay you two hundred thousand, in cash.'

'Why on earth would you do that?'

She shrugged a shoulder. 'My quarrel is with the upstart Baron and his subjects − not the White Council. I would prefer to demonstrate my respect to your people, instead of causing an untoward altercation with them over the matter of your death.'

'Uh-huh.'

Her smile turned sharper. 'If it pleases you, I might offer to entertain you, once business is done.'

I let out a harsh burst of laughter. 'Oh,' I said, still chortling. 'Oh, oh, oh. That's funny.'

She blinked and stared at me, uncomprehending.

The expression made me laugh even harder. 'You . . . you want me to . . . I mean, Hell's bells, do you think I don't *know* what happens to a mantis's mate once the deed is done?'

She bared her teeth in sudden anger. They were shiny and black.

'You want me to trust you,' I went on, still laughing, 'and you think waving some bling and some booty at me is going to get it done? God, that's so cute I could just put you in my pocket.'

'Do not deny me what is mine, wizard,' she snarled. 'I *will* have them. Make a pact with me. I will honor it.'

'Yeah,' I said. 'I've seen the way you people honor your pacts. Let me make you a counteroffer. Give me Marcone, safe and whole, and get out of town, now, and I'll let you live.'

'Suppose your offer appeals. Why should I believe you would allow us to leave in peace?'

I gave her a faint smile and quietly paraphrased a dead friend. 'Because I know what your word is worth, Denarian. And you know the worth of mine.'

She stared at me for a moment. Then she said, 'I will consult my companions and return in five minutes.'

I bowed my head slightly to her. She returned the gesture and started up the stairs again.

She vanished from sight. Glass broke somewhere upstairs.

Then a red-and-black blur flashed down the stairs toward us, simultaneously with a chorus of hellish cries from outside.

Treachery doesn't work so well when the other guy expects it, and I'd had the spell ready to go since the second she'd turned her back. Mantis Girl didn't get to the bottom of the stairs before I pointed my staff at her and snarled, '*Forzare!*'

A hammer of pure kinetic energy slammed against her. She went flying back the way she'd come, and when she reached the top of the stairs she kept going, crashing through the wall of the house with a tremendous crunch.

No time to lose. Something came charging through the doorway, to be met by Thomas's sword and pistol. I didn't get a good look at it, but got an impression of spiraling antlers and green scales. I drew in my will, pointed my staff at the front wall of the house and murmured, '*Forzare,*' sending out a slow pulse of motion. I let it press up against the front wall of the house, and then fed more energy into it, hardening it into a single striking surface.

Then I drew back and really let loose, roaring '*Forzare!*' at the top of my lungs. I unleashed everything I had into a blast of energy, which struck against the plate of force I'd just created. There was an enormous sound of screaming wood and steel, and the entire front wall of the house blasted free from its frame.

Demonic voices howled. I turned to find Thomas taking advantage of the distraction to whip his saber through scything arcs, rondello-style, cutting his opponent to ribbons. The Denarian bounded away, screaming in brassy pain.

'Dammit!' Thomas screamed at me. 'That's a brand-new car!'

'Quit whining and go!' I shouted back, suiting words to action. The front wall of the house had come down like a tidal wave, shattering into a small ocean of rubble, covering the hood of the Hummer. Somewhere beneath the rubble I could hear the other Denarians trying to get free.

We rushed for the Hummer and piled in. Thomas got it

started just as Mantis Girl sailed down from overhead and landed on the hood of the Hummer, denting it in sharply.

'God*dammit!*' Thomas snarled. He slapped the Hummer into reverse and started driving backward – while emptying his gun into Mantis Girl. Bursts of fluttering insect forms flew up from the gunshots instead of sprays of blood, but judging by the screaming it hurt her plenty. She tumbled back off the hood and vanished.

Thomas manhandled the Hummer into a turn, and we left, heading back out into the heavy snowfall.

We all rode in silence for several moments while our heart rates slowed and the terror-fueled adrenaline rush faded.

Then Thomas said, 'I don't think we learned much.'

'The hell we didn't,' I said.

'Like what?'

'We know that there are more than five Denarians in town. *And* we know that they're signatories of the Accords – who apparently object to Marcone's recent elevation.'

Thomas grunted acknowledgment. 'What now?'

I shook my head wearily. That last spell had been a doozy. 'Now? I think . . .' I turned my head and studied the unconscious Gard. 'I think I'd better call the Council.'

14

Now that I had not one, but two supernatural hit squads with a good reason to come after me, my options had grown sort of limited. In the end there was really only one place I could take Gard and Hendricks without endangering innocent lives: St. Mary of the Angels Church.

Which was why I told Thomas to drive us to the Carpenter house.

'I still think this is a bad idea,' Thomas said quietly. The plow trucks were working hard, but so far they'd barely been keeping even with the snow, ensuring that the routes to the hospitals were clear. The streets in some places looked like World War I trenches, snow piled up head-high on either side.

'The Denarians know that we use the church as a safehouse,' I said. 'They'll be watching it.'

Thomas grunted and checked the rearview mirror. Gard was still unconscious, but breathing. Hendricks's eyes were shut, his mouth slightly open. I didn't blame him. I hadn't been standing watch over a wounded comrade all night, and I felt like I could have taken a nap, too.

'What were those things?' Thomas asked.

'The Knights of the Blackened Denarius,' I replied. 'You remember Michael's sword? The nail worked into the hilt?'

'Sure,' Thomas said.

'There are two others like it,' I said. 'Three swords. Three nails.'

Thomas's eyes widened for a moment. 'Wait. *Those* nails? From the Crucifixion?'

I nodded. 'Pretty sure.'

'And those things were what? Michael's opposite number?'

'Yeah. Each of those Denarian bozos has a silver coin.'

'Three silver coins,' Thomas said. 'I'm drawing a blank.'

'Thirty,' I corrected him.

Thomas made a choking sound. *'Thirty?'*

'Potentially. But Michael and the others have several of them hidden away at the moment.'

'Thirty pieces of silver,' Thomas said, understanding.

I nodded. 'Each coin has the spirit of one of the Fallen trapped inside. Whoever possesses one of the coins can draw upon the Fallen angel's power. They use it to shapeshift into those forms you saw, heal wounds, all kinds of fun stuff.'

'They tough?'

'Certifiable nightmares,' I said. 'A lot of them have been alive long enough to develop some serious talent for magic, too.'

'Huh,' Thomas said. 'The one who came through the door didn't seem like such a badass. Ugly, sure, but he wasn't Superman.'

'Maybe you got lucky,' I said. 'As long as they have the coins, "hard to kill" doesn't begin to describe it.'

'Ah,' Thomas said. 'That explains it, then.'

'What?' I asked.

Thomas reached into his pants pocket and drew out a silver coin a little larger than a nickel, blackened with age, except for the shape of a single sigil, shining cleanly through the tarnish. 'When I gutted Captain Ugly, this went flying out.'

'Hell's bells!' I spat, and flinched away from the coin.

Thomas twitched in surprise, and the Hummer went into a slow slide on the snow. He turned into it and regained control of the vehicle without ever taking his eyes off me. 'Whoa, Harry. What?'

I pressed my side up against the door of the Hummer, getting as far as I physically could from the thing. 'Look, just . . . just don't move, all right?'

He arched an eyebrow. 'Ooookay. Why not?'

'Because if that thing touches your skin, you're screwed,' I said. 'Shut up a second and let me think.'

The gloves. Thomas had been wearing gloves earlier, when fingering Justine's scarf. He hadn't touched the coin with his skin, or he'd already know how much trouble he was in. Good. But the coin was a menace, and I strongly suspected that the entity trapped inside it might be able to influence the physical world around it in subtle ways – enough to go rolling away from its former owner, for example, or to somehow manipulate Thomas into dropping or misplacing it.

Containment. It had to be contained. I fumbled at my pockets. The only container I was carrying was an old Crown Royal whiskey bag, the one that held my little set of gaming dice. I dumped them out into my pocket and opened the bag.

I already had a glove on my left hand. My paw had recovered significantly from the horrible burns it had gotten several years before, but it still wasn't what you'd call pretty. I kept it covered out of courtesy to everyone who might glance at it. I held the little bag open with two fingers of my left hand and said, 'Put it in here. And for God's sake, don't drop it or touch me with it.'

Thomas's eyes widened further. He bit his lower lip and moved his hand very carefully, until he could drop the inoffensive little disk into the Crown Royal bag.

I jerked the drawstrings tight the second the coin was in, and tied the bag shut. Then I slapped open the Hummer's ashtray, stuffed the bag inside, and slammed it closed again.

Only then did I draw a slow breath and sag back down into my seat.

'Jesus,' Thomas said quietly. He hesitated for a moment and then said, 'Harry . . . is it really that bad?'

'It's worse,' I said. 'But I can't think of any other precautions to take yet.'

'What would have happened if I'd touched it?'

'The Fallen inside the coin would have invaded your consciousness,' I said. 'It would offer you power. Temptation. Once you gave in enough, it would own you.'

'I've resisted temptation before, Harry.'

'Not like this.' I turned a frank gaze to him. 'It's a Fallen angel, man. Thousands and thousands of years old. It knows how people think. It knows how to exploit them.'

His voice sharpened a little. 'I come from a family where everyone's an incubus or a succubus. I think I know a little something about temptation.'

'Then you should know how they'd get you.' I lowered my voice and said gently, 'It could give Justine back to you, Thomas. Let you touch her again.'

He stared at me for a second, a flicker of wild longing somewhere far back in his eyes. Then he turned his head slowly back to the road, his expression slipping into a neutral mask. 'Oh,' he said quietly. After a moment he said, 'We should probably get rid of the thing.'

'We will,' I said. 'The Church has been up against the Denarians for a couple of thousand years. There are measures they can take.'

Thomas glanced down at the ashtray for a second, then dragged his eyes away and glowered at the dented hood of his Hummer. 'They couldn't have shown up six months ago. When I was driving a Buick.'

I snorted. 'As long as you've got your priorities in order.'

'I just met them, but already I hate these guys,' Thomas said. 'But why are they here? Why now?'

'Offhand? I'd say that they were out to wax Marcone and prove to the other members of the Accords that vanilla mortals have no place among us weirdos – I mean, superhumans.'

'They're members of the Accords?'

'I'd have to look it up,' I said. 'I doubt they're signed on as the "Order of Demon-possessed Psychotics." But from the way Mantis Girl was talking, yeah.'

Thomas shook his head. 'So what do they get out of it? What does taking Marcone prove?'

I shrugged. I had already asked myself the same questions and hadn't been able to come up with any answers. 'No clue,' I said. 'But they've got what it takes to have torn that building apart, and to get around or go through the kind of muscle Marcone keeps around him.'

'And what the hell are the Faerie Queens doing getting involved?' Thomas asked.

I shrugged again. I'd already asked myself that, too. I hate it when I have to answer my own questions like that.

We went the rest of the way to Michael's place in grey-and-white silence.

His street was on one of the routes being kept plowed, and we had no trouble rolling right up into his driveway. Michael himself was there with his two tallest sons, each of them wielding a snow shovel as they labored to clear the driveway and the sidewalk and the porch of the ongoing snow.

Michael regarded the Hummer with pursed lips as Thomas pulled in. He said something to his sons that made them trade a look with each other, then hurry inside. Michael walked down the driveway to my side of the truck and looked at my brother, then at the passengers in the backseat.

I rolled down the window. 'Hey,' I said.

'Harry,' he said calmly. 'What are you doing here?'

'I just had a conversation with Preying Mantis Girl,' I said. I held up a notebook, where I'd scribbled down the angelic sigil while it was still fresh in my memory.

Michael took a deep breath and grimaced. Then he nodded. 'I had a feeling they might be in town.'

'Oh?' I asked.

The front door of the house opened, and a large, dark-skinned man appeared, dressed in blue jeans and a dark leather jacket. He wore a gym bag over one broad shoulder, and had one hand resting casually inside it. He paced out into the cold and the snow as if he'd been wearing full winter-weather gear, rather than casual traveling clothes, and stalked over toward us.

Once he got close enough to make out the details his face split into a broad, brief grin, and he hurried to stand beside Michael. 'Harry!' he said, his voice deep, rich, and thick with a Russian accent. 'We meet again.'

I answered his grin. 'Sanya,' I replied, offering my hand. He shook it with enough force to crack bones. 'What are you doing here?'

'Passing through,' Sanya said, and hooked a thumb up at the snow. 'I was on the last flight in before they closed the airport. Looks like I am staying for a few days.' His eyes went from my face to the notebook, and the pleasant expression on his dark face turned to a brief snarl.

'Somebody you know?' I asked.

'Tessa,' he said. 'And Imariel.'

'You've met, huh?'

His jaw clenched again. 'Tessa's second . . . recruited me. Tessa is here?'

'With friends.' I sketched the sigil I'd seen on the blackened denarius a few moments before and held it up to them.

Sanya shook his head and glanced at Michael.

'Akariel,' Michael said at once.

I nodded. 'He's in a Crown Royal bag in the ashtray.'

Michael blinked. Sanya too.

'I hope you have one of those holy hankies. I'd have taken it to Padre Forthill, but I figured they'd have him under observation. I need someplace quiet to hole up.'

Sanya and Michael traded a long, silent look.

Sanya frowned, examining my brother. 'Who is the vampire?'

I felt Thomas stiffen in surprise. As a rule, even members of the supernatural world can't detect what a vampire of the White Court truly is, unless he's actually in the middle of doing something vampity. It's a natural camouflage for his kind, and they rely upon it every bit as much as a leopard does its spots.

But it can be tough to hide things from a Knight of the Cross. Maybe it's a part of the power they're given, or maybe it's just a part of the personality of the men chosen for the job – don't ask me which. I'm fuzzy on the whole issue of faith and the Almighty, and I swim those waters with extreme caution and as much brevity as possible. I just know that the bad guys rarely get to sneak up on a Knight of the Cross, and that the Knights have a propensity for bringing the truth to light.

I met Sanya's gaze for a moment and said, 'He's with me. He's also the reason Akariel has a date with the inside of a vault.'

Sanya seemed to consider that for a moment. He glanced at Michael, who gave a grudging nod.

The younger Knight pursed his lips thoughtfully at that, his gaze moving to the backseat.

Hendricks had woken up, but he hadn't moved. He watched Sanya with steady, beady eyes.

'The woman,' Sanya said, frowning. 'What is she?'

'Hurt,' I said.

Something like chagrin flickered over his features. '*Da*, of course. You would not bring her here if you thought her a danger.'

'Not to you or me,' I said. 'Tessa might have a different opinion.'

Sanya's eyebrows went up. 'Is that how she was wounded?'

'That was *after* she was wounded.'

'Really.' Sanya peered a little more closely at Gard.

'Back off,' Hendricks rumbled. 'Comrade.'

Sanya flashed that swift smile again and displayed open palms to Hendricks.

Michael nodded to Thomas. 'Pull the truck around to the back of the house. With all this snow piled up it should be hidden from the street.'

'Thank you, Michael,' I said.

He shook his head. 'There's a heater in the workshop, and a couple of folding cots. I'm not exposing the children to this.'

'I understand.'

'Do you?' Michael asked gently. He thumped the truck's dented hood once, lightly, and waved Thomas toward the back of the house.

Twenty minutes later we were all warm, if a bit crowded in Michael's workshop.

Gard lay on a couch, sleeping, her color improving almost visibly. Hendricks sat down with his back to the wall beside Gard's cot, presumably to stand watch, but he'd started snoring within a few minutes. Sanya, with the help of Molly and her siblings, was off rounding up food.

I watched as Michael wrapped Akariel up in a clean white hankie embroidered with a silver cross, muttering a prayer under his breath the whole while. Then he slipped the hankie into a plain wooden box, also adorned with a silver cross. 'Excuse me,' he said. 'I need to secure this.'

'Where do they keep those things?' Thomas asked, after Michael had departed.

I shrugged. 'Some big warehouse with a gazillion identical boxes, probably.'

Thomas snorted.

'Don't even think it,' I said. 'It isn't worth it.'

Thomas ran his gloved fingers over the white scarf. 'Isn't it?'

'You saw how these things operate. They'll manipulate your emotions and self-control, and something bad would happen to Justine. Or they'd wait until they had you hook, line, and sinker and you were their meat puppet. And something bad would happen to Justine.'

Thomas shrugged. 'I've got one demon in my head already. What's one more?'

I studied his profile. 'You've got one monster in your head already,' I countered. 'She barely survived it.'

He was still for a moment. Then he slammed his elbow back against the workshop wall, a gesture of pure frustration. Wood splintered, and a little cold air whooshed in.

'Maybe you're right,' he said in a dull voice.

'Holy crap,' I said. An idea crystallized in my head, and a chill went down my spine.

Thomas rubbed his elbow lightly. 'What?'

'I just had a really unpleasant thought.' I gestured at Marcone's exhausted retainers. 'I don't think the Denarians took Marcone so that they could erase him and make an example of him.'

My brother shrugged. 'Why else would they do it?'

I bit my lip, my stomach turning in uncomfortable flips.

'Because,' I said, 'maybe they want to recruit him.'

15

Thomas stood watch over our sleeping beauties while I went inside to talk with Michael and Sanya at the Carpenter kitchen table.

I laid all the cards down. See above regarding the general futility of lying to Knights of the Cross – and besides, they'd both more than earned my trust. It didn't take me very long.

'So,' I said, 'I think we've got to move fast, and get Marcone away from them before he's forced to join up.'

Michael frowned and folded his broad, work-scarred hands on the table before him. 'What makes you think he's going to tell them no?'

'Marcone's scum,' I said. 'But he's his own scum. He doesn't work for anyone.'

'You are sure?' Sanya asked, frowning thoughtfully.

'Yeah,' I said. 'I think that's why they wanted to grab Hendricks and Gard instead of killing them. So they could force him to take the coin or they'd kill his people.'

Michael grunted. 'It's a frequently used tactic.'

'Not for Tessa,' Sanya said, his voice absolutely certain. 'She prefers to find those already well motivated to accept a coin. She regards their potential talents as a secondary factor to raw desire.'

Michael acceded the point with a nod. 'Which would mean that Tessa isn't giving the orders.'

Sanya showed his teeth in a sudden, fierce grin. 'Nicodemus is here.'

'Fu—' I started to swear, but I glanced at Michael and changed it to, 'Fudgesicles. Nicodemus nearly killed us all last time he was in town. And he *did* kill Shiro.'

Both of the Knights nodded. Michael bowed his head and murmured a brief prayer.

'Guys,' I said, 'I know that your first instincts tend to be to stand watch against the night, turning the other cheek, and so on. But he's here with maybe twice the demon-power he had on his last visit. If we wait for him to come to us, he'll tear us apart.'

'Agreed,' Sanya said firmly. 'Take the initiative. Find him and hit the snake before he can coil to strike.'

Michael shook his head. 'Brother, you forget our purpose. We are not given our power so that we can strike down our enemies, no matter how much they might deserve it. Our purpose is to rescue the poor souls trapped by the Fallen.'

'Nicodemus doesn't want to be rescued,' I said. 'He's in full collaboration with his demon.'

'Which changes nothing about our duty,' he said. 'Anyone, even Nicodemus, can seek redemption, no matter what they've done, as long as they have breath enough to ask forgiveness.'

'I don't suppose a pair of sucking chest wounds could get us around that?' I asked him. 'Because if they would, I'd be tickled to provide them.'

Sanya let out a bark of laughter.

Michael smiled, but it was brief and strained. 'My point is that we can undertake such an aggressive move in only the direst of circumstances.'

'Faerie stands poised on the brink of an internal war,' I said. 'Which would probably reignite the war between the Council and the Vampire Courts – and in the bad guys' favor, I might add. One of the most dangerous men I've ever known is about to have involuntary access to the knowledge and power of a Fallen angel, which would give the Denarians access to major influence within the United States. Not to mention the serious personal consequences for me if they succeed in making it happen.' I looked back and forth between the two Knights, and held up one hand straight over my head. 'I vote dire. All in favor?'

Michael caught Sanya's hand on the way up, and pushed it gently back down to the table. 'This isn't a democracy, Harry. We serve a King.'

Sanya frowned for a moment, glancing at me. But then he settled back in his chair, a silent statement of support for Michael.

'You want to *talk* to them?' I asked Michael. 'You've got to be kidding me.'

'I didn't say that,' Michael replied. 'But I will not set out to simply murder them and have done. It's a solution, Harry. But it isn't good enough.'

I settled back in my chair and rubbed at my head with one hand. An ache was forming there. 'Okay,' I said quietly, trying to make up a plan as I went along. 'What if . . . I set up a talk? Could you be lurking nearby for backup?'

Michael sighed. 'There's a measure of sophistry in that. You know they'll try to betray you if it seems to be to their advantage.'

'Yeah. And it'll be their choice to do it. That's what you're looking for, isn't it? Some way to deal with the problem while still giving them a choice about what to do? Preferably in some manner that will get as few good guys killed as possible?'

He looked pained, but Michael nodded.

'Fine,' I said. 'I'll try to set it up.'

'How?' Sanya asked.

'Let me worry about that,' I said. I checked the clock on the wall. 'Crap. I'm late for a meeting. Can I borrow your phone?'

'Of course,' Michael said.

I glanced around the quiet house on my way to the phone and frowned. 'Where is everyone?'

'Charity took them elsewhere for a few days,' Michael said. 'There won't be school in this mess, anyway.'

I grunted. 'Where's Molly?'

Michael paused and then shook his head. 'I'm not sure. I don't think she went with them.'

I thought about it for a moment and thought I knew where

she'd be. I nodded around the kitchen. 'How do you keep things running around here with Molly under the roof? I figured things would be breaking down left and right.'

'Lots and lots of preventive maintenance,' Michael replied steadily. 'And about twice as much repair work as I usually do.'

'Sorry.'

He smiled. 'Small price. She's worth it.'

The reasons I like Michael have nothing to do with swords and the smiting of evil.

I got on the phone and dialed McAnally's Pub.

'Mac,' answered Mac, the ever-laconic owner.

'It's Harry Dresden,' I said. 'Is Sergeant Murphy there?'

Mac grunted in the affirmative.

'Put a beer on my tab and tell her I'm on the way?'

Mac grunted yes again.

'Thanks, man.'

He hung up without saying good-bye.

I made another call and spoke to a humorless-sounding man with a Slavic accent. I muttered my password, so that no one in the kitchen would overhear it, but the connection was so bad that I wound up all but screaming it into the receiver. That kind of thing is to be expected when you've got a wizard on both ends.

It only took the Jolly Northman about ten minutes to get my call through to my party.

'Luccio,' said a young woman's voice. 'What's gone wrong, Harry?'

'Hey!' I protested. 'That's a hell of a thing to say to a man, Captain. Just because I'm calling in doesn't mean that there's some kind of crisis.'

'Technically true, I suppose. Why are you calling?'

'Well. There's a crisis.'

She made an *mmmmmm* sound.

'A group known as the Knights of the Blackened Denarius has kidnapped Baron Marcone.'

'The crime lord you took it upon yourself to assist in joining the Accords?' Luccio asked, amusement in her voice. 'In what way is that relevant to the White Council?'

'These Denarian creeps are also signatories of the Accords,' I said. 'Marcone's retainers are crying foul. They've asked me to formally protest the abduction and summon an Emissary to resolve the dispute.'

Seconds of silence ticked by.

'In what way,' Luccio repeated, her voice much harder this time, 'is that relevant to the White Council?'

'The Accords don't mean anything if they aren't enforced and supported,' I said. 'In the long run, it's in our own best interests to make sure they're supported now, before a precedent is set and—'

'Don't bullshit me,' the captain of the Wardens snarled, a hint of an Italian accent creeping into her speech. 'If we take formal action it could provoke a war – a war we simply cannot afford. We all know the Red Court is only catching its breath. We can ill afford the losses we've already taken, much less those we might assume in a new conflict.'

I made sure to keep my voice steady, grim. 'Mab has contacted me personally. She has indicated that it is strongly in our own best interests to intervene.'

It wasn't *exactly* a lie. I hadn't ever specified who *we* meant. And with any luck the mention of Mab would keep Luccio's attention completely. The only reason the Red Court hadn't wiped us out in the years-long war was that Mab had given the Council right-of-way through the portions of the Nevernever under her control, allowing us wizards to stay as mobile as our opponents, who had considerably less difficulty employing mortal vehicles to maneuver its soldiery.

'*Jesu Christi,*' Luccio spat. 'She means to withdraw our right-of-way through Winter if we don't accede to her demands.'

'Well,' I said, 'she never actually came out and *said* that.'

'Of course she didn't. She never speaks plainly at all.'

'She does keep her deals, though,' I pointed out.

'She doesn't make deals she can't slide out of. She's forbidden the Ways to her people but also to the Wyldfae as a gesture of courtesy. All she needs to do is relax her ban against the Wyldfae, and we'd be forced to travel in strength every time we went through the Ways.'

'She's a sneaky bitch,' I agreed. I crossed my fingers.

Luccio exhaled forcefully through her nose. 'Very well. I will forward the appropriate notifications, pending approval by the Senior Council. Which Emissary would you prefer?'

'The Archive. We have a working relationship.'

Luccio *mmmmm*ed again. I heard a pencil scratching. 'Dresden,' she said, 'I cannot stress to you enough how vital it is that we avoid general hostilities, even with a relatively small power.'

Translation: *Don't start another war, Harry.*

'But,' she continued, 'we can afford to lose the paths through Winter even less.'

Translation: *Unless you really have to.*

'I hear you,' I said. 'I'll do my best.'

'Do better,' Luccio said, her tone blunt. 'There are those on the Senior Council who hold the opinion that we're already fighting one war because of your incompetence.'

I felt heat flush up my neck. 'If they bring that up, remind them that my incompetence is the only reason they weren't all blasted to molecules by a newborn god,' I shot back. 'And after that, remind them that because of my incompetence, we're enjoying a cease-fire that we desperately needed to replace our losses. And after *that*—'

'That is enough, Warden,' the captain snapped.

I fought down my frustration and clamped my mouth shut.

Hey, we were coming up on the holidays. They're a time of miracles.

'I'll notify you when I learn something,' Luccio said, and hung up the phone.

I hung up too, harder than I really needed to. I turned to find Michael and Sanya staring at me.

'Harry,' Michael said quietly, 'that was Captain Luccio, was it not?'

'Yeah,' I said.

'You never told us that Mab threatened to go back on her bargain.'

'Well, no.'

Michael watched me with troubled eyes. 'Because she didn't. You just lied to Luccio.'

'Yeah,' I said shortly. 'Because I need the Council's say-so to set up the meeting. Because I've *got* to set up the meeting so that the gang of murdering bastards who tortured Shiro to death will have a chance to prove to you that they've still got it coming.'

'Harry, if the Council learns that you've misled them—'

'They'll probably charge me with treason,' I said.

Michael rose from his seat. 'But—'

I stabbed a finger at him. 'The longer we delay, the longer those creeps stay in town, the longer Summer's hit men keep coming after me, and the more likely it is that innocent people are going to get hurt in the cross fire. I've got to move fast, and the best way to get the Council to move is to let it think its own ass is about to fall into the fire.'

'Harry—' Michael began.

'Don't,' I said. 'Don't give me the speech about redemption and mercy and how everyone deserves a second chance. I'm all for doing the right thing, Michael. You know that. But this isn't the time.'

'Then what is right changes because we're in a hurry?' he asked gently.

'Even your Book says that there's a time for all things,' I said. 'A time to heal – and a time to kill.'

Michael looked from me to the corner by the back door, where the broadsword *Amoracchius* rested in its humble leather scabbard, its plain, crusader-style hilt bound in wire. 'It isn't that, Harry. I've seen more of what they've done than you have. I have no qualms with fighting them, if it comes to that.'

'They've already blown up a building, tried to murder me, and set off a situation that nearly got your own children

burned down in the cross fire. In what way has it *not* come
to *that?*'

Instead of answering, Michael shook his head, took up
Amoracchius, and walked further into the house.

I scowled after him for a minute and muttered darkly under
my breath.

'You confused him,' Sanya rumbled.

I glanced at the dark-skinned Knight. 'What?'

'You confused him,' Sanya repeated. 'Because of what you
did.'

'What? Lying to the Council? I don't see that I had much
choice.'

'But you did,' Sanya said placidly. He reached into the gym
bag on the floor next to him and drew out a long saber, an old
cavalry weapon – *Esperacchius*. A nail worked into the hilt declared
it a brother of Michael's sword. He started inspecting the blade.
'You could have simply moved to attack them.'

'By myself? I'm bad, but I'm not that bad.'

'He's your friend. He would have come with you. You know
that.'

I shook my head. 'He's my friend. Period. You don't do that
to your friends.'

'Precisely,' Sanya said. 'So instead you have placed your own
life in jeopardy in order to protect his beliefs. You risk your body
to preserve his heart.' He brought out a smooth sharpening stone
and began stropping the saber's blade. 'I suppose he considers it
a particularly messianic act.'

'That's not why I did it,' I said.

'Of course it isn't. He knows that. It isn't easy for him. Usually
he's the one protecting another, willing to pay the price if he
must.'

I exhaled and glanced after Michael. 'I don't know what else
I could have done.'

'*Da*,' Sanya agreed. 'But he is still afraid for you.' He fell
quiet for a moment, while his stone slid along the sword's blade.

'Mind if I ask you something?' I said.

The big man kept sharpening the sword with a steady hand. 'Not at all.'

'You looked a little tense when Tessa's name came up,' I said.

Sanya glanced up at me for a second, his eyes shadowed and unreadable. He shrugged a shoulder and went back to his work.

'She do you wrong?'

'Barely ever noticed me. Or spoke to me,' Sanya said. 'To her I was just an employee. One more face. She did not care who I was.'

'This second of hers, though. The one who recruited you.'

The muscles along his jawline twitched. 'Her name is Rosanna.'

'And she done you wrong,' I said.

'Why do you say that?'

''Cause when you talk about her, your face says that you been done wrong.'

He gave me a brief smile. 'Do you know how many black men live in Russia, Dresden?'

'No. I mean, I figure they're kind of a minority.'

Sanya stopped in midstrop and glanced at me for a pregnant moment, one eyebrow arched. 'Yes,' he said, his tone dry. 'Kind of.'

'More so than in the States, I guess.'

He grunted. 'For Moscow I was very, very odd. If I went out to any smaller towns when I was growing up, I had to be careful about walking down busy streets. I could cause car accidents when drivers took their eyes off the road to stare at me. Literally. Many people in that part of the world had never seen a black person with their own eyes. That is changing slowly, but growing up I was a minority the way Bigfoot is a minority. A freak.'

I started putting things together. 'That's the kind of thing that is bound to make a young man a little resentful.'

He went back to sharpening the sword. 'Oh, yes.'

'So when you say that Tessa prefers to take recruits she knows will be eager to accept a coin . . .'

'I speak from experience,' Sanya said, nodding. 'Rosanna was everything that angry, poor, desperate young man could dream of. Pretty. Strong. Sensual. And she truly did not care about the color of my skin.' Sanya shook his head. 'I was sixteen.'

I winced. 'Yeah. Good age for making really bad decisions. I speak from experience, too.'

'She offered me the coin,' Sanya said. 'I took it. And for five years the creature known as Magog and I traveled the world with Rosanna, indulged in every vice a young man could possibly imagine, and . . . obeyed Tessa's commands.' He shook his head and glanced up at me. 'By the end of that time, Dresden, I wasn't much more than a beast who walked upright. Oh, I had thoughts and feelings, but they were all slaves to my baser desires. I did many things of which I am not—' He broke off and turned his face away from me. 'I did many things.'

'She was your handler,' I said quietly. 'Rosanna. She was the one getting you to try the drugs, to do the deeds. One little step at a time. Corrupting you and letting the Fallen take control.'

He nodded. 'And the whole time I never even suspected it. I thought that she cared about me as much as I cared about her.' He smiled faintly. 'Mind you, I never claimed to be of any particular intelligence.'

'Who got you out?' I asked him. 'Shiro?'

'In a way,' Sanya said. 'Shiro had just driven Tessa from one of her projects in . . . Antwerp, I believe. She came storming into Rosanna's apartment in Venice, furious. She and Rosanna had an argument I never completely understood – but instead of leaving when I was told to do so, I stayed to listen. I heard what Rosanna truly felt about me, heard her report about me to Tessa. And I finally understood what an idiot I'd been. I dropped the coin into a canal and never looked back.'

I blinked at him. 'That must have been difficult.'

'My entire life has been one of a snowball in Hell,' Sanya said cheerfully. 'Though the metaphor is perhaps inverted. At the time I judged the action to be tantamount to suicide, since Tessa was certain to track me down and kill me – but Shiro had followed her to Venice, and he found me instead. Michael – not the Chicago Michael, the other one – met us at Malta and brought *Esperacchius*, here, with him, offering me the chance to work against some of the evil I'd helped to create. From there I have been Knighting. Is good work. Plenty of travel, interesting people, always a new challenge.'

I shook my head and laughed. 'That's putting a positive spin on it.'

'I am making a difference,' Sanya said with simple and rock-solid conviction. 'And you, Dresden? Have you considered taking up *Fidelacchius*? Joining us?'

'No,' I said quietly.

'Why not?' Sanya asked, his tone reasonable. 'You know for what we fight. You know the good we do for others. Your cause runs a close parallel to ours: to protect those who cannot protect themselves; to pit yourself against the forces of violence and death when they arise.'

'I'm not really into the whole God thing,' I said.

'And I am an agnostic,' Sanya responded.

I snorted. 'Hell's bells. Tell me you aren't still clinging to that. You carry a holy blade and hang out with angels.'

'The blade has power, true. The beings allied with that power are . . . somewhat angelic. But I have met many strange and mighty things since I took up the sword. If one called them "aliens" instead of "angels," it would only mean that I was working in concert with powerful beings – not necessarily the literal forces of Heaven, or a literal Creator.' Sanya grinned. 'A philosophical fine point, true, but I am not prepared to abandon it. What we do is worthy, without ever bringing questions of faith, religion, or God into the discussion.'

'Can't argue with that,' I admitted.

'So tell me,' Sanya said, 'why have you not considered taking up the sword?'

I thought about it for a second and said, 'Because it isn't for me. And Shiro said I would know who to give it to.'

Sanya shrugged and nodded his head in acquiescence. 'Reason enough.' He sighed. 'We could use *Fidelacchius*'s power in this conflict. I wish Shiro were with us now.'

'Good man,' I agreed quietly. 'He was a king, you know.'

'I thought he just liked the King's music.'

'No, no,' I said. 'Shiro himself. He was a direct descendent of the last king of Okinawa. Several generations back, but his family was royalty.'

Sanya shrugged his broad shoulders. 'There have been many kings over the centuries, my friend, and many years for their bloodlines to spread through the populace. My own family can trace its roots back to Salahuddin.'

I felt my eyebrows rise. 'Salahuddin. You mean Saladin? King of Syria and Egypt during the Crusades?'

Sanya nodded. 'The same.' He paused in midstrop and looked up at me, his eyes widening.

'I know you're agnostic,' I said. 'But do you believe in coincidence?'

'Not nearly so much as I once did,' Sanya replied.

'That can't be a coincidence. Both of you descended from royalty.' I chewed on my lip. 'Could that have something to do with who can take up one of the swords?'

'I am a soldier and an amateur philosopher,' Sanya said. 'You are the wizard. Could such a thing be significant?'

I waggled a hand in midair. 'Yes and no. I mean, there are a lot of factors that tie magic to matters of inheritance – genetic or otherwise. A lot of the old rites were intimately bound up with political rulers.'

'The king and his land are one,' Sanya intoned solemnly.

'Well, yeah.'

Sanya nodded. 'Michael showed me that movie.'

'Merlin was the only good thing about that movie. That and Captain Picard kicking ass in plate mail with a big ax.' I waved my hand. 'The point is that in many cultures, the king or sultan or whatever held a position of duty and authority that was as much spiritual as physical. Certain energies could have been connected to that, giving the old kings a form of metaphysical significance.'

'Perhaps something similar to the power of the Swords?' Sanya asked.

I shrugged. 'Maybe. By the time I was born the planet was running a little low on monarchs. It isn't something I've looked at before.'

Sanya smiled. 'Well. Now you need only find a prince or princess willing to lay down his or her life over matters of principle. Do you know any?'

'Not so much,' I said. 'But I've got a feeling that we're onto something.' I glanced at the clock on the wall. 'It's getting late. I'll be back here in about two hours, or I'll call.'

'*Da*,' Sanya said. 'We will watch over your criminals for you.'

'Thanks,' I said, and went back out to the workshop. Hendricks had slumped to the floor and was sleeping. Gard was actually snoring. Thomas had been pacing restlessly when I entered.

'Well?' he asked.

'Gotta get to Mac's and meet Murphy,' I said. 'Let's roll.'

Thomas nodded and headed for the door.

I reached into the trash can by the door, took out an empty motor oil can, and tossed it into the least cluttered corner of the workshop. It bounced off something in midair, and Molly let out a soft yelp, appearing there a moment later, rubbing a hand to her hip.

'Where'd she come from?' Thomas demanded crossly.

'What did I miss?' Molly demanded, her tone faintly offended. 'I had all the senses covered. Even Thomas didn't know I was there.'

'You didn't miss anything,' I said. 'I just know how you think, grasshopper. If I can't make you stay where it's safe, I might as well keep you where I can see you. Maybe you'll even be useful. You're with us.'

Molly's eyes gleamed. '*Excellent*,' she said, and hurried over to join me.

16

I was more than an hour late, and Murphy was not amused.

'Your nose looks worse than it did yesterday,' she said when I sat down at the table. 'I think the black eyes have grown, too.'

'Gosh, you're cute when you're angry,' I responded.

Her eyes narrowed dangerously.

'It makes your little button nose all pink and your eyes get bloodshot and even bluer.'

'Did you have any last words, Dresden, or should I just choke you now?'

'Mac!' I called, raising a hand. 'Two pale!'

She fixed me with a steady look and said, 'Don't think you can buy your way out of this with good beer.'

'I don't,' I said, rising. 'I'm buying my way out of it with really, *really* good beer.'

I walked over to the bar as Mac set two bottles of his micro-brewed liquid nirvana down and took off the caps with a deft twist of his hand, disdaining a bottle opener. I winked at him and picked up both bottles, then sauntered back over to Murphy.

I gave her my bottle, took mine, and we drank. She paused after the first taste and blinked at the bottle before drinking again more deeply. 'This beer,' she pronounced after that, 'just saved your life.'

'Mac's a master beeromancer,' I replied. I'd never tell him, but at the time I wished he'd serve his brew cold. I'd have loved to hold a frosty bottle against my aching head for a moment. You'd think the pain from the damned broken nose would fade eventually. But it just kept on stubbornly burning.

We had settled down at a table along one wall of the pub. There are thirteen tables in the room, and thirteen wooden pillars, each extensively carved with scenes mostly out of Old World fairy tales. The bar is crooked and has thirteen stools, and thirteen ceiling fans whir lazily overhead. The setup of the entire place is designed to diffuse and refract random magical energies, the kind that often gather around practitioners of magic when they're grumpy or out of sorts. It offers a measure of protection from accumulated negative energies, enough to make sure that annoying or depressing 'vibes,' for lack of a more precise term, don't adversely affect the moods and attitudes of the pub's clientele.

It doesn't keep out any of the supernatural riffraff – that's what the sign by the door is for. Mac had the place legally recognized as neutral ground among the members of the Unseelie Accords, and members of any of the Accorded nations had a responsibility to avoid conflict in such a place, or at least to take it outside.

Still, neutral ground is safe only until someone thinks they can get away with violating the Accords. It's best to be cautious there.

'On the other hand,' Murphy said, more quietly, 'maybe you're too pathetic to beat to death right now.'

'My nose, you mean. Compared to the way my hand felt, it's nothing,' I said.

'Still can't be much fun.'

'Well. No.'

She watched me through her next sip and then said, 'You're about to play the wizard card and tell me to butt out.'

'Not exactly,' I said.

She gave me her cop eyes, all professionally detached neutrality, and nodded once. 'So talk.'

'Remember the guys from the airport a few years back?'

'Yeah. Killed the old Okinawan guy in the chapel. He died real bad.'

I smiled faintly. 'I think he'd probably argue the point, if he could.'

She shrugged and said, tone quietly flat, 'It was a mess.'

'The guys behind it are back. They've abducted Marcone.'

Murphy frowned, her eyes distant for a moment, calculating. 'They're grabbing his business?'

'Or forcing him onto their team,' I said. 'I'm not sure yet. We're working on it.'

'We?'

'You remember Michael?' I asked.

'Charity's husband?'

'Yeah.'

'I remember that at the airport we found a couple of men with no tongues and fake identification. They'd been killed with long blades. Swords, if you can believe that in this day and age. It was messy, Harry.' She put her hands flat on the table and leaned toward me. 'I don't *like* messy.'

'I'm all kinds of sorry about that, Murph,' I said. It's possible that a grain or two of sarcasm was showing in my reply. 'I'll be sure to ask them to put on the kid gloves. If I survive asking the question, I'll let you know what they say.'

Murphy regarded me calmly. 'They're back, then?'

I nodded. 'Only this time they brought more friends to the party.'

She nodded. 'Where are they?'

'No, Murph.'

'Where are they, Harry?' Murph asked, her voice hard. 'If they're that dangerous, I'm not waiting for them to choose their ground so that we have to rush into a hostile situation in response to them. We'll go after them right now, before they have a chance to hurt anyone else.'

'It'd be a slaughter, Murphy.'

'Maybe,' she said. 'Maybe not. You'd be surprised what kinds of resources the department has gotten its hands on, what with the whole War on Terror.'

'Right. And you're going to tell your bosses what?'

'That the same terrorists who attacked the airport and murdered a woman in the marina are in the city, planning another operation. That the only way to ensure the safety of its citizens is to preemptively assault them. Then show up with SWAT, SI, every cop in town, anyone we can get from the Bureau, and all the military backup available on short notice.'

I sat back in my chair at that, startled at Murphy's tone – and at the possibilities.

Hell. The kind of firepower she was talking about might give even the Denarians pause. And given the current climate, *terrorist plot* was all but synonymous with *respond with overwhelming force*. Oh, sure, most modern weaponry was far less effective on supernatural targets than anyone without knowledge of them would expect – but even reduced to the effectiveness of bee stings, *enough* bee stings can be just as deadly as a knife in the heart.

Humanity, at large, enjoys a dichotomous role in supernatural politics. On the one hand they are sneered at and held in contempt for being patently unable to come to grips with reality, to the point where the supernatural world hardly needed to bother to hide from them. Given half a chance, the average human being would rationalize the most bizarre of encounters down to 'unusual but explainable' events. They are referred to as herd animals by a lot of the things that prey on them, and often toyed with and tormented.

On the other hand, no one wants to get them stirred up, either. Humanity, when frightened and angry, is a force even the supernatural world does not wish to reckon with. The torches and pitchforks are just as deadly, in their numbers and their simple rage, as they ever were – and it was my opinion that most of the supernatural crowd had very little appreciation for just how destructive and dangerous mankind had grown in the past century.

Which is why I found myself sorely tempted to let the Denarians get a big old faceful of angry cop. Five or six rifles like Gard's might not kill Mantis Girl – but if you followed them up with thirty or forty pairs of stompy combat boots for all the little bugs, Little Miss Clamphands could go down for the count.

Of course, all that was predicated on the idea that the humans involved a) knew what they were up against and b) took it seriously and worked together tightly enough to get the job done. Murphy and the guys in SI might have a pretty good grasp of the situation, but the others wouldn't. They'd be expecting a soldier movie, but they'd be getting something out of a horror flick instead. I didn't for one second believe that Murphy or Stallings or anyone else in Chicago could make everyone involved listen to them once they started talking about demons and monsters.

I rubbed at my head again, thinking of Sanya. Maybe we could try to explain it in more palatable terms. Instead of 'shapeshifting demons' we could tell them that the terrorists were in possession (ha-ha, get it?) of 'experimental genetically engineered biomimetic armored suits.' Maybe that would give them the framework they needed to get the job done.

And maybe it wouldn't. Maybe they'd run into something out of a nightmare and start screaming in fear. Coordination and control would go right out the window, especially if the Denarians had anyone with enough magical juice to start blowing out technology. Then would come the panic and slaughter and terror.

'It's an idea,' I said to Murphy. 'Maybe even a workable idea. But I don't think its time has come. At least, not yet.'

Her eyes flashed very blue. 'And you're the one who decides.'

I took another sip of beer and set the bottle down again, deliberately. 'Apparently.'

'Says who?' Murphy demanded.

I leaned back in my chair. 'In the first place,' I said quietly, 'even if you brought in all that firepower, the best you could hope for is a hideously bloody, costly victory. In the second place, there's a chance that I can resolve this whole thing through Council channels – or at least make sure that when the fur starts flying, we're not in the middle of the bloody town.'

'But you—'

'And in the third place,' I continued, 'I don't know where they are.'

Murphy narrowed her eyes, and then some of the tension abruptly left her features. 'You're telling me the truth.'

'Usually do,' I said. 'I could probably track them down, given a day or so. But it might not come to that.'

She studied my face for a moment. 'But you don't think that talk will stop them from whatever they're doing here.'

'Not a chance in hell. But hopefully I'll talk them out of the woodwork to someplace a little more out of the way.'

'What if someone gets hurt while you're scheming?' she asked. 'Those encounters people were having last night are getting attention. No one's been hurt so far, but that could change. I'm not prepared to tolerate that.'

'Those were something else,' I said tiredly. 'Something I don't think will be a threat to the public.' I told her about Summer's hitters.

She drank the rest of her beer in a single tip, then sighed. 'Nothing's ever simple with you.'

I shrugged modestly.

'Here's the problem, Harry,' she said quietly. 'Last time these maniacs were around, there were bodies. And there were reports. Several witnesses gave a fairly good description of you.'

'And nothing came of it,' I said.

'Nothing came of it because I was in charge of the investigation,' Murphy corrected me, her tone slightly sharpening. 'The case was never closed. And if similar events bring it up again, there's no way I can protect you.'

'Stallings wouldn't . . . ?'

'John would probably try,' Murphy said. 'But Rudolph's been ladder climbing over in Internal Affairs, and if he gets an opening he'll start screaming about it and the case will get kicked up the line and out of SI's control.'

I frowned at that, turning my bottle around slowly in my fingers. 'Well,' I said, 'that could complicate things.'

Murphy rolled her eyes. 'You think? Dammit, Harry. A long time ago I agreed with you that there were some things that it was better the department didn't get involved in. I promised not to go blowing whistles and raising alarms every time things got spooky.' She leaned forward slightly, her eyes intent. 'But I'm a cop, Harry. Before everything else. My job is to defend and protect the people of this city.'

'And what do you think I'm doing?'

'The best you know how,' she said without heat. 'I know your heart is in the right place. But you can be as sincere as hell and still be *wrong*.' She paused to let that sink in. 'And if you're wrong it could cost lives. Lives I'm sworn to protect.'

I said nothing.

'You asked me to respect your limits and I have,' she said quietly. 'I expect you to return the favor. If for one second I think that letting you handle this is going to cost innocent lives, I'm not going to stand quietly in the wings. I'm going in and bringing everything I can get my hands on with me. And if I do that, I expect your complete support.'

'And you're the one who gets to decide when that is?' I demanded.

She faced me without flinching, not a millimeter. 'Apparently.'

I leaned back in my seat and sipped beer with my eyes closed.

Murphy didn't know everything that was at stake here. More than anyone else on the force, sure, but she was operating under only partial knowledge. If she made the wrong call, she could really screw things up beyond all ability to conceive.

She'd probably had that same exact thought about *me*, and on more than one occasion.

I'd asked Murphy for a lot when I'd asked her to trust me.

How could I *not* return the favor and still call myself her friend?

Simple.

I couldn't.

Hell, if she decided to go in, she'd do it with or without me. In that circumstance my presence could mean the difference between a bloody victory and a disaster, and . . .

And I suddenly felt a lot more empathy for Michael's confusion.

I opened my eyes again and said quietly, 'You decide to bring CPD in, you'll have my cooperation. But you've got to believe me: This isn't the time for that kind of solution.'

She ran her thumb over a scar in the wooden table. 'What if that building had been full of people, Harry? Families. These Denarians could have killed hundreds.'

'Give me time,' I said.

She put her hands on the table's edge and rose, facing me with those same neutral eyes again. As she started to speak I got a twisty feeling in the pit of my stomach. 'I wish I could,' she said, 'but—'

The door to the pub slammed open hard enough to strain its hinges and leave marks against the old wooden wall.

A . . . thing . . . came through the door. It was hard for me to tell what it was at first. Imagine a big man trying to squeeze into a doghouse. He has to crouch down and go in sideways, one shoulder at a time, moving very carefully to avoid harming himself on the door frame. That's what this huge, grey-furred thing looked like. But with horns and cloven hooves.

The enormous gruff – several feet taller than any ogre or troll I'd ever seen – squeezed all the way through the door and then rose to a crouch. His head, shoulders, and the top part of his back pressed against the ceiling. Hunched awkwardly, he slowly scanned the room, his golden eyes gleaming around their rectangular pupils. Each knuckle of his closed fists was the size of a freaking cantaloupe, and a heavy, pungent animal scent filled the air.

Thanks to the snow, the pub wasn't crowded – just a few regulars, plus Murphy and me. But even so, this wasn't something you saw every day, and the room went totally still.

The gruff's gaze settled on me.

Then he duckwalked toward my table. Mac raced for the switch that turned off the fans, but the first couple of spinning blades the gruff passed struck sharply against his curling horns – and shattered. He did not so much as blink. He stopped beside my table and surveyed Murphy, then turned his huge, heavy gaze to me.

'Wizard,' he rumbled in a voice so deep that I could *feel* it better than I could hear it. 'I have come hence to speak to thee about mine younger brothers.' The gruff's huge eyes narrowed, and its knuckles creaked like shipping hawsers as its fists tightened. 'And the harms thou hast wrought upon them.'

17

I picked up my staff and rose to face the enormous gruff.

Murphy watched me with very, very wide eyes.

'This is neutral ground,' I said quietly.

'Aye,' the gruff agreed. 'The Accords alone keep thy neck unbroken, thy skull uncracked.'

'Or your enormous ass uncooked,' I replied, staring up and setting my jaw. 'Don't start thinking it would be easy, Tiny.'

'Mayhap, and mayhap not,' the gruff rumbled. ' 'Tis a question answered only by the field.'

I breathed as shallowly as I could. The huge gruff didn't smell *bad*, precisely – but he sure as hell smelled a *lot*. 'Speak.'

'We find ourselves at odds, friend of Winter,' the gruff rumbled.

'Friend of Summer, too,' I said. 'They gave me jewelry and everything.'

'Aye,' the huge gruff said. 'You have done good service to my Court, if not to my Queen. I am surprised, then, at your use of the bane 'pon two of my younger kin.'

'The bane?' Murphy said quietly.

'Iron,' I clarified. I turned back to the gruff. 'They were trying to kill me. I wanted to survive.'

'No friend of either Court would so employ the bane, wizard,' the gruff growled. 'Did you not know this? It is more than a mere weapon, and the pain it causes more than simple discomfort. It is a poison, body and spirit, that you have used 'pon us.'

I glared at the big idiot. 'They were trying to *kill* me,' I repeated, only more slowly, you know, so it would be all insulting. 'I wanted to survive.'

The gruff narrowed its eyes. 'Then you intend to continue as you have begun?'

'I intend to survive,' I replied. 'I didn't ask for this fight. I didn't begin it.'

'Thou'rt fated to die in any case, mortal, soon or late. Why not face it with honor and make thy passing more peaceful thereby?'

'Peaceful?' I asked, barely containing a laugh. 'If I go down fighting, Tiny, I plan for it to be about as unpeaceful as things *get*.' I jabbed a finger at him. 'I've got nothing against you and your brothers, Tiny, except that you keep trying to freaking *kill* me. Back off, and it won't have to get any uglier than it already has.'

The gruff growled. It sounded like a dump truck grinding its gears. 'That I will not do. I will serve my Queen.'

'Then don't expect anything but more of the same from me,' I replied.

'You would behave this way in the service of *Winter*?' the gruff demanded, incredulous. 'You, who struck the heart of Arctis Tor? What hold has the Dark Queen 'pon you, mortal?'

'Sorry, Tiny, but you aren't nearly as special as you think you are. This is pretty much the way I behave every time someone tries to whack me.' I gestured at him with my staff. 'So if you came here to try to talk me into lying down and dying, you can leave the way you came in. And if you're the one coming after me next, you'd better have more brains than your brothers did, or I'm going to leave you as a great big pile of cold cuts and spare ribs.'

The gruff growled again and gave me a stiff nod. 'Then come out. And let us settle this.'

Uh. Uh-oh.

Showing bravado to the bad guys – or the not-so-bad guys, as the case may be – is a given, a part of the territory. But I'd never taken on anything with the sheer mass of Tiny the gruff, and I really didn't think I'd care to try my hand against him without one hell of a lot of preparation first. I also had to remember that big didn't necessarily equal stupid, not given the circles he apparently moved in.

In fact, most of the higher reaches of the Summer Court knew a formidable amount of countermagic. If Tiny here had half the ability I'd seen demonstrated in the past, I would be in real trouble in a straight fight. All he had to do was stand outside and wait. Mac's place had only the one door.

Worse, Thomas and Molly were waiting outside in Thomas's barge, and they would be sure to join in. I wasn't sure what could happen at that point. Leaving totally aside the fact that we'd be brawling in the middle of Chicago in broad daylight, I had to think that the gruff might have backup waiting nearby to intervene if anyone outside the business of the Courts of Winter and Summer tried to interfere. Molly was of limited capability in a fight, and Thomas tended to believe that the best way to approach any given combat was with a maximum of power, speed, and aggressive ferocity.

Things could get really messy, really fast.

I was trying to think of a way of getting out of this without getting anyone killed when Murphy put her gun on the table and said in a very clear, loud, challenging tone, 'I don't think so.'

The gruff turned to stare at her in surprise.

So did Mac.

So did everyone else there.

Heck, so did I.

Murphy stood straight up and turned to face the enormous gruff with her feet spread. 'I will not let this challenge to my authority pass.'

The gruff tilted its head to one side. Its horns dug furrows in the wooden ceiling.

Mac winced.

'Lady?' it rumbled.

'Do you know who I am?' Murphy asked.

'A lady knight, a shield bearer of this mortal demesne,' the gruff replied. 'An . . . officer of the law, or so I believe it is called.'

'That's right,' she said calmly.

'I make no challenge to your authority, Dame . . .'

'Murphy,' she said.

'Dame Murphy,' rumbled the gruff.

'But you do,' Murphy said. 'You have threatened one I am sworn to protect.'

The gruff blinked – a considerable gesture on his scale – and glanced at me. 'This wizard?'

'Yes,' Murphy said. 'He is a citizen of Chicago, and I am sworn to protect and defend him against those who would harm him.'

'Dame Murphy,' the gruff said stiffly, 'this matter is not one of mortal concern.'

'The hell it isn't,' Murphy said. 'This man lives in Chicago. He pays taxes to the city. He is beholden to its laws.' She glanced aside at me, and her mouth quirked wryly. 'If he is to suffer the headaches of citizenry, as he must, then it is fair and lawful that he should enjoy the protections offered to every citizen. He is therefore under my protection, and any quarrel you have with him, you also have with me.'

The gruff stared at her for a moment, eyes narrowed in thought. 'Art thou quite certain of thy position, Dame Murphy?'

'Quite certain,' she replied.

'Even knowing that the duty solemnly charged unto me and my kin might require us to kill thee?'

'Master Gruff,' Murphy replied, laying a hand on her gun for the first time, 'consider for a moment what a steel-jacketed round would feel like as it entered your flesh.'

The gruff flicked its ears in surprise. A number of napkins were blown from the surface of a nearby table. 'Thou wouldst aim such weapons of the bane at a lawful champion of the Seelie Court?'

'In your case, Master Gruff,' Murphy said, 'I would hardly *need* to aim.' Then she picked up the gun and aimed it at the gruff's eyes.

I started to panic. Then I saw where I thought Murph was

going with this one, and I had to work to keep myself from letting out a cheer.

The gruff's knuckles popped again. 'This,' it growled, 'is neutral ground.'

'Chicago,' she replied, 'has never signed any Accords. I will fulfill my duty.'

'Attack me here,' the gruff said, 'and I will crush you.'

'Crush me here,' Murphy said, 'and you will have broken the Accords while acting on behalf of your Queen. Was that your intention in coming here?'

The gruff ground its teeth, a sound like creaking millstones. 'My quarrel is not with you.'

'If you attempt to take the life of a citizen of Chicago, whom I am sworn to protect, you have *made* it my quarrel, Master Gruff. Does your Queen wish to declare war upon the mortal authorities of Chicago? Would she wish *you* to decide such a thing?'

The gruff stared at her, evidently pondering.

'Lady has a point, Tiny,' I drawled. 'There's nothing to be gained here but trouble, and nothing to be lost but a little time. Walk away. You'll find me again soon enough.'

The gruff stared at Murphy, and then at me. If I'd been less intrepid and fearless, I would have held my breath, hoping I'd avoided a fight. As it was, I held my breath mostly to cut down on the smell.

Finally the gruff bowed its head toward Murphy, with more scraping of ceilings and wincing of bartenders. 'Courage,' he rumbled, 'should be honored. Though thou art less a man than I thought, wizard, hiding behind a mortal, however valiant she may be.'

I let out a long breath as silently as I could and said, 'Gosh. Somehow I'll try to live with myself.'

'It will not o'erburden you long. This I promise.' The gruff nodded once to Murphy, then turned and scuttled out the way he'd squeezed in. He even shut the door behind him.

Murphy let out her breath and put her gun away in its shoulder holster. It took her two or three tries.

I sank into my chair on weak legs. 'You,' I said to Murphy, 'are so hot right now.'

She gave me a weak smile. 'Oh, now you notice.' She glanced at the door. 'Is he really gone?'

'Yeah,' I said. 'I figure he is. The Summer Court aren't exactly sweetness and light, but they do have a concept of honor, and if any faerie gives his word, he's good for it.'

Mac did something I'd rarely seen him do.

He got three black bottles out from beneath the bar and brought them over to the table. He twisted the tops off and put one down in front of me, and another in front of Murphy, then kept the third for himself.

I took up the bottle and sniffed at it. I wasn't familiar with the brew, but it had a rich, earthy aroma that made my mouth water.

Without a word Mac held up his bottle in a salute to Murphy.

I joined him. Murphy shook her head tiredly and returned the salute.

We drank together, and my tongue decided that any other brew it ever had would probably be a bitter disappointment from this day forward. Too many flavors to count blended together into something I couldn't describe if I'd had a week to talk about it. I'd never had anything like it. It was God's beer.

Mac drained the bottle in a single pull, with his eyes closed. When he lowered it, he looked at Murphy and said, 'Bravely done.'

Murphy's face was flushed with relief and with a reaction to her beer that was at least as favorable as mine. I doubt Mac could have seen it, but I'd known Murph long enough to see that she started blushing, too.

Mac went back to the bar, leaving Murphy and me to finish our bottled ambrosia.

'Okay,' Murphy said in a weak voice. 'Where were we?'

'You were about to tell me how you thought I was wrong and that the Chicago PD needed to intervene.'

'Oh,' Murph said. 'Right.' She stared after the departed gruff for a moment. 'You said that that thing was from the nicer of the two groups causing us grief?'

'Yep,' I said.

'We've gone up against the supernatural three times,' she said quietly. 'It's ended badly twice.'

We meaning the cops, of course. I nodded. One of those occasions had killed her partner, Ron Carmichael. He hadn't been an angel or anything, but he had been a good man and a solid cop.

'All right,' she said quietly. 'I'm willing to hold off for now. On one condition.'

'Name it.'

'I'm in from here on out. You obviously need someone to protect you from the big, bad billy goats.'

I snorted. 'Yeah, obviously.'

She held up the last of her beer. I held up mine.

We clinked them, finished them, and went back out into the winter cold together.

18

'All right,' I said. 'I hearby call this war council to order.'

We were all sitting around my tiny living room, eating Burger King. Thomas and Molly had voted for McDonald's, but since I was paying, I sternly informed them that this was not a democracy, and Burger King it was.

Hail to the King, baby.

Murphy rolled her eyes over the whole thing.

'War council?' Molly asked, wide-eyed. 'Are we going to start another war?'

'I sort of meant it as a metaphor,' I said, as I made sure the ketchup-mustard ratio on my burger was within acceptable parameters. 'I need to decide on my next step, and I've been hit in the head a few times lately. Figured my brain could use a little help.'

'Just now worked that out, did you?' Thomas murmured.

'Quiet, you,' I growled. 'The idea is to generate useful thoughts here.'

'Not funny ones,' Molly said, suppressing a laugh.

I eyed her. She ate a french fry.

Murphy sipped at her Diet Coke. 'Well,' she said, 'I don't know how much advice I can give you until I know what you're up against.'

'I told you in the car,' I said. 'The Knights of the Blackened Denarius.'

'Fallen angels, old tarnished coins, psychotic killers, got it,' Murphy said. 'But that doesn't tell me what their capabilities are.'

'She's got a point,' Thomas said quietly. 'You haven't said much about these guys.'

I blew out a breath and took a big bite of hamburger to give me a moment to think while I chewed. 'There's a lot that these things can do,' I said afterward. 'Mostly, the coins seem to allow their users to alter their physical form into something better suited for a fight than a regular human body.'

'Battle shapeshifting,' Molly said. *'Cool.'*

'It isn't cool,' I told her. Then I paused and admitted, 'Okay, maybe a little. It makes them harder to hurt. It makes them faster. It arms them with various forms of weaponry. Claws, fangs, that kind of thing. Cassius looked like he might have had a poisonous bite, for example. Ursiel's wielder could shift into this huge bear thing with claws and fangs and horns. Another one turned her hair into about a million strips of living titanium blade, and they were whipping all over the place and shooting through walls. Stretched out like twenty or thirty feet.'

'I have some customers like that,' Thomas quipped.

Murphy blinked and glanced at him.

I cleared my throat and gave Thomas another glare. 'Another one of them, Nicodemus, didn't seem to do any shapeshifting, but his freaking shadow could leap off the wall and strangle you. Creepy as hell.'

'They don't all have, like, a uniform or something?' Molly asked.

'Not even close,' I replied. 'Each of the Fallen seems to have its own particular preferences. And I suspect that those preferences adapt themselves differently to different holders of the coins. Quintus Cassius's Fallen had this whole serpent motif going, and Cassius's magic was pretty snake-intensive, too. But he was totally different from Ursiel, who was totally different from Mantis Girl from this morning, who was different from the other Denarians I've seen.'

Murphy nodded. 'Anything else?'

'Goons,' I said. 'More like a cult, really. Nicodemus had a number of followers whose tongues had been removed. They were fanatics, heavily armed, and crazy enough to commit suicide rather than be captured by his enemies.'

She winced. 'The airport?'

'Yeah.'

'That it?'

'No,' I said. 'Nicodemus also had these . . . call them guard dogs, I guess. Except that they weren't dogs. I don't know what they were, but they were ugly and ran fast and had big teeth. But all of that isn't what makes them dangerous.'

'No?' Thomas said. 'Then what is?'

'The Fallen,' I replied.

The room fell silent.

'They're beings older than time who have spent two thousand years learning the ins and outs of the mortal world and the mortal mind,' I said quietly. 'They understand things we literally could not begin to grasp. They've seen every trick, learned every move, and they're riding shotgun for each coin holder – if they aren't in the driver's seat already. Every one of them has a perfect memory, a library of information at his immediate disposal, and a schemer that makes Cardinal Richelieu look like Mother Teresa hanging around in his brain as an adviser.'

Thomas stared at me very hard for a moment, frowning. I tried to ignore him.

Murphy shook her head. 'Let's sum up: an unknown number of enemies with unknown capabilities, supported by a gang of madmen, packs of attack animals, and superhumanly intelligent pocket change.' She gave me a look. 'It's sort of tough to plan for that, given how much we don't know.'

'Well, then that's what we do next, isn't it?' Molly asked tentatively. 'Find out more about them?'

Thomas flicked a glance at Molly and nodded once.

'To do that we'd have to find them,' I said.

'A tracking spell?' Molly suggested.

'I don't have any samples to work with,' I replied. 'And even if I did, somebody on their team was able to obscure *Mab's* divining spells. I'm nowhere close to Mab's league. My spells wouldn't have a prayer.'

'If they've got that much of an entourage, they're going to

stick out anywhere even vaguely public,' Murphy mused. 'A gang of toughs with no tongues? If the Denarians are in town, that should make them relatively easy to locate.'

'Last time they were holed up in Undertown,' I said. 'Believe me, there's plenty of room for badness down there.'

'What about the spirit world?' Thomas asked quietly. 'Surely there's an entity or two who could tell us something.'

'Possibly,' I said. 'I'm on speaking terms with one or two of the *loa*. But that kind of information is either expensive or unreliable. Sometimes both. And remember who we're talking about. The Fallen are heavyweights in the spirit world. No one wants to cross them.'

Molly made a frustrated sound. 'If we can't track them with magic, and we can't find them physically, then how are we supposed to learn more about them?'

'Exactly, kid,' I said. 'Hence the whole "war council" concept.'

We ate in silence for a few minutes. Then Murphy said, 'We're coming at this from the wrong angle.'

'Eh?' I said wittily.

'We're thinking like the good guys. We should be thinking like the bad guys. Figuring out what they had to face and get around.'

I leaned forward a little and nodded at her to go on.

'I don't know as much about the supernatural aspects of this situation,' she said. 'I don't know much of anything about these Denarians. But I *do* know some things about Marcone. For example, I know that even if he has some underlings who want to take over the franchise, he's got more who are personally loyal or who will figure that bailing him out will reap them some major profits.'

'Yeah,' I said, tilting my head at her. 'So?'

'So wherever they took him, it has to be somewhere Marcone's network can't reach. We can be virtually certain that they aren't hiding in plain sight.'

I grunted. 'Hell's bells, yeah. Not only that, but Marcone plans ahead. He had that panic room ready to go. In fact . . .'

My eyes widened. 'The location of your secret hidey-hole ought to be awfully secret, don't you think?'

'Sure,' Molly said. 'What good is a hiding place if everyone knows where it is?'

'The Denarians knew exactly where he was going,' I said. 'The spell they set up to tear down that building's defenses was no spur-of-the-moment magic – it was too complex. It had been planned out *ahead of time*.'

'Son of a bitch,' Thomas swore. 'Someone inside Marcone's organization ratted him out.'

'So if we find the rat . . .' Murphy said, catching on.

'We might find a trail that leads back to the Nickelheads,' I finished with a fierce grin. 'Was this war council concept a brilliant idea or what?'

Molly tittered. 'Nickelheads.'

'I have a gift,' I said modestly. Then I added in a low voice, 'And stop giggling. Wizards don't giggle. Bad for the image.'

Molly buried her giggle in another mouthful of fries.

I slurped on my Coke and turned to Murphy. 'So, what we need to do is figure out who's going to backstab Marcone. Someone highly placed enough to know the location of the safehouse, and who will profit by Marcone's absence.'

'You're assuming the informant was complicit,' Murphy said. 'That wouldn't necessarily be true. Someone could have inadvertently given information away, or been compelled to cooperate.'

I paused to think about that. 'True. So we'll have to start by looking at who *could* have given away the safe house.'

Murphy raked her fingers through her dark-golden hair, frowning in thought. 'To be honest, SI doesn't cross trails with the outfit all that often. I'd have to make some calls to find out.'

Thomas drummed his fingers on the arm of his chair. 'The FBI would have more, wouldn't they?'

'And you know that guy Rick, right?' Molly said. 'The one who was helping that jerk interrogate me?'

Murphy's eyes narrowed. She made a noise that wasn't quite an agreement, but wasn't quite a denial, either. Murphy has issues with her ex-husband.

It took Molly about half a second to figure out the expression on Murphy's face. She looked around the room somewhat desperately for a moment. 'Uh, so, Harry, what's with Mister? He's been sleeping like a log the whole time we've been here.'

'Which brings us to the second part of the problem,' I said. 'The hitters from the Summer Court. I think odds are good that they've got my place under surveillance.'

Thomas arched an eyebrow. 'I didn't sense anything coming in.'

'You didn't sense anything walking through the front door of the pub, either,' Murphy said archly.

'I was circling the block,' Thomas said crossly. 'Middle of a damned blizzard and you still can't find a parking spot. I hate this town.'

'I've got warning spells spread out all around this place,' I said. 'Anything gets within a block and I'll probably know about it. And you've got to get up early in the morning to sneak past Mouse.'

Mouse, who was sitting in front of Molly making soulful eyes at her chicken sandwich, glanced at me and wagged his tail.

'If they were very close, I'd know it. They're probably spread out in a loose ring, watching who comes and goes,' I said. 'The gruffs don't really want to kick my apartment door down – not yet, at any rate. They'd rather fight where there won't be collateral damage. But I've got a feeling that they aren't at their best in all this snow.'

Molly frowned. 'You think Mab is influencing the weather for you?'

'Maybe the ongoing record snowfall is a coincidence,' I said. 'But if so, it's awfully convenient.'

'Nothing's ever convenient with you, Dresden,' Murphy said.

'Exactly my point.' I rubbed at my jaw. I needed to shave, but my throbbing nose was bad enough without adding a couple of razor nicks to the mess. I didn't trust my hands to be steady. There were too many scary things moving around, and if I stopped long enough to think about how far in over my head I was getting, I might just crawl into a hole and pull it in after me.

Don't think, Harry. You know too much about what you're up against.

Analyze, decide, and act.

'Okay. We can assume that the Summer crew saw us come in. As long as we don't leave, they'll assume that we're still here.'

Molly said, 'Aha. I wondered why you asked me along.'

I winked at her. 'Know thyself, grasshopper. Yeah. When we leave, I want you to make sure that the gruffs and their crew don't notice. Hopefully that will buy us some more time while they play patient hunter and wait for me to expose myself again.'

'Heh,' Thomas sniggered. 'Expose yourself.'

Murphy tossed an onion ring at him, which he caught and popped in his mouth.

'Meanwhile, I've got a new toy for you to play with, Thomas.'

My brother arched his eyebrows and focused his attention on me.

I went into my tiny bedroom and came back out with a small figurine, a rough figure of clay that resembled Gumby more than anything. I lifted it to my mouth and breathed on it, then murmured a word and said, 'Catch.'

I tossed it to Thomas. My brother caught it and—

—suddenly a tall man, too lanky to look altogether healthy and with too many rough edges to be handsome, sat in Thomas's chair, dressed in his clothes. His hair had short waves in it, and looked perpetually rumpled. His eyes were a bit sunken in a permanent state of too little sleep, but the line of his chin, strong and clean, made him look harder and sharper than he might otherwise have appeared.

Hell's bells. Did I really look like that? Maybe I needed a makeover or something.

Murphy sucked in a breath and looked back and forth between Thomas, in his new look, and me. Molly didn't bother trying to hide her reaction, and just said, '*Cool*.'

'What?' Thomas asked. Though the figure speaking looked like me, the sound of my brother's voice was unchanged, and a spot of ketchup from his burger still speckled one side of his mouth. He looked around for a moment, then scowled, rose, and ducked into my bedroom to look at himself in the little shaving mirror in the drawer in my bathroom. 'You've invented a doll that turns people into their ugly half brothers, eh?'

'Get over yourself, prettyboy,' I called.

'If you think I'm letting you break my nose to complete the look, you're insane.'

I grunted. 'Yeah, that's a problem. I had to set it up to look like I looked the day I finished it.'

'It isn't a problem,' Molly said at once. 'I'll get my makeup kit and fix up his eyes for him, at least. I don't know what we can do for his nose, but from a distance he should look right.'

'If he looks like you, Harry,' Murphy said, 'doesn't that mean he's going to be attracting some sort of hostile attention?'

Thomas snorted and appeared in the doorway to my bedroom, his face ketchup-free. 'Harry walks around looking like this all the *time*. Now, *that* would be awful. I can handle it for a few hours.'

'Don't get cute on me,' I said. 'Give us two or three hours' lead time, and then head out. Stay on the roads and keep moving. Don't give them a chance to surround you. You've got your cell phone?'

'I suppose,' he said. 'But given how much I've been hanging around you two and the bad weather, I'd say the odds were against its working.' I grunted and tossed him my leather duster and my staff. He caught them and frowned. 'You sure you don't want these?'

'Just don't lose them,' I said. 'If the gruffs saw a double of me who wasn't wearing the coat, they'd know something was up in a heartbeat. The idea is to keep them from getting suspicious in the first place. The charm should be good for another six, maybe seven hours. Once it drops, get back here.'

'Yeah, yeah,' Thomas said, sliding into my duster. The illusion magic didn't make the thing fit him, and he had to fiddle with the sleeves, but it *looked* like it always did on me. 'Karrin, don't let him do anything stupid.'

Murphy nodded. 'I'll try. But you know how he is.' She picked up her coat and shrugged into it. 'Where are we going?'

'Back to Gard,' I said. 'The Carpenter place. I'm betting Marcone left her a sample of his hair to use to track him down, for just such an occasion as this.'

'But you said you couldn't get through the, uh . . . the obscuring magic that the Nickelheads have.'

'Probably not. But if I know Marcone, he also collected samples of hair or blood from his people. To find them if they ever needed help or . . .'

Murphy grimaced. 'If they rated early retirement.'

'I'm hoping Gard can give us an inside track on finding the leak, too,' I said.

Meanwhile, Molly hurried over to Thomas with her makeup kit and began modifying his face. Thomas's face was about level with the chin of the illusion-me, if not a little lower, but I'd taught Molly the basics behind my illusion magic – such as it was. My skill with illusions was pretty basic, and it wouldn't stand up to any serious examination. Molly was able to scrunch up her eyes and see past it.

Of course, you didn't have to make the illusion utterly convincing if you could manage to keep people from having a good reason to take a hard look at it in the first place. The illusion doesn't have to be fancy – it's the misdirection behind it that really matters.

Molly had been caught in a Goth undertow of the youth culture, and it showed in her makeup. She had plenty of blues and purples and reds to darken Thomas's eyes with, and the illusion of my face assumed an appearance fairly close to my own, sans the swollen nose.

'It'll do,' I said. 'Murph, you're driving. Molly, if you don't mind.'

My apprentice grinned as she hurriedly pulled on her coat. Then she stuck her tongue between her teeth, frowned fiercely, and waved her hand at me with a murmur. I felt the kid's veil congeal about me like a thin layer of Jell-O, a wobbly and slippery sensation. The world went a little bit blurry, as if I were suddenly looking at everything through hazy green water, but Murphy's face turned up into a grin.

'That's very good,' she said. 'I can't see him at all.'

Molly's face was set with concentration as she maintained the spell, but she glanced at Murphy and nodded her head in acknowledgment.

'Right,' I said. 'Come on, Mouse.'

My dog hopped to his feet and trotted over eagerly, waving his tail.

Murphy looked in my general direction, and arched an eyebrow.

'If the gruffs don't buy it, I want all the early warning I can get,' I told her.

She lowered her voice and murmured, 'And maybe you're a little nervous about going out without the coat and the staff?'

'Maybe,' I said.

It was only a half lie. Insulting nickname or not, coat and staff or not, the more I thought about what we were up against, the more worried I became.

I wasn't nervous.

I was pretty much *terrified*.

19

It was dark by the time we got to Chez Carpenter, and we were beginning to slow down to turn into the driveway when Murphy said, 'Someone's tailing us.'

'Keep driving,' I snapped at once, from where I was crouched down in the back of Murphy's Saturn. I felt like a groundhog trying to hide in a golf divot. 'Go past the house.'

Murphy picked up speed again, accelerating very slowly and carefully on the snowbound streets.

I poked my head up just enough to peer into the night behind us. Mouse sat up with me and looked solemnly and carefully out the back window when I did. 'The car with one headlight pointing a little to the left?' I asked.

'That's the one. Spotted him about ten minutes ago. Can you see his plates?'

I squinted. 'Not through this snow and with his lights in my eyes.'

Molly turned and knelt in the passenger seat, peering through the back window. 'Who do you think it is?'

'Molly, sit down,' Murphy snapped. 'We don't want them to know that we've seen—'

The headlights of the car behind us grew brighter and began to sweep closer. 'Murph, they saw her. Here they come.'

'I'm sorry!' Molly said. 'I'm sorry!'

'Get your seat belts on,' Murphy barked.

Murphy began accelerating, but our pursuer closed the distance within a few seconds. The headlights grew brighter, and I could hear the roar of a big old throaty engine. I scrambled up to the backseat and clawed at the seat belt, but Mouse was sitting on the other side of the buckle, and before I could get it out from under him Murphy screamed, 'Hang on!'

Collisions are always louder than I expect, and this one was no exception. The pursuing car smashed into the rear of the Saturn at maybe forty miles an hour.

Metal screamed.

Fiberglass shattered.

I got slammed back against my seat and then whiplashed into the back of the driver's seat.

Mouse bounced around, too.

Molly screamed.

Murph swore and wrenched at the steering wheel.

It could have been worse. Murphy had gained enough speed to mitigate the impact, but the Saturn went into a spin on the snowy streets and revolved in a graceful, slow-motion ballet.

Slamming my nose into the back of Murphy's seat didn't feel very good. In fact, it felt so not-good that I lost track of what was going on for a few seconds. I was vaguely aware of the car spinning and then crunching broadside into an enormous mound of snow.

The Saturn's engine coughed and died. My pounding heart sent thunder to my ears and agony to my nose. I barely heard the sound of a car door opening and closing somewhere nearby.

I heard Murphy twist around in her chair and gasp, 'Gun.' She drew her weapon, unfastened her seat belt, and tried her door. It was pressed into a solid wall of white. She snarled and crawled across a stunned Molly's lap, fumbling at the door.

I lurched to the other side of the car and clawed at the door until it opened. When it did I saw a slightly smashed-up car in the middle of the street, idling with both doors open. Two men stalked toward us through the snow. One was holding what looked like a shotgun, and his partner had an automatic in either hand.

Murphy threw herself out of the car and darted to one side. It wasn't hard to figure out why – if she'd started shooting immediately, Molly would have been in the line of any return fire. Murphy moved swiftly, crouched as close to the ground as she could get, but to do so cost her a precious second.

The shotgun roared and spat fire.

The blast smashed Murphy to the ground like a blow from a sledgehammer.

At the sight my scrambled brain congealed. I drew up my will, flung out a hand, and screamed, '*Ventas servitas!*'

Wind roared forth from my outstretched fingers. I directed it at the snow-covered ground in front of our attackers, and a sudden storm of flying bits of ice and snow engulfed the gunmen.

I kept the pressure on them, maintaining the spell, as I shouted, 'Molly! Get to Murphy! Veil and first aid!'

Molly shook her head and gave me a glassy-eyed stare, but she climbed out of the car and staggered over to Murphy. A second later both of them vanished from sight.

I let up on the wind spell. Moving enough air to keep a gale-force wind going is a lot more work than anyone thinks. The air went still again except for swirling eddies of wind, frost devils that danced about in half a dozen whirling helices of snow. The two gunmen were revealed, crouching low, their arms still upraised to shield their eyes from the wind and stinging flakes of ice.

I missed my staff. I missed my duster. But I wasn't missing the .44 revolver I drew from my coat's pocket and aimed at the bad guys, while I raised my left hand, shaking the shield bracelet there out from under the sleeve of my coat.

I recognized one of the two gunmen, the one with the brace of pistols. His name was Bart something or other, and he was muscle for hire — cheap muscle, at that, but at least you got what you paid for. Bart was the kind of guy you called when you needed someone's ribs broken on a budget.

The other guy was familiar, too, but I couldn't put a name to him. Come on, it wasn't like I hung around in outfit bars, getting to know everyone. Besides, all I really needed to know was that he'd shot Murphy.

I started walking forward, straight at them, and stopped when

I was maybe fifteen feet away. By the time I got there they were finally getting the ice and snow out of their eyes. I didn't wait for them to get their vision back. I aimed carefully and put a bullet through shotgun boy's right knee.

He went down screaming, and kept screaming.

Bart turned toward me and raised both guns, but my shield bracelet was ready. I made an effort of will, and a hemisphere of shimmering, translucent silver force flickered to life between Bart and me. He emptied both automatics at me, but he might as well have been shooting water pistols. My shield caught every shot, and I angled it to deflect the rounds up into the air rather than into one of the houses in the neighborhood around us.

Bart's guns clicked empty.

I lowered the shield and lifted my revolver as he fumbled at his pockets for fresh magazines. 'Bart,' I chided him, 'Think this one through.'

He froze in place, and then slowly moved his hands away from his pockets.

'Thank you. Guess what I want you to do next?'

He dropped his guns. Bart was in his late thirties and good-looking, tall, with the frame of a man who spent a lot of his time at the gym. He had little weasel eyes, though, dark and gleaming. They darted left and right, as if seeking possible avenues of escape.

'Don't make me shoot you in the back, Bart,' I said. 'Bullet could hit your spine, paralyze you without killing you. That would be awful.' I moseyed over to him, keeping the gun trained on him and making sure I always had a clear view of the other gunman. He was still screaming, though it had a hoarse, thready sound to it now. 'Do you know who I am?'

'Dresden, Jesus,' Bart said. 'Nothing personal, man.'

'You tried to kill me, Bart. That's just about as personal as it gets.'

'It was a job,' he said. 'Just a job.'

And I suddenly remembered where I'd seen the other guy before: unconscious in the hallway outside Demeter's office at

Executive Priority. He was one of Torelli's flunkies, and he did not appear to have much more savvy than his boss.

'Job's gonna get you killed one day, Bart,' I said. 'Maybe even right now.' I called out, 'Molly? How is she?'

Murphy's voice came back to me instead of Molly's. 'I'm fine,' she said. The words were clipped, as if she were in pain. 'Vest stopped all but one of the balls, and that one isn't bad.'

'Her arm is bleeding, Harry,' Molly said, her voice shaking. 'It's stopping, but I don't think there's anything else I can do.'

'Murph, get back to the car. Stay warm.'

'Like hell, Harry. I will—'

I completed the sentence for her. '—go into *shock*. Don't be stupid, Murph. I can't lug your unconscious body around *and* keep these guys under control.'

Murphy growled something vaguely threatening under her breath, but I heard Molly say, 'Here, let me help you.'

Bart's beady eyes were all but bugging out of his head as he searched for the source of the sound of Molly's voice. 'What? What the hell?'

By now, I was sure, people in the houses around us had called the police. I was sure that the cops would be a few moments longer than usual arriving, too. I wanted to be gone by then, which meant that I didn't have much time. But Bart didn't have to know that. Just like Bart didn't have a clue what he'd gotten himself involved in.

I most likely didn't have time to grill even one of the gunmen. Torelli's goon was hurt and probably mad as hell at me. He was probably more loyal to Torelli, too, if he was a personal retainer. That really left me only one smart option for gathering information.

I stepped forward, shifting my gun to my left hand, and held out my right. I spoke a quiet word and a sphere of fire, bright as a tiny sun, kindled to life in the air above my right hand. I turned a slow stare on Bart and stepped close to him.

The thug flinched and fell onto his ass in the snowy street.

I released the sphere of fire, and it drifted closer to Bart.

'Look, big guy,' I said in an amiable tone. 'I've had a tense couple of days. And I've got to tell you, burning someone's face off sounds like a great way to relax.'

'I was just a hire!' Bart stammered, scooting back on his buttocks from the little sphere of fire. 'Just a driver!'

'Hired to do what?' I asked him.

'I was just supposed to put you off the road and cover the shooter,' Bart half screamed. He pointed a finger at the wounded man. 'Him.'

I spread my fingers a little wider, and the flaming sphere jumped a few inches closer to the goon's face. 'Bart, Bart. Let's not change the focus here. This is about you and me.'

'I'm just a contractor!' Bart all but screamed, writhing to get his face farther away from the fire. 'They don't tell guys like me shit!'

'Guys like you always know more than you're told,' I said. 'So you've got something you can give the cops to keep yourself out of jail.'

'I don't!' Bart said. 'I swear!'

I smiled at him and pushed the fire sphere a little closer. 'Inhale blue,' I said. 'Exhale pink. Hey, this *is* relaxing.'

'Torelli!' Bart screamed, throwing up his arms. 'Jesus, it was Torelli! Torelli wanted the job done! He's been getting ready to move on Marcone!'

'Since when?' I demanded.

'I don't know. Couple of weeks, maybe. That's when they brought me in! Oh, Jesus!'

I closed my hand and snuffed out the sphere of fire before it could do more than scorch the sleeves of Bart's coat. He lay there on the ground breathing roughly, and refused to lower his arms.

The sound of sirens ghosted through the streets. It was time to go.

'He been talking to anyone lately?' I demanded. 'Anyone new? Setting up an alliance?'

Bart shook his head, shuddering. 'I ain't one of his full-timers. I ain't seen nothing like that.'

'Harry!' Molly screamed.

I'd gotten too intent on the conversation with Bart, and I'd been too worried about Murphy to remember to take everybody's guns away. The gunman on the ground had recovered his shotgun and worked the action, ejecting a spent shell and loading a new round. I spun toward him, raising my shield bracelet. The problem was that my spiffy redesigned bracelet, while better in a lot of ways than the old one, took a lot more power to use, and as a result I could bring it up only so fast. I threw myself to the ground and tried to put Bart between me and Torelli's hitter. Bart scrambled frantically to clear the line of fire, and I knew that I wasn't going to get the shield up in time.

Mouse must have darted off to the side at the beginning of the confrontation, because he appeared out of the shadows and came bounding through nearly three feet of snow as if he'd been running on racetrack turf. He was moving so fast that a bow wave of flying snow literally preceded him, like when a speedboat cuts through the water. He hit Torelli's hitter just as the man pulled the trigger.

Shotguns are *loud*. Bart screamed an impolite word.

Mouse seized Torelli's man by his wounded leg, the one I'd shot a minute ago, and began wrenching him around by it, shaking him as easily as a terrier shakes a rat. The goon had another ear-piercing scream left in him, a high-pitched thing that sounded like it had come from a slaughterhouse hog. The shotgun flew from his fingers, and he began flopping like a rag doll, unconscious from the pain.

The sirens grew louder, and I pushed myself back to my feet. Bart lay on the ground, rocking back and forth and screaming. The wild shotgun blast had hit him right in the ass. There was a lot of blood on his jeans, but he didn't seem to be gushing anything from a major artery. Granted, depending on how much of the shot he'd caught, the wound could potentially maim, cripple, or maybe even kill him if there was any internal bleeding. But there are worse places to get hit, and with all the adrenaline surging through me, it seemed pretty hilarious.

Cackling, I called to Mouse and ran for the car.

Molly already had Murph buckled into the passenger seat. I had to crawl across her to get to the driver's side. She let out a blistering curse as I accidentally bumped her arm. The driver's chair was practically touching the steering wheel, and for a second I thought I was going to have to push down the pedals with one hand and drive with the other, but I managed to find the lever that made the seat slide back, and the car started on the first try.

'Dammit, Dresden,' Murphy wheezed. 'There were weapons involved. We have to go back.'

Mouse sailed into the backseat through the open door, and Molly closed both doors on that side of the car. I rocked the steering wheel and wiggled the Saturn loose from the snow, then started off down the street. I still had an irrational smile plastered on my face. My cheeks hurt. 'Not a chance, Murphy.'

'We can't just let them *go*.'

I suppressed another round of adrenaline giggles. 'They aren't going anywhere. And I'm persona non grata, remember? You want to get caught at the scene of a shooting with me mixed up in it?'

'But—'

'Dammit, Murphy,' I said, exasperated. 'Do you *want* me to go to jail? If we go back now, Torelli's goon tells them I shot him. They take my gun, and if they can find the bullet, or if it's still in his leg, it's assault with a deadly weapon.'

'Not if you were defending yourself,' Murphy grated.

'In a fair world, maybe,' I said. 'As it is, if there's no one but outfit goons there, two guys with records and a known association, both of them wounded, the cops are going to assume that they quarreled and shot each other. Two bad guys go away, you keep your job, and I don't get pulled off of this case – which is the same thing as getting killed.' I glanced aside at her. 'Who loses?'

Murphy didn't say anything for a moment. Then she said, 'Everyone loses, Harry. The law is there to protect everyone. It's supposed to apply equally to everyone.'

I sighed and paid attention to the road. I'd drive for a few minutes to be sure we were in the clear, and then circle back to Michael's place. 'That's wishful thinking, Murph, and you know it. Pretty sure Marcone's lawyers love that attitude.'

'The law isn't perfect,' she replied quietly. 'But that doesn't mean that we shouldn't try to make it work.'

'Do me a favor,' I said.

'What?'

'Hold your nose shut, put on a Philadelphia accent, and say, "I *am* the law."'

Murphy snorted and shook her head. I glanced aside at her. Her face was pale with pain, her eyes a little glassy. Her left arm was wrapped up in what looked like strips torn from Molly's T-shirt.

I checked the rearview. My apprentice was, indeed, wearing nothing but a green lace bra under her winter coat. She was crouched down with both arms around Mouse, her face buried in his snow-frosted fur.

'Hey, back there,' I said. 'Anyone hurt?'

Mouse yawned, but Molly checked him over anyway. 'No. We're both fine.'

'Cool,' I said. I looked over my shoulder for a second to give Molly a smile. 'Nice veil back there. Fast as hell. You did good, grasshopper.'

Molly beamed at me. 'Did my face look like that when you did that little ball-of-fire thing to me?'

'I prefer to think of it as a little ball of sunshine,' I said. 'And you were stoic compared to that guy, grasshopper. You did a good job too, furface,' I told Mouse. 'I owe you one.'

Mouse opened his mouth in a doggy grin and wagged his tail. It thumped against Molly, scattering a little snow against bare skin. She yelped and burst into a laugh.

Murphy and I traded a look. If the gunman had squeezed the trigger a hundredth of a second sooner or later, Murphy would be dead. The blast could have taken her in the head or neck, or torn into an artery. Without Mouse I'd probably be dead, too.

And if they'd gotten me and Murphy, I doubted they'd have left Molly behind to testify against them.

That one had been close – no supernatural opposition necessary. Molly might not realize that yet, but Murphy and I did.

'How's the arm, Murph?' I asked quietly.

'Just hit muscle,' she said, closing her eyes. 'It hurts like hell, but it isn't going to kill me.'

'You want me to drive you to the emergency room?'

Murphy didn't answer right away. There was a lot more to the question than the words in it. Doctors are required by law to report any gunshot wound to the authorities. If Murph went in for proper medical treatment, they'd report it to the cops. And, since she *was* a cop, it would mean that she had to answer all kinds of questions, and it would probably mean that the truth of what happened behind us would come out.

It was the responsible, law-abiding thing to do.

'No, Harry,' she said finally, and closed her eyes.

I exhaled slowly, relieved. That answer had cost her something. My hands had started shaking on the wheel. Generally speaking I'm fine when there's a crisis in progress. It's afterward that it starts getting to my nerves. 'Sit tight,' I said. 'We'll get you patched up.'

'Just drive,' she said wearily.

So I drove.

20

'This is getting awfully murky, Harry,' Michael said, worry in his voice. 'I don't like it.'

Snow crunched under our feet as we walked from the house to the workshop. The daylight was fading as a second front hit the city, darkening the skies with the promise of more snow. 'I don't like it much either,' I replied. 'But nobody came rushing up to present me with options.' I stopped in the snow. 'How's Murphy?'

Michael paused beside me. 'Charity is the one who's had actual medical training, but it seemed a simple enough injury to me. A bandage stopped the bleeding, and we cleaned the wound thoroughly. She should be careful to monitor her condition for the next few days, but I think she'll be all right.'

'How much pain is she in?' I asked.

'Charity keeps some codeine on hand. It isn't as strong as the painkillers at a hospital, but it should let her sleep, at least.'

I grimaced and nodded. 'I'm going to hunt up the Denarians, Michael.'

He took a deep breath. 'You're going to attack them?'

'I should,' I said, a little more sharply than I'd meant to. 'Because there are people who don't deserve a second chance, Michael, and if these losers don't qualify for the permanent shit list, I don't know who does.'

Michael gave me a small smile. 'Everyone does, Harry.'

A little shiver went through me, but I didn't let it show on my face. I just rolled my eyes. 'Right, right. Original sin, God's grace, I've heard this part before.' I sighed. 'But I'm not planning to assault them. I just want to learn whatever I can about them before we square off.'

Michael nodded. 'Which is why we're standing out in the snow talking, I take it.'

'I need whatever information you can give me. And I don't need another philosophical debate.'

Michael grunted. 'I already got in touch with Father Forthill. He sent over a report on who we think might be in town with Tessa.'

I spent a couple of seconds feeling like an argumentative jerk. 'Oh,' I said. 'Thank you. That . . . that could help a lot.'

Michael shrugged. 'We've learned to be wary of even our own intelligence. The Fallen are masters of deception, Harry. Sometimes it takes us centuries to catch one of them lying.'

'I know,' I said. 'But you must have something solid.'

'A little,' he said. 'We are fairly certain that Tessa and Imariel are the second-eldest of the Denarians. Only Nicodemus and Anduriel have been operating longer.'

I grunted. 'Are Tessa and Nicodemus rivals?'

'Generally,' Michael replied. 'Though I suppose it bears mentioning that they're also husband and wife.'

'Match made in Hell, eh?'

'Not that it seems to mean much to either of them. They very rarely work together, and when they do it's never good. The last time they did so, according to the Church's records, was just before the Black Plague came to Europe.'

'Plagues? The Nickelheads did that last time they were in town.' I shook my head. 'You'd expect a different tune or two in a husband-and-wife act that had been running that long.'

'Variety is the key to a happy marriage,' Michael agreed solemnly. His mouth quivered. 'Nickelheads?'

'I decided their name gave them too much dignity, given what they are. I'm correcting that.'

'Those who underestimate them generally don't survive it,' Michael said. 'Be careful.'

'You know me.'

'Yes,' he said. 'Where were we?'

'Plagues.'

'Ah, yes. The Nickelheads have used plagues to instigate the most havoc and confusion in the past.'

I fought off a smile that threatened my hard-ass exterior as Michael continued.

'It's proven a successful tactic on more than one occasion. Once a plague has gained momentum, there's almost no limit to the lives they can claim and the suffering they can inflict.'

I frowned and folded my arms. 'Sanya said that Tessa preferred choosing eager . . . subjects, I suppose, over talented ones.'

Michael nodded. 'The Fallen who follow Imariel go through bearers very quickly. None of them are kind to those they bond with, but Imariel's crew are the monsters among the monsters. Tessa chooses their hosts from among the downtrodden, the desperate, those who believe that they have nothing to lose. Those who will succumb to temptation the most rapidly.'

I grunted. 'Lot of those around in the wake of a big nasty plague. Or any kind of similar chaos.'

'Yes. We believe that it is one reason she collaborates with Nicodemus from time to time.'

'She's focused on short-term,' I said, getting it. 'He's all about the long view.'

'Exactly,' Michael said. 'When he threw Lasciel's coin at my son, it was a calculated gesture.'

'Calculated to rope me in,' I said.

'You,' Michael said, 'or my son.'

A chill that had nothing to do with the air went through me. 'Give the coin to a child?'

'A child who couldn't defend himself. Who could be raised with the voice of a Fallen angel whispering in his ear. Shaping him. Preparing him to be used as a weapon against his own family. Imagine it.'

I stared around the yard that had been the scene of so much merriment only a few hours before. 'I'd rather not,' I said.

Michael continued quietly. 'In general, the families of the bearers of the Swords are sheltered against such evils. But things like that have happened before. And Nicodemus has borne a coin for a score of centuries. He has no difficulty with the notion of waiting ten or fifteen or twenty years to attain his goals.'

'That's why you think he's here,' I said. 'Because going after someone like Marcone isn't Tessa's style.'

'It isn't,' Michael said. 'But I believe that if by helping it happen she could create the kind of environment she loves best, full of chaos and despair, it would be reason enough for her to join forces with her husband.'

'How many?'

'Tessa keeps a group of five other Fallen around her.' He gave me a quick smile. 'Sorry. Four, now.'

'Thank Thomas,' I said. 'Not me.'

'I intend to,' Michael said. 'Nicodemus . . .' Michael shook his head. 'I believe you've been told before that Nicodemus makes it a point to destroy any records the Church manages to build concerning him. That's not going to be as easy to arrange in the future—'

'Hail the information age,' I interjected.

'—but our accounts regarding him are sketchy. We thought he had only three regular companions – but then he produced Lasciel's coin, which had supposedly been in secure storage in a Chilean monastery. I think it would be dangerous to assume anything at this point.'

'Worst-case scenario,' I said, 'how many other coins might he have with him?'

Michael shrugged. 'Six, perhaps? But it's just a guess.'

I stared at him. 'You're saying that they could have a dozen walking nightmares with them this time.'

He nodded.

'Last time they came to party, all three Swords were here. There were *four* Denarians. And we barely came out of it alive.'

'I know.'

'But you're used to this, right?' I asked him. 'The Knights take on odds like this all the time.'

He gave me an apologetic glance. 'We like to outnumber them two to one if possible. Three to one when we can arrange it.'

'But Shiro said he had fought several duels against them,' I said. 'One-on-one.'

'Shiro had a gift,' Michael said. 'It was as simple as that. Shiro knew swordplay like Mozart knew music. I'm not like him. I'm not afraid of facing a single Denarian alone, but I would generally consider us evenly matched. My fate would be in God's hands.'

'Super,' I sighed.

'Faith, Harry,' Michael said. 'He will not abandon us. There will be a way for good to overcome.'

'Good overcame last time,' I said quietly. 'More or less. But that didn't stop them from killing Shiro.'

'Our lives belong to the Almighty,' Michael said evenly. 'We serve and live for the sake of others. Not for our own.'

'Yeah,' I said. 'I'm sure that will comfort your kids when they have to grow up without a father.'

Michael abruptly turned to face me squarely, and his right hand closed into a fist. 'Stop talking,' he said in a low, hard tone. 'Right now.'

So help me God, I almost took a swing at him out of sheer frustration. But sanity grabbed the scruff of my neck and turned me around. I stalked several paces away through the snow and stood with my back to him.

Sanity invited shame over for tea and biscuits. Dammit. I was supposed to be a wizard. Connected with my inner light, master of the disciplined mind, all of that kind of crap. But instead I was shooting my mouth off at a man who didn't deserve it because . . .

Because I was scared. Really, really scared. I always started shooting my mouth off when something scared me. It had been an asset before, but it sure as hell wasn't right now. When something scared me I almost always embraced my anger as a weapon against it. That, too, was usually an asset. But this time I'd let that fear and anger shape my thinking, and as a result I'd torn into my friend in the most tender spot he had, at a time when he could probably have used my support.

Then I realized why I was angry at Michael. I had wanted him to come flying in like Superman and solve my problems, and he'd let me down.

We're always disappointed when we find out someone else has human limits, the same as we do. It's stupid for us to feel that way, and we really ought to know better, but that doesn't seem to slow us down.

I wondered if Michael had ever felt the same way about me.

'My last remark,' I muttered, 'was out of line.'

'Yes,' Michael said. 'It was.'

'You want to duke it out or arm wrestle or something?'

'There are better ways for us to spend our time. Nicodemus and Tessa should be our focus.'

I turned back to him. 'Agreed.'

'This isn't over,' he said, a harsh edge in his voice. 'We'll discuss it after.'

I grunted and nodded. Some of the tension left the air between us. Back to business. That was easier. 'You know what I don't get?' I said. 'How do you step from Nicodemus's end of recruiting Marcone all the way to Tessa's end of a society steeped in chaos and despair?'

'I don't know,' Michael said. He moved his hand to the hilt of the sword he now wore belted to his side, an unconscious gesture. 'But Nicodemus thinks he does. And whatever he's doing, I've got a bad feeling that we'd better figure it out before he gets it done.'

21

'If I knew of any trusted lieutenants preparing to betray my employer,' Miss Gard said with exaggerated patience, 'they wouldn't be *trusted*, now, would they? If you ask politely, I'm sure you can get someone to read the definition of *treachery* to you, Dresden.'

Michael smiled quietly. He sat at the workbench with one of his heavy daggers and a metal file, evidently taking some burrs out of the blade. Hendricks sat on a stool at the other end of the workbench. The huge enforcer had disassembled a handgun and was cleaning the pieces fastidiously.

'Okay, then,' I said to Gard. 'Why don't we start with everyone who knew the location of Marcone's panic room.'

Gard narrowed her eyes, studying me. She looked better. Granted, it's difficult to look much *worse* than disemboweled, but even so, she'd been reduced from ten miles of bad road to maybe two or three. She was sitting up in her cot, her back resting against the wall of the workshop, and though she looked pale and incredibly tired, her blue eyes were clear and sharp.

'I don't think so,' she said quietly.

'There's not going to be much need to keep Marcone's secrets once he's dead, or under the control of one of the Fallen.'

'I can't,' she said.

'Oh, come on,' I said, throwing up my hands. 'Hell's bells, I'm not asking you for the launch codes to nuclear missiles.'

She took a deep breath and enunciated each word. 'I. Can't.'

From the workbench Hendricks rumbled, 'S'okay. Tell him.'

Gard frowned at his broad back but nodded once and turned to me. 'Comparatively few people in the organization were directly aware of the panic room, but I'm not sure that's our biggest concern.'

The change in gears, from stonewall to narration, made me blink a little. Even Michael glanced up, frowning at Gard.

'No?' I asked. 'If that's not our biggest concern, what is?'

'The number of people who could have pieced it together from disparate facts,' Gard replied. 'Contractors had to be paid. Materials had to be purchased. Architects had to be hired. Any of a dozen different things could have indicated that Marcone was building something, and piqued someone's curiosity enough to dig deeper.'

I grunted. 'At which point he could probably find out a lot by talking to the architects or builders.'

'Exactly. In this instance he was unusually lax in his standard caution when it came to matters of security. I urged him to take conventional measures, but he refused.'

'Conventional measures,' I said. 'You're talking about killing everyone who worked on it.'

'Secret passages and secret sanctums are quite useless if they aren't *secret*,' Gard replied.

'Maybe he didn't feel like killing a bunch of his employees to cover his own ass.'

Gard shrugged. 'I'm not here to make moral judgments, Dresden. I'm an adviser. That was my advice.'

I grunted. 'So who would know? The builders. People handling books and paychecks.'

'And anyone they talked to,' Gard said.

'That makes the suspect pool a little larger than is useful,' I said.

'Indeed it does.'

'Stop,' I said. 'Occam time.'

Gard gave me a blank stare. Maybe she'd never heard of MC Hammer.

'Occam?' she asked.

'Occam's razor,' I said. 'The simplest explanation is most often correct.'

Her lips quivered. 'How charming.'

'If we define a circle of suspects that includes everyone who might possibly have heard anything, we get nowhere. If we limit the pool to the most likely choices, we have something we can work with, and we're much more likely to find the traitor.'

'We?' Gard asked.

'Whatever,' I said. 'Who would have had a lot of access? Let's leave the contractors out of it. They generally aren't out for blood, and Marcone owns half the developers in town anyway.'

Gard nodded her head in acceptance. 'Very well. One of three or four accountants, any of the inner circle, and one of two or three troubleshooters.'

'Troubleshooters?' Michael asked.

'When there's trouble,' I told him, 'they shoot it.'

Gard let out a quick snort of laughter – then winced, clutching at her stomach with both hands.

'Easy there,' I said. 'You all right?'

'Eventually,' Gard murmured. 'Please continue.'

'What about Torelli?' I asked.

'What about him?'

'Could he be our guy?'

Gard rolled her eyes. 'Please. The man has the intellect of a lobotomized turtle. Marcone's been aware of his ambition for some time now.'

'If he's been aware of it,' I asked, 'how come Torelli is still paying taxes?'

'Because we were using him to draw any other would-be usurpers into the open, where they could be dealt with.'

'Hungh,' I said, frowning. 'Could he have put pressure on any of the people in the know?'

'The bookkeepers, perhaps, but I think it highly unlikely. Marcone has made it clear that they enjoy his most enthusiastic protection.'

'Yeah, but Yurtle the Lobotomized isn't all that bright.'

Gard blinked. 'Excuse me?'

'My God, woman!' I protested. 'You've never read Dr. Seuss?'

She frowned. 'Who is Dr.—'

I held up a hand. 'Never mind, forget it. Torelli isn't all that bright. Maybe he figured he could strong-arm a bookkeeper and knock off Marcone before Marcone got a chance to demonstrate his enthusiasm.'

Gard pursed her lips. 'Torelli has stupidity enough and to spare. But he's also a sniveling, cowardly little splatter of rat dung.' She narrowed her eyes. 'Why are you so focused on him?'

'Oh,' I said, 'I can't put my finger on any one thing. But my finely tuned instincts tell me that he's hostile.'

Gard smiled. 'Tried to kill you, did he?'

'He started trying to put the muscle on Demeter while I was there this morning. I objected.'

'Ah,' she said. 'I had wondered how you found us.'

'Torelli's goons tried shooting me up right before I came here.'

'I see,' Gard said, narrowing her eyes in thought. 'The timing of his uprising is rather too precise to be mere coincidence.'

'I'm glad I'm not the only one who thought of that.'

She tapped a finger against her chin. 'Torelli is no genius, but he *is* competent at his job. He wouldn't be operating that high in the organization if he weren't. I suppose it's possible that Torelli might have secured the information if he applied enough mean cunning to the task.' She glanced up at me. 'You think the Denarians recruited him to be their man on the inside?'

'I think they had to get their information about Marcone's panic room somewhere,' I said.

'Worked that out, did you?' Gard said with a wan smile.

'Yeah. Turned your own hidey-hole into a fox trap. That's gotta sting the old ego, Miss Security Consultant.'

'You wouldn't believe how much,' Gard said, a flinty light in her eyes. 'But I'll deal with that when it's time.'

'You aren't dealing with anything but more sleep for a little while,' I noted.

Her face twisted into a scowl. 'Yes.'

'So let me do the heavy lifting,' I said.

'How so?'

I glanced around the workshop. 'Could we speak privately for a moment?'

Hendricks, who had been reassembling his gun, turned his overdeveloped brow ridges toward me, scowling in suspicion. Michael glanced up, his face a mask.

Gard looked at me for a while. Then she said, 'It's all right with me.'

Hendricks finished putting the pistol back together, loaded it, and then loaded a round into the chamber. He made it a point to stare straight at me the entire while. Then he stood up, tugged on his coat, and walked straight toward me.

Hendricks wasn't as tall as me, which cut down on the intimidation factor. On the other hand, he had muscle enough to break me in half and we both knew it. He stopped a foot away, put the gun in his pocket, and said, 'Be right outside.'

'Michael,' I said. 'Please.'

He rose, sheathing the dagger, and followed Hendricks out into the snow. The two kept a careful, even distance between them as they went, like dogs who aren't yet sure whether they're going to fight or not. I closed the door behind them and turned to Gard.

'Give me what I need to find and question Torelli.'

She shook her head. 'I can get you his address and the locations of the properties he owns, places he frequents, known associates, but he won't be at any of those places. He's been in the business too long to make a mistake like that.'

'Oh, please,' I said, rolling my eyes. 'You've got blood or hair samples for all of your people somewhere. Get me Torelli's.'

Gard stared at me with her poker face.

'For that matter,' I added, 'get me Marcone's. If I can get close enough, it might help me find him.'

'My employer keeps them under intense security. He's the only one who can access them.'

I snorted. 'So get me samples from the second collection.'

'Second collection?'

'You know, the one you're keeping. The one Marcone doesn't know about.'

Gard brushed a stray lock of gold from her cheek. 'What makes you think I have any such samples?'

I showed her my teeth. 'You're a mercenary, Gard. Mercenaries have to be more cautious with their own employers than they do with the enemy they've been hired to fight. They take out insurance policies. Even if Marcone didn't have samples collected, I'm betting you did.'

Her eyes drifted over to the door for a moment, and then back to me. 'Let's pretend, for a moment, that I have such a collection,' she said. 'Why on earth would I hand it over to you? You're antagonistic to my employer's business, and could inflict catastrophic damage on it with such a thing in your possession.'

'Gosh, you're squeamish, considering the catastrophic damage his business inflicts on thousands of people every day of the year.'

'I'm merely protecting my employer's interests.' She showed me her teeth. 'Almost as though I'm a mercenary.'

I sighed and folded my arms. 'What if I only took Torelli's and Marcone's samples?'

'Then you would still be capable of using that against Marcone in the future.'

'If I want to hurt Marcone,' I said, 'all I need to do is sit down with a six-pack of beer and a bag of pretzels and let him twist in the wind.'

'Perhaps,' Gard admitted. 'Swear to me that you will use none of the samples but Torelli's and Marcone's, that you will use neither of them for harm of any kind, and that you will return both to me immediately upon my request. Swear it by your power.'

Oaths in general carry a lot of currency among the preternatural crowd. They're binding in more senses than the theoretical. Every time you break a promise, there's a kind of backlash of spiritual energies. A broken promise can inflict horrible pain on supernatural entities, such as the Sidhe. When a wizard breaks a promise, particularly when sworn by his own power, the backlash is different: a diminishing of that magical talent. It isn't a crippling effect by any means – but break enough promises and sooner or later you'd have nothing left.

As dangerous as the world had been for wizards over the past few years, any of us would have been insane to take the chance that our talents, and thus our ability to defend ourselves, might be hampered, even if that reduction was relatively slight.

I squared my shoulders and nodded. 'I swear, by my own power, that I will abide by those restrictions.'

Gard narrowed her eyes as I spoke, and when I finished she gave me a single nod. She reached into her pocket, moving very gingerly, and withdrew a single silver key. She held it out to me. 'Union Station, locker two fourteen. Everything is labeled.'

I reached out to take the key, but Gard's fingers tightened on it for a second. 'Don't let anything you care about stand directly in front of it when you open it.'

I arched an eyebrow at her as she released the key. 'All right. Thank you.'

She gave me a quick, tight smile. 'Stop wasting time here. Go.'

I frowned. 'You're that worried about your boss?'

'Not at all,' Gard said, closing her eyes and sagging wearily down on the cot. 'I just don't want to be in the vicinity the next time someone comes to kill you.'

22

Murphy's car looked like it might have been through a war zone, and there were odd-colored stains in the snow underneath it. As a result we'd taken Michael's truck. I rode in the cab with Michael, while Mouse rode in the back. Yeah, I know, not safe, but the reality of the situation is that you don't fit two people our size and a dog Mouse's size into the cab of a pickup. There wouldn't be any room left for oxygen.

Mouse didn't seem to be the least bit distressed by the cold as we sallied forth to Union Station. He actually walked to the side of the truck and stuck his head out into the wind, tongue lolling happily. Not that there was a lot of wind to be had – Michael drove patiently and carefully in the bad weather.

After the third or fourth time we passed a car that had slid up onto a sidewalk or into a ditch, I stopped tapping my foot and mentally urging him to hurry. It would take a hell of a lot longer to walk to Union Station than it would to drive with what was obviously appropriate caution.

We didn't talk on the way. Don't get me wrong. It isn't like Michael is a chatterbox or anything. It's just that he usually has something to say. He invites me to go to church with him (which I don't, unless something is chasing us) or has some kind of proud-papa talk regarding something one of his kids has done. We'll talk about Molly's progress, or weather, or sports, or something.

Not this time.

Maybe he wanted to focus his whole attention on the road, I told myself.

Yeah. That was probably it. It couldn't have anything to do with me opening my big fat mouth too much, obviously.

A mound of plowed snow had collapsed at the entrance of the parking garage, but Michael just built up a little speed and rumbled over and through it, though it was mostly the momentum that got him inside.

The parking garage's lights were out, and with all that piled snow around the first level, very little of the ambient snow-light got inside. Parking garages are kind of intimidating places even when you can see them. They're even more intimidating when they're entirely black, except for the none-too-expansive areas lit by the glare of headlights.

'Well,' I said, 'at least there's plenty of available spaces.'

Michael grunted. 'Who wants to travel in weather like this?' He wheeled into the nearest open parking space and the truck jerked to a stop. He got out, fetched the heavy sports bag he used to carry *Amoracchius* in public, and slung the bag from his shoulder. I got out, and Mouse hopped out of the back to the ground. The truck creaked and rocked on its springs, relieved of the big dog's weight. I clipped Mouse's lead on him, and then tied on the little apron thing that declared him a service dog. It's an out-and-out lie, but it makes moving around in public with him a lot easier.

Mouse gave the apron an approving glance, and waited patiently until his disguise was in place.

'Service dog?' Michael asked, his expression uncomfortable. He had a flashlight in his right hand, and he shone it at us for a moment before sweeping it around us, searching the shadows.

'I have a rare condition,' I said, scratching the big dog under the chin. 'Can't-get-a-date-itis. He's supposed to be some kind of catalyst or conversation starter. Or failing that, a consolation prize. Anyway, he's necessary.'

Mouse made a chuffing sound, and his tail thumped against my leg.

Michael sighed.

'You're awfully persnickety about the law all of a sudden,' I said. 'Especially considering that you're toting a concealed weapon.'

'Please, Harry. I'm uncomfortable enough.'

'I won't tell anyone about your Sword if you won't tell anyone about my gun.'

Michael sighed and started walking. Mouse and I followed.

The parking garage proved to be very cold, very dark, very creepy, and empty of any threat. We crossed the half-buried street, Mouse leading the way through the snow.

'Snow's coming down thicker again now that the sun's down,' Michael noted.

'Mab's doing, maybe,' I said. 'If it is, Titania would be less able to oppose her power after the sun went down. Which is also when Titania's agents would be able to move most freely through town.'

'But you aren't certain it's Mab's doing?' Michael asked.

'Nope. Could just be Chicago. Which can be just as scary as Mab, some days.'

Michael chuckled and we went into Union Station. It doesn't look like that scene in *The Untouchables*, if you were wondering. That was shot in this big room they rent out for well-to-do gatherings. The rest of the place doesn't look like something that fits into the Roaring Twenties. It's all modernized, and looks more or less like an airport.

Sorta depressing, really. I mean, of all the possible aesthetic choices out there, airports must generally rank in the top five or ten most bland. But I guess they're cost-effective. That counts for more and more when it comes to beauty. Sure, all the marble and Corinthian columns and soaring spaces were beautiful, but where do they fall on a cost-assessment worksheet?

The ghost of style still haunts the bits of the original Union Station that have been permitted to stand, but, looking around the place, I couldn't help but get the same feeling I had when I looked at the Coliseum in Rome, or the Parthenon in Athens – that once, it had been a place of splendor. Once. But a long, long time ago.

'Which way are the lockers?' Michael asked quietly.

I nodded toward the northeast end of the building and started walking. The ticketing counters were closed, except for one, whose clerk was probably in a back room somewhere. There weren't a lot of people walking around. Late at night train stations in general don't seem to explode with activity. Particularly not in weather like ours. One harried customer-service representative from Amtrak was dealing with a small knot of angry-looking travelers who had probably just been stranded in town by the storm. She was trying to get them a hotel. Good luck. The airport had been closed since yesterday, and the hotels would be doing a brisk business already.

'You know your way around the station,' Michael commented.

'Trains are faster than buses and safer than planes,' I said. 'I took a plane to Portland once, and the pilot lost his radio and computer and so on. Had to land without instruments or communications. We were lucky it was a clear day.'

'Statistically, it's still the safest—' he began.

'Not for wizards it isn't,' I told him seriously. 'I've had flights that went smoothly. A couple of them just had little problems. But after that trip to Portland . . .' I shook my head. 'There were kids on that plane. I'm going to live a long time. I can take a little longer to get there. Hey, Joe,' I said to a silver-haired janitor, walking by with a wheeled cart of cleaning supplies.

'Harry,' Joe said, nodding with a small smile as he passed by.

'I've been here a lot lately,' I said to Michael. 'Traveling to support the Paranet, mostly. Plus Warden stuff.' I rolled my eyes. 'I didn't want the job, but I'll be damned if I'll do it half-assed.'

Michael looked back at the janitor thoughtfully for a moment, and then at me. 'What's that like?'

'Wardening?' I asked. I shrugged. 'I've got four other Wardens who are, I guess, under my command.' I made air quotes around the word. 'In Atlanta, Dallas, New York, and Boston. But I mostly just stay out of their way and let them do their jobs, give them help when they need it. They're kids. Grew up hard in the war, though that didn't give them brains enough to keep from looking up to me.'

Mouse suddenly stopped in his tracks.

Me too. I didn't rubberneck around. Instead I focused on the dog.

Mouse's ears twitched like individual radar dishes. His nose quivered. One paw came up off the ground, but the dog only looked around him uncertainly.

'Lassie would have smelled something,' I told him. 'She would have given a clear, concise warning. One bark for gruffs, two barks for Nickelheads.'

Mouse gave me a reproachful glance, put his paw back down, and sneezed.

'He's right,' Michael said quietly. 'Something is watching us.'

'When isn't it?' I muttered, glancing around. I didn't see anything. My highly tuned investigative instincts didn't see anything either. I hate feeling like Han Solo in a world of Jedi. 'I'm supposed to be the Jedi,' I muttered aloud.

'What's that?' Michael asked.

The station's lights went out. All of them. At exactly the same time.

The emergency lights, which are supposed to come on instantly, didn't.

Beside me Michael's coat rustled and something clicked several times. Presumably he was trying his flashlight, and presumably it didn't work.

That wasn't good. Magic could interfere with the function of technology, but that was more of a Murphy effect: Things that naturally could go wrong tended to go wrong a lot more often. It didn't behave in a predictable or uniform fashion. It didn't shut down lights, emergency lights, and battery-powered flashlights all at the same time.

I didn't know what could do that.

'Harry?' Michael asked.

Mouse pressed up against my leg, and I felt his warning growl vibrating through his chest.

'You said it, Chewie,' I told my dog. 'I've got a bad feeling about this.'

23

People started screaming.

I reached for the amulet around my neck and drew it forth as I directed an effort of will at it to call forth light in the darkness.

And nothing happened.

I'd have stared at my amulet if I could have seen it. I couldn't believe that it wasn't working. I shook the necklace, cursed at it, and raised it again, forcing more of my will into the amulet.

It flickered with blue-white sparks for a moment, and that was it.

Mouse let out a louder snarl, the one I hear only when he's identified a real threat. Something close. My heart jumped up hard enough to bounce off the roof of my mouth.

'I can't call a light!' I said, my voice high and thin.

A zipper let out a high-pitched whine in the dark next to me, and steel rasped against steel, then rang like a gently struck bell. 'Father,' Michael's voice murmured gently, 'we need Your help.'

White light exploded from the sword.

About a dozen things crouching within three or four yards of us started screaming.

I'd never seen anything like them before. They were maybe five feet tall, but squat and thick, with rubbery-looking muscle. They were built more or less along the lines of baboons, somewhere between pure quadruped and biped, with wicked-looking claws, long, ropy tails, and massive shoulders. Some of them carried crude-looking weapons: cudgels, stone-headed axes, and stone-bladed knives. Their heads were apelike and nearly skeletal, black skin stretched tight over muscle and bone. They had ugly, almost sharklike teeth, so oversized that you could see where they were cutting their own lips and—

And they didn't have any eyes. Where their eyes should have been there was nothing but blank, sunken skin.

They screamed in agony as the light from Michael's sword fell on them, reeling back as if burned by a sudden flame – and if the sudden, smoldering reek that filled the air was any indicator, they had been.

'Harry!' Michael cried.

I knew that tone of voice. I crouched as quickly as I could, as low as I could, and barely got out of the way before *Amoracchius* swept through the space where my head had been—

—and slammed into the leaping form of one of the creatures that had been about to land on my back.

The thing fell back away from me and landed on the floor, thrashing. Its blood erupted into blue-white fire as it spurted from the wound.

I snapped my head around to stare at *Amoracchius*. More blood sizzled on the blade of the sword like grease on a hot skillet.

Iron.

These things were faeries.

I'd never seen them face-to-face before, but I'd read descriptions of them – including when I had been boning up on my book learning to figure out the identity of the gruffs. Given that this beastie was a faerie, there was only one thing it could be.

'Hobs!' I screamed at Michael as I drew the gun from my coat pocket. 'They're hobs!'

After that I didn't have time to talk. A couple of the hobs around us had recovered enough from the shock of sudden exposure to light to fling themselves forward. Mouse let out his deep-chested battle roar and collided with one of them in midair. They went down in a tangle of thrashing limbs and flashing teeth.

The next hob leapt over them at me, stone knife in its knobby hand. I slipped aside from the line of his jump and pistol-whipped him with the barrel of the heavy revolver. The steel smashed into the hob's eyeless face, scorching flesh and shattering teeth. The hob screamed in pain as it flew by, crashing into one of its fellows.

'*In nomine Dei!*' Michael bellowed. I felt his shoulder blades hit mine, and the light from the great sword bobbed and flashed, followed by another scream from a hob's throat.

The hob wrestling with Mouse slammed the huge dog to the floor and rose up above him, baring its fangs.

I took a step toward it, jammed the revolver into its face, screamed, 'Get off my dog!' and started pulling the trigger. I wasn't sure what hurt the hob more – the bullets or the muted flashes of light from the discharge. Either way it recoiled so hard that it flung itself completely off of Mouse, who came to his feet still full of fight. I grabbed him by the collar and hauled him back with me until I felt Michael at my back again.

The hobs withdrew to the shadows, but I could still hear them all around us. As bright as Michael's sword was, I should have been able to see the ceiling far overhead, but it spread out for only twenty feet or so – far enough to keep the hobs from leaping onto us in a single bound, but not much more than that.

I could hear screams still, drifting through the interior of the station. I heard a gun go off, something smaller than my .44, the rapid shots of panic fire. Whoever was packing was presumably shooting blindly into the dark. Hell's bells, this was going to turn into a real mess if I didn't do something, and fast.

'We've got to get out of the open,' I said, thinking out loud. 'Michael, head for the ticketing counter.'

'Can't you clear the way?' Michael asked. 'I can cover you.'

'I can't *see* in this crap,' I said. 'And there are other people in here. If I start tossing power around I could kill somebody.'

'Then stay close,' Michael said. He moved out at a stalk, sword held high over his head, ready to sweep down on top of anything stupid enough to come leaping at him. We went over two dead hobs, both of them covered in blue flames that gave off barely any light but consumed the bodies with voracious rapidity. I heard a scuffle of claws on the floor and shouted a wordless cry.

Michael pivoted smoothly as a hob armed with a pair of stone axes rushed into the light of the holy sword. The dark faerie flung one of the axes at Michael on the way. My friend slapped it aside with a contemptuous flick of his sword, and met the hob with a horizontal slash that shattered its second ax and split open its torso all the way back to its crooked spine. The hob dropped, spewing flame, and Michael kicked its falling body back into its companions, scattering them for a moment and gaining us another twenty feet.

'Nice,' I said, keeping close, trying to watch the bobbing shadows all around us. 'You been working out? You look good.'

Michael's teeth flashed in a quick smile. 'Wouldn't speaking give these creatures a fine means of tar—' He broke off as *Amoracchius* flicked in front of my face, deflecting a tumbling stone knife. 'Targeting us,' he continued.

Me and my big mouth. I shut up the rest of the way to the ticketing counter.

I led Michael around behind it and all but tripped over the form of a wounded man in a business suit. He let out a choked scream of pain and clutched at the bloodied cloth over his lower leg. There was the broken shard of a stone blade still protruding from the man's leg.

'Harry,' Michael said, 'keep moving. They're gathering for a rush.'

'Okay,' I said. I knelt down by the wounded businessman and said, 'Come on, buddy; this is no place to be sitting around.' I grabbed him underneath the arms and started backpedaling down the counter. 'There's a doorway back here somewhere, goes to the rear area.'

'Perfect,' Michael said. 'I can hold that for as long as you need.'

The wounded man struggled to help me, but mostly all he did was make it harder to move him. He was making continuous sounds of terror and pain. I was glad that we had the barrier of the counter between us and the encroaching hobs. I didn't particularly care to find out what getting hit with a sharp stone ax felt like.

We reached the door behind the ticketing counter, which was closed. I jiggled the handle, but it was apparently locked. I didn't have time for this crap. I lifted my right hand and focused on one of the energy rings I wore. There was one of them on each finger, a band made of three rings woven into a braid. The rings stored energy, saving back a little every time I moved my arm, and allowing me to unleash that stored energy all in one spot.

I brought my will to bear on the door as I lifted my hand in a closed fist, focusing the energy of the rings into as small an area as I could. I hadn't designed them for this kind of work. They'd been made to shove things roughly away from me before they could rip my face off. But I didn't have a lot of time to waste putting together something neater.

So I aimed as best I could, triggered the ring, and watched it rip the doorknob, the lock, and the plate they were all mounted in right out of the door, to send them tumbling into the room beyond. Unimpeded by any of those pesky metal security fittings, the door swung inward.

'Come on!' I said to Michael, seizing the wounded man again. 'Mouse, lead the way.'

My dog padded through the doorway, crouched low and with his teeth bared. I practically walked on his tail as I came in behind him, and Michael was all but treading on the wounded man's bloodied leg.

As the light from *Amoracchius* illuminated the room we entered, it revealed the harried customer-service rep we'd seen a few minutes before. She knelt on the floor, crucifix in hand, her head bowed as she frantically recited a prayer. As the light fell over her she blinked and looked up. The white fire of the holy sword painted the tear streaks on her face silver as her mouth dropped open in an expression of shock and stunned joy. She looked down at her crucifix, and back up at him again.

Michael took a quick glance around the room, smiled at the woman, and said, 'Of course He's there. Of course He listens.' He paused, then admitted, 'Granted, He doesn't always answer quite this quickly.'

There were other people in the room – the customers she'd been trying to find a hotel room for. When things had gone dark and scary she had somehow rounded them up and gotten them into the room. That took a lot more moxie than most people had. I also noted that she had been kneeling between the customers and the doorway. I liked her already.

'Carol,' I said, sharply enough to make her tug her gaze from Michael, who now stood in the doorway, holy Sword in hand. 'Carol, I need you to give me a hand here.'

She blinked and then nodded jerkily and rose. She helped me drag the wounded man over to where the others were seated against the wall. 'H-how did you know my name?' she stammered. 'Are y-you two angels?'

I sighed and tapped a fingernail on the name tag she wore. 'I'm sure as hell not,' I said. I jerked my head at Michael. 'Though he's about as close to one as you're ever likely to see.'

'Don't be ridiculous, Harry,' Michael said. 'I'm just a—' He broke off and ducked. Something solid whizzed past him and slammed a hole the size of my head into the drywall above us. Bits of dust rained down, and frightened people cried out.

Michael slammed the door shut, but without, you know, all those pesky metal security fittings, it swung open again. He slammed it closed and leaned one shoulder against it, panting. Something struck the door with a heavy thump. Then there was silence.

I ripped open the wounded man's pant leg along the seam. The knife had hit him in the calf and he was a bloody mess, but it could have been worse. 'Leave it in,' I told Carol, 'and make sure he stays still. That's close to some big veins, and I don't want to open them trying to take it out. Stay close to him and keep *him* from trying to take it out. Okay?'

'I . . . Yes, all right,' Carol said. She blinked her eyes at me several times. 'I don't understand what's happening.'

'Me either,' I responded. I rose and went to stand beside Michael.

'Those things are quite a bit stronger than I am,' he said in a low rumble that the people behind us couldn't hear. 'If they rush this door I won't be able to hold it shut.'

'I'm not sure they will,' I said.

'But you're here.'

'I don't think they're after *me*,' I said. 'If they were, they wouldn't be going after everyone else, too.'

Michael frowned at me. 'But you said they were faeries.'

'They are,' I said. 'But I don't think this was supposed to be a hit. There are too many of them for that. This is a full-blown assault.'

Michael grimaced. 'Then there are people in danger. They need our help.'

'And they're going to get it,' I said. 'Listen, hobs can't stand light. Any kind of light. It burns them and it can kill them. That's why they called up this *myrk* before they came in.'

'*Myrk?*'

'It's matter from the Nevernever. Think of it as a cellophane filter, only instead of being around a light, it is spread all through the air. That's why we couldn't see the light from my amulet, and why the muzzle flash of my gun was so muted. And that's how we're going to take them out.'

'We get rid of the *myrk*,' Michael said, nodding.

'Exactly,' I said. I raked my fingers back through my hair and started fumbling through my pockets to see what I had on me. Not much. I keep a small collection of handy wizarding gear in the voluminous pockets of my duster, but the pockets of my winter coat contained nothing but a stick of chalk, two ketchup packages from Burger King, and a furry, lint-coated Tic Tac. 'Okay,' I said. 'Let me think a minute.'

Something slammed into the other side of the door and shoved Michael's work boots a good eighteen inches across the floor. A claw flashed through the opening at me. I got out of the way, but the sleeve of my coat didn't. The hob's claws ripped three neat slits in the fabric.

Michael lifted *Amoracchius* in one hand and drove its blazing length *through* the sturdy door. The hob screamed and pulled away. Michael slammed the door shut again and jerked the weapon clear. Dark blood sizzled on the holy blade. 'I don't mean to rush you,' he said calmly, 'but I don't think we *have* a minute.'

24

'Dammit!' I swore. 'This is my only winter coat!' I closed my eyes for a second and tried to focus my mind to the task. A *myrk* wasn't like other forms of faerie glamour. Those could create appearance, and could simulate emotional states related to that appearance. The *myrk* was a conjuration, something physical, tangible, that actually did exist and would continue to do so as long as the hobs gave it enough juice, metaphorically speaking.

Wind might do it. A big enough wind could push the *myrk* away – but it would have to be an awful lot of wind. The little gale I'd called up to handle Torelli's hitters would barely make a dent in it. I could probably do something more violent and widespread, but when it comes to moving matter around, you don't get something for nothing. There was no way I'd be able to maintain that kind of blast long enough to get the job done.

I might be able to cut the *myrk* off from the hobs. If I could sever that connection it would prevent them from pouring constant energy into it, and poof, the *myrk* would resume its natural state as ectoplasm. Of course, cutting them off wouldn't be a cakewalk. I would need some means of creating a channel to each and every hob in order to be sure I got the job done. I didn't have anything I could use as a focus, and I had no idea how many of them were out there, anyway.

An empowered circle could cut the power to the spell from the other side of the equation, isolating the hobs from the flow of energy outside the circle. But the circle would need to encompass the entire freaking building. I doubted the hobs would be considerate enough to let me run outside and sprint around an entire Chicago city block to fire up a circle. Besides, I didn't have that much chalk. Running water can ground out a spell if there's enough of it, but given that we were inside a building, that wasn't in the cards. So how the hell was I supposed to cut off this stupid spell, given the pathetic resources I had? It isn't like there are a whole lot of ways to rob a widespread working of its power.

My nose throbbed harder, and I leaned my head back, turning my face upward. Sometimes doing that seemed to reduce the pressure and ease the pain a little. I stared up at the office ceiling, which had been installed at a height of ten or eleven feet, rather than leaving the place open to the cavernous reaches of the old station, and beat my head against the proverbial wall. The ceiling was one of those drop-down setups, a metal framework supporting dreary yet cost-effective rectangles of acoustic material, interrupted every few yards by the ugly little cowboy spur of an automatic firefighting sprinkler.

My eyes widened.

'Ha!' I said, and threw my arms up in the air. 'Ha-ha! Ah-hahahaha! I am wizard; hear me roar!'

Mouse gave me an oblique look and sidled a step farther away from me.

'And well you should!' I bellowed, pointing at the dog. 'For I am a fearsome bringer of fire!' I held up my right hand and with a murmur called up the tiny sphere of flame. The spell stuttered and coughed before it coalesced, and even then the light was barely brighter than a candle.

'Harry?' Michael asked in that tone of voice people use when they talk to crazy people. 'What are you doing?'

The drywall to one side of the door suddenly buckled as a hob's claws began ripping through it. Michael bobbed to one side, temporarily leaving the door, held his thumb up to the wall, as if judging where the stud would be, and then ran *Amoracchius* at an angle through the drywall. The Sword came back hissing and spitting, while another hob howled with pain.

'Without the *myrk*, these things are in trouble,' I said. 'Carol, be a dear and roll that chair over here.'

Carol, her eyes very wide, her face very pale, did so. She gave the chair a little push, so that it came the last six feet on its own.

Michael's shoulder hit the door as another hob tried to push in. The creature wasn't stupid. It didn't keep trying to force the door when *Amoracchius* plunged through the wood as if it had been a rice-paper screen, and Michael's Sword came back unstained. 'Whatever you're going to do, sooner would be better than later.'

'Two minutes,' I said. I rolled the chair to the right spot and stood up on it. I wobbled for a second, then stabilized myself and quickly unscrewed the sprinkler from its housing. Foulsmelling water rushed out in its wake, which I had expected and mostly avoided. Granted, I hadn't expected it to smell quite so overwhelmingly stagnant, though I should have. Many sprinkler systems have closed holding tanks, and God only knew how many years that water had been in there, waiting to be used.

I hopped down out of the chair and moved out from under the falling water. I pulled one of the pieces of chalk out of my pocket, knelt, and began to draw a large circle all around me on the low-nap carpet. It didn't have to be a perfect circle, as long as it was closed, but I've drawn a lot of them, and by now they're usually pretty close.

'E-excuse me,' Carol said. 'Wh-what are you doing?'

'Our charming visitors are known as hobs,' I told her, drawing carefully, infusing the chalk with some of my will as I did so. 'Light hurts them.'

A hob burst through the already broken drywall, this time getting its head and one shoulder through. It howled and raked at Michael, who was still leaning on the door. Michael's hip got ripped by a claw, but then *Amoracchius* swept down and took the hob's head from its shoulders in reply. Dark, blazing blood spattered the room, and some of it nearly hit my circle.

'Hey!' I complained. 'I'm working here!'

'Sorry,' Michael said without a trace of sarcasm. A hob slammed into the door before he could return to it, and drove him several paces back. He recovered in time to duck under the swing of a heavy club, then swept *Amoracchius* across the creature's belly and followed it up with a heavy, thrusting kick that shoved the wicked faerie out of the room and back into its fellows. Michael slammed the door shut again.

'B-but it's dark,' Carol stammered, staring at Michael and me alternately.

'They've put something in the air called *myrk*. Think of it as a smoke screen. The *myrk* is keeping the lights from hurting the hobs,' I said. I finished the circle and felt it spring to life around me, an intangible curtain of power that walled away outside magic – including the *myrk* that had been caught inside the circle as it formed. It congealed into a thin coating of slimy ectoplasm over everything in the circle – which is to say, me. 'Super,' I mumbled, and swiped it out of my eyes as best I could.

'S-so,' Carol said, 'what are you doing, exactly?'

'I'm going to take their smoke screen away.' I held the sprinkler head in my right hand and closed my eyes, focusing on it, on its texture, its shape, its composition. I began pouring energy into the object, imagining it as a glowing aura of blue-white light with dozens of little tendrils sprouting from it. Once the energy was firmly wrapped around the sprinkler, I transferred it to my left hand and extended my right again.

'B-but we don't have any lights.'

'Oh, we have lights,' I said. I held out my right hand and called forth my little ball of sunshine. In the *myrk*-free interior of the circle, it was as white-hot and as bright as usual, but I could see that outside of the circle it didn't spread more than five or six feet through the *myrk* out there.

'Oh, my God,' Carol said.

'Actually, all the regular lights are on too – they're just being blocked. The *myrk* isn't shutting down the electricity. These computers are all on, for example – but the *myrk* is keeping you from seeing any of the indicator lights.'

'Harry!' Michael called.

'You rush a miracle worker, you get lousy miracles!' I called back in an annoyed tone. The rest of the spell was going to be a little tricky.

'H-how are you doing that?' Carol breathed.

'Magic,' I growled. 'Hush.' I wore a leather glove over my left hand, as usual, which should offer my scarred skin a little protection. All the same, this wouldn't be much fun. I murmured, *Ignus, infusiarus,*' and thrust the end of the sprinkler into the flame floating over my right hand.

'How does this help us?' Carol demanded, her voice shaking and frightened.

'This place still has electricity,' I said. Maybe I was imagining the smell of burned leather as the heat from the flame poured into the metal sprinkler. 'It still has computers. It still has phones.'

'Harry!' Michael said, swinging his head left and right, staring up at the ceiling. 'They're climbing. They're going to come through the roof.'

I began to feel the heat, even in the nerve-damaged fingers of my left hand. It was going to have to be hot enough. I drew up more of my will, lifted the sprinkler and the flame, and visualized what I wanted, the tendrils of energy around it zipping out to every other sprinkler head in the whole building. 'And it still has its sprinklers.'

I broke the circle with my foot, and energy lashed out from the sprinkler to every other object shaped like it in the surrounding area. Heat washed out of me in a wave, headed in dozens of different directions, and I poured all the energy I could into the little ball of sunshine, which suddenly had several dozen sprinkler heads to absorb its energy instead of only one.

It took maybe ten seconds before the fire detector let out a howl and the sprinkler system chattered to life. People let out surprised little shrieks, and a steady emergency klaxon wound to life somewhere out in the station. Sparks flew up from several phones, monitors, and computers.

'Okay,' I said. 'So the office doesn't have computers. But the rest still applies.'

Michael looked up at me and showed me his teeth in a ferocious grin. 'When?'

I watched my little ball of sunshine intensely as the water came down. For maybe half a minute nothing happened, except that we got drenched. It was actually kind of surprising how much water was coming down – surprising in a good way, I mean. I wanted lots of water.

Somewhere around the sixty-second mark I felt my spell begin to flicker, its power eroded away by the constant downpour.

'Wait for it,' I said. 'Ready . . .'

At two minutes my spell buckled, the connection to the other sprinklers snapping, the fire in my hand snuffing out. 'Michael!' I shouted. 'Now!'

Michael grunted and flung open the door. Before he'd stepped through it there was a sudden flutter of faltering power in the air, and the holy blade blazed with light brighter than the heart of the sun itself.

He plunged through the door, and as the burning light of *Amoracchius* emerged into the station at large, dozens or hundreds of hob throats erupted into tortured cries. The sound of the wicked faeries' screams was so loud that I actually felt the pressure it put on my ears, the way you can at a really loud concert.

But louder still was the voice of Michael Carpenter, Knight of the Cross, avenging angel incarnate, bearer of the blade that had once belonged to a squire called Wart. '*Lava quod est sordium!*' Michael bellowed, his voice stentorian, too enormous to come from a human throat. '*In nomine Dei, sana quod est saucium!*'

After the Sword had left the room, I could see that all the office lights had come back, as well as those outside. 'Mouse!' I screamed. 'Stay! Guard the wounded!' I hurried after Michael and glanced back behind me. Mouse trotted forward and planted himself in the doorway between the hobs and the people in the office, head high, legs braced wide to fill the space.

Outside the sprinklers were doing a credible impersonation of a really stinky monsoon. I slipped in a puddle of water and burning hob blood a few feet outside the door. The light from the Sword was so bright, so purely, even painfully *white* that I had to shield my eyes with one arm. I couldn't look directly at Michael, or even anywhere near him, so I followed him by the pieces of hob he left in his wake.

Several wicked faeries had been struck down by Michael's sword.

They were the lucky ones.

Many more – dozens that I could see – had fallen too far away for Michael to have reached them with the blade. Those were simply lumps of smoldering charcoal spewing columns of greasy smoke, their meat flash-cooked away from bone. Some of the soon-to-be-former hobs were still thrashing as they burned.

Hell's bells.

I don't call him the Fist of God as a pet name, folks.

I followed Michael, alert for any dimming of the Sword's light. If any of the sprinklers in the building were a different model from the one I'd used to focus my spell, it wouldn't have been able to heat them and trigger them. If Michael wound up plunging back into the *myrk*, then the hobs, afforded a measure of protection from the light, would gang up on him – and fast.

But as luck (or maybe fate, or maybe God, but probably a cheap city contractor) would have it, it looked like they'd all been the same. Water came down everywhere, washing away the *myrk* as if it had been a layer of mud, replacing it with thousands upon thousands of fractured rainbows as the pure illumination of *Amoracchius* shone through the artificial downpour.

For the hobs, there was nowhere to hide.

I followed the trail of smitten fiends. Smiten fiends? Smited fiends? Smoted fiends? Don't look at me. I never finished high school. Maybe learning the various conjugations of *to smite* had been in senior-year English. It sure as hell hadn't been on my GED test.

I stopped and peered around as best I could through the blinding light and steady fall of water from the sprinklers, trying to get an idea of where Michael was headed.

I felt a sudden, swift vibration that rose through the soles of my shoes, and then a heavy thud accompanying a second such tremor. I whirled to face the front of the building as glass and brick and stone exploded from the entry door. Behind it was a vague flicker of haze in the air, but as whatever was behind the veil entered the glare of *Amoracchius* and my impromptu thundershower, the spell faltered and vanished.

Twenty feet and four or five tons of Big Brother Gruff erupted from the veil.

He wore armor made of some kind of translucent crystal, and the sword in his hand was longer than my freaking car. His mouth opened, and I *felt* his battle roar rather than hearing it over the cacophony of combat, a sound so deep and loud that it should have been made by a freaking whale.

'Oh, yeah,' I muttered. 'Today just keeps getting better and better.'

25

Anybody with an ounce of sense knows that fighting someone with a significant advantage in size, weight, and reach is difficult. If your opponent has you by fifty pounds, winning a fight against him is a dubious proposition, at best.

If your opponent has you by eight *thousand* and fifty pounds, you've left the realm of combat and enrolled yourself in Roadkill 101. Or possibly in a Tom and Jerry cartoon.

My body was already in motion, apparently having decided that waiting on my brain to work things through was counterproductive to survival. It was thinking that the cat-and-mouse analogy was a pretty good one. While I was nimbler and could accelerate more swiftly than the huge gruff, he could build up more speed on a straightaway. Physically speaking, I had almost no chance of seriously harming him, while even a love tap from him would probably collapse my rib cage – another similarity.

Jerry wins on television, but in real life Tom would rarely end up with the short end of the stick. I don't remember Mister ever coming home nursing mouse-inflicted wounds. For that matter, he hardly ever came home from one of his rambles hungry. Playing cat and mouse is generally only fun for the cat.

My body, meanwhile, had flung itself to one side, forcing Tiny to turn as he pursued me, limiting his speed and buying me a precious second or three – time enough for me to sprint toward a section of floor marked off by a pair of yellow caution signs, where Joe the janitor had been waxing the floor. I crossed the wet, slick floor at a sprint and prayed that I wouldn't trip. If I went down it would take only one stomp of one of those enormous hooves to slice me in half.

Footgear like that isn't so hot for slippery terrain, though.

As soon as I crossed to the other side of the waxed floor I juked left as sharply as I could, changing direction. Tiny tried to compensate and his legs went out from under him.

That isn't a big deal, by itself. Sometimes when you run something happens and you trip and you fall down. You get a skinned knee or two, maybe scuff up your hands, and very rarely you'll do something worse, like sprain an ankle.

But that's at human mass. Increase the mass to Tiny's size, and a fall becomes another animal entirely, especially if there's a lot of velocity involved. That's one reason why elephants don't ever actually run — they aren't capable of it, of lifting their weight from the ground in a full running stride. If they fell at their size, the damage could be extreme, and evidently nature had selected out all those elephant wind sprinters. That much weight moving at that much speed carries a tremendous amount of energy — enough to easily snap bones, to drive objects deep into flesh, to scrape the ground hard enough to strip a body to the bone.

Tiny must have weighed twice what an elephant does. Five *tons* of flesh and bone came down all along one side of his body and landed hard — then slid, carrying so much momentum that Tiny more resembled a freight train than any kind of living being. He slid across the floor and slammed into the wall of a rental car kiosk, shattering it to splinters — and went right on through it, hardly even slowing down.

Tiny dug at the floor with the yellow nails of one huge hand, but they didn't do anything but peel up curls of wax as he went sliding past me.

I slammed on the brakes and tried to judge where Tiny looked like he'd coast to a halt. Then I drew in my will.

It was difficult as hell in the falling water, but I didn't need a lot of it. When it comes to intentionally screwing up technology, I've always had a gift.

I focused on the lights above the entire section of the station Tiny slid into, lifted my right hand, and snarled, '*Hexus!*' Some of them actually exploded in showers of golden sparks. Some of them let out little puffs of smoke – but every single one of them went out.

Michael had advanced down the concourse far behind me, and the light of *Amoracchius* was now shielded by the station's interior walls. When I took out the electric lights, it created a genuine swath of heavy shadows.

The sudden island of darkness drew hobs like corpses draw flies: burned, terrified, furious hobs whose tidbit-filled night on the town had suddenly turned into a nightmare. They didn't have eyes, but they found their way to the dark easily enough, and I saw more than a dozen rush in, one of them passing within a couple of feet of me without ever slowing down or taking note of my presence.

Tiny started bellowing a second later, his huge voice blending with the vengeful howls of angry hobs.

'Ain't so big now,' I panted, 'are you?'

But as it turned out, Tiny was just as big.

A crushed hob flew out of the shadows and splattered the floor maybe twenty feet away. I don't mean that he was just rag-doll limp. He was crushed, *crushed* like a beer can, where Tiny's huge fist had simply seized the hob, squeezed it hard enough to empty it of various internal liquids, and then thrown it away.

Light flashed in the shadows, a long streak of sparks, like flint drawn along a long, long strip of steel, and suddenly low blue flames surrounded the blade of Tiny's sword. They were guttering, barely able to stay alight beneath the falling water, but they cast enough light to let me see what was happening.

The hobs had gone mad with hate.

It had been inevitable, I suppose. The minions of Winter and those of Summer do *not* play well with one another, and the denizens of Faerie do not behave like human beings. Their natures are far more primal, more immutable. They are what they are. Predators are swift to attack prey that has fallen and is vulnerable. Winter fae hate the champions of Summer. The hobs were both.

Several of them threw themselves at Tiny's head, while the

others just started hacking with their crude weapons or biting with their sharklike teeth. Tiny's armor served him well in that mess, defending the most critical areas, and as hobs went for his throat the gruff started throwing his head back and forth. I thought it was panic for a second, until he slammed one of his horns into a hob with such power that it broke the wicked faerie's skull. His sword slewed back and forth in two quick, precise motions, and half a dozen hobs fell, dead and burning.

The others let out shrieks of terror and bounded away, their hatred insufficient to the task of withstanding the fallen gruff. Tiny rolled to his knees and began to push himself up, and though his expression was contorted with pain his inhuman eyes swept around until they spotted me.

Oh, crap.

I didn't wait for him to get up and kill me. I ran.

Of all the times to do without my jacket and staff. For crying out loud, what had I been thinking? That I had Summer so thoroughly outwitted that I wouldn't need them? That life just hadn't been challenging enough until now? *Stupid, Harry. Stupid, stupid.* I swore that if I lived through this, I'd make up dummy copies of my gear for when I needed Thomas to play stalking horse.

The ground started shaking as Tiny took up the chase behind me.

My options were limited. To my right was the exterior wall of the building, and I couldn't go outside into the deepening snow. My imagination treated me to a dandy image of me floundering in hip-deep snow while Tiny, with his far greater height and mass, cruised effortlessly up behind me and beer-canned me. Ahead of me was an empty hallway leading to another wall, and on my left were nothing but rows and rows of . . .

. . . storage lockers.

I fumbled in my pocket again as I ran through the water sheeting the floor, and started trying to get a look at the numbers on the lockers. I spotted the one corresponding to Gard's key, and I skidded to a halt on the watery floor. I jammed the key in the lock frantically as Tiny, running with a limp but still running, closed the last dozen yards between us.

I had to time it perfectly. I raised my right hand, aimed at the hoof on his wounded leg, and waited for all of his weight to come forward onto it before triggering every energy ring on my right hand, unleashing a rushing column of force that hit him with the power of a speeding car.

The gruff's hoof went out from under him again on the wet floor, and he pitched forward with a roar of frustration. He dropped his blade and reached for me with both hands as he fell.

I waited until the last second to jump back, ripping open the door to Gard's locker as I went.

I could only describe what happened next as a bolt of lightning. It wasn't lightning – not really. Real lightning did not have the raw, savage intensity of this . . . thing, and I realized with a startled flash of insight that this energy, whatever it was, was *alive*. White-hot power tinged with flashes of scarlet streaked out of the locker like a hundred hyperkinetic serpents, zig-zagging with impossible speed. That living lightning ripped into Tiny, cutting through his crystalline armor as if it had been made of soft wax. It burned and slashed and pounded the flesh beneath in a long line from Tiny's shoulder to his lower leg, letting out a screaming buzz of sound unlike anything I had ever heard before.

In the last fraction of a second before it vanished, the energy snapped back and forth like the tip of a whip, and Tiny's left leg came off at the knee.

The gruff screamed. Whatever that thing had been, it had taken the fight out of Tiny.

Hell's bells.

I stared at the maimed Summer champion and then at the open, innocent-looking locker. Then I walked slowly forward.

Tiny had only one eye open, and it didn't look like it would focus on anything. His breathing was rough, quick, and ragged, which translated into a seething, oat-scented breeze anywhere within ten or fifteen feet of his head.

Tiny blinked his other eye open, and though they still wouldn't focus he let out a weak-sounding grunt. 'Mortal,' he rasped, 'I am bested.' One of his ears flicked once and he exhaled in a sigh. 'Finish it.'

I walked past the fallen gruff without stopping, noting as I did that the stroke of energy that had severed his leg had cauterized it shut, too. He wasn't going to bleed to death.

I peered cautiously into the locker.

It was empty except for a single, flat wooden box about the size of a big backgammon kit. The back wall of the locker sported something else – the blackened outline of some sort of rune. It wasn't the first time I'd seen Gard employing some kind of rune-based magic, but I'd be damned if I knew how it was done. I reached out with my wizard's senses cautiously, but felt nothing. Whatever energy had been stored there was gone now.

What the hell? I reached in and grabbed the box. Nothing ripped me into quivering shreds.

I scowled suspiciously and slowly withdrew the box, but nothing else happened. Evidently Gard had considered her security measures to be adequate for dealing with a thief. Or a dinosaur. Whichever.

Once I had the case, I turned back to the gruff.

'Mortal,' Tiny wheezed, 'finish it.'

'I try not to kill anything unless it's absolutely necessary,' I replied, 'and I've got no need to kill you today. This wasn't a personal matter. It's done. That's the end of it.'

The gruff focused his eyes and just stared at me for a startled moment. 'Mercy? From a Winterbound?'

'I'm *not* bound,' I snapped. 'This is purely temp work.' I squinted around. 'I think the hobs have mostly cleared out. Can you leave on your own, or do you need me to send for someone?'

The gruff shuddered and shook his huge head. 'Not necessary. I will go.' He spread the fingers of one hand on the ground and started sinking into it as if it were quicksand. As portals to Faerie went, that was a new one for me.

'This is a onetime offer,' I told him just before he was completely gone. 'Don't come back.'

'I shan't,' he rumbled, his eyes sagging closed in weariness. 'But mark you this, wizard.'

I frowned at him. 'What?'

'My elder brother,' he growled, 'is going to kill thee.'

Then Tiny sank into the floor and was gone.

'*Another* one?' I demanded of the floor. 'You've got to be *kidding* me!'

I leaned against the lockers, banging my head gently against the steel for a moment. Then I pushed myself back onto my feet and started jogging back toward where I had parted with Michael. Just because the hobs were gone from this part of the station didn't mean that there wasn't still a fight going on. Michael might need my help.

I picked up the trail of body parts again, though by this time most of them were mounds of dark powder, like charcoal dust, pounded to a gooey paste by the building's sprinklers. The patches of gunk got thicker as I continued in the direction I thought Michael had gone.

I followed the trail to the base of a ridiculously broad flight of stone stairs – the one that actually had been in *The Untouchables*. The parts were still recognizable as parts here. These hobs hadn't been dead for long. They lay in a carpet of motionless, burning corpses on the stairs. Judging by the way they'd fallen they had been facing up the stairs when they died.

Several fallen hobs bore wounds that indicated that Michael had hewed his way through them from behind. White knight he might be, but once that sword comes out, Michael puts his game face on, and he plays as hard as almost anyone I've ever seen.

Not that I could blame him. Not all the remains I'd passed had been those of hobs.

Three security guards were down, one maybe ten feet from the stairs, the other two on the stairway itself. They had fallen separately in the darkness.

I'd passed several other bloodstains that had almost certainly been fatal to their donors, unless the falling water had made them look more extensive than they actually were. I'd never encountered hobs face-to-face before, but I knew enough about them to hope that whoever had spilled that blood was dead.

Hobs had a habit of hauling victims back into their lightless tunnels.

I shuddered. I'd give the troubleshooters from Summer that much: All the gruffs wanted to do was kill me, clean, and that would be the end of it. I'd been carried into the darkness by monsters before. It isn't something I'd wish on anyone. Ever.

You don't really live through it, even if you survive. It changes you.

I pushed away bad memories and tried to ignore them while I thought. Some of the hobs had obviously taken their victims and run. According to the books it was their modus operandi. Though this entire attack seemed to indicate a higher level of organization than the average rampage, obviously whoever was behind it wasn't in complete control. Faeries share one universal trait – their essential natures are actively contrary, and they are notoriously difficult to command.

The hobs on the stairs were different from the ones I'd had to contend with at the front of the station. These all bore more advanced cutlery, probably made of bronze, and wore armor made of some kind of hide. To be clustered this thickly on the stairs, they had to have been at least a little organized, fighting in ranks, too.

Something had compelled these hobs to attack in unison. Hell, if the numbers of fallen hobs in front of me were any indication, the gang that came after Michael and me were probably stragglers who had gone haring off on their own, looking for a little carryout to take home.

So what had been the purpose of the attack? What the hell had drawn them all to the stairway?

Whatever was at the top, obviously.

Above me the light of the holy Sword flickered and began

to fade. I chugged up the stairs as it did, still holding my fingers up to shield my eyes until the light dwindled, and caught up to Michael. He was breathing hard, Sword still raised over his head in a high guard and ready to come sweeping down. I noted, idly, that the stench of stagnant water had vanished, replaced by the quiet, strong scent of roses. I lifted my face again and felt cool, clean, rose-scented water fall on my face. Falling through the light of the holy Sword had improved it, it would seem.

The last hob to fall, a big brute the size of a freaking mountain gorilla, lay motionless near Michael's feet. What was left of a bronze shield and sword lay in neatly sliced fragments around the body. Its blood spread sluggishly down the stairs, coated with blue-white flame as its body was slowly consumed by more of the same.

'Everybody can relax,' I panted as I caught up to Michael. 'I'm here.'

Michael greeted me with a nod and a quick smile. 'Are you all right?'

'Not bad,' I said, barely resisting the temptation to turn the second word into a barnyard sound. 'Sorry I wasn't much use to you once you waded in.'

'It couldn't have happened without your help,' Michael said seriously. 'Thank you.'

'*De nada*,' I replied.

I went up the last few stairs and got a look at what the hobs had been after.

Children.

There must have been thirty kids around ten years old up at the top of the stairs, all of them in school uniforms, all of them huddled together in a corner, all of them frightened, most of them crying. There was one dazed-looking woman in a blazer that matched those of the children, together with two women dressed in the casual uniforms of Amtrak stewards.

'A train had just arrived,' I murmured to Michael as I realized what had happened. 'It must have gotten in through the weather somehow. That's why the hobs were here now.'

Michael flicked *Amoracchius* to one side, shaking off a small cloud of fine black powder from the blade as he did. Then he put the weapon away. 'It should be safe now, everyone,' he said, his voice calm. 'The authorities should be here any minute.' He added in a quieter tone, 'We should probably go.'

'Not yet,' I said quietly. I walked into the Great Hall far enough to see the area behind the first of the row of Corinthian pillars that lined the walls.

Three people stood there.

The first was a man, of a height with Michael, but built more leanly, more dangerously. He had hair of dark gold that fell to his shoulders, and the shadow of a beard resulting from several days without shaving. He wore a casual, dark-blue sports suit over a white T-shirt, and he held the bronze sword of a hob, stained with their dark blood, in either hand. He regarded me with the calm, remote eyes of a great cat, and he showed me some of his teeth when he saw me. His name was Kincaid, and he was a professional assassin.

Next to him was a young woman with long, curling brown hair and flashing dark eyes. Her jeans were tight enough to show off some nice curves, but not too tight to move in, and she held a slender rod maybe five feet long in one hand, carved with runes and sigils not too unlike mine. Captain Luccio had a long plastic tube hanging from a strap over one of her shoulders, its top dangling loose. Odds were good her silver sword was still stowed inside it. I knew that when she smiled, she had killer dimples – but from the expression on her face I wasn't going to be exposed to that hazard anytime soon. Her features were hard and guarded, though they did not entirely hide a fierce rage. I hoped it was reserved for the attacking hobs and not for me. The captain was not someone I wanted angry at me.

Standing between and slightly behind the two adults was a girl not much older than all the other children who had taken refuge in the Hall. She'd grown more than a foot since the last time I'd seen her, about five years ago. She still looked like a neatly dressed, perfectly groomed child – except for her eyes.

Her eyes were creepily out of place in that innocent face, heavy with knowledge and all the burdens that come with it.

The Archive put a hand on Kincaid's elbow, and the hired killer lowered his swords. The girl stepped forward and said, 'Hello, Mister Dresden.'

'Hello, Ivy,' I responded, nodding politely.

'If these creatures were under your command,' the little girl said in a level tone, 'I'm going to execute you.'

She didn't make it a threat. There wasn't enough interest in her voice for it to be that. The Archive just stated it as a simple and undeniable fact.

The scary part was that if she decided to kill me, there'd be little I could do about it. The child wasn't simply a child. She was the Archive, the embodied memory of humanity, a living repository of the knowledge of mankind. When she was six or seven I'd seen her kill a dozen of the most dangerous warriors of the Red Court. It took her about as much effort as it takes me to open the wrapper on a stack of crackers. The Archive was Power with a capital P, and operated on an entirely different level than I did.

'Of course they weren't under his command,' Luccio said. She glanced at me and arched an eyebrow. 'How could you even suspect such a thing?'

'I find it unlikely that an attack of this magnitude could be anything but a deliberate attempt to abduct or assassinate me. Mab and Titania have involved themselves in this business,' the Archive said in a matter-of-fact tone. 'Mister Dresden is currently Winter's Emissary in this affair – and need I remind you that hobs are beholden to Winter – to Mab?'

She hadn't needed to remind me, though I'd been putting that thought off for a while. The fact that the hobs were Mab's subjects meant that matters were even murkier than I thought, and that now was probably a reasonably good time to start panicking.

But first things first: Prevent the scary little girl from killing me.

'I have no idea who was ordering these things around,' I said quietly.

The Archive stared at me for an endless second. Then that ancient, implacable gaze moved to Michael. 'Sir Knight,' she said, her tone polite. 'Will you vouch for this man?'

Maybe it was just my imagination that it took Michael a second longer to answer than he might have done in the past. 'Of course.'

She stared at him as well, and then nodded her head. 'Mister Dresden, you remember my bodyguard, Kincaid.'

'Yeah,' I said. My voice didn't exactly bubble with enthusiasm. 'Hi, tough guy. What brings you to Chicago?'

Kincaid showed me even more teeth. 'The midget,' he said. 'I hate the snow. If it was up to me, I'd much rather be somewhere warm. Say, Hawaii, for example.'

'I am not a midget,' the Archive said in a firmly disapproving tone. 'I am in the seventy-fourth percentile for height for my age. And stop trying to provoke him.'

'The midget's no fun,' Kincaid explained. 'I tried to get her to join the Girl Scouts, but she wasn't having any of it.'

'If I want to glue macaroni to a paper plate, I can do that at home,' said the Archive. 'It's hours past my bedtime, and I have no desire to entangle ourselves with the local authorities. We should leave.' She frowned at Kincaid. 'Obviously our movements have been tracked. Our quarters here are probably compromised.' She turned her eyes back to me. 'I formally request the hospitality of the White Council until such time as I can establish secure lodgings.'

'Uh,' I said.

Luccio made a quick motion with one hand, urging me to accept.

'Of course,' I said, nodding at the Archive.

'Excellent,' the Archive said. She turned to Kincaid. 'I'm soaked. My coat and a change of clothes are in my bag on the train. I'll need them.'

Kincaid gave me a skeptical glance but, tellingly, he didn't argue with the Archive. Instead he vanished quickly down the stairs.

The Archive turned to me. 'Statistically speaking, the emergency services of this city should begin to arrive in another three minutes, given the weather and the condition of the roads. It would be best for all of us if we were gone by then.'

'Couldn't agree more,' I said. I grimaced. 'Whoever did this is taking awful chances, moving this publically.'

The Archive's not-quite-human gaze bored into me for a moment. Then she said, 'Matters may be quite a bit worse than that. I'm afraid our troubles are just beginning.'

26

Michael stopped in his tracks when he saw the gaping hole Tiny the gruff had left in the east wall of Union Station. 'Merciful God,' he breathed. 'Harry, what happened?'

'Little problem,' I said.

'You didn't say anything to me.'

'You looked busy,' I told him, 'and you already had a couple of hundred bad guys to handle.' I nodded at the hole. 'I only had the one.'

Michael shook his head bemusedly, and I saw Luccio look at the hole with something like mild alarm.

'Did you get it?' Michael asked.

Luccio cocked her head at Michael when he spoke, and then looked sharply at me.

I gave Michael a level look and said, 'Obviously.' Then I turned on my heel and whistled sharply. 'Mouse!'

My dog, soggy but still enthusiastic, came bounding toward us over the water-coated marble floors. He slid to a stop, throwing up a little wave that splashed over my feet as he did. The Archive peered intently at Mouse as he arrived, and took a step toward him – but was prevented from going farther by Kincaid's hand, which came to rest on her slender shoulder.

Michael frowned at the girl and then at the dog. 'This,' he said, 'brings up a problem.'

There was only so much room in the cab of Michael's truck.

All of us were soaking wet, and there was no time to get dry before the authorities arrived. I didn't think it completely fair that I got a number of less than friendly looks on the walk to the garage, after I explained that it had been me who set off the sprinkler system, but at least no one could claim that I

hadn't been willing to suffer the consequences right along with
them.

The Archive might have been a creepy Billy Mumy-in-*The
Twilight Zone* kind of child, but she was still a child. By general
acclamation she was in the cab. Michael had to drive.

'I'm not letting her sit in there alone,' Kincaid stated.

'Oh, come on,' I said. 'He's a Knight of the freaking Cross.
He isn't going to hurt her.'

'Irrelevant,' Kincaid said. 'What about when someone starts
shooting at her on the way there? Is he going to throw his body
in front of her to keep her from harm?'

'I—' Michael began.

'You're damned right he will,' I growled.

'Harry,' Michael said, his tone placating, 'I'd be glad to protect
the child. But it would be somewhat problematic to do that and
drive at the same time.'

Mouse let out a low, distressed sound, which drew my attention to the fact that the Archive had fallen uncharacteristically
silent. She was standing beside Kincaid, shuddering, her eyes
rolling back in her head.

'Dammit,' I said. 'Get her into the truck. Go, Kincaid,
Michael.'

Kincaid scooped her up at once, and he and Michael got into
the cab of the truck.

'I-is y-your h-house far from here, Warden?' Luccio asked me.

She didn't look good. Well, she looked good given the circumstances. But she also looked soaked and half-frozen already,
kneeling to hug Mouse, ostensibly rubbing his fur to help dry
it and fluff it out. I'd seen Luccio in action, as captain of the
Wardens of the White Council, and I had formed my opinion
of her accordingly. When I looked at the woman who'd faced
Kemmler's disciples without batting an eye, whom I'd once seen
stand in the open under fire from automatic weapons to protect
the apprentices under her care, I tended to forget that she was
about five-foot-four and might have checked in at a hundred
and thirty or forty pounds soaking wet.

Which she was.

In the middle of a blizzard.

'It isn't far,' I said. Then I went up to the door beside Kincaid and said, 'Put the kid on your lap.'

'She wears the seat belt,' Kincaid said. 'She's in danger enough from exposure already.'

'Luccio doesn't weigh much more than Ivy does,' I said in a flat tone. 'She's in almost as much danger as the kid. So you're holding Ivy on your lap and letting my captain ride in the cab, like a gentleman.'

Kincaid gave me a level look, his pale eyes cold. 'Or what?'

'I'm armed,' I said. 'You're not.'

He looked at me levelly, then at my hands. One of them was in my coat pocket. Then he said, 'You think I believe that you'd kill me?'

'If you try to make me choose between you and Luccio,' I said, with a brittle smile, 'I'm pretty sure whom I'm going to bid aloha.'

His teeth flashed in a sudden, wolfish smile. And he moved over, drawing the freezing child onto his lap.

By the time I got back to Luccio she was upright only because Mouse sat placidly in the cold, supporting her. She mumbled some kind of protest in a faint, commanding tone, but since she said it in Italian I declared her brain frozen and assumed command of the local Warden detachment, which was handy, since it consisted of only me anyway. I bundled her into the truck's cab and got her buckled in beside Kincaid. He helped with it – my fingers were too cold and stiff to manage very quickly.

'Harry,' Michael said. He reached back, drew a rolled-up thermal blanket from behind the truck's front seat, and tossed it to me. I caught it and nodded my thanks with the cold already starting to chew at my belly.

That left me and Mouse in the back of the truck, both of us soaking wet, in the middle of winter, in the middle of a blizzard. The cold moved from my belly to my chest, and I curled up into a ball because I didn't have much choice in the matter.

Magic wasn't an option. My palm-sized ball of flame wouldn't get along well with the back of a moving truck, especially given how much I was already shaking. I wanted to get warm, not set myself on fire.

'S-s-s-sometimes ch-ch-ch-chivalry s-s-s-sucks,' I growled to Mouse, teeth chattering.

My dog, whose thick winter coat wasn't much good after it had gotten a good soaking, leaned against me as hard as I leaned against him, underneath the rough blanket, while the cab of the truck heated up nicely, its windows fogging. I felt like a Dickens character. I thought about explaining that to Mouse, just to occupy my thoughts, but he was suffering enough without being forced to endure Dickens, even by proxy. So we made the trip in miserable, companionable silence. There might have been emergency lights going by us. I was too busy enjoying the involuntary rhythmic contractions of every muscle cell in my freaking body to notice.

Thirty seconds into the trip I was fairly certain that I was going to black out and wake up five hundred years in the future, but as it turned out I had to endure only a miserable twenty minutes or so before Michael pulled up outside my apartment.

Both vehicle doors opened to the weary but authoritative ring of Luccio's voice. 'Get him to the door while he can still let us in through his wards.'

'I'm fine,' I said, rising. Only it came out sounding more like, 'Mmmmnnngh,' and when I tried to stand up I all but fell out of the truck. Michael caught me, and Kincaid moved quickly to help him lift me to the ground.

I dimly felt one of Kincaid's hands enter my jacket pocket and turn it out empty. 'Son of a bitch,' he said, grinning. 'I knew it.'

Luccio emerged from the truck's cab, carrying the entirely limp form of the Archive draped over one hip. The girl's arms and legs flopped loosely, her mouth hung open in sleep, and her cheeks were bright pink. 'Get up, Dresden,' she stated. Her voice was firm, but though warmed by the trip, she was still nearly as damp as she had been at the station, and I saw her buckle as the cold sank its teeth into her. 'Hurry.'

I moved my feet in a vague shuffle, and remembered somewhere that when you walked, you moved them alternately. This improved our progress considerably. We reached a door, and someone said something about dangerous wards.

No kidding, I thought. *I've got some wards on my place that'll fry you to greasy spots on the concrete. But you should see the ones Gard can do.*

Luccio snapped something to me about the wards, and I thought she looked cold. I had a fire at my place, which she could probably use. I opened the door for her, the way you're supposed to for a lady, but the damned thing was stuck until Michael shoved it open with his shoulder and muttered something disparaging about amateur work.

Then everything got sort of muddled, and my arms and legs hurt a lot.

I ended up thinking: *Man, my couch feels nice.*

Mouse snuffled at my face and then all but squashed me as he laid his head and most of his upper body across mine. I thought about chewing him out for it, but opted for sleep on my wonderful couch instead.

Blackness ensued.

I woke up to a room illuminated only by the light from my fireplace. I was toasty, though my fingers and toes throbbed uncomfortably. There was a gentle weight pressing down on me that proved to be virtually every blanket I owned. The deep, slow, steady sound of my dog's breathing whispered from the rug in front of the couch, and one of my hands was lying on the rough, warm, dry fur of Mouse's back.

Water trickled nearby.

Luccio sat on a footstool in front of the fire, facing the flames. My teapot hung on its latch over the fire. A basin of steaming water sat upon the hearth. As I watched, she dipped a cloth in the hot water and slid it over her shoulder and down the length of one arm, her face in profile to me. Her eyes were closed in an expression of simple pleasure. The light of the fire made lovely, exquisitely feminine shadows along the slender lines of her naked back, down to the waist of her jeans as she moved, muscles shifting beneath soft skin that shimmered golden like the firelight for a second after the warm cloth glided over it, leaving little wisps of vapor in its wake.

Something else had never really occurred to me before, either. Luccio was beautiful.

Oh, she wasn't cover-girl pretty, though I suspected that with the right preparation she'd be damned close. Her features were appealing, particularly around her little Cupid's bow of a mouth, framed by its dimples, contrasted with a rather squared-off chin that stopped half an eyelash shy of masculinity. She had dark eyes that flashed when she was angry or amused, and her medium-brown hair was long, curling, and lustrous. She obviously took really good care of it – but there was too much strength in that face for her to be conventionally pretty.

Beauty runs deeper than that.

There was an inexpressible quality of femininity about her that appealed to me tremendously – some critical mixture of gentle curves, quiet grace, and supple strength that I had only that second realized happened to reside in the same place as the head of the Wardens. Maybe more important, I knew the quality of the person under the skin. I'd known Luccio for years, been in more than one tight spot with her, and found her to be one of the only veteran Wardens whom I both liked and respected.

She shook her hair to the other side of her back and washed the other shoulder and arm just as slowly, and just as evidently taking pleasure in doing so.

It had been a while since I'd seen a woman's naked back and shoulders. It had been considerably rarer than my views of the various nightmares my job kept exposing me to. I guess even among all the nightmares, sooner or later you'll get lucky enough to catch a glimpse of a beautiful dream. And despite the trouble I was in, for just that moment there, under all those blankets,

I looked at something beautiful. It made me wish I had the talent to capture the sight with charcoal or inks or oils – but that had never been my gift. All I could do was soak up that simple sight: beautiful woman bathing in firelight.

I didn't actually notice when Luccio paused and turned her head to face me. I just noticed, suddenly, that she was returning my gaze, her dark eyes steady. I swallowed. I wasn't sure what I had been expecting. Sudden outrage, maybe, or a biting remark, or at least a blush. Luccio didn't do any of that. She just returned my stare, calm and poised and lovely as you please, one arm folded across her breasts while the other dipped the cloth into the steaming basin again.

'Sorry,' I said finally, lowering my eyes. I was probably blushing. Dammit. Maybe I could pass it off as mild frostbite, heroically suffered on her behalf.

She let out a quiet little murmur of sound that was too relaxed to be a chuckle. 'Did it displease you?'

'No,' I said, at once. 'God, no, nothing like that.'

'Then why apologize?' she said.

'I, uh . . .' I coughed. 'I just figured that a girl who came of age during the reign of Queen Victoria would be a little more conservative.'

Luccio let out a wicked little laugh that time. 'Victoria was British,' she said. 'I'm Italian.'

'Bit of a difference, then?' I asked.

'Just a little,' she replied. 'When I was young, I posed for a number of painters and sculptors, you know.' She tilted her head back and washed her throat as she spoke. 'Mmm. Though that was in my original body, of course.'

Right. The one that had been stolen by an insane necromancer, leaving Luccio's mind permanently trapped in a loaner. A really young, fit, lovely loaner. 'I don't see how the one you're in now could possibly come up short by comparison.'

She opened her eyes and flashed me a smile that was entirely too pleased and girlish. 'Thank you. But I would not have you misunderstanding me. I'd avail myself of your shower, after being soaked in that foul soup, but the Archive is on your bed, and Kincaid has closed the door. He's resting too, and I'd rather not have him go for my throat before he wakes. And you were asleep, so . . .' She gave a little shrug of her shoulders.

It did really interesting things to the shadows the fire cast upon her skin, and I was suddenly glad of all the blankets piled on me.

'Are you feeling all right?' Luccio asked me.

'I'll live,' I said.

'It was gallant of you to face down Kincaid like that.'

'No problem. He's an ass.'

'A very dangerous one,' Luccio said. 'I wouldn't have traveled with him if I had not seen him pass through the security check-point in Boston.' She rose, dropped the washcloth in the basin, and pulled her shirt on, giving me a rather intriguing view of her back and waist silhouetted against the firelight.

I sighed. Moment over. Back to business.

'What *were* you doing traveling with them?' I asked.

'Bringing them here for the parley,' she replied.

'Parley?'

'The Archive contacted Nicodemus Archleone regarding our accusations. He agreed to meet with us here, in Chicago, to discuss the matter. You are the initiating party in this instance, and I am here to serve as your second.'

I blinked at her. 'You? *My* second?'

She turned to face me as she finished buttoning her shirt and smiled faintly. 'Duty before ego. Relatively few of the Wardens with sufficient seasoning for the role were willing. I thought it might be best if you worked with me instead of Morgan.'

'That's why they pay you the big bucks, Cap. That keen inter-personal insight.'

'That and because I'm quite good at killing things,' Luccio said, nodding. She turned to the fireplace and took Gard's little wooden box off the mantel. 'Dresden . . .'

'Hell's bells,' I breathed, sitting up. 'Captain, that thing is dangerous. Put it *down*.' I snapped out that last in a tone of pure authority, one I'd gotten used to when working with Molly and various folks I'd met through the Paranet.

She froze in her tracks and arched an eyebrow at me, but only for a split second. Then she smoothly replaced the box and stepped away from it. 'I see. You were holding it when we dragged you in here. You wouldn't let it go, in fact.'

'Well,' I said, 'no.'

'Which, I take it, explains what *you* were doing at the station.'

'Well,' I said, 'yes.'

'Quite a coincidence,' she said.

I shook my head. 'In my experience, when there's a Knight of the Cross around, there's no such thing as coincidence.'

She frowned at that. 'It's been a very long time since I've been to confession. Nearly a century, in fact. I'm not aware that the Almighty owes me any favors.'

'Mysterious ways,' I said smugly.

She laughed. 'I take it they've used that line on you before?'

'Constantly,' I said.

'A good man,' she said. 'You're lucky to have him as a friend.'

I frowned and said quietly, 'Yeah. I am.' I shook my head. 'When's the parley?'

'Noon, tomorrow.' She nodded at the mantel. 'Can you tell me what's in there?'

'Options,' I said. 'If the parley fails.'

'Out with it, Dresden,' she said.

I shook my head.

She put a fist on one hip. 'Why not?'

'Gave my word.'

She considered that for a moment. Then she nodded once and said, 'As you wish. Get some more rest. You'll need it.' Then she prowled over to my love seat, sank wearily down into it, and, without another word, curled up under a blanket. She was apparently asleep seconds later.

I thought about getting up and checking out Gard's case, maybe calling Michael and Murphy, but the weariness that suddenly settled on my limbs made all of that sound impossibly difficult. So I settled in a little more comfortably and found sleep coming swiftly to me as well.

The last thing I noticed, before I dropped off, was that under all the blankets I was entirely undressed.

And I was clean.

27

'I still don't see why I can't go,' Molly said, folding her arms crossly.

'You know how you told me how much you hate it when your parents quote scripture at you to answer your questions?' I asked her.

'Yeah.'

'I'm not gonna do that. Because I don't know this one well enough to get the quote right.'

She rolled her eyes.

'But it's something about the best way to defeat temptation is to avoid it.'

'Oh, please,' Molly said.

'Actually, he's right,' Thomas said, passing over my duster. 'Seriously. I know temptation.'

Molly gave my brother a sidelong look and blushed faintly.

'Stop that,' I told him.

Thomas shrugged. 'Can't help it. I'm hungry. I wound up jumping rooftop to rooftop for half an hour, dodging a bunch of three-foot-tall lunatics with bows and arrows.'

'Elves,' I murmured. 'Someone on Summer's team was calling in backup, too. Interesting. I wonder which side tipped the scales first.'

'You're welcome,' Thomas said.

'Hey,' Molly snapped. 'Can we get back on topic? I know how to handle myself, Harry. This is supposed to be a talk, not a fight.'

I sighed, turning to her. We were talking to each other in the Carpenters' kitchen, while everyone else geared up in the workshop. Thomas had sneaked in the front door of the house to pass my staff and coat back to me, after his evening of decoy work.

'Grasshopper,' I said, 'think who we're going to be talking to.'

'Nicodemus. The head of the Denarians,' she said. 'The man who tried to kill my father and my teacher, and did his best to put a demon inside my little brother's head.'

I blinked. 'How did you know about—'

'The usual, eavesdropping on Mom and Dad,' she replied impatiently. 'The point being that I'm *not* going to be tempted to pick up one of his coins, Harry.'

'I'm not talking about *you* being tempted, kid,' I said. 'I'm worried about Nicodemus. Given everything that's going on, I'd rather not wave a Knight of the Cross's brushed-with-darkness daughter under his nose. We're trying to avoid a huge fight, not find new reasons to start one.'

Molly gave me a steady stare.

'Hey,' I said, 'how's that homework I gave you coming?'

She stared some more. She'd learned from Charity, so she was pretty good at it. I'd gotten Charity's stare plenty, though, so I'd been inoculated. She turned in silence and stalked out of the kitchen.

Thomas snorted quietly.

'What?' I asked him.

'You really think you're going to avoid a fight?'

'I think I'm not going to hand them any of Michael's family as hostages,' I said. 'Nicodemus has got something up his sleeve.' As I spoke, I made sure the little holdout knife in its leather sheath was still secured up mine. 'The only question is who is going to start the music and where.'

'Where's the meeting?'

I shrugged. 'Neither party knows. Kincaid and the Archive are picking a neutral spot. They left my place early this morning. They're going to call. But I doubt they'll start it this soon. My money says that Nicodemus will want something in exchange for Marcone. That's when he'll make his move.'

'At the exchange?' Thomas asked.

I nodded. 'Try to grab the whole tamale.'

'Uh-huh,' Thomas said. 'Speaking of, I came by your place after I was done playing tag with assassin midgets last night. Got a whiff of perfume on the doorway and checked through the window on the south side of the house.' He gave me a sly grin. 'About fucking time, man.'

I frowned at him. 'What?'

The grin faded. 'You mean you *still* didn't . . . Oh, empty *night*, Harry.'

'What did you *see?*'

'I saw *you*, talking to a woman who had already taken half her *clothes* off for you, man.'

'Oh, come on,' I said. 'Thomas, it wasn't like that. She was just getting clean.' I gave him the short version of the previous evening.

Thomas gave me a look of his own. Then he thwapped me gently upside the head.

'Hey!' I said.

'Harry,' he said. 'You were sleeping for *hours*. She had *plenty* of time to get clean. You think she sat around for all that time because she wasn't tired just yet? You think she didn't *plan* on you seeing her?'

I opened my mouth to answer and left it that way.

'For that matter, she could have settled down behind the couch, where you couldn't have seen her if you *did* wake up,' Thomas continued. 'Not right by the fire, where she made what I thought was quite a nice little picture for you.'

'I . . . I didn't think she . . .'

He stared at me. 'You didn't make a move.'

'She's . . . Luccio is my commanding officer, man. We . . . we *work* together.'

Thomas rolled his eyes. 'That's a twenty-first-century attitude, man. She's a nineteenth-century girl. She doesn't draw the lines the same way you and I do.'

'But I never thought—'

'I can't believe this,' Thomas said. 'Tell me you aren't that stupid.'

'Stupid?' I demanded.

'Yeah,' he said bluntly. 'Stupid. If she offered and you turned her down because you had a reason you didn't want to, that's one thing. Never realizing what she was talking about, though – that's just pathetic.'

'She *never* said—'

My brother threw up his hands. 'What does a woman need to do, Harry? Rip her clothes off, throw herself on top of you, and shimmy while screaming, "Do me, baby!"?' He shook his head. 'Sometimes you're a frigging idiot.'

'I . . .' I spread my hands. 'She just went to sleep, man.'

'Because she was being thoughtful of you, you knob. She didn't want to come on too strong and make you uncomfortable, especially given that she's older and more experienced than you are, and your commanding officer to boot. She didn't want to make you feel pressured. So she left you plenty of room to turn her down gracefully.' He rolled his eyes. 'Read between the lines once in a while, man.'

'I . . .' I sighed. 'I've never been hit on by a woman a hundred and fifty years older than me,' I said lamely.

'Try to use your brain around women once in a while, instead of just your juju stick.' Thomas tossed me my staff.

I caught it. 'Everyone's a critic.'

My brother purloined an apple from the basket on the island in the kitchen on his way to the door, glanced over his shoulder, and said, 'Moron. Thank God Nicodemus is a man.'

He left, and I stood there for a second being annoyed at him. I mean, sure, he was probably right – but that only made it more annoying, not less.

Something else he was right about: Anastasia had looked simply amazing in front of that fire.

Huh.

I hadn't really thought of her in terms of her first name before. Just as 'Luccio' or 'the captain' or 'Captain Luccio.' Come to think of it, she'd been out of the dating game for even longer than I had. Could be that she hadn't exactly been brimming with self-confidence last night, either.

The situation bore thinking upon.

Later.

For now, there was intrigue and inevitable betrayal afoot, and I had to focus.

I headed out to the workshop. The day was brighter than the one before, but the cloud cover still hadn't gone. It had stopped snowing, though the wind kicked up enough powder to make it hard to tell. A check of the mirror had revealed that the tip of my nose, the tops of my ears, and the highest parts of my cheeks were rough and ruddy from exposure to cold and my brush with hypothermia. They looked like they'd suffered from a heavy sunburn. Added to my raccoon eyes, I thought them quite charming.

No wonder Luccio had thrown herself at me with such wanton abandon.

Dammit, Harry, focus, focus. Danger is afoot.

I opened the door to the workshop just as Michael folded his arms and said, 'I still don't see why I can't go.'

'Because we're trying to avoid a fight,' Luccio said calmly, 'and an atmosphere of nervous fear is not going to foster a good environment for a peaceful exchange.'

'I'm not afraid of them,' Michael said.

'No,' Luccio said, smiling faintly. 'But they're afraid of you.'

'In any case,' Gard said, 'neither the Church nor the Knights are signatories of the Accords. Not to put it too bluntly, Sir Michael, but this is quite literally none of your business.'

'You don't know these people,' Michael said quietly. 'Not the way I do.'

'I do,' I said quietly. 'At least in some ways.'

Michael turned to give me a steady, searching look. 'Maybe,' he said quietly. 'Do you think I should stay away?'

I didn't answer him immediately. Gard watched me from where she sat on the edge of her cot, now dressed and upright, if not precisely healthy-looking. Hendricks sat at the workbench again, although he was sharpening a knife this time. Weapons nuts are always fiddling with their gear. Murphy, seated down the bench from Hendricks, was cleaning her gun. She wasn't moving her wounded arm much, though she apparently had full use of that hand. Sanya loomed in a corner near the workbench, patiently working some kind of leather polish into *Esperacchius*'s scabbard.

'I don't *think* this is where they'll try to stick in the knife,' I said quietly. I turned my eyes to Luccio. 'I also don't think it would be stupid to have a couple of Knights on standby, in case I'm wrong.'

Luccio's head rocked back a little.

'No reason not to hedge our bets,' I told her quietly. 'These people don't play nice like the Unseelie fae, or the Red Court. I've seen them in action, Captain.'

She pursed her lips, and her eyes never wavered from my face. 'All right, Warden,' she said, finally. 'It's your city.'

'I did *not* agree to this,' Gard said, rising, her expression dark.

'Oh, deal with it, blondie,' I told her. 'Beggars and choosers. The White Council is backing you up on this one, but don't start thinking it's because we work for you. Or your boss.'

'I'm going to be there too,' Murphy said quietly, without looking up from her gun. 'Not just somewhere nearby. There. In the room.'

Pretty much everyone there said, 'No,' or some variant of it at that point, except for Hendricks, who didn't talk a lot, and me, who knew better.

Murphy put her gun back together during the protests and loaded it in the silence afterward.

'If you people want to have your plots and your shadowy wars in private,' she said, 'you should take them to Antarctica or somewhere. Or you could do this in New York, or Boise, and this isn't any of my business. But you aren't in any of those places. You're in Chicago. And when things get out of hand, it's the people I'm sworn to protect who are endangered.' She rose, and though she was the shortest person in the room, she wasn't looking up at anyone. 'I'm going to be there as a moderating influence with your cooperation. Or we can do it the other way. Your choice, but I know a lot of cops who are sick and tired of this supernatural bullshit sneaking up on us.'

She directed a level gaze around the room. She hadn't put the gun away.

I smiled at her. Just a little.

Gard looked at me and said, '*Dresden.*'

I shrugged and shook my head sadly. 'What? Once we gave them the vote, it went totally out of control.'

'You're a pig, Harry,' Murphy growled.

'But a pig smart enough to bow to the inevitable,' I said. I looked at Gard and said, 'Far as I'm concerned, she's got a legitimate interest. I'll back it.'

'Warden,' Luccio said in a warning tone, 'may I speak to you?'

I walked over to her.

'She can't possibly know,' Luccio said quietly, 'the kind of grief she could be letting herself in for.'

'She can,' I replied as quietly. 'She's been through more than most Wardens, Captain. And she's sure as hell covered my back enough times to have earned the right to make up her own mind.'

Luccio frowned at me for a moment, and then turned to face Murphy. 'Sergeant,' she said quietly. 'This could expose you to a . . . considerable degree of risk. Are you sure?'

'If it were your town,' Murphy said, 'your job, your duty? Could you stand around with your fingers in your ears?'

Luccio nodded slowly and then inclined her head.

'Besides,' Murphy said, half smiling as she put her gun in her shoulder holster, 'it's not as if I'm leaving you people much choice.'

'I like her,' Sanya rumbled in his deep, half-swallowed accent. 'She is so tiny and fierce. I don't suppose she knows how to—'

'Sanya,' Michael said, his voice very firm. 'We have talked about this.'

The dark-skinned Russian sighed and shrugged. 'It could not hurt to ask.'

'*Sanya.*'

He lifted both hands in a gesture of surrender, grinning, and fell silent.

The door to the house banged shut, and running footsteps crunched through the snow. Molly opened the door to the workshop and said, 'Harry, Kincaid's on the phone. He's got the location for the meeting.'

'Kincaid?' Murphy said in a rather sharp voice.

'Yeah, didn't I mention that?' I asked her, my tone perfectly innocent as I headed for the door. 'He showed up last night.'

Her eyes narrowed. 'We'll talk.'

'Tiny,' Sanya rumbled to Michael, clenching a demonstrative fist. 'But *fierce.*'

28

People think that nothing can possibly happen in the middle of a big city – say, Chicago – without lots of witnesses seeing everything that happened. What most people don't really understand is that there are two reasons why that just ain't so – the first being that humans in general make lousy witnesses.

Take something fairly innocuous, like a minor traffic accident at a busy pedestrian intersection. *Beep-beep, crunch,* followed by a lot of shouting and arm waving. Line up everyone at that intersection and ask them what happened. Every single one of them will give you a slightly different story. Some of them will have seen the whole thing start to finish. Some of them will have seen only the aftermath. Some of them will have seen only one of the cars. Some of them will tell you, with perfect assurance, that they saw *both* cars from start to finish, including such details as the expressions on the drivers' faces and changes in vehicle acceleration, despite the fact that they would have to be performing simultaneous feats of bilocation, levitation, and telepathy to have done so.

Most people will be honest. And incorrect. Honest incorrectness isn't the same thing as lying, but it amounts to the same thing when you're talking about witnesses to a specific event. A relative minority will limit themselves to reporting what they actually saw, not things that they have filled in by assumption, or memories contaminated by too much exposure to other points of view. Of that relative minority, even fewer will be the kind of person who, by natural inclination or possibly training, has the capacity for noticing and retaining a large amount of detail in a limited amount of time.

The point being that once events pass into memory, they

already have a tendency to begin to become muddled and cloudy. It can be more of an art form than a science to gain an accurate picture of what transpired based upon eyewitness descriptions – and that's for a matter of relative unimportance, purely a matter of fallible intellect, with no deep personal or emotional issues involved.

Throw emotions into the mix, and mild confusion turns into utter havoc. Take that same fender-bender, make it an accident between a carload of neoskinhead types and some gangbangers at a busy crosswalk in a South Side neighborhood, and you've got the kind of situation that kicks off riots. No matter what happens, you probably aren't going to be able to get a straight story out of anyone afterward. In fact, you might be hard-pressed to get *any* story out of *anyone*.

Once human emotions get tossed into the mix, everything is up for grabs.

The second reason things can go unnoticed in the middle of the big city is pretty simple: walls. Walls block line of sight.

Let me rephrase that: Walls block line of involvement.

The human animal is oriented around a sense of sight. Things aren't real until we see them: Seeing is believing, right? Which is also why there are illusionists – they can make us see things that aren't real, and it seems amazing.

If a human being actually sees something bad happening, there's a better chance that he or she will act and get involved than if the sense of sight isn't involved. History illustrates it. Oh, sure, Allied governments heard reports of Nazi death camps in World War II, but that was a far cry from when the first troops actually *saw* the imprisoned Jews as they liberated the camps. Hearst had known it before that: *You furnish the pictures, and I'll furnish the war.* And according to some, he did.

Conversely, if you don't *see* something happening, it isn't as real. You can hear reports of tragedies, but they don't hit you the way they would if you were standing there in the ruins.

Nowhere has as many walls as big cities do, and walls keep

you from seeing things. They help make things less real. Sure, maybe you hear loud, sharp noises outside some nights. But it's easy to tell yourself that those aren't gunshots, that there's no need to call the police, no need to even worry. It's probably just a car backfiring. Sure. Or a kid with fireworks. There might be loud wailing or screams coming from the apartment upstairs, but you don't *know* that the drunken neighbor is beating his wife with a rolling pin again. It's not really any of your business, and they're always fighting, and the man is scary, besides. Yeah, you know that there are cars coming and going at all hours from your neighbor's place, and that the crowd there isn't exactly the most upright-looking bunch, but you haven't *seen* him dealing drugs. Not even to the kids you see going over there sometimes. It's easier and safer to shut the door, be quiet, and turn up the TV.

We're ostriches and the whole world is sand.

Newbies who are just learning about the world of wizards and the unpleasant side of the supernatural always think there's this huge conspiracy to hide it from everyone. There isn't. There's no need for one, beyond preventing actual parades down Main Street. Hell's bells, from where I'm standing, it's a miracle anyone *ever* notices.

Which is why I was fairly sure that our parley with the Archive and the Denarians in the Shedd Aquarium was going to go unremarked. Oh, sure, it was right in the middle of town, within a stone's throw of the Field Museum and within sight of Soldier Field, but given the weather there wasn't going to be a lot of foot traffic – and the Aquarium was in its off-season. There might be a handful of people there caring for the animals, but I felt confident that Kincaid would find a way to convince them to be somewhere else.

Murphy had rented a car, since hers was so busted-up. The past few days of snow had seen a load of accidents, and there weren't any compact cars left, so she'd wound up with a silver Caddy the size of a yacht, and I'd called shotgun. Hendricks and Gard rode in the backseat. Gard had gotten to the car under her own power, though she had been moving carefully. Luccio sat beside Gard with her slender staff and her silver rapier resting on the floorboards between her feet, though my own staff was a lot longer and had to slant back between the front seats and past Gard's head, up into the rear window well.

City work crews were still laboring to clear roads and access to critical facilities. An off-season tourist attraction was not high on anyone's priority list. For that matter, the Field Museum had been closed due to the weather, which meant that there really weren't any functioning public buildings for several hundred yards in any direction.

That could be a problem. Michael's white truck wasn't going to be able to get anywhere close without being spotted, which meant that he and Sanya were going to be two, maybe three minutes away from helping, provided they could be signaled at all. That was practically the other side of the world, where a violent confrontation is concerned. On the other hand, it also meant that the bad guys weren't going to be able to bring in any help without being spotted, either.

Provided they were driving cars, of course.

Glass half-full, Harry, glass half-full. There was no profit to be had in a fight – not yet, anyway. Whatever Nicodemus was after, he'd have to make his demands before he had a chance to double-cross us out of whatever he wanted us to bring him. Besides, given what I'd seen of the Archive in action, he'd be freaking insane to try anything where she was officiating. She didn't brook slights to her authority lightly.

The nearest street had been cleared by city trucks, but none of the parking lots had been done, and the excess snow from the streets formed small mountains on either side of the road.

'Looks like we're going to have to walk in,' Murphy said quietly.

'Keep circling. They keep the animals here year-round,' I said quietly. 'And they've got to be fed every day. The staff will have broken a trail in somewhere.'

'Perhaps they let the exhibits go hungry during the storm,'

Gard suggested. 'Few would venture into this for the sake of their paychecks.'

'You don't do oceanography for the money,' I said. 'And you sure as hell don't take up working with dolphins and whales for the vast paycheck and the company car.' I shook my head. 'They love them. Someone's gone in every day. They'll at least have broken a foot trail.'

'There,' Murphy said, pointing. Sure enough, someone had hacked a narrow opening into the mounded snow at the side of the road and dug out a footpath on the other side. Murph had to park at the side of the road, with the doors of the rental car just an inch from the snow walls. If someone came along going too fast, given the condition the streets were in, the Caddy was going to get smashed, but it wasn't like she had a lot of choice.

We all piled out of the driver's side of the car into the wan light of early afternoon. Luccio and I both paused to put on our grey Warden's cloaks. Cloaks look cool and everything, but they don't go well with cars. Luccio buckled on a finely tooled leather belt that held a sword on her left hip and a Colt on her right.

My .44 was back in my duster pocket, and the weight of both the coat and the gun felt greatly comforting. The wind caught my coat and the cloak both, and almost knocked me over until I got them gathered in close to my body again and under control. Hendricks, stolid and huge in his dark, sensible London Fog winter coat, went by me with a small smile on his face.

Hendricks took point, and the rest of us followed him through what could only generously be called a trail. Instead of the snow being up to our chests, on the trail we sank only to our knees. It was a long, cold slog up to the Aquarium, and then around the entire building, where the snow had piled up to truly impressive depths in the lee of the wind on the south side of the structure. Wind hustling in over the frozen lake felt like it had come straight from outer space, and everyone but Gard hunched up miserably against it. The trail led us to an employee's door in the side of the building, which proved to have had the lock housing on its frame covered in duct tape, leaving it open.

Hendricks opened the door, and I stuck my head in and took a quick look around. The building was dark beneath its smothering blanket of snow, except for a few dim night-lights set low on the walls. I didn't see anyone, but I took an extra moment or two to extend my senses into the building, searching for any lurking presences or hostile magicks.

Nothing.

But a little paranoia never hurts in a situation like this.

'Captain,' I said quietly, 'what do you think?'

Luccio moved up beside me and studied the hall beyond the doorway, her dark eyes flickering alertly back and forth. 'It seems clear.'

I nodded, said, 'Excuse me,' and went through the door in a burst of raging anticlimax. I stomped the snow off my boots and jeans as best I could as the others came in behind me. I moved farther down the hall, straining to sense anyone approaching, which meant that I heard the soft scuff of deliberately obtrusive footsteps two or three seconds before Kincaid rounded the far corner. He was dressed in his customary black clothing again, fatigue pants, and a hunting jacket over body armor, and he had enough guns strapped to his body to outfit a terrorist cell, or a Texan nuclear family.

He gave his chin a sharp little lift toward me by way of greeting. 'This way, ple . . .' His eyes focused past me and his voice died in midcourtesy. He stared over my shoulder for a second, sighed, and then told me, 'She can't be here.'

I felt my eyebrows rising. The corners of my mouth went along for the ride. I leaned in a little to Kincaid and murmured, 'You tell her.'

His gaze went from Murphy to me. A less charitable man than I might have called his expression sour. He drummed one thumb on the handle of a sidearm and asked, 'She threaten to call in the constabulary?'

'She's got this funny thing where she takes her oath to protect the city and citizens of Chicago seriously. It's as if her promises mean something to her.'

Kincaid grimaced. 'I'll have to clear it with the Archive.'

'No Murphy, no meeting,' I said. 'Tell her I said that.'

The assassin grunted. 'You can tell her yourself.'

He led me through the halls of the Shedd, to the Oceanarium. It was probably the most popular exhibit there – a great big old semicircular building containing the largest indoor aquatic exhibits in the world. Its outer ring of exhibits sported a number of absolutely huge pools containing millions of gallons of water and a number of dolphins and those little white whales whose names I can never remember. The same as the caviar. Beluga, beluga whales. There were rocks and trees built up around the outsides of the pools, complete with moss and plants and everything, to make it look like the Pacific Northwest. Although I was fairly sure that the bleacher seats, where the audience could marvel at whales and dolphins who would show up and do their usual daily health inspections for their trainers to the sound of applause, weren't indigenous to the Pacific Northwest. I think those were actually Floridian in origin.

A pair of dolphins swept by us in the water, flicking their heads out to get a look at us as they went. One of them made a chittering sound that wasn't very melodic. The other twitched its tail and splashed a little water our way, all in good fun. They weren't the attractive Flipper kind of dolphins. They were regular dolphins that aren't as pretty and don't get cast on television. Maybe they just refused to sell out and see a plastic surgeon. I held up a fist to them. Represent.

Kincaid scanned the bleachers, frowning. 'She's supposed to be sitting here. Dammit.'

I sighed and circled back toward the stairs to the lower level. 'She might be the Archive but she's still a kid, Kincaid.'

He frowned and looked at me. 'So?'

'So? Kids like cute.'

He blinked at me. 'Cute?'

'Come on.'

I led him downstairs.

On the lower level of the Oceanarium there's an inner ring of exhibits, too, containing both penguins and – wait for it – sea otters.

I mean, come on, sea otters. They open abalone with rocks while floating on their backs. How much cuter does it get than small, fuzzy, floating, playful tool users with big, soft brown eyes?

We found Ivy standing in front of one of the sea otter habitats, dressed much more warmly and practically this time, and carrying a small backpack. She was watching two otters chase each other around the habitat, and smiling.

Kincaid stopped in his tracks when he saw that. Just to see what he'd do, I tried to step past him. He shot me a look like he'd murder me if I tried to interrupt her, and my opinion of him went up a notch. I eased back and waited. No skin off my teeth to let the girl watch the otters for a minute.

It had been hard sometimes, when I was a kid, after my magic had started coming in. I'd felt weird and different – alone. It had gradually distanced me from the other kids. But Ivy had never had the luxury of belonging, even temporarily. From what I understood, she'd been the Archive since she was born, fully aware and stuffed full of knowledge from the time she'd opened her eyes. I couldn't even imagine how hideous *that* would be.

Hell, the more I learned as I got older, the more I wished I were ignorant again. Well. Innocent, anyway. I remembered what it was like, at least.

Ivy had never been innocent.

I could let her smile at sea otters. You bet.

A shadow moved behind me, and I willed myself not to be creeped out. I turned and saw the two dolphins from the tank above cruise by, observing us again. The huge tanks contained observation windows running the whole length of the second-level gallery, so you could see the cute things on one side, and ogle the homely dolphins and the caviar whales on the other.

From down here you could also see the far wall of the big tank, which was a curved wall of glass that faced the open waters of Lake Michigan. That always seemed a little sadistic to me. I mean, here were animals whom nature had equipped to roam the open vastness of the deep blue sea, being kept in a mere three million gallons or so of water. Bad enough to do that to them without giving them a window seat onto all that open water too.

Or maybe it wasn't. I hear it kind of sucks to be a whale or a dolphin in the open ocean these days, given the state of the fishing industry.

'I guess they're looking at a can one way or another,' I muttered.

'Hmmm?' Kincaid said.

'Nothing.'

Ivy let out her breath in a satisfied sigh a moment later as the otters vanished into their den. Then she turned toward us and blinked. 'Oh,' she said. Her cheeks colored slightly, and for a moment she looked very much like a young girl. 'Oh.' She smoothed wrinkles that didn't exist in her trousers, nodded at Kincaid, and said, 'Yes?'

Kincaid nodded toward me. 'Local law enforcement wants a representative present to observe. Dresden's supporting it.'

She took that in for a moment. 'Sergeant Murphy?'

'Yes,' I said.

'I see.' She frowned. When she spoke, her tone was careful, as if she was considering each word before she spoke it. 'Speaking as arbiter, I have no objection, provided both parties involved in the parley give their assent.'

'Right,' Kincaid said. He turned and started walking.

I nodded to Ivy, who returned the gesture. Then I turned and hurried to catch up to Kincaid. 'So?' I asked him as we climbed the stairs.

'So,' he said, 'let's go talk to Nicodemus.'

*   *   *

Kincaid led me down the way from the Oceanarium and out to the main entry hall. It's another grandiose collection of shining stone floor and towering Corinthian columns, arranged around a huge tank the size of a roller rink. It's full of salt water and coral and seaweed and all kinds of tropical fish. Sometimes there's a diver with a microphone built into his or her mask feeding the little sharks and fish and talking to gawking tourists. Diffused light floods in through an enormous, triangular-paneled cupola overhead.

The recent snow had blackened the panes of the cupola and drifted up over most of the glass front doors, so the only light in the room came from the little colored lights in the huge tank. Fish glided through the tank like wraiths, the odd light casting sinister shades over their scales, and their shadows drifted disembodied over the walls of the room, magnified by the distance and the glass walls of the aquarium.

It was eerie as hell.

One of the shadows drew my attention as some instinct picked out a strong, subtle sense of menace about it. It took me a couple of seconds to realize that this particular shadow disturbed me because it was human, and moving in a perfect, gliding pace around the wall, behind the shadow of one of the tank's small but genuine sharks – even though the man who cast the shadow was standing perfectly still.

Nicodemus turned from contemplating the fish swimming in the tank so that I could see the outline of his profile against the softly colored lights. His teeth gleamed orange-red in the light of the nearest underwater lamp.

I stopped myself from taking an involuntary step back, but just barely.

'It is a metaphor,' he said quietly. He had a good voice, mellow and surprisingly deep. 'Look at them. Swimming. Eating. Mating. Hunting, killing, fleeing, hiding, each to its nature. All of them so different. So alien to one another. Their world in constant motion, always changing, always threatening, challenging.' He moved one arm, sweeping it in a wider gesture. 'They cannot know how fragile it is, or that they are constantly surrounded by beings with the power to destroy their world and kill them all with the twitch of a finger. It is no fault of theirs, of course.' Nicodemus shrugged. 'They are simply . . . limited. Very, very limited. Hello, Dresden.'

'You're playing the creepy vibe a little hard,' I said. 'Might as well go for broke, put on a black top hat and pipe in some organ music.'

He laughed quietly. It didn't sound evil as much as it did rich and supremely confident. 'There's some irregularity with the meeting, I take it?'

Kincaid glanced at me and nodded.

'Local law enforcement wishes a representative to be present,' I said.

Nicodemus's head tilted. 'Really? Who?'

'Does it matter?' Kincaid asked, his tone bored. 'The Archive is willing to permit it, if you have no objections.'

Nicodemus turned all the way around finally. I couldn't see his expression, just his outline against the tank. His shadow, meanwhile, kept circling the room behind the shark. 'Two conditions,' he said.

'Go on,' Kincaid said.

'First, that the representative be unarmed, and that the Archive guarantee his neutrality in the absence of factors that conflict with matters of law-enforcement duty.'

Kincaid glanced at me. Murphy wouldn't like the 'unarmed' part, but she'd do it. If nothing else, she wouldn't want to back down in front of me – or maybe Kincaid.

But I had to wonder, what was Nicodemus's problem with an armed cop? Guns did not bother the man. Not even a little. Why that stipulation?

I nodded at Kincaid.

'Excellent,' Nicodemus said. 'Second . . .' He walked forward, each footstep sounding clearly upon the marble floors, until we could see him in the nearest floorlights. He was a man of medium height and build, his features handsome, strong, his eyes dark and intelligent. Hints of silver graced his immaculate hair, though he was holding up pretty well for a man of two thousand. He wore a black silk shirt, dark pants, and what could have been mistaken for a grey Western tie at his throat. It wasn't. It was an old, old rope from the same field as his coin. 'Second,' he said, 'I want five minutes alone with Dresden.'

'No offense, Nick,' I said, 'but that's about five minutes longer than I want to spend with you.'

'Exactly,' he replied, smiling. It was the kind of smile you see at country clubs and in boardrooms and on crocodiles. 'There's really never a good opportunity for us to have a civilized conversation. I'm seizing the chance for a chat.' He gestured at the building around us. 'Sans demolition, if you think you can refrain.'

I scowled at him.

'Mister Archleone,' Kincaid said, 'are you offering a peace bond? If so, the Archive will hold you to it.'

'I offer no such thing,' Nicodemus said without looking away from me. 'Dresden would count it as worthless coin, and his is the only opinion that really matters in this particular situation.' He spread his hands. 'A talk, Dresden. Five minutes. I assure you, if I wished to do you harm, even the Hellhound's reputation' – he paused deliberately to glance at Kincaid with naked contempt in his gaze – 'would not make me hesitate for an instant. I would have killed you already.'

Kincaid gave Nicodemus a chill little smile, and the air boiled with potential violence.

I held up a hand and said quietly, 'Easy there, Wild Bill. I'll talk with him. Then we'll have our sit-down. All nice and civilized.'

Kincaid glanced at me and arched a shaggy, dark-gold eyebrow. 'You sure?'

I shrugged a shoulder.

'All right,' he said. 'I'll be back in five minutes.' He paused, then added, 'If either of you initiates violence outside of the strictures of a formal duel, you'll be in violation of the Accords. In addition, you will have offered an insult to the reputation and integrity of the Archive – which I will take personal action to amend.'

The wintry chill in his blue eyes was mostly for Nicodemus, but I got some of it too. Kincaid meant it, and I'd seen him in action before. He was one of the scarier people I knew; the more so because he went about matters with ruthless practicality, unhindered by personal ego or the pride one often encountered in the supernatural set. Kincaid wouldn't care if he looked into my eyes as he killed me, if that was what he set out to do. He'd be just as happy to put a bullet through my head from a thousand meters away, or wire a bomb to my car and read about my death on the Internet the next morning. Whatever got the job done.

That kind of attitude doesn't help you when it comes to finding flashy or dramatic ways to do away with your enemies, but what it lacks in aesthetics it makes up in economy. Marcone, whom this whole mess was about, worked the same way, and it had taken him far. You crossed such men at *extreme* peril.

Nicodemus let out another quiet, charming laugh. He didn't look impressed by Kincaid. Maybe that was a good thing. Too much pride can kill a man.

On the other hand, from what I'd seen of him, maybe Nicodemus really *was* that tough.

'Run along, Hellhound,' Nicodemus said. 'Your mistress's honor is quite safe.' He drew an X on his chest. 'Cross my heart.'

Maybe it was an inside reference. Kincaid's eyes flashed with something hot and furious before they went glacial again. He nodded to me, then precisely the same way to Nicodemus, and left.

I'm pretty sure the room didn't actually become darker and scarier and more threatening when I was left alone with the most dangerous man I'd ever crossed.

But it sure felt that way.

Nicodemus turned that toothy predator's smile to me as his shadow began to glide around the walls of the entry hall. Circling me. Like a shark.

'So, Harry,' he said, walking closer, 'what shall we talk about?'

29

'You're the one who wanted a conversation,' I said. 'And don't call me Harry. My friends call me Harry.'

He turned one hand palm up. 'And who is to say I cannot be your friend?'

'That would be me, Nick. I say. Here, I'll show you.' I enunciated: 'You can't be my friend.'

'If I am to call you Dresden, it is only fair that you should call me Archleone.'

'Archleone?' I asked. 'As in "seeking whom he may devour"? Kinda pretentious, isn't it?'

For half of a second, the smile turned into something almost genuine. 'For a godless heathen, you are entirely too familiar with scripture. You know that I can kill you, do you not?'

'We'd make a mess,' I said. 'And who knows? I might get lucky.'

Really, really, really lucky.

Nicodemus moved a hand in acknowledgment. 'But barring luck.'

'Yeah,' I said.

'And you offer such insouciance regardless?'

'Habit,' I said. 'It doesn't make you special or anything, believe me.'

'Oh, I picked the right coin for you.' He started to walk in a slow circle around me, the way you might a car at the dealership. 'There are rumors that a certain Warden has been flinging Hellfire at his foes. How do you like it?'

'I'd like it better if it came in Pine Fresh and New Car instead of only Rotting Egg,' I said.

Nicodemus completed his circuit of me and arched an eyebrow. 'You haven't taken up the coin.'

'I would, but it's in my piggybank,' I said, 'and I can't break the piggy, obviously. He's too cute.'

'Lasciel's shadow must be slipping,' Nicodemus said, shaking his head. 'It has had years to reason with you, and still you refuse our gifts.'

'What with the curly little tail and the big, sad brown eyes,' I said, as if he hadn't said anything.

One of his heels hit the ground with unnecessary force, and he stopped walking. He inhaled through his nose and out again. 'Definitely the proper coin for you.' He folded his hands carefully behind his back. 'Dresden, you have a skewed image of us. We were operating at cross-purposes the first time we met, and you probably learned everything you know about us from Carpenter and his cohorts. The Church has always had excellent propaganda.'

'Actually, the murder, torture, and destruction you and your people perpetrated spoke pretty loudly all by themselves.'

Nicodemus rolled his eyes. 'Dresden, please. You have done all of those things at one time or another. Poor Cassius told me all about what you did to him in the hotel room.'

'Gosh,' I said, grinning. 'If someone had walked in on us in the middle of that sentence, would my face be red or what?'

He stared at me for a second, and the emotion and expression drained out of his features like dewdrops vanishing under a desert sunrise. What was left behind was little more than desolation. 'Harry Dresden,' he said, so softly that I could barely make it out. 'I admire your defiance of greater powers than your own. I always have. But *tempus fugit*. For all of us.'

I blinked.

For all of us? What the hell did he mean by that?

'Have you not seen the signs around you?' Nicodemus asked. 'Beings acting against their natures? Creatures behaving in ways that they should not? The old conventions and customs being cast aside?'

I narrowed my eyes at him. 'You're talking about the Black Council.'

He tilted his head slightly to one side. Then his mouth

twitched at a corner and he nodded his head very slightly. 'They move in shadows, manipulate puppets. Some of them may be on your Council, yes. As good a name as any.'

'Stop playing innocent,' I spat at him. 'I saw the leftovers of the Black Council attack on Arctis Tor. I know what Hellfire smells like. One of yours was in on it.'

Nicodemus.

Blinked.

Then he surged forward – fast. So fast that by the time I'd registered that he was moving, my back had already hit the wall that had been twenty feet behind me. He hadn't been trying to hurt me. If he had, the back of my head would have splattered open. He just pinned me there against the wall with one hand on my throat, tighter and harder than a steel vise.

'*What?*' he demanded, his voice still a whisper. His eyes, though, were very wide. Both sets of them. A second set, these glowing faintly green, had opened just above his eyebrows – Anduriel's, I presumed.

'Ack,' I said. 'Glarghk.'

His arm quivered for a second, and then he lowered his eyelids until they were almost closed. A moment later he very, very slowly relaxed his arm, allowing me to breathe again. My throat burned, but air came in, and I wheezed for a second or two while he stepped back from me.

I glared up at him and debated slamming him through one of those Corinthian columns by way of objecting to being manhandled. But I decided that I didn't want to piss him off.

Nicodemus's lips moved, but an entirely different voice issued from them – something musical, lyrical, and androgynous. 'At least it has *some* survival instinct.'

Nicodemus shook his head as if buzzed by a mosquito and said, 'Dresden, speak.'

'I'm not your friend,' I said, my voice rough. 'I'm not your damned dog, either. Conversation over.' I took a few steps to one side so that I could move around him without taking my eyes off him, and started to leave.

'Dresden,' Nicodemus said. 'Stop.'

I kept walking.

I was almost out of the room before he spoke again, resignation in his tone. 'Please.'

I paused, without turning around.

'I . . . reacted inappropriately. Especially for this venue. I apologize.'

'Huh,' I said, and looked over my shoulder. 'Now I wish I *had* brought Michael. He'd have fainted.'

'Your friend and his brethren are tools of an organization with its own agenda, and they always have been,' Nicodemus said. 'But that's not the issue here.'

'No,' I said. 'The issue is Marcone.'

Nicodemus waved a hand. 'Marcone is an immediate matter. There are long-term issues in play.'

I turned to face him and sighed. 'I think you're probably full of crap. But okay, I'll bite. What long-term issues?'

'Those surrounding the activities of your Black Council,' Nicodemus said. 'Are you *certain* you saw evidence of Hellfire in use at the site of the attack on Arctis Tor?'

'Yes.' I didn't add the word *dummy*. Who says I ain't diplomatic?

Nicodemus's fingers flexed into the shape of claws and then relaxed again. He pursed his lips. 'Interesting. Then the only question is if the contamination is among standing members of our Order or . . .' He let the thought trail off and glanced at me, lifting an eyebrow.

I followed the logic to the only other people in possession of any of the coins. 'Someone in the Church,' I whispered, with a sick feeling in my stomach.

'Historically speaking, we get about half of the coins back that way,' Nicodemus noted. 'What would you say if I told you that you and I might have a great many common interests in the future?'

'I wouldn't say much of anything,' I said. 'I'd be too busy laughing in your face.'

Nicodemus shook his head. 'Shortsighted. You can't afford that. Come with me for a week and see if you feel the same way when we're done.'

'Even assuming I was stupid enough to go anywhere with you for an hour, much less a week, I saw how you treated Cassius. I'm not real eager to slide my nameplate onto his office door.'

'He didn't adjust to the times,' Nicodemus replied with a shrug. 'I wouldn't have been doing him any favors by coddling him. We live in a dangerous world, Dresden. One adapts and thrives or one dies. Living on the largesse of others is nothing but parasitism. I respected Cassius too much to let him devolve to that.'

'Gosh, you're chatty,' I said. 'You were right. This is so much fun. It's almost like . . .'

A horrible thought hit me.

Nicodemus was many things, but he wasn't a fool. He knew I wasn't going to sign on for his team. Not after the way he treated me the last time we'd met. He knew that nothing he said was going to sway me. I might have surprised him with that little nugget of information about Arctis Tor, but that could have been an act, too. All in all, odds were high that this conversation was accomplishing absolutely nothing, and Nicodemus had to know that.

So why was he having it? I asked myself.

Because the goal of the conversation doesn't have anything to do with the subject or the context of the conversation, I answered.

He wasn't here to talk to me about anything or convince me of anything.

He wanted to talk to me and keep me *here*.

Which meant that something else was about to happen somewhere else.

Wheels within wheels.

My God, it was a metaphor.

This *conversation* was a metaphor for the parley as a whole. Nicodemus hadn't come to talk to us about violations of the Accords. He'd *engineered* the parley, and his motivation had nothing to do with subverting Marcone's talents to the service of a Fallen angel.

He was after bigger game.

I whipped my staff toward Nicodemus, slamming my will through it in a surge of panicked realization, screaming *'Forzare!'* as I did. Unseen force lifted him from his feet and slammed him into one of the huge Corinthian columns like a cannonball. Stone shattered with a deafening crash like thunder, and a lot of rock started to fall.

I didn't stick around to see how much. It wouldn't kill him. I only hoped it would slow him down enough for me to get to the others.

'Kincaid!' I shouted as I ran. My voice boomed through the empty halls in the wake of the collapsing rubble. 'Kincaid!'

I knew I had only seconds before all Hell broke loose.

'Kincaid, get the kid out of here!' I screamed. *'They're coming for Ivy!'*

30

My brain flew along a lot faster than my feet.

Given the heavy snow outside, the first line of retreat the Archive would take would be into the Nevernever. The spirit world touches on the mortal world at all places and at all times. It gets weird once you realize that totally alien regions of the Nevernever might touch upon relatively close points in the real world. Crossing into the Nevernever is dangerous unless you know exactly where you're going – I don't use it as a fallback very often at all. But if you've really got your back to the wall, and you have more experience than I do at crossing over, you can get a feel for the crossing and almost always get to someplace relatively benign.

I figured it was safe to assume that the Archive would be savvy enough to feel comfortable stepping over – in fact, she would have chosen this location for the parley for precisely that reason. The Denarians would know it too, and they didn't want the Archive to escape their ambush and come back loaded for bear. They would have prepared countermeasures, much as they had for Marcone.

No, scratch that. *Exactly* the way they had for Marcone, I realized. The huge spell that had been used to tear apart the defenses of the crime lord's panic room hadn't simply been a way for the Denarians to secure the bait in this scheme. It had been a field test for their means to cut off the magical energy from a large area, and access to the Nevernever with it – and to imprison something *big* at the same time.

It was a bear trap, custom-designed for Ivy. They were going to spring that monstrous pentagram again.

Only this time I was going to be standing inside it when it happened.

Fortunately, the Shedd was a lot squattier and more stable than Marcone's old apartment building had been – though that didn't mean pieces big enough to kill people wouldn't fall when the beam ripped through the walls. And though a lot of stonework was used, there was still the danger of fire.

Fire. In an aquarium. Breathe in the irony.

But more important, once that pentagram came up – and it was coming now; I could feel it, a faint stirring of power that slid along the edges of my wizard's senses like some huge and hungry snake passing by in the darkness – it was going to shut the building off from the rest of the world, magically speaking. That meant that I wasn't going to be able to draw in any power to use to defend myself, any more than I'd be able to breathe if someone plunged my head underwater.

Usually, when you work a spell, you reach out into the environment around you and pull in energy. It flows in from everywhere, from the fabric of life in the whole planet. You don't create a 'hole' in the field of energy we call 'magic.' It all pours in together, levels out instantly, all across the world. But the circle about to go up was going to change that. The relatively tiny area inside the Shedd would contain only so much energy. Granted, it would be a fairly rich spot – there was a lot of life in the building, and it had hosted a lot of visitors generating a lot of emotions, especially the energy given off by all those children. But even so, it was a sealed box, and given the number of people present who knew how to use magic, the local supply wasn't going to last long.

Try to imagine a knife fight in an airtight phone booth – lots of heavy breathing and exertion, but not for long.

One way or the other, not for long.

That was their plan, of course. Without magic to draw upon, I was pretty much just a scrappy guy with a gun, whereas Nicodemus was still a nigh-invincible engine of destruction.

For a few seconds my steps slowed.

Put that way, it almost sounded a little crazy of me to be rushing into this. I mean, I was basically opting for a cage match with a collection of demons, and one that I would have to win within a matter of seconds or not at all – and I hadn't been all that impressive against the Denarians when I'd had relatively few constraints on what power I could wield against them.

I did some mental math. If the symbol the Denarians were using was approximately the same size as the one at Marcone's place, it would be big enough to encompass only the Oceanarium itself in the pentagram at its center. Murphy and the others, if they'd stayed where we'd come in, would probably be safe. More to the point, if they'd stayed where they were, they would have no way to enter the Oceanarium.

That meant it would be just me and Ivy and maybe Kincaid – against Nicodemus, Tessa, and every Denarian they could beg, borrow or steal. Those were long odds. Really, really long odds. Ridiculously long odds, really. When you have to measure them in astronomical units, it probably isn't a good bet.

So, going in there would be bad.

If I didn't go in, though, it would be just Ivy and Kincaid against all of them. In a deadly business, Kincaid was one of the deadliest, at the top of the field for centuries – but there was only one of him. Ivy had vast knowledge to draw upon, of course, but once she'd been cut off and expended whatever magic she had immediately available to her, the only thing she'd be able to do with all that knowledge would be to calculate her worsening odds of escape.

Every hair on my body tried to stand up all at the same time, and I knew that the symbol was being energized. In seconds it would howl to life.

I guess in the end it came down to a single question: whether or not I was the kind of man who walks away when he knows a little kid is in danger.

I'd been down this road before: *Not* going in there would be worse.

Heat shimmers filled the air in the hall in front of me as I sprinted toward the Oceanarium.

Fight smarter, not harder, Harry. I drew in power on the way

– a *lot* of power. If there wasn't going to be any magic available for the taking once the symbol went up, I'd just have to bring my own.

Usually I draw in power only when it's ready to flow directly out of me again, channeling the energy through my mind and into the structure of a spell. This time I brought it in without ever letting it out, and it built up as a pressure behind my eyes. My body temperature jumped by at least four or five degrees, and my muscles and bones screamed with sudden pain while my vision went red and flickered with spots of black. Static electricity crackled with every single motion of my limbs, bright green and painfully sharp, until it sounded like I was running across a field of bubble wrap. My head pounded like every New Year's hangover I'd ever had, all in the same spot, and my lungs felt like the air had turned to acid. I concentrated on keeping my feet underneath me and moving. One step at a time.

I pounded through the entry to the Oceanarium, felt a shivering sensation as I ran right through a veil I had not sensed was there, and all but barreled into a demonic figure crouched down on the floor. I skidded to a stop, and there was an instant of surprise as we stared at each other.

The Denarian was basically humanoid, as most of them were, a gaunt, even skeletal grey-skinned figure. Spurs of bone jutted out from every joint, slightly curved and wickedly pointed. Greasy, lanky hair hung from its knobby skull to its skinny shoulders, and its two pairs of eyes, one very human brown and one glowing demonic green, were both wide and staring in shock.

It was crouched amidst the preparations of a spell of some kind – a candle, a chalk circle on the floor, a cup made from a skull and filled with water – and it wore a heavy canvas messenger bag slung across one shoulder. One hand was still down in the bag, as if it had been in the midst of drawing something out of it when I'd come charging up.

Fortunately for me, my mind had been in motion. His had been tangled up in whatever spell he was doing, and he was slower to get back into gear than I was.

So I kicked him in the face.

He went down with a grunt, and a chip of broken tooth skittered across the floor. I didn't know what spell he was getting together, but it seemed a good bet that I didn't want him to finish it. I broke his circle with my will as I crossed it with my body, unleashing a ripple of random and diffused energies that had never had the chance to coalesce into something more coherent. I knocked his skull goblet into one of the enormous nearby tanks with my staff as I raised it and pointed one end of it at the stunned Denarian, snarling, 'Forzare!'

Some of that searing storm of power I was holding in screamed out of my body and down through my staff, hurtling at the Denarian, an invisible cannonball surrounded by a cloud of static discharge. It was more power than I'd meant to unleash. If it hit him it was going to throw him halfway across Lake Michigan.

But while the Denarian's mortal set of eyes may have still been blank with shock and surprise, the glowing green set was bright with rage. The thorny Denarian lifted his left hand in a sweeping gesture, made a rippling motion of his fingers, drawing his hand toward his mouth, and . . .

. . . and he just *ate* my spell.

He *ate* it. And then that gaunt, skeletal face spread in a toothy smile.

'That,' I muttered, 'is incredibly unfair.'

I lifted my left hand just as the Denarian crouched and vomited out a spinning cloud of black threads that came whirling through the air in dozens of tiny, spiraling arcs. I brought up my shield, but none of the threads actually came down to touch me – they landed all around me instead, in a nearly perfect circle.

And an instant later my shield stuttered and shorted out. I still had the energy for it – I hadn't been cut off. But somehow the Denarian's weird spell had disrupted the magic as it left my body. I tried to throw another bolt of force at him, and got to feel supremely silly, waving my staff around to absolutely zero effect.

'Interruptions,' the Denarian said in an odd accent. 'Always the interruptions.'

His left hand returned to rummaging in his bag, while his mortal eyes went back to the now-scattered remnants of the spell, evidently dismissing my existence. The green eyes remained focused on me, though, and darkness suddenly gathered around the forefinger of his upraised right hand.

Time slowed down.

Dark light leapt toward me.

Sheer defiance made me step forward, trying to brush past the little spinning columns of shadow that surrounded me, only to find them as solid as steel bars, and colder than a yeti's fridge. I threw my magic against those bars to no avail as a shaft of dark lightning streaked toward my heart.

Something happened.

I don't know how to describe it. I was trying to slam another bolt of force between the bars of my conjured prison when something . . . else . . . got involved. Ever been carrying something and had someone intentionally, unexpectedly jostle your elbow? It felt something like that – a tiny but critically timed nudge just as I threw my will into a last futile effort of defiance.

Power screamed as it wrenched its way out of my body. It shattered the black-thread bars of my prison and left a streak of metallic light on the air behind it for an instant, reflective, like a trail of liquid chrome. It caught the falling Denarian in a massive silvery simulacrum of my own fist.

I actually felt my fingers close over the gaunt, skeletal, grey-skinned figure, felt the numerous spurs of bone jutting from its joints press painfully into my flesh. I flung it away from me with a cry, and the huge silver hand flung the Denarian into the nearest wall, ripping through several feet of expensive stone terracing and carefully simulated Pacific Northwest.

I stared for a second, first at the stunned Denarian, and then at my own spread fingers – and at the floating silvery hand beyond, mirroring my movements. Then the skeletal Denarian gathered itself and rose, fast as hell – until I shoved the heel of my hand forward and drove his bony ass six inches into the wall of rock behind him.

'Oh, yeah, baby!' I heard myself howl, elated. 'Talk to the hand!'

I picked up the thorny fiend by a leg and laughed as it raked and bit and scrabbled at the construct that held it. I could feel the pain of it – but it was a small thing, really, something I might have gotten from a rat. Unpleasant as hell, but I'd felt much, much worse, and it was *nothing* compared to the agony of the power still burning inside me. I slammed him into the wall again, then swung him twenty feet through the air, shoved him through a pane of unbroken three-inch-thick glass on the outer wall of the Oceanarium, drew him back through, and then rammed him through the next one, and the next one, and the one after that, cutting him to tatters as I did.

I had maybe half of a second's warning, as my already over-loaded nerves screamed that the circle was closing, that the Sign was rising, as I felt the surge of energy approaching from no more than a dozen yards away. There was still no time for a shield.

So Spinyboy would have to do.

I flung him between me and where my instinct warned me the inbound power was coming from, and then there was a roar like a dozen turbine engines howling to life in synchronization. Thirty feet from me the walls exploded in light and Hellfire. Heat, light, and sheer, intangible power slammed against my senses and threw me from my feet. Bits of molten rock hissed through the air, deadlier than any bullet.

Spinyboy caught a bunch of those. They flew out his back and left gaping, smoking, cauterized holes in it. I could see them through the silvery haze of the construct hand that still held him, could feel the heat as they bored through the construct, and—

—and then my head bumped the ground hard enough to make me see stars. I rolled to my feet and nearly wobbled over the railing and into the pool with the whales. I slammed the end of my staff into the ground with my left hand and leaned heavily against it, panting.

I was still alive. I still retained an agonizing amount of energy. So far, I thought woozily, everything was going exactly according to plan.

The skeletal, spiny Denarian lay twitching on the ground ten or twelve feet in front of me. There were big smoking holes in its body. One of its arms was moving. So was its head. But its legs and its lower body were completely limp. I could see the bones of its spine standing out sharply from its gaunt, emaciated back. Two of the smoking holes intersected that spine precisely. He – or she, I supposed, if it mattered – wasn't going anywhere.

Great currents of energy, eight or nine feet thick, intersected maybe fifty feet away. It was like . . . looking at the cross-section of a river in flood – if the river had been made of fire instead of water, and if two rivers could have intersected and passed through each other without affecting each other's courses. I turned my head and saw, through the walls of glass that I'd broken, more of the same beams, all around the Oceanarium in an unbroken wall.

The eerie part was that the fiery current of energy was silent. Absolutely silent. There was no crackle of flame, no roar of superheated air, no hiss of steam as snow and ice melted. I heard some rubble falling, stone landing on stone. I heard a broken electrical line somewhere, spitting and snapping for a few seconds before it, too, went silent.

That was when I realized a couple of things.

The silver energy construct that had gripped the Denarian was gone.

And I couldn't feel my right hand.

I looked down in a panic, but found that it was still there, at least, flopping loosely at the end of my arm. I couldn't feel anything below my wrist. My fingers were slightly curled and didn't respond when I told them to move.

'Crap,' I muttered. Then I gathered my wits about me, gripped my staff more firmly in my left hand, and took several rapid steps until I stood over Spinyboy.

Then I bashed him over the head with the solid length of oak until he stopped moving.

Immobilized wasn't the same as unconscious. He wouldn't be the only one of his kind in the building, and I didn't want him shouting my location to anybody the second my back was turned.

One down. Who knew how many to go.

I crouched in the walkway with the wall on my right, the windows facing the outside of the Oceanarium on my left, and the beam of Hellfire at my back. It was the most secure position I was likely to get. There was still no sound, which meant that they hadn't tried to take the Archive yet. Kincaid would not go down quietly.

But they were in here with me. They had to be.

But they didn't necessarily know *I* was in here with them.

That could be an advantage. Maybe even a huge advantage.

Sure, Harry. What cat ever expects the mouse to come after it?

I stuffed my numb right hand in my duster pocket, tried to ignore the bone-deep ache of unspent power racking my body and the limb-weakening tremors of raw terror radiating through my guts, and stalked silently forward to sucker punch some Fallen angels.

31

I've read that dolphins are as smart as people. I've even read one article by a researcher who claimed that her results indicated that the dolphins she'd been working with had been throwing the tests, and it had taken us years to realize it – that in fact, they might be *smarter* than us. I'd read other positions that said that they were quite a bit dumber than that. Being as how I'd never really sat down for a game of checkers with a dolphin, my own personal meter for such things, I didn't really have an opinion until that day in the Shedd.

That was when those ugly little dolphins swam by me in perfect silence, except for the swish of their dorsal fins breaking the surface to get my attention – and then raised holy hell seventy feet farther down the path beside the pool, around the curve and out of my sight, splashing and chattering and squeaking for all they were worth.

I stared stupidly for about half a second before the message got through: Bad guys sighted, and close. Evidently the aquatic Americans had decided that I was on the home team. As quickly as the chattering had begun it ended, the dolphins vanishing beneath the surface.

I heard a creaking, skittering sound, and instinct drew my face up. Shadows moved on the snow-covered glass roof of the Oceanarium.

More of Nicodemus's plan in delaying me became clear. He'd needed time to let his people get into position within and atop the building, once he'd been able to determine generally where the Archive was within the Aquarium.

I threw myself into the heavy ferns planted next to the foot-path beside the outer pools, crouching down in the thickest bunch of greenery I could find. I held on hard to the power I'd drawn into me and hoped I could make my sucker punch last for more than a single hit.

A breath later, glass shattered and fell. Dark, inhuman forms dropped silently from overhead.

I picked the outermost of the invading Denarians, the one farthest from the center of action and attention, pointed my staff at him from my hiding spot amidst the green, and snarled, '*Forzare!*' unleashing a moderate effort of will. Invisible force caught the shapeshifted fiend as he was falling. I never got much of a look at him, beyond the fact that he had a lot of muscle and a ridge of leathery plates running down his spine.

Muscle doesn't do you any good in free fall, no matter how many Fallen angels you've got inside you. Unless you've got some wings to put it to use, you're in the hands of Mother Earth and Sir Isaac Newton.

I wasn't trying to smash him into the middle of the lake. I applied just enough force to alter his trajectory, shoving the falling Denarian thirty feet off course, and he landed in one of those beams of titanic energy.

There was a flash of white light, a brief shadow of a human skeleton burned onto my vision, and then a white-hot something went spinning out from the beam. It landed in one of the pools in an angry gush of steam. The dolphins darted away from it.

Then I froze, not moving.

Denarians fell like rain, more than a dozen of them, landing with heavy-sounding thumps and a couple of splashes . . .

. . . and a splat. One of them, a lizard-looking thing, had fallen into the foliage behind me and not five feet from my hiding spot, with about two-thirds of its head simply missing from its shoulders. It twitched wildly for several seconds, pumping very human-looking blood all over the place before it slowly went still and simply started draining.

My eyes tracked up to the roof and found a darkened corner.

Kincaid hung in it like a spider, suspended from some sort of harness and perfectly still, and I realized that he'd had the same idea I had: Remove them before they'd realized that the battle was well and truly begun, while they were still holding back all their power to unleash in concentration. He gave me a grim little smile, moved his head in an 'after you' sort of gesture, and raised a rifle sporting a heavy, outsized silencer to his cheek.

Kincaid had once informed me, quite calmly, that if he ever wanted to kill me, it would be with a rifle from more than a mile away. This was more like a hundred feet, maybe less, but Kincaid had dropped the Denarian with a shot to the head, maybe *more* than one, while it fell to the ground amidst a shower of broken glass. He was deadly as hell, and he could just as easily be coming after me as my enemies, but somehow my terror had dwindled to something familiar – and ferocious.

Sure, I might be outnumbered, but I was no longer at all certain that I was outclassed. When the Fallen were calling the shots they were arrogant to the extreme, and they weren't at all used to playing it by ear and adjusting to changes in the tempo. When the coin bearers were running things, they could be more dangerous – but no more so than anyone else I had crossed metaphorical swords with.

Nicodemus, then, was dangerous because he was Nicodemus – not because of a Fallen angel or a lack of one. And while I would be a fool to think him anything less than a deadly threat, I had survived him once, and seen the trap coming this time, even if it had been at the last minute.

I spared a glance for the splattered, twitching remains of the decapitated Denarian in the ferns. These creeps might have scary angels looking over their shoulders – but for the next couple of minutes, at least, so did I.

It didn't make them any less dangerous. It just made me see that I had a chance of standing up to them.

No flash and thunder, then. I had no energy to spare for them. No wasted time, either. I rose and stole through the ferns toward where I thought the next-nearest Denarian had come down, up a steep hillside that was murder to move over silently. The Denarian who had landed hadn't stayed immobile, though. I found the spread talon prints in the earth where it had touched down, like those of a turkey, but larger.

I froze as water splashed off to my right. From the corner of my eye I saw a Denarian haul herself out of the water of the dolphin pool – Mantis Girl, Tessa. She pulled herself over the pedestrian guardrail, moving fast and warily. I saw a flash of silver in the talons of one hand. She'd recovered the coin of the Denarian I'd shoved into the beam. She knew they weren't alone. I didn't have much in the way of cover between her and me, but I didn't move, and I didn't think she spotted me.

Mantis Girl landed on the concrete and vanished down the path and out of my sight. Something let out a chittering, monkey-like sound from somewhere in the vast room, but other than that everything remained silent.

I ghosted forward again, straining to hear. Where was the drama? Where were the explosions, the howling screams, the deafening soundtrack? This was just one big, eerie game of hide-and-seek.

Which, I suddenly realized, must have been the Archive's counterstrategy. The energy output of the enormous symbol was too high to maintain for long. If she could simply remain hidden from her enemies until the symbol could no longer be maintained, she could depart at will. There would then be no need for her to burn through her precious little available energy in a last-ditch, desperate effort to defend herself – provided she could stay calm and focused enough to maintain a veil under these circumstances, of course. It would force the Denarians to hunt Ivy – expending their efforts on trying to pierce her veil, while Kincaid concentrated on isolating them and killing them while they were distracted. It was a deucedly clever countertactic.

On the far side of the room one of the Denarians started screaming, a wail of agony. My eyes snapped up to Kincaid's position. He was gone. A rope now dangled down over the foliage below where he'd hung, but he'd abandoned the exposed shooting position after taking down one more enemy, it would seem.

I found myself grinning. Fine. If that was the game, I could play too. *Ready or not, here I come.*

I pressed on through the ferns, angling over toward the amphitheater seats, and dropped into a sudden crouch as the low mutter of voices came to me.

'Where *is* she?' demanded a heavy, thick-sounding man's voice.

I couldn't see the source of the voices from amidst the fake wilderness until I glanced up. Light and shadow played together in the room and conspired to create a reflective surface for me upon one of the panels of glass on the ceiling. Three of the Denarians had gathered on the bleacher seats. The one who spoke looked like nothing so much as a big, leathery gorilla, except for the goat's horns and heavy claws.

'Shut up, Magog,' snarled Mantis Girl. 'I can't think with you running your stupid mouth.'

'We're nearly out of *time*,' Magog growled.

'She knows that,' snapped a third Denarian. I recognized this one, which looked like a woman, except for the reverse-jointed legs ending in panther claws, the bright red skin, and the mass of metallic, ten-foot-long, independently moving blades in place of hair. Deirdre, Nicodemus's darling daughter. She turned back to Tessa. 'But Magog has a point, Mother. Scent tracking has been useless.' She held up a small pink sock. 'Bits of clothing with her scent on them have been scattered everywhere.'

'That's the Hellhound's work,' Magog spat, bright green eyes glowing brightly over dull, animalistic brown ones. 'He's fought us before.'

'He hunts us,' Deirdre said, 'while she forces us to focus on piercing a veil. They work too well together. He's killed two of us. Three if you count Urumviel.'

Tessa bounced the silver coin in her palm. 'Urumviel's vessel may have been killed by his own idiocy,' she said. Her insectoid eyes seemed to narrow. 'Or perhaps the wizard managed to return before the Sign was raised.'

'You think *that* pathetic sot bested *Father*?' Deirdre said with scorn.

I bristled.

'He wouldn't need to best him, you moron,' Tessa said. 'Only to run faster. And it would explain why Thorned Namshiel hasn't appeared as well.'

Yeah. If Spinyboy ever woke up, it would be with one hell of a Dresden hangover. *Stick that in your pipe and smoke it, Deedee.*

'The wizard is nothing,' Magog growled. 'If the girl is not found, and swiftly, none of this will matter to us.'

Tessa snapped her fingers and once again did that disgusting little trick where the mouth of the mantis form opened and the head of a pretty young girl emerged, smiling. 'Of course,' she said, looking at Deirdre. 'I should have thought of it sooner.'

Deirdre tilted her head. Blades whispered murderously against one another at the gesture. 'Of what?'

'The entire strength of this plan is predicated upon attacking the child, not the Archive,' Tessa said, her smile turning vicious. 'Ignore the girl. Bring me the Hellhound.'

32

It took me about a second to see what Mantis Bitch had in mind, and half that long to hate her for it.

Ivy didn't have a family. Until I'd given one to her, she hadn't even had a name. She'd just been 'the Archive.' What she had was a world of power and responsibility and knowledge and danger – and Kincaid. While the Archive would know that the proper decision would be to allow Kincaid to die in order to protect the sanctity of the Archive, *Ivy* wouldn't be making the decision with the same detached calm. Kincaid was the closest thing she had to family. She wouldn't let them hurt him. She couldn't.

Damn them, to take a little girl's loneliness and use it against her like that.

Grand schemes and sweeping plans to bring doom and darkness are all fine and scary, but they at least have the advantage of being impersonal. This was simple, calculated, cruel malice deliberately aimed at a child – a *child* – and it pissed me off.

Deirdre was closest. Fine.

I stepped out of the ferns, swept my staff in a broad back-handed swing, and unleashed some of the power I'd been painfully holding back, snarling, *'Ventas servitas!'*

A burst of wind gathered underneath Deirdre, lifting her out of the amphitheater seats and throwing her out over the pool like a dart shot from a child's air gun. I'd thrown her at the nearest section of the pentagram's beam, but the instant she'd gone airborne those snakelike strips of her hair had fanned out like a tattered parachute and begun thrashing at the air, slowing her and changing her course.

I didn't stop to watch where she landed. Magog spun before

Deirdre's feet were more than a yard off the ground and broke into one of those diagonal simian charges, coming right up the bleachers as smoothly as if they'd been level ground. Forget what I'd said about not reacting quickly. Magog's reaction time had been nothing, if not a little less. He had to have checked in at seven or eight hundred pounds, and he covered the forty feet between us in the space of a couple of seconds, the acceleration incredible.

Of course, reacting quickly isn't always the same thing as reacting intelligently. Magog looked like he was used to being an unstoppable force.

I brought up my shield bracelet, slamming my will through it, pushing most of the painful load of power still remaining to me into the barrier that sprang to life. I shouted out in wordless challenge, my voice thin and strained beside the deep-chested bellow that Magog unleashed in answer. Normally my shield manifests as a shimmering dome of mixed blue and silver light.

This time I left it transparent, on the theory that what Magog didn't know would hurt him. The shapeshifted Denarian slammed into the invisible barrier in an explosion of silver sparks and found it as immovable as the side of a mountain. The force of the gorilla-thing's charge was not simply physical, though, and ugly red light clung to the silver power of my defenses. Excess energy bled through my bracelet as heat, scalding my skin – but the barrier held, and Magog staggered back, stunned.

'Hey,' I said as I let the shield fall. 'Where's an eight-hundred-pound gorilla sit?' I took a step forward and kicked him as hard as I could, right in the coconuts, then followed up with a stomping kick to the neck. Magog shrieked in agony and went tumbling back down the bleachers. 'Somewhere with lots of extra cushions, I guess, eh, Monkeyboy?'

My instincts screamed a warning at me, and I threw myself down behind the last row of bleacher seats just as Mantis Bitch pointed a finger at me and screamed, '*Amal-bijal!*' There was a crash of thunder, a flash of light, a wash of heat, and a cloud of glowing splinters flew up a few feet away, where a section of seating had been a second before.

Hell's bells. A sorceress. A damned dangerous one, too.

I readied my shield, already acutely aware of how little energy remained to me. I kept it small, maybe three feet across, and had started to rise when I saw a shape flit into my peripheral vision above me: Tessa, in the middle of an airborne leap. She cried out again, and I yelped and pulled into a tight fetal curl behind my shield as another bolt of lightning ripped through the air.

Pressure slammed my shoulders against concrete floor. Light blinded me, and sound deafened me, leaving my world nothing but one long white tone. My lungs forgot their job for a couple of seconds, but my legs were on the ball, scrambling to get beneath me.

I had just managed to sort out where I was when another deafening flash and crack hit somewhere close and flung me to the ground again. And then a third. I tried to keep my shield up, but I couldn't *see* anything but yellow spots, and there wasn't anything left to put into it, anyway. It was like walking along and suddenly finding myself without any floor – which happened more literally a second later, when I tripped over a bleacher seat and fell a couple of rows down, banging myself up pretty well in the process.

Some dazed part of me realized that I'd made a mistake in my assumptions. Tessa wasn't trying to take me out. She was just trying to keep me dazed and disoriented long enough for her people to arrive. That same part of me realized, even more belatedly, that I'd let myself be goaded into attacking by their words, let my heart rule my decision instead of playing it smart.

Something slapped my staff out of my hand. I went for my gun, only to be slammed to the ground by another terrific physical force. Then something like an iron bar slammed across my throat.

The light spots began to clear away in time for me to see a

Denarian I'd never seen before atop me, this one like an androgynous, naked, bald statue of obsidian, green eyes glowing above human eyes of bright blue. A second shapeshifted creature, this one covered in a shaggy coat of grey, dusty-looking feathers, its face a grey mass of fleshy, hanging tendrils, had my wrists pinned to the ground.

Tessa stood over me, watching something on the far side of the room, her eyes narrowed. 'Don't choke him out,' she snapped. 'He can't talk if he's unconscious.'

The obsidian statue eased up the pressure on my neck a little.

'Report,' Tessa said.

'We think the Hellhound is hiding in the bathrooms,' came a strained-sounding, harsh woman's voice.

'You think?'

'Varthiel and Ordiel are down and McKullen is dead. They were searching there. The exit is watched. There's no way for him to escape the room.'

'Their coins?' Tessa asked.

'Recovered, my lady.'

'Thank you, Rosanna. Any other word?'

'We've found Thorned Namshiel, unconscious and gravely wounded. There was extensive damage all around the area in which he fell.'

'Yes. And yet it was done fairly quietly. It seems our intelligence on our young wizard thug was faulty.'

Someone, presumably Mantis Bitch, kicked me in the ribs. It hurt. There wasn't much I could do about it other than try to suck in a breath.

'Very well,' Tessa said. 'Take Magog and Deirdre for the Hellhound. Take him alive. Do it within the next five minutes.'

'Yes, my lady,' Rosanna rasped. What sounded like hooves clopped away.

Tessa stepped into view again, sweetly pretty face visible atop the monstrous body. She was smiling. 'You're all kinds of feisty, boy. It's cute. The sort of thing my husband likes in his recruits.' She kicked me again. 'I find it endlessly annoying, personally.

But I'm willing to play nice, since we might work together in the future. I'll give you this chance to cooperate. Tell me where the little girl is.'

'I wish I knew,' I panted. 'That way I could exercise free will while telling you to go fuck yourself.'

She let out a playful little laugh and reached down to tweak my broken nose.

Okay.

Ow.

'They say to give a man three chances to say no,' she said.

'Save us both time and breath,' I said. 'No, twice. That's three.'

'Suit yourself,' Tessa said.

She reached into the pocket of my duster, withdrew my revolver, pointed it at my head, and pulled the trigger.

I had just enough time to gawk and think, *Wait, wait, this isn't right.*

The muzzle flashed.

There was a loud noise.

I reached for power, tried to shield, but there was simply nothing there, nothing to use. The magic was *gone*.

So it had to be someone else's spell that neatly intersected the bullet's course and bounced it into the shaggy-feathered thing holding my arms.

My stomach sank as I realized what was happening.

Ivy must have been there all along, quietly sitting on the bleachers, hidden by her veil from everything that was going on. Now she stood perhaps ten feet away, just a young girl, her expression solemn – but her eyes and cheeks were bright with tears.

'Get away from him,' she said quietly. 'All of you. I will not permit you to hurt him.'

I hadn't really extended my line of thinking beyond Kincaid. But of all the people who had dealt with the Archive, I'd been one of the only ones to take any interest in her as anything but a font of knowledge. I'd been the one to inquire after her personally. I'd been the one to give her a name. Sad but true, I was the closest thing that little girl had to a friend.

She couldn't have let anything happen to me, either.

I'd just handed her to the Denarians.

Tessa threw back her head and loosed a long, triumphant cry.

33

'Ivy,' I said in that tone you use with children who are up past their bedtime. I'm better at it than you'd think, after so much time working with an apprentice. 'Get that veil back up and get out of here.'

Tessa kicked me in the ribs again, hard enough to keep me from breathing much or talking at all. 'When I want an opinion from you, Dresden,' she said, 'I'll read it in your entrails.'

Ivy took two steps forward at Tessa's gesture and narrowed her blue eyes. 'For the benefit of the slow, Polonius Lartessa, I will repeat myself. I will not allow you to harm him. Step away.'

Tessa's eyes narrowed suddenly. 'You know my name.'

'I know everything about you, Lartessa,' Ivy said, her tone flat, passionless. 'It was all recorded, of course. Everything was, in Thessalonica in those days. Your father's failing business. Your sale to the temple of Isis. If you like, I could draw you a cost-benefit analysis of your training versus your earnings in your first year at the temple, before Nicodemus came. I could use charts to make it easier for you to understand. And color them in with crayons. I enjoy crayons.'

I wasn't certain, but it sounded like the kid was trying to give the bad guys some guff on my behalf. She needed to work on her technique, but it was the thought that counted. If I could breathe, I might have gotten a little choked up.

'Do you think I'm intimidated that you know where I come from, child?' Tessa snarled.

'I know more about you than you do,' Ivy replied, her voice steady. 'I know far more precisely than you how many you've harmed. How many bad situations you've made worse. Cambodia,

Colombia, and Rwanda most recently, but whether in this century, the Wars of the Roses or the Hundred Years' War, your story is the same stupid little story, told over and over again. You learned your lessons when you were a child, and you've never swerved from them. You're a vulture, Lartessa. A maggot. You survive on diseased flesh and rotting meat. Anything whole and healthy frightens you.'

The little girl didn't see the Denarian that came creeping through the ferns behind her and flung itself at her back, several hundred pounds of scales and fangs.

'Ivy!' I choked out.

She had it covered. There was a flash of light, an overwhelming scent of ozone and fresh laundry, and a silver denarius rolled away from a mound of ash that fell to the ground without ever getting within three feet of the small form of the Archive. The coin rolled past her, on a straight line toward Tessa – but Ivy stomped on it with one small shoe, flattening it to the floor and preventing it from returning to Tessa's grasp.

'Tiny,' I said, in an overblown imitation of Sanya's Russian accent, unable to keep a crazed giggle out of my voice. 'But *fierce*.'

Tessa regarded the fallen coin with a faint smile. 'Costly. How many such spells do you think you can manage before you are out of energy, little one?'

Ivy shrugged. 'How many minions can you throw away? How many will be willing to die for you?'

Tessa called out, 'Around her, everyone. Make sure she knows where you are.'

And nightmarish forms rose around the little girl, huge beside her single, slender little form. Deirdre, soaked and smelling of dead fish and seawater, gave me a sullen glare as she mounted the steps beside her mother. The shaggy-feathered thing that still held my hands bled quietly, keening under its breath. It was wounded, but it still kept my arms pinned. Magog came monkeying up over a bit of landscaping, grinning an evil grin, and I wondered where the hell Kincaid had wandered off to.

The obsidian statue shifted its weight, keeping one hand resting on my chest – I had the feeling it could have shoved it right through to my spine if it wanted to.

There were half a dozen others. Rosanna proved to be a rather beautiful-looking woman, the classical demoness with scarlet skin and a goat's legs, complete with leathery black wings and delicately curling horns – though her deep brown eyes were haunted beneath the demonic green glowing set. She had a bag slung on a strap over her shoulder, just like Spinyboy – Tessa had called him Thorned Namshiel – had carried with him. Most of the others just looked big and mean, in various unsettling flavors.

I guess even in Hell, it's easier to find strong backs than strong brains.

Ivy faced them and lifted her arms into a pose that vaguely resembled a defensive martial arts stance. It wasn't. She was preparing to manipulate defensive energies. I just hadn't ever seen anyone getting ready to do two entirely separate spells in either hand at the same freaking time before.

Two questions occurred to me at that point. First, if the plan was for the Denarians to wear Ivy's magic down and then take her by main force before their trap ran out of power, why weren't they doing it already? And second . . .

What was that hissing sound?

It rose up around us, something I could just barely hear until I focused my senses on it, tuning out the musty reek and iron blood-scent of Shaggy Feathers and the cold solidity of Obsidian Statue's hand.

A definite, steady hissing sound, like air escaping from a tire or . . .

Or hairspray issuing forth from a can.

I lifted my head, twisting around enough to see through the crouched limbs of Shaggy Feathers, which seemed to be neither arms or legs, but something that served it as both, like the extremities of a spider. I couldn't see what it had my wrists pinned with, and I didn't want to. What I *could* see was a couple of leaves trembling on a nearby fern, and a gleam of metal from somewhere near the source of the mysterious hiss.

Gas.

The entire strength of this plan is predicated upon attacking the child, not the Archive.

Children have very low body mass, compared to adults.

A toxin dispersed in the air would be far more effective against Ivy than one of the Denarians – or even a grown person. All the bad guys had to do was pick something that caused unconsciousness and skewed heavily toward body mass, and they'd have an ideal weapon to use against her. Tessa and Nicodemus must have had several of their more capable lackeys carry in canisters of the stuff, whatever it was. Then all they had to do was open the cans and wait for her to fall.

My thoughts flashed back to Thorned Namshiel's spell, the one he'd been carrying out behind his concealing veil. A detail I'd barely noticed at the time suddenly leapt out at me. I'd been worried about what spell he was getting ready. I should have been paying attention to *where* he was getting ready to cast it – directly underneath a set of large vents. He'd probably been getting ready to set a wind spell in motion, to keep air pumping through the vents and spreading the gas through the Oceanarium.

Could I smell something sort of mediciney? Had the end of my nose gone numb? *Hell's bells, Harry, this is no time either to panic or to suddenly pass out.* I had to warn Ivy.

I turned my head back toward her and caught Tessa's gaze halfway. 'Worked it out, did you?' Mantis Girl murmured. 'If he speaks,' she said, presumably to Obsidian Statue, 'crush his chest.'

A weirdly modulated voice issued from the general area of the androgynous statue's head. 'Yes, mis—'

And then there was a *whup* and a slap of air pressure against my skin, and Statue's head – and Shaggy Feathers's too – exploded in simultaneous eruptions of distinctly different forms of gore. The statue went out like some kind of faulty street-paving machine, splattering black sludge that looked like hot asphalt everywhere in a steadily spurting stream. It flung itself onto its back, then bounded to its hands and knees and started hammering its fists at the concrete. I guess it intended to smash me. I guess without a head, it didn't know that it was actually six feet away, and digging a hole through the bleachers and into the material beneath.

Shaggy Feathers just fell in a welter of very human-looking, -smelling, and -tasting blood, and maybe three hundred pounds of limp, rubbery muscle landed on my chest.

'Ivy!' I screamed. 'Gas! Get clear!'

And *then* things got noisy.

A series of cracking thumps came down faster than you could rapidly snap your fingers, and Denarians began to scream in pain and rage. I was vaguely aware of them bounding left and right, and saw a muzzle flash from the far side of the Oceanarium. At least I knew where Kincaid had been – getting into a position to kill *both* demon-taken madmen holding me down with a single freaking bullet, since anything less would have meant my certain death.

'He is nothing!' howled Tessa. 'Tarsiel, take the Hellhound! Everyone else, the girl!'

Come on, Harry. Time to pay Kincaid back by getting the kid clear. Somehow. My right hand wasn't moving much, and my singed left arm didn't like it, but I heaved and strained and got enough of the dead Denarian off me to let me begin to squirm out from under it. Just as I was about to pull free, a silver coin rolled out from amidst the ruined tentacles that had passed for the thing's head and dropped toward my face. I jerked my head aside in a panic.

The falling coin missed touching my bare flesh by a hair and bounced off the concrete floor. My left hand moved, faster and smoother than I would have thought possible, snapping the coin from the air on the bounce as smoothly and nimbly as if it had been whole and healthy and not burned and scarred and covered in a leather glove.

I looked between it and my numb-tingling right hand for a quarter of a second.

What. The hell.

That was *not* normal.

Worry about it later, Harry. I mean, sure, obviously Something Has Happened to you, but now is not the time to get distracted. Focus. Save the girl.

I jammed the cursed relic in my pocket, hoped to God my 501s didn't have a hole in them, and spun toward Ivy.

I know I'm a wizard, a card-carrying member of the White Council and all. I know I'm a Warden, a certified combat expert of wizardkind, a cop, a soldier – have staff, will kick ass, if you will. I thought I'd seen some real professionals in action, the top of the wizarding game.

I was wrong.

It wasn't that Ivy was slinging around a ton of power. She wasn't. But think about this one for a moment: What's really more impressive? A giant truck rumbling around on a great big old smoking engine? Or a little car just barely big enough to get the job done that's powered by a couple of AA batteries?

Seven of them were going after Ivy with magic, and she was countering them. All of them.

Magog had charged her as he had me, but she hadn't slammed him to a stop with a brick wall. She'd trapped him inside some kind of frictionless bubble, and he was spinning uselessly in circles half an inch off the floor, every motion making him spin faster. Whatever additional metaphysical mass he'd brought to the fight hadn't cramped her style much. Her arms, bobbing and weaving continuously between all the workings she had up, flicked by the field containing him every few seconds and, I swear, struck his whirling snare for no reason other than to impart an additional, nausea-inducing vector to his spin.

Deirdre's tangle of living locks danced with purple Saint Elmo's fire, lashing out in a deadly webwork, but Ivy constantly cast out a spinning cat's cradle of light, tiny, tiny threads of power that did not so much stop any of Deirdre's attacks as they fouled any one of her locks with others near it, tangling them together into useless clumps – sort of an enforced bad-hair day. On the opposite side of Ivy, Rosanna launched more traditional lances of flame from her open palms, much like the ones I—

—a savage pain went through my skull for a second – *son of a bitch*—

—but Ivy dispersed them with delicately applied wedges of air, intercepting each burst of fire far enough short of her body to prevent the bloom of heat as they died from scorching her – though the two more physical Denarians who strained to force their way past the barrier of snapping sparks that formed whenever they tried to get close had far less luck. The Hellmaid's flames scorched them badly.

The sixth, a wizened little thing that looked like a caricature of a woman carved from a dried tree root, seemed to be holding the end of a rope of liquid shadow that curled like a hungry serpent, darting now and then toward Ivy's head. Ivy faced it down steadily, moving her head calmly in a dodge once, swatting it aside with a little burst of silver energy a second later.

But mostly she faced an amused-looking Tessa, who, apparently just for the fun of it, threw another thunderbolt at her now and again. That told me something right there. It told me Tessa was no punk sorceress. She was White Council material herself, if she could make that much flash and bang while expending that little energy. Either that or she'd been able to hold back one whale of a lot more power than I had when she took her deep breath before the battle. Either way she was a big-leaguer, and Ivy's response to the attack confirmed it. Each time the Archive turned to fully face Tessa, and each time she dedicated one of her hands entirely to the defensive measure used to stop the incoming spell.

Gulp.

Holy moly. It was one thing to have an academic appreciation that I still had a lot to learn about magic. It was another to see a demonstration of exactly how much I still couldn't do. In another circumstance it would be humbling. In this one it was freaking terrifying. For maybe ten seconds I stood there, trying to figure out how the hell to help without getting myself incinerated, skewered, or otherwise obliterated without accomplishing anything.

I felt a little surge of dizziness. The gas levels must be rising. *Screw it.* The only reason someone hadn't killed me already was because I was so impotent, at the moment, that nobody gave a damn what I did. I might be able to get the kid to another part of the building, out of the gas – and if someone killed me on the way, I could try to level my death curse on them, maybe get her out of this mess.

So I rushed toward her, trying to use the hot zone and the trapped Magog as shields, and said, 'Ivy, come on!'

Something took a swipe at me, and several feet away my gun went off. I ducked, but I guess Tessa wasn't much of a shot. I didn't get hit. A second later I grabbed Ivy by the waist and lifted her to my hip.

'Keep clear of my arms, please!' Ivy commanded.

I made sure to. I was getting dizzier, but anywhere was better than here.

'His legs!' Tessa commanded.

I had a feeling that those people tried to do a lot of disturbing things to my pins, but I didn't stop to watch them try it. I ran for the stairs, trusting the skill of the Archive to keep me mobile. It was a good bet. Ivy murmured and waved her arms the whole while, and I felt her little body tingling with the live current of the energy she was working.

She was using what power she had left for all it was worth, but it wasn't bottomless. She was running dry. This fight was almost over.

Time, I thought muzzily, panting. We just needed a little more time.

Gravity suggested that I keep on going down, and it seemed an excellent idea. I staggered down the stairs into the lower level, running past the underwater vistas of the whale and dolphin tanks, past the cute penguins and the sea otters, the Denarians in pursuit, their sorceries flashing past us while Ivy shielded us with the last bits of energy in her reservoir. I felt it when she ran dry, and labored to keep my legs moving, to keep ahead of the pursuit.

Then the ground hit me with an uppercut. Everyone else in the Oceanarium suddenly fell sideways.

Or wait. Maybe it was me.

I realized belatedly that, given that I'd been at ground level near that one container, and breathing hard with pain and exertion to boot, I'd probably given myself a nice large dose before I'd ever gotten up. Furthermore, if the gas was heavier than air, there was probably even more of it down here than there had been up in the bleachers.

I had bought us a few seconds. It just hadn't been time enough.

Ivy landed beside me. She blinked, and her eyes abruptly went wide with panic. She lifted her arms again, but they came up slowly, sluggishly, and her fingers stayed half-closed, like a sleepy child's.

The black rope-spell wrapped around Ivy's throat, and dozens of Deirdre's tendrils twined around her arms and legs. They jerked her out of my sight.

I looked up to find the Denarians standing as a group in the hallway, lit by the eerie blue light coming in from the big tanks. Rosanna stared intently at Ivy for a moment before she shuddered and folded her dark bat wings around herself, shivering as if with cold, and turned away from the scene, her glowing eyes narrowed. She reached into the bag and produced another canister. She offered it to Tessa without being prompted.

Tessa took it, twisted something on the nozzle, and gave Ivy a polite smile. Then she quite literally jammed the nozzle into the little girl's mouth and held it there.

Ivy panicked and cried out. I saw her kick and twist. She must have bitten her tongue or cut her lip on one of her teeth. Blood ran from her mouth. She bucked and fought uselessly for a few seconds, and then went rag-doll limp.

'Finally,' Tessa said, expelling her breath in irritation. 'Could it have been any more annoying?'

'Damn you,' I slurred. I shoved myself up to one knee and glared at Tessa. 'Damn you all. You can't have her.'

'Clichéd,' Tessa singsonged. 'Boring.' She tapped her chin with one claw-hand. 'Let me see. Where were we when we were so rudely interrupted? Ah!' She stepped closer, smiling cheerily, and lifted my .44.

Just then, I felt the snap of magic rushing back into the Oceanarium as the enormous symbol collapsed and the circle fell.

I took my frustration and rage and turned it into raw force, screaming, '*Forzare!*'

I didn't direct it at Tessa and her crew.

I aimed it at the glass wall that was the only thing between all of us and three million gallons of seawater.

The force of my will and my rage lashed out and shattered the wall into powder.

The sea came in with a roar, one enormous impact that felt like the strike of a hammer being applied to every square inch of my body at once.

Then it was cold.

And black.

34

The next thing I knew, I was coughing, and my chest hurt, and my head hurt, and everything else hurt, and I was colder than hell. I choked in a breath and felt my body getting ready to send up everything. I tried to roll onto my side and couldn't, until someone pulled on my coat and helped me.

Fishy salt water and whatever had been in my stomach came out in equal proportions.

'Oh,' someone said. 'Oh, thank You, God.'

Michael, then.

'Michael!' Sanya shouted from somewhere nearby. 'I need you!'

Work boots pounded away at a sprint.

'Easy, Harry,' Murphy said. 'Easy.' She helped me turn back over when I was done puking. I was lying at the top of the stairs to the lower level. My lower legs were actually on the stairs. My left foot was in cold water to the ankle.

I put a hand to my chest, wincing. Murphy smoothed a hand over my head, brushing hair and water away from my eyes. The lines in her face looked a little deeper, her eyes worried.

'CPR?' I asked her. My voice felt weak.

'Yeah.'

'Guess we're even,' I said.

'Like hell we are,' she said quietly. 'I only spit fruit punch into *your* mouth.'

I laughed weakly, and that hurt, too.

Murphy leaned down and rested her forehead gently against mine. 'You are such an enormous pain in my ass, Harry. Don't scare me like that again.'

Her fingers found mine and squeezed really tight. I squeezed back, too tired to do anything else.

Something brushed my foot, and I nearly screamed. I sat up, reaching for power, raising my right hand, while invisible force gathered around it in shimmering waves.

A corpse floated in the water, nude, facedown. It was a man I'd never seen before, his hair long, grey, and matted. His limp, outstretched hand had bumped against my foot.

'Jesus, Harry,' Murphy said, her voice shaking. 'He's dead. Harry, it's okay. He's dead, Harry.'

My right hand remained where it was, fingers outspread, ripples of light flickering over them. Then they started shaking. I lowered my hand again, releasing the power I'd gathered, and as I did I felt my fingers tingle and go numb once more.

I stared at them, puzzled. That wasn't right. I was fairly sure that I should be a lot more worried about that than I was at the moment, but I couldn't put together enough cohesive thought to remember why.

Murphy was still talking, her voice steady and soothing. I dimly realized, a minute later, that it was the tone of voice you use with crazy people and frightened animals, and that I was breathing hard and fast despite the lack of any exertion to explain it.

'It's all right, Harry,' she said. 'He's dead. You can let go of me.'

That was when I realized that my left arm had pulled Murphy tight against me, drawing her across my body and away from the corpse as I'd gotten ready to do . . . whatever it was I had been about to do. She was, at the moment, more or less sitting across my lap. Wherever she was touching me, I was warm. It took me a moment to figure out exactly why it was a good idea to let her go. Eventually, though, I did.

Murphy slid carefully away from me, shaking her head. 'God,' she said. 'What happened to you, Harry? What did they do to you?'

I slumped, too tired to move my foot out of the water, too tired to try to explain that I'd failed to stop the demons from carrying away a little girl.

After a moment of silence Murphy said, 'That's it. I'm getting you to a doctor. I don't care who these people think they are. They can't just waltz into town and tear apart my—' She broke off suddenly. 'Hngh. What do you make of this, Harry?'

She took a step down into the water and bent over.

'No!' I snapped.

She froze in place.

'Jesus, those things get predictable,' I muttered. 'Silver coin just fall out of the corpse's fingers?'

Murphy blinked and looked at me. 'Yes.'

'Evil. Cursed. Don't touch it.' I shook my head and stood up. The wall had to help me, but I made it all the way up, thinking out loud on the way. 'Okay, we've got to make sure there's no more of these lying around, first thing. I'm already carrying one. We limit the risk. I carry them all for now. Until they can be properly disposed of.'

'Harry,' Murphy said in a steady voice. 'You're mumbling, and what's coming through is making a limited amount of sense.'

'I'll explain. Bear with me.' I bent over and found another stained denarius gleaming guiltily in the water. 'Moron,' I muttered at the coin, then picked it up with my gloved hand and put it in my pocket along with the other one. *In for a penny, in for a pound, ah hah hah.*

Damn, I'm clever.

Footsteps sounded, brisk and precise, and Luccio walked into view beside Gard. There was a subtle difference in Gard's body language toward Luccio, something a shade more respectful than was there before. The captain of the Wardens was wiping her sword clean on her grey cloak – blood wouldn't stain it, which made it handy for such things. Luccio paused for a moment upon seeing me, her expression carefully guarded, then nodded. 'Warden. How are you feeling?'

'I'll live,' I rasped. 'What happened?'

'Two Denarians,' Gard replied. She nodded her head briefly to Luccio. 'Both dead.'

Luccio shook her head. 'They'd been half-drowned,' she said.

'I only finished them off. I shouldn't have liked to fight them fresh.'

'Take me to the bodies,' I said quietly. 'Hurry.'

There was a sighing sound from behind us. I didn't freak out about it this time, but Murphy did, her gun appearing in her hand. To be fair, Luccio had her sword half out of its sheath, too. I checked and found what I'd more or less expected: The body of the former Denarian, relieved of its coin, was decomposing with unnatural speed, even in the cold water. The Fallen angel in the coin might have been holding off the ravages of time, but the old man with the hourglass is patient, and he was collecting his due from the fallen Denarian with compounded interest.

'Captain, we've got to get every single coin we possibly can, and we've got to do it now.'

Luccio cocked her head at me. 'Why?'

'Look, I don't know what arrangements Kincaid made, but somebody is going to notice something soon, and then emergency services will be all over this place. I don't want some poor fireman or cop accidentally picking up one of these things.'

'True enough,' she said, nodding – and then glanced at Murphy. 'Sergeant, do you concur?'

Murphy grimaced. 'Dammit, there's always something. . . .' She held up her hands as if pushing away a blanket that was wrapped too tightly around her and said, 'Yes, yes. Round them up.'

'Michael,' I said. 'Sanya?'

'When we got here,' Murphy said, 'a bunch of those things were pulling you out of the water.'

'They ran. We went different directions, pursuing them,' Gard supplied.

'Where's Cujo?' I asked.

Gard gave me a blank look.

'Hendricks.'

'Ah,' she said. 'Lookout. He'll give us a warning when the authorities begin to arrive.'

At least someone was thinking like a criminal. I suppose she was the right person for the job.

I raised my voice as much as I could. It came out sort of furry and rough. 'Michael?'

'Here,' came the answer. He came walking around the curving path toward us a few moments later, wearing only his undershirt beneath his heavy denim jacket. I hadn't seen him wearing that little before. Michael had some serious pecs. Maybe I should work out. He was carrying with both hands part of his blue-and-white denim shirt folded into a careful bundle in front of him.

Sanya came along behind Michael, soaking wet, his chest bare underneath his coat. Never mind Michael's pecs. Sanya made us both look like we needed to eat more wheat germ or something. He was carrying *Esperacchius* and *Amoracchius* over one shoulder – and Kincaid over the other.

Kincaid wasn't moving much, though he was clearly trying to support some of his weight. His skin was chalk white. He was covered in blood. The rest of Michael's shirt, and both of Sanya's, had been pressed into service as emergency bandages – and layers of duct tape had been wrapped around and around them, sealing them into place around both arms, over his belly, and around one leg.

Murphy hissed and went to him, her voice raw. 'Jared.'

Jared. Huh.

'Dresden.' Kincaid gasped. 'Dresden.'

They laid him down, and I shambled over. I managed not to fall down on him as I knelt beside him. I'd seen him wounded before, but it hadn't been as bad as this. He'd used the tape the same way, though. I checked. Sure enough, there was a roll of tape hanging from a loop on Kincaid's equipment harness.

'Just like the vampire lair,' I said quietly.

'No claymores here,' Kincaid said. 'Should have had claymores.' He shook his head and blinked his eyes a couple of times, trying to focus them. 'Dresden, not much time. The girl. They got out with her. She's alive.'

I grimaced and looked away.

His bloody hand shot out and seized the front of my coat. '*Look* at me.'

I did.

I expected rage, hate, and blame. All I got was a look of . . . just, desperate, desperate fear.

'Go after them. Bring her back. Save her.'

'Kincaid . . .' I said softly.

'Swear it,' he said. His eyes went out of focus for a second, then glittered coldly. 'Swear it. Or I'm coming for you. Swear it to me, Dresden.'

'I'm too damned tired to be scared of you,' I said.

Kincaid closed his eyes. 'She doesn't have anybody else. No one.'

Murphy knelt down by Kincaid across from me. She stared at me for a moment, then said quietly, 'Jared, rest. He's going to help her.'

I traded a faint, tired smile with Murphy. She knows me.

'But—' Kincaid began.

She leaned down and kissed his forehead, blood and all. 'Hush. I promise.'

Kincaid subsided. Or passed out. One of the two.

'Dresden, get out of the way,' Gard said in a patient voice.

'Don't tell me you're a doctor,' I said.

'I've seen more battlefield injuries than any bone-saw-flourishing mortal hack,' Gard said. 'Move.'

'Harry,' Murph said, her voice tight. 'Please.'

I creaked to my feet and shambled over to Michael and Sanya, who stood looking out at the dolphins and the little whales in the big pool. The water level had dropped seven or eight feet, and the residents were giving the newly inundated area of the pool a wide berth. If the presence of the rotting thing behind me made the water feel anything like the air was starting to smell, I couldn't blame them.

'He looks pretty bad,' I told them.

Michael shook his head, his eyes distant. 'It isn't his time yet.'

I spocked an eyebrow and gave him a look. Sanya gave him one very nearly as dubious as mine.

Michael glanced at me and then back out at the water. 'I asked.'

'Uh-huh,' I said quietly.

Sanya smiled faintly and shook his head.

I glanced at him. 'Still agnostic, huh?'

'Some things I am willing to take on faith,' Sanya said with a shrug.

'Luccio took down two,' I told Michael. 'What's the count?' I didn't need to be any more specific than that.

Sanya's grin broadened. 'That is the good news.'

I turned to face Sanya. 'Those assholes just carried off a child that they plan to torture into accepting a Fallen angel,' I said quietly. 'There isn't any good news.'

The big Russian's expression sobered. 'Good is where you find it,' he seriously.

'Eleven,' Michael said quietly.

I blinked at him. 'What?'

'Eleven,' he repeated. 'Eleven of them fell here today. Judging from the wounds, Kincaid killed five of them. Captain Luccio killed two more. Sanya and I caught a pair on the way out. One of them was carrying a bag with the coins of those who had already fallen.'

'We found the coin of Urumviel, which we knew to be in possession of a victim,' Sanya said, 'but we were short by one body.'

'That one was mine,' I said. 'He's tiny pieces of soot and ash now. And that only brings us to ten.'

'One more drowned when that tank collapsed,' Michael said. 'They're floating down there. Eleven of them, Harry.' He shook his head. 'Eleven. Do you realize what this means?'

'That if we whack one more, we get the complimentary steak knives?'

He turned to me, his eyes intent and bright. 'Tessa escaped with only four other members of her retinue, and Nicodemus was nowhere to be found. We have recovered thirteen coins already — and eleven more today, assuming we can find them all.'

'Only six coins remain free to do harm,' Sanya said. 'Only six. Those six are the last. And they are all *here* in Chicago. Together.'

'The Fallen in the coins have been waging a war for the minds and lives of mankind for two thousand years, Harry,' Michael said. 'And we have fought them. That war could end. It could all be *over*.' He turned back to the pool and shook his head, his expression that of a man baffled. 'I could go to Alicia's softball games. Teach little Harry to ride a bicycle. I could build *houses*, Harry.'

The longing in his voice was so thick, I could practically feel it brushing against my face.

'Let's round up the coins and get out of here before the flashing lights show up,' I said quietly. 'Michael, open up the bundle.'

He frowned at me but did, revealing disks of tarnished silver. I drew the pair of coins I'd found from my pocket with my gloved hand and added them to the pile. 'Thanks,' I said. 'Let's get moving.'

I turned and walked away as Michael folded the cloth closed around the coins again, his eyes distant, presumably focused on some dream of shoving those coins down a deep, dark hole and living a boring, simple, normal life with his wife and kids.

I let him have it while he could.

I was going to have to take that dream away from him, dammit.

Whether he wanted to go along with the idea or not.

35

I slept in the cab of Michael's truck all the way back to his place, leaning against the passenger-side window. Sanya had the middle seat. I was dimly aware that they were speaking quietly to each other on the way home, but their voices were just low rumbles, especially Sanya's, and I tuned them out until the truck crunched to a halt.

'It doesn't matter,' Michael was saying in a patient voice. 'Sanya, we don't recruit members. We're not a chapter of the Masons. It's got to be a calling.'

'We act in the interests of God on a daily basis,' Sanya said in a reasonable voice. 'If He is being slow to call a new wielder for *Fidelacchius*, perhaps it is a subtle hint that He wishes us to take on the responsibility for ourselves.'

'Don't you keep assuring me you are undecided on whether or not God exists?' Michael asked.

'I am speaking to you in your idiom, to make you comfortable,' Sanya said. 'She would make a good Knight.'

Michael sighed. 'Perhaps the reason no new wielder has been called is because our task is nearly complete. Perhaps one isn't needed.'

Sanya's voice turned dry. 'Yes. Perhaps all evil, everywhere, is about to be destroyed forever and there will be no more need for the strength to protect those who cannot protect themselves.' He sighed. 'Or perhaps . . .' he began, glancing at me. He saw me blinking my eyes open and hurriedly said, 'Dresden. How are you feeling?'

'Nothing a few days in a hospital, a new set of lungs, a keg of Mac's dark, and a pair of feisty redheads couldn't cure,' I mumbled. I tried for cavalier, but it came out a little flatter and darker than I'd meant it to. 'I'll live.'

Michael nodded and parked the truck. 'When do we go after them?'

'We don't,' I said quietly. 'They've developed some kind of stealth defense against being found or scried upon magically.'

Michael frowned. 'Are you sure?'

'I'm sure it's really hard to defeat someone you can't *find*, Michael.' I rubbed at my eyes and all but slapped my own hand away, it hurt so much. *Ow. Stupid broken nose. Stupid Tessa tweaking it.*

'You need to get some sleep, Harry,' Michael said quietly.

'And perhaps a shower,' Sanya suggested.

'You smell like dolphin water too, big guy,' I shot back.

'But not nearly so much,' he said. 'And I didn't throw up on myself.'

I glowered at him for a second. 'Isn't Sanya a girl's name?'

Michael snorted. 'Get some sleep first, Harry.'

'After,' I said. 'First things first. War council in the kitchen. And if someone doesn't make me a cup of coffee, I'm going to shimmy dry all over everything, like Mouse.'

'Mouse is too polite to do that in my house,' Michael said.

'Like somebody else's dog then,' I said. 'Crap, I forgot my staff.'

Michael swung out of the truck, reached into the bed of the pickup, and lifted my staff out of it. I got out, and he tossed it to me across the back of the truck. I caught it in my left hand and nodded to him. 'Bless you. It's a real pain to make one of these. Way harder to carve out than, uh . . .' I shook my head as my thoughts wandered off-track. 'Sorry. Long day.'

'Get inside before you take a chill,' Michael said quietly.

'Good idea.'

We trooped in. The others arrived over the next twenty minutes or so. Gard had insisted on taking Kincaid by one of Marcone's buildings – probably someplace where he kept medical supplies for those times when he didn't want the police wondering why his employees came in with gunshot or knife wounds. To my amusement, Murphy had insisted on accompanying Kincaid – which meant that the cops were about to learn the location of another of Marcone's secret stashes, maybe even the name of whatever doctor he had on his payroll. And since it was Murphy's car, and Murphy was with me, and Gard needed my help, there wasn't diddly Gard could do about it.

That's my Murphy, manufacturing her own damned silver lining when the clouds didn't cough one up.

Mouse was delighted to see me, and greeted me with much fond twitching and bumping against my legs and tail wagging. He, at least, thought I merely smelled interesting. Molly greeted us with only slightly less enthusiasm, and immediately set about making food for everyone. It turns out that Molly wasn't her mother's daughter in that respect. Charity was like the MacGyver of the kitchen. She could whip up a five-course meal for twelve from an egg, two spaghetti noodles, some household chemicals, and a stick of chewing gum. Molly . . .

Molly once burned my egg. My boiled egg. I don't know how. She could, however, make a mean cup of coffee.

Once Kincaid had been settled down on the guest bed in Charity's sewing room, everyone else gathered in the kitchen. Murphy looked strained. I poured her a cup of joe, and she came to stand next to me. I offered Luccio one as well. She accepted with a small, grateful nod.

'How is he?' she asked Murphy.

'Sleeping,' Murphy said. 'Gard got him some painkillers.'

I guzzled coffee, fighting off a round of chills. 'Okay, people. Here's the situation. We are bent over, greased up, and Nicodemus and his crew are about to drive one of those Japanese bullet trains right up our collective ass.'

The room went quiet.

'They took Ivy,' I said. 'That's bad.'

'Harry,' Murphy said, 'I know I'm the new kid, but you're going to have to explain this thing with the little girl to me again.'

'Ivy is the Archive,' I said quietly. 'A long time ago – we

don't know when – somebody – we don't know who – created the Archive. A kind of intellectual construct.'

'What?' Sanya asked.

'A kind of entity composed of pure information. Think of it as software for the brain,' Luccio said. 'Like a very advanced database management system.'

'Ah,' Sanya said, nodding.

I arched an eyebrow at Luccio in surprise.

She shrugged, smiling a little. 'I like computers. I read all about them. It's . . . my hobby, really. I understand the theory behind them.'

'Right,' I said. 'Ahem. Okay. The Archive is passed from one generation to the next, mother to daughter – all the memories of the previous bearers of the Archive, and all the facts they have gathered.

'All that knowledge makes the Archive powerful – and it was created as a repository of learning, a safeguard against the possibility of a cataclysm of civilization, a loss of all knowledge, the destruction of all learning. It was bound to neutrality, to the preservation and *gathering* of knowledge.'

'Gathering?' Murphy said. 'So . . . the Archive reads a lot?'

'It goes deeper than that,' I said. 'The Archive is a magic so complex that it's practically alive – and it just *knows*. Anything that gets printed or written down, the Archive knows.'

Hendricks said a bad word.

'Sideways,' I agreed. 'That's what Nicky and the Nickelheads have taken.'

'With that kind of information at their disposal,' Murphy said, 'they could . . . My God, they could blackmail officials. Control governments.'

'Launch nuclear warheads,' I said. 'Stop thinking so small.' I nodded at Michael. 'Remember, you told me that Nicodemus was playing Armageddon lotto. He makes big plans, but he plots them out so that he can make an incremental profit along the way. This was just one more scheme.'

Michael frowned. 'He was after the Archive all along? He

deliberately came here and provoked a confrontation to get you to call her in to arbitrate?'

'That isn't much of a plan,' Luccio said. 'You could have chosen any one of a dozen neutral arbiters.'

Murphy snorted. 'But it's Dresden. He's lived in the same apartment since I first met him. Drives the same car. Drinks at that same little pub. Favorite restaurant is Burger King. He gets the same damned meal every time he goes there, too.'

'You can't improve on perfection,' I said. 'That's why it's called perfection. And what's your point?'

'You're a creature of habit, Harry. You don't like change.'

There wasn't much use denying that. 'Even if I hadn't called Ivy, Nicodemus still could realize some gains. Maybe recruit Marcone. Maybe kill off Michael or Sanya. Maybe ditch some deadwood within his own organization. Who knows? The point is, I *did* call Ivy in, he *did* get the opportunity to take her down, and it paid off.'

'But the Archive was created neutral,' Sanya said. 'Constrained. You said so yourself.'

'The Archive was,' I said. 'But Ivy wasn't, and Ivy controls the Archive. She's still a *child*. That child can be hurt. Frightened. Coerced. Tempted.' I rubbed at the spot between my eyes. 'They want to make her one of them. Probably hoping to gobble up Marcone along the way.'

'God help us if they're taken,' Murphy said quietly.

'God help *them* if they're taken,' Michael murmured. 'We have to find them, Harry.'

'Not even Mab could locate the Denarians with magic,' I said. 'Gard. Could your firm do any better?'

She shook her head.

I glanced at Michael. 'I don't suppose anyone's drawn a big flashing arrow in the sky for you two to see?'

Michael shook his head, his expression sober. 'I looked.'

'Okay, then. Barring divine intervention we have no way of finding them.' I took a deep breath. 'So. We're going to make them find us.'

'That would be a good trick if we could do it,' Sanya said. 'What did you have in mind?'

Hendricks lifted his head suddenly. 'Coins.'

Everyone turned to stare at him.

Hendricks counted on his fingers for a second. 'They only got six. And six people. So how they gonna get the creepy little girl a coin? Or one for the boss?'

'Good thinking, Cujo,' I said. 'It'll only hurt for a minute. But we've got to move fast to make it work. Nicodemus can't afford to throw away any more manpower, but his conscience won't hesitate for one itty-bitty second to kill one of his own people for their coin, if it comes to that. So we're going to offer him a trade. Eleven old nickels in exchange for the girl.'

Michael and Sanya both came to their feet in an instant, speaking loudly and in two different languages. It was hard to make out individual words, but the gestalt of their protest amounted to, *Are you out of your mind?*

'Dammit all, Michael!' I said, swinging around to face him, thrusting out my jaw. 'If Nicodemus manages to take the Archive, it won't *matter* how many of the damned coins you have locked away.'

Silence. The clock in the entry hall ticked very loudly.

I didn't back down. 'Right now six demons are torturing an eleven-year-old girl. The same way they tortured me. The same way they tortured Shiro.'

Michael flinched.

'Look me in the eye,' I told him, 'and tell me you think that we should let that child suffer when we have the means to save her.'

Tick, tock.

Tick, tock.

Michael shook his head.

Sanya subsided, sinking back to lean against a cabinet again, his expression pensive and solemn.

'Nicodemus will never accept that trade,' Michael said quietly.

Luccio smiled, showing a lot of teeth. 'Of course he will. Why sacrifice a useful retainer when he can show up for the exchange, double-cross us, steal the coins, and keep the Archive?'

'Bingo,' I said. 'And we'll be ready for him. Captain, do you know how to contact him through the channels outlined in the Accords?'

'Yes,' she said.

'Harry,' Michael said gently, 'we're taking a terrible risk.'

He and Luccio exchanged a glance pregnant with silence, swayed by deep undercurrents.

'At this point,' Luccio said, 'the only riskier thing we can do is . . .' She shrugged and spread her hands. 'Nothing.'

Michael grimaced and crossed himself. 'God be with us.'

'Amen,' Sanya said, winking over Michael's shoulder at me.

'Call Nicodemus,' I said. 'Tell him I want to make a deal.'

36

It takes time to go through channels.

The last thing I wanted to do was get wet again, but I was still freezing, and shaky, and as it turns out, there are a number of other inconvenient and unpleasant side effects to accidentally gulping down gallons of salt water. It's the little things that get to you the most.

It took me a couple of hours to get my system straightened out, get showered, and get horizontal, and by the time I finally did it I was so tired that I could barely focus my eyes. Molly was committing dinner by that time, aided and abetted by Sanya, who seemed to take some kind of grim Russian delight in watching train wrecks in progress. I fell down on the couch to debate whether or not I wanted to risk putting anything else in the pipes, and Rip van Winkled my way right through the danger.

I didn't want to wake up. I was having a dream where I wasn't hurt, and no one was kicking me around. The walls were white and smooth and clean, lit only by frosty moonlight, and someone with a gentle voice was speaking quietly to me. But my right hand had broken into fierce tingling, all pins and needles, and sleep began to retreat. I started to wake slowly. Voices murmured in the room.

'. . . can she possibly be *sure*?' Murphy demanded in a heated whisper.

'It isn't my area of knowledge,' Michael rumbled back. 'Ma'am?'

Luccio's tone was cautious. 'It is a delicate area of the art,' she said. 'But the girl does have a gift.'

'Then we need to say something.'

'You can't,' Molly said, her tone quiet and sad. 'It wouldn't help. It might make things worse.'

'And you know that?' Murphy demanded. 'You know that for a fact?'

I was so tired, I'd probably missed a sentence or three in there. I blinked my eyes open and said muzzily, 'The kid knows what she's talking about.' I fumbled about and found Mouse lying on the floor beside the couch, immediately under my arm. I decided sitting up could wait for a minute. 'What are we talking about?'

Molly gave Murphy a look that said, *There, see?*

Murphy shook her head and said, 'I'm going to see if Kincaid is awake yet.' She left, her expression set in stony displeasure.

Mouse set about industriously licking my right hand, a canine grooming ritual he sometimes pursued. It broke up the pins and needles a bit, so I didn't argue. I still had no idea what was up with my hand. I'd never heard of anything like this happening to anyone – but it wasn't terribly uncomfortable, and all things considered it wasn't anywhere near the top of my priority list at the moment.

Nobody answered my question, though.

The silence got awkward. I coughed uncomfortably. 'Uh. Anyone know what time it is?'

'Almost midnight,' Luccio said quietly.

I waited for a minute, but apparently no one was going to do me a favor and knock me unconscious again, so I did my best to ignore the aches and pains and sat up. 'What's the word from Nicodemus?'

'He hasn't returned our call,' Luccio said.

'Not really a surprise,' I muttered, raking my fingers through my hair. I'd gone to sleep wearing one of Michael's old pairs of sweats and one of his T-shirts, so my ankles stuck way out, and both shirt and sweats fit me as well as a tent. 'Whatever they're doing to keep Ivy restrained, it's got to be pretty elaborate. I'd hold my calls until I was sure it was solid, too.'

'As would I,' Luccio agreed.

'Is she really *that* dangerous?' Michael asked.

'Yes,' Luccio said calmly. 'The Council regards her as a signifi-cant power in her own right, on par with the youngest Queens of the Sidhe Courts.'

'If anything, I think that profile in the Wardens' files under-estimates her,' I said quietly. 'She had barely anything to work with, and she was making Tessa and her crew look like pygmies trying to capture an elephant. If she hadn't been cut off so entirely, I think she'd have eaten them alive.'

Luccio frowned, disturbed. 'Truly?'

'You had to have seen it,' I said. 'I've never seen anyone . . . You had to have seen it.'

'If she's that powerful,' Michael said quietly, 'can she be contained?'

'Oh, yes,' I said. 'Absolutely. But it would take a greater circle – heavy-duty ritual stuff in a prepared location. And it would have to be freaking flawless, or she could break it.'

Molly screwed up her face in distress. 'She won't . . . won't take one of the coins. Will she?' She glanced back and forth between Luccio and me and shrugged a little. 'Because . . . it would be bad if she did.'

I looked at Michael. 'The Fallen can't just jump in and over-whelm someone, can they? Outright, nonconsensual possession?'

'Not normally,' Michael replied. 'There are circumstances that can change that, though. Mentally damaged people can be suscep-tible to it. Other things can open a spirit to possession. Drugs, involvement with dark rituals, extended, deliberate contact with spiritual entities. A few other things.'

'Drugs,' I said tiredly. 'Jesus.'

Michael winced.

'Sorry.'

'Even if a soul is made vulnerable to assault,' Michael said, 'the mind and will can fight against an invasive spirit. Surely the Archive qualifies as a formidable mind and will.'

'Sure. But that doesn't necessarily mean that *Ivy* does. Since she was born she's been the Archive. She's never had a chance to develop her own mind, her own personality.' I stood up, shaking my head, and started to pace restlessly around the room. 'She's going to be helpless, probably for the first time since she could walk. Alone. Scared.' I looked at Michael. 'You think that those . . . people . . . won't know how to terrify a little girl?'

He grimaced and bowed his head.

'And then along comes the Fallen and tells her how it can help her. How it wants to be her friend. How it can make the bad people stop hurting her.' I shook my head and clenched my hands. 'Maybe she'll know the facts. But those facts aren't going to be much comfort to her. They aren't going to *feel* tr—'

I blinked and looked at Michael. Then Molly. Then I stormed past them into the kitchen and grabbed the pad of paper Charity kept stuck to the fridge with a magnet to use to make grocery lists. I found a pencil on top of the fridge and sat down at the kitchen table, writing furiously.

Ivy,

You are not alone.

Kincaid is alive. I'm all right. We're coming after you.

Don't listen to them. Hang on.

We're coming.

You are not alone.

Harry

'Oh,' said Molly, reading over my shoulder. 'That's clever.'

'If it works,' Luccio said. 'Will she know it?'

'I don't know,' I said. 'But I don't know what else I can do.' I rubbed at my forehead. 'Is there any food?'

'I made pot roast,' Molly said.

'But is there any food?'

She swatted me on the back of the head, though not too hard, and went to the refrigerator.

I made a sandwich out of things. I'm an American. We can eat anything as long as it's between two pieces of bread. With enough mustard I almost couldn't taste the roast. For a few minutes I paid attention to eating, and was hungry enough to actually enjoy part of the experience – the part where Molly's pot roast finally terrified my growling stomach into silence.

The phone rang.

Michael answered. He listened for a moment and then said gently, 'It isn't too late to seek redemption. Not even for you.'

Someone laughed merrily on the other end of the phone.

'Just a moment,' Michael said a breath later. He turned, holding his hand over the phone, and said, 'Harry.'

'Him,' I said.

Michael nodded.

I went to the phone and took it from him. 'Dresden.'

'I'm impressed, Dresden,' Nicodemus said. 'I expected the Hellhound to make a good showing, of course, but you surprised me. Your skills are developing quite rapidly. Tessa is furious with you.'

'I'm tired,' I replied. 'Do you want to talk deal or not?'

'I wouldn't have called, otherwise,' Nicodemus replied. 'But let's keep this a bit simpler, shall we? Just you and me. I have no desire to drag Chicago's underworld or the rest of the White Council into this ugly little affair. Mutually guaranteed safe passage, of course.'

'We did that once,' I said.

'And despite the fact that you betrayed the neutrality of the meeting well before I or any of my people took action – which I take as a highly promising act on your part – I am willing to extend my trust to you once more.'

I bit out a little laugh. 'Yeah. You're a saint.'

'One day,' Nicodemus said. 'One day. But for now, let's say a face-to-face meeting. A talk. Just you and I.'

'So you and your posse can jump me alone? No, thanks.'

'Come now. As you say, I *do* want to talk deal. If you're willing to extend your word of safe passage, we can even have it on your own ground.'

'Oh?' I asked. 'And where would that be?'

'It doesn't matter to me, as long as I don't have to be seen with you while you're wearing that ridiculous borrowed ensemble.'

The hairs on the back of my neck started crawling up into my hairline. I turned my head around very slightly. The windows to the Carpenters' backyard had blinds and curtains, but neither was wholly drawn. The kitchen lights made the windows into mirrors. I couldn't see beyond them.

'What is it going to be, Dresden?' Nicodemus asked. 'Will you give me your word of safe passage for our talk? Or shall I have my men open fire on that lovely young lady at the kitchen sink?'

I glanced over my shoulder to where Molly was drying dishes. She watched me out of the corner of her eye, clearly interested in the discussion, but trying not to look like it.

I couldn't possibly warn anyone before Nick's men could open fire — and I believed that he had them there. Probably up in the tree house. It had a reasonably good view of the kitchen.

'All right,' I said, speaking so that everyone there could hear me. 'I'm giving you my word of safe passage. For ten minutes.'

'And hope to die?' Nicodemus prompted.

I gritted my teeth. 'At the rate we're going, someone will.'

He laughed again. 'Keep the subject matter of this conversation between you and I, and it won't have to be anyone in the kitchen.'

The phone disconnected.

A beat later someone knocked at the front door.

Mouse's growl rumbled through the whole house, even though he'd remained in the front room.

'Harry?' Michael asked.

I found my shoes and stuffed my bare feet into them. 'I'm going out to talk to him. Keep an eye on us, but don't do anything if he doesn't start it. And watch your back. The last chat with him was a distraction.' I stood up, pulled on my duster, and picked up my staff. I met Michael's eyes and said, 'Watch your back.'

Michael's head tilted slightly. Then he looked past me, to the windows to the backyard. 'Be careful.'

I took my shield bracelet out of my duster pocket and fastened it on, wincing as it went over the mild burns on my wrist. 'You know me, Michael. I'm always careful.'

I walked to the front door and looked out the window.

The lights on the street were all out, except for the street-light in front of Michael's house. Nicodemus stood in the center of the street outside. His shadow stretched out long and dark to one side of him – the side opposite the one it should have been on, given the position of the light.

Mouse came to my side and planted himself there firmly.

I rested my hand on my dog's thick neck for a moment, searching the darkness outside for anything or anyone else. I saw nothing – which meant nothing, really. Anything could be out there in the dark.

But the only thing I *knew* was out there was a scared little girl.

'Let's go,' I said to Mouse, and stalked out into the snow.

37

It was snowing again. Five or six inches had fallen since the last time anyone cleared the Carpenters' front walk. My footsteps crunched through the silent winter air. You could have heard them a block away.

Nicodemus waited for me, stylishly casual in a deep green silk shirt and black trousers. He watched me come with a neutral expression, his eyes narrowed.

I shivered when a breath of cold wind touched me, and my weary muscles threatened to go out of control. Dammit, *I* was the one working for the Winter Queen. So how come everyone *else* got to be perfectly comfortable in the middle of a blizzard?

I stopped at the end of Michael's driveway and planted my staff on the ground. Nicodemus stared silently at me for a while. The shadows had shifted to mask his expression, and I couldn't see his face very well.

'What,' he said in a low, deadly tone, 'is that?'

Mouse stared at Nicodemus, and let out a growl so low that individual snowflakes jumped up off the ground all around him. My dog bared his teeth, showing long white fangs, and his snarl rose in volume.

Hell's bells. I'd never seen Mouse react like that, except in earnest combat.

And it looked like Nicodemus didn't like Mouse much, either.

'Answer my question, Dresden,' Nicodemus growled. 'What is *that*?'

'A precaution against getting stuck in deep snow,' I said. 'He's training to be a Saint Bernard.'

'Excuse me?' Nicodemus said.

I mimed covering one of Mouse's ears with my hand and stage-whispered, 'Don't tell him that they don't actually carry kegs of booze on their collars. Break his little heart.'

Nicodemus didn't move, but his shadow shifted until it lay in a shapeless little pool between him and Mouse. His face came into view again, and he was smiling. 'It's been a little while since anyone was quite that insolent to my face. May I ask you a question?'

'Why not?'

'Do you always retreat into insouciance when you're frightened, Dresden?'

'I don't think of it as retreating. I think of it as an advance to the cheer. May I ask you a question?'

The smile widened. 'Oh, why not?'

'How come some of you losers seem to have personal names, and the others just get called after the Fallen in the coin?'

'It isn't complicated,' Nicodemus said. 'Some of our order are active, willing minds, with strength enough to retain their sense of self. Others are' – he shrugged a shoulder, an elegant, arrogant little motion – 'of little consequence. Disposable vessels, and nothing more.'

'Like Rasmussen,' I muttered.

Nicodemus looked puzzled for a moment. Then his eyes narrowed suddenly, focusing intently upon me. His shadow stirred again, and something made a noise that sounded like a disturbingly serpentine whisper. 'Oh, yes, Ursiel's vessel. Precisely.' He looked past me to the house. 'Have your friends begun whispering behind your back yet?'

They sure as hell had, though I had no idea why. I hung on to my poker face. 'Why would they?'

'Try to imagine the Aquarium from their point of view. They enter a building with you, along with someone they would not normally bring along – but you have insisted that the police detective accompany your group. As a result, you walk away to a private conference with just you, me, and the Archive's guard dog. Then the sign goes up, and they can hear a terrible conflict raging. They race to the scene as quickly as possible and find my people dragging you out of the water – to take back the coin you had in your pocket, but your friends had no way of knowing that. They find the Archive gone, her body-guard wounded or dead, and you being apparently assisted by my people.

'And *they never saw what happened,*' Nicodemus continued. 'To a suspicious mind, you might seem an accomplice to the act.'

I swallowed. 'I doubt that.'

'Oh?' Nicodemus said. 'Even though you're about to propose giving me back the coins you took at the Aquarium? Eleven coins, Dresden. Should I recover them, everything you and your people have done during the past few days will mean nothing. I'll be just as strong and possess the power of the Archive to boot. It is hardly a stretch to consider that you would be ideally positioned to betray them at a critical moment – which this is.'

I . . . hadn't thought of it like that.

' "What if he's finally falling to the influence of her shadow?" they're thinking. "What if he's not wholly in control of his own decisions?" they're thinking. Treachery is a more dangerous weapon than any magic, Dresden. I've had two thousand years to practice arranging it, and your friends the Knights know it.'

Suddenly Michael's attitude began to make a lot more sense, and the pot roast fought to come back up. I tried to keep my poker face, but it wouldn't stick.

'Ouch,' Nicodemus said, his eyes widening. 'After all those years of baseless suspicion and hostility from your own Council, *that* must be a painful realization.' He smirked at Mouse and then at me. 'Your little heart must be breaking.'

Mouse pressed his shoulder against my leg and snarled savagely at Nicodemus, taking a step forward.

Nicodemus ignored him, his focus all on me. 'It's a tempting offer,' he said. 'Exchanging the coins for the Archive? Presenting me with an opportunity to walk away with every jewel in the vault? It's something I can hardly ignore. Well-done.'

'So?' I said. 'Where do you want to set it up?'

He shook his head. 'I don't,' he said quietly. 'This is endgame, Dresden, even if you and yours can't accept it. Once I have the Archive, the rest is simply an exercise. Losing the coins will hurt, true, but I don't need them. Thorned Namshiel is of no real use to me in his current condition, and I haven't worked for two thousand years only to take a gamble at the last second. No deal.'

I swallowed. 'Then why are you here?'

'To give you a chance to reconsider,' Nicodemus said. 'I think you and I are not so very different. Both of us are creatures of will. Both of us live our lives for ideals, not material things. Both of us are willing to sacrifice to attain our goals.'

'Maybe we should wear matching outfits.'

He spread his hands. 'I could be an ally far more effective and dangerous than any you have now. I'm willing to compromise with you, and make some of your goals my own. I can provide you with support beyond anything your own Council has ever done for you. The material gain of such a partnership is a passing matter, ultimately, but wouldn't you enjoy living in something other than a musty basement? Don't you get tired of coming home to cold showers, cheap food, and an empty bed?'

I just stared at him.

'A great deal of work needs to be done, and not all of it is repugnant to you. In fact, I should imagine that some of it would prove to be quite satisfying to your personal sense of right and wrong.'

To hell with the poker face. I sneered at him. 'Like what?'

'The Red Court is one example,' Nicodemus said. 'They're large, well organized, dangerous to my plans, a plague upon mankind, and aesthetically repugnant. They're parasites who are inconvenient in the short term, dangerous in the middle distance, and fatal to any long-range plan. They need to be destroyed at some point, in any case. I should have no objection to giving my assistance to you, and through you to the White Council in their efforts to do so.'

'Make the Council into cat's-paws to wipe out the Red Court?' I asked.

'As if you have not been made into their tool on many occasions.'

'The Council doesn't need my help to be a bunch of tools,' I muttered.

'And yet the reversal appeals to your sense of justice, as does the notion of visiting destruction upon the Red Court. Especially given what they did to Susan Rodriguez.' He tilted his head to one side. 'It may be possible to help her, you know. If anyone might know of a means to free her of her condition, it is the Fallen.'

'Why not just offer me floating castles and world peace while you're at it, Nick?'

He spread his hands. 'I only suggest possibilities. Here is what is concrete: You and I share a great many foes. I am willing to help you fight them.'

'Let me get this straight,' I said. 'You're telling me that you want me to work with you, and that I still get to keep being one of the good guys.'

'Good and evil are relative. You know that by now. But I would never ask you to work against your conscience. I have no need to do so in order to make use of your talents. Consider how many people you could help with the power I'm offering you.'

'Yeah. You seem like a real philanthropist.'

'As I said, I'm willing to work with you, and I am quite sincere.' He met my eyes. 'Look upon my soul, Dresden. See for yourself.'

My heart ripped out about a thousand beats in two seconds, and I jerked my eyes away from him, terrified. I didn't want to see what was behind Nicodemus's dark, calm, ancient eyes. It could have been something monstrous, his soul, something that ripped away my sanity and left a stain of itself on my own like a smear of grease.

Or it could be even worse.

What if he was telling the truth?

I glanced back at the Carpenter house, feeling very cold and very tired. Tired of everything. Tired of all of it. I looked down at my borrowed clothes and my bare ankles, covered with snow just like my shoes.

'I don't have anything against you personally, Dresden,' he said. 'I respect your integrity. I would enjoy working with you. But make no mistake: If you stand in my way, I'll mow you down beside everyone else.'

Silence reigned.

I thought about what I knew of Nicodemus.

I thought about my friends and those whispers behind my back. I thought about the awkward silences.

I thought about what the world might become if Nicodemus turned Ivy.

I thought about how scared the little girl must be right now.

And I thought about a little old man from Okinawa who had literally laid down his life for my own.

'You and I,' I said quietly, 'are both willing to give things up to reach our goals.'

Nicodemus tilted his head, waiting.

'But we have real different ideas when it comes to deciding who does the sacrificing and who gets sacrificed.' I shook my head. 'No.'

He took a slow, deep breath and said, 'Pity. Good evening, Dresden. Best of luck to you in the new world. But I expect we won't meet again in this life.'

He turned to go.

And my heart sped up again.

Shiro said I would know who to give the sword to.

'Wait,' I said.

Nicodemus paused.

'I've got more than coins to offer you.'

He turned, his face a mask.

'You give me Ivy and I give you eleven coins,' I said quietly, 'plus *Fidelacchius*.'

Nicodemus froze. His shadow twisted and twitched. 'You have it?'

'Yeah.'

That ugly whispering sound came again, louder and faster. Nicodemus glanced down at his shadow, frowning.

'Suppose you get Ivy,' I said. 'Suppose you turn her and manage to control her. It's a great scheme. Suppose you get your apocalypse and your neo Dark Age. Do you think that's going to stop the Knights? Do you think that, one after the other, new men and women won't take up the Swords and fight you? You think Heaven's just going to sit there letting you do whatever you want?'

Nicodemus had a better poker face than me, but I had him. He was listening.

'How many times have the Swords broken up your plans?' I asked. 'How many times have they forced you to abandon one position or another?' I took a stab in the dark that seemed worth it. 'Don't you get tired of waking up from nightmares about taking a sword through the heart or the neck? Turning you into one more discarded Dixie cup for the Fallen? Terrified of what you're going to face once you shuffle off the mortal coil?

'I've got the Sword,' I said. 'I'm willing to trade it and the coins alike.'

His teeth showed. 'No, you aren't.'

'I'm just as willing to give you the Sword and the coins as you are to give me the Archive,' I said. 'I'm handing you an opportunity, Nick. A chance to destroy one of the Swords forever. Who knows? If things go well you might have a shot at taking out the other two at the same time.'

The whispering increased in volume and speed again.

Nicodemus stared at me. I couldn't read his expression, but

his right hand was slowly clenching and unclenching, as if eager to take up a weapon, and hate poured off him like heat from an oven.

'So,' I said as nonchalantly as I could, 'where do you want to do the exchange?'

38

I walked back up to the house again a few minutes later, Mouse at my side. Michael had been right: Before we went inside, the big dog shook himself thoroughly. I decided to follow his example and stomped whatever snow I could off my numb feet, then went in.

I walked into the living room and found everyone there waiting for me – Luccio, Michael, Molly, Sanya, and Murphy. Everyone looked at me expectantly.

'He went for it. We're going to have to haul ass in a minute. But I need to speak with you first, Michael.'

Michael raised his eyebrows. 'Oh, certainly.'

'Alone,' I said quietly. 'And bring your Sword.'

I turned and walked on through the house, out the barely functioning back door the gruff had damaged before all this began, and on to the workshop. I didn't stop to look behind me. I didn't need to look to know that everyone was trading Significant Glances.

If Nicodemus actually did have people in the tree house, they were gone now. I wouldn't put it past the bastard to have been lying about them, just to keep me honest. I went inside the workshop and laid my staff down on the workbench. It had a lot of dings and nicks in it. It could benefit from a set of wood-carving tools, sandpaper, and patient attention.

Michael came in silently a moment later. I turned to face him. He wore his fleece-lined denim coat again, and bore *Amoracchius* in its sheath, attached to a belt he'd slung over one shoulder.

I took my duster off and put it next to the staff. 'Draw it, please.'

'Harry,' Michael said. 'What are you doing?'

'Making a point,' I said. 'Just do it.'

He frowned at me, his expression uncertain, but he drew the blade.

I added my energy rings to the pile on the workbench. Then my shield bracelet. Finally I took off my mother's silver pentacle necklace and put it down there too. Then I turned and walked over to Michael.

I met his eyes steadily. I'd already looked upon Michael's soul. I knew its quality, and he knew that of mine.

Then I reached down with my left hand, gently grasped *Amoracchius*'s blade, and lifted it to rest against the left side of my neck, just below my ear. The jugular vein. Or the carotid artery. I get them confused.

Michael went pale. 'Harry—'

'Shut up,' I said. 'For the past couple of days you've done all kinds of not-talking. You can do a little bit more of it until I've said my piece.'

He subsided, his eyes troubled, and stood very, very still.

What can I say? I have a gift for getting people's attention.

I stared at him down the length of shining, deadly steel, and then, very slowly, took my hand off the Sword, leaving its wickedly sharp edge resting against the beat of my life. Then I spread my hands and just stood there for a minute.

'You are my friend, Michael,' I said, barely louder than a whisper. 'I trust you.'

His eyes glittered and he closed them.

'And you want to know,' he said heavily, looking up again, 'if I can say the same.'

'Talk is cheap,' I said, and moved my chin a little to indicate the Sword. 'I want to know if you'll show me.'

He lowered the Sword carefully from my neck. His hands shook a little, but mine didn't. 'It isn't that simple.'

'Yes, it is,' I told him. 'I'm your friend, or I'm not. You trust me – or you don't.'

He sheathed the Sword and turned away, facing the window.

'That's the real reason you didn't want to hat up and go

gunning for the Denarians right at first, the way I wanted to.
You were worried I was leading you into a trap.'

'I didn't lie to you, Harry,' Michael said. 'But I'd be lying
right now if I didn't admit that, yes, the thought had crossed
my mind.'

'Why?' I asked, my voice perfectly calm. 'What reason have
I ever given you for that?'

'It isn't that *simple*, Harry.'

'I've fought and bled to defend you and your family. I put
my neck in a noose for Molly, when the Council would have
killed her. I can't even tell you how much business I've missed
out on because of the time I've got to spend teaching her. What
was it that tipped you off to my imminent villainhood?'

'Harry . . .'

Nicodemus had been right about one thing: It hurt to be
suspected by my friends. It hurt like hell. I didn't even realize
I had raised my voice until I'd already screamed, 'Look at me
when I'm talking to you!'

Michael turned his face to me, his expression grim.

'Do you think I've decided to side with Nicodemus and his
buddies?' I snarled. 'Do you really think that? Because if you do,
you might was well put that Sword through my neck right now.'

'I don't know what to think, Harry,' he said quietly. 'There's
a lot you haven't said.'

'I don't share everything with you,' I retorted. 'I don't share
everything with anyone. That's nothing new.'

'I know it isn't,' he said.

'Then *why*?' Some of the fire went out of my voice, and I felt
like a half-deflated balloon. 'You've known me for years, man.
We've covered each other plenty of times. Why are you doubting
me now?'

'Because of Lasciel's shadow,' Michael said quietly. 'Because
as long as it's in you it will tempt you – and the longer it stays,
the more able it will be to do so.'

'I gave Forthill the coin,' I said. 'I figured that pretty much
said it all.'

Michael grimaced. 'The shadow can show you how to summon the coin. It's happened before. That's why we're so careful not to touch them.'

'It's over, Michael. There is no more shadow.'

Michael shook his head, his eyes filled with something very like pity. 'It doesn't work like that, Harry.'

The fire came back. The one thing I didn't want or need was pity. I'd made my own choices, lived my own life, and even if they hadn't all been smart choices, there weren't many of them that I regretted. 'How do you know?' I asked.

'Because in two thousand years, *no one* has rid themselves of the shadow of one of the Fallen – except by accepting the demon into them entirely, taking up the coin, and living to feel remorse and discarding it. And you claim that you never took up the coin.'

'That's right,' I said.

'Then either the shadow is still there,' Michael said, 'still twisting your thoughts. Still whispering to you. Or you're lying to me about taking up the coin. Those are the only options.'

I just stared at him for a minute. Then I said, 'Hell's bells. And I thought wizards had a monopoly on arrogance.'

He blinked.

'Or do you really expect me to believe that the Church has been there to document every single instance of anyone picking up any of the cursed coins. That they've followed through with everyone tempted by a Fallen's shadow, taken testimony. Made copies. Hell, gotten it notarized. Especially given that you've told me that Nicodemus has worked as hard as he could to destroy the Church's records and archives through the years.'

Michael's weight settled back on his heels. He frowned.

'This is what they want, Michael. They want us at one another's throats. They want us to distrust one another.' I shook my head. 'And right now is *not* the time to give it to them.'

Michael folded his arms, studying me. 'It could have done something to your mind,' Michael said quietly. 'You might not be in control of yourself, Harry.'

I took a deep breath. 'That's . . . possible,' I admitted. 'Anybody's head can be messed with. But if you go rewiring someone's brain, it damages them, badly. The bigger the changes you make, the worse it disorders their mind.'

'The way my daughter did to her friends,' Michael said. 'I know.'

'So there are signs,' I said. 'If you know the person well enough, there are almost always signs. They act differently. Have I been acting differently? Have I suddenly gone crazy on you?'

He arched an eyebrow.

'More so than usual,' I amended.

He shook his head. 'No.'

'Then odds are pretty good no one has scrambled my noggin,' I said. 'Besides which, it isn't the sort of thing one tends to overlook, and as a grade-A wizard of the White Council, I assure you that nothing like that has happened to me.'

For a second he looked like he wanted to speak, but he didn't.

'Which brings us back to the only real issue here,' I said. 'Do you think I've gone over to them? Do you think I *could* do such a thing, after what I've seen?'

My friend sighed. 'No, Harry.'

I stepped up to him and put my hand on his shoulder. 'Then trust me for a little longer. Help me for a little longer.'

He searched my eyes again. 'I will,' he whispered, 'if you answer one question for me.'

I frowned at him and tilted my head. 'Okay.'

He took a deep breath and spoke carefully. 'Harry,' he said quietly, 'what happened to your blasting rod?'

For a second the question didn't make any sense. The words sounded like noises, like sounds infants make before they learn to speak. Especially the last part of the sentence. 'I . . . I'm sorry,' I said. 'What did you say?'

'Where,' he said gently, 'is your blasting rod?'

This time I heard the words.

Pain stabbed me in the head, ice picks plunging into both temples. I flinched and doubled over. Blasting rod. Familiar words. I fought to summon an image of what went with the words, but I couldn't *find* anything. I *knew* I had a memory associated with those words, but try as I might, I couldn't drag it out. It was like a shape covered by some heavy tarp. I knew an object was beneath, but I couldn't get to it.

'I don't . . . I don't . . .' I started breathing faster. The pain got worse.

Someone had been in my head.

Someone had been in my *head*.

Oh, God.

I must have fallen at some point, because the workshop's floor was cold underneath one of my cheeks when I felt Michael's broad, work-calloused hand gently cover my forehead.

'Father,' he murmured, humbly and with no drama whatsoever. 'Father, please help my friend. Father of light, banish the darkness that he may see. Father of truth, expose the lies. Father of mercy, ease his pain. Father of love, honor this good man's heart. Amen.'

Michael's hand felt suddenly red-hot, and I felt power burning in the air around him – not magic, the magic I worked with every day. This was something different, something more ancient, more potent, more pure. This was the power of faith, and as that heat settled into the spaces behind my eyes, something cracked and shattered inside my thoughts.

The pain vanished so suddenly that it left me gasping, even as the image of a simple wooden rod, a couple of feet long, heavily carved with sigils and runes, leapt into the forefront of my thoughts. Along with the image of the blasting rod came thousands of memories, everything I had ever known about using magic to summon and control fire in a hurry, evocation, combat magic, and they hit me like a sledgehammer.

I lay there shuddering for a minute or two as I took it all back in. The memories filled a hole inside me I hadn't even realized was there.

Michael left his hand on my head. 'Easy, Harry. Easy. Just rest for a minute. I'm right here.'

I decided not to argue with him.

'Well,' I rasped weakly a moment later. I opened my eyes and looked up to where Michael sat cross-legged on the floor beside me. 'Somebody owes somebody here an apology.'

He gave me a small, concerned smile. 'You don't owe me anything. Perhaps I should have spoken sooner, but . . .'

'But confronting someone who's had his brain twisted out of shape about the fact can prove traumatic,' I said quietly. 'Especially if part of the twisting was making damned sure that he didn't remember any such thing happening.'

He nodded. 'Molly became concerned sometime yesterday. I asked her to have a look at you while you were sleeping earlier. I apologize for that, but I didn't know any other way to be sure that someone had tampered with you.'

I shivered. Ugh. Molly playing in my head. That wasn't necessarily the prettiest thing to think about. Molly had a gift for neuromancy, mind magic, but she'd used it to do some fairly nasty things to people in the past – for perfectly good reasons, true, but all the same it had been honest-to-evilness black magic. It was the kind of thing that people got addicted to, and it wasn't the kind of candy store that I would ever want that kid to play in.

Especially considering that the inventory was me.

'Hell's bells, Michael,' I murmured. 'You shouldn't have done that to her.'

'It was her idea, actually. And you're right, Harry. We can't afford to be divided right now. What can you remember?'

I shook my head, squinting while I sorted through the dump-truckload of loose memories. 'The last time I remember having it was right after the gruffs attacked us here. After that . . . nothing. I don't know where it is now. And no, I don't remember who did it to me or why.'

Michael frowned but nodded. 'Well. He doesn't always give us what we want. Only what we need.'

I rubbed at my forehead. 'I hope so,' I said sheepishly. 'So. Um. This is a little awkward. After that thing with putting your Sword to my throat and all.'

Michael let his head fall back and belted out a warm, rich laugh. 'You aren't the sort of person to do things by halves, Harry. Grand gestures included.'

'I guess not,' I said quietly.

'I have to ask,' Michael said, studying me intently. 'Lasciel's shadow. Is it really gone?'

I nodded.

'How?'

I looked away from him. 'I don't like to talk about it.'

He frowned but nodded slowly. 'Can you tell me why not?'

'Because what happened to her wasn't fair.' I shook my head. 'Do you know why the Denarians don't like going into churches, Michael?'

He shrugged. 'Because the presence of the Almighty makes them uncomfortable, or so I always supposed.'

'No,' I said, closing my eyes. 'Because it makes the Fallen *feel*, Michael. Makes them remember. Makes them sad.'

I felt his startled glance, even with my eyes closed.

'Imagine how awful that would be,' I said, 'after millennia of certainty of purpose. Suddenly you have doubts. Suddenly you question whether or not everything you've done has been one enormous, futile lie. If everything you sacrificed, you sacrificed for nothing.' I smiled faintly. 'Couldn't be good for your confidence.'

'No,' Michael said thoughtfully. 'I don't suppose it would be.'

'Shiro told me I'd know who to give the Sword to,' I said.

'Yes?'

'I threw it into the deal with Nicodemus. The coins and the Sword for the child.'

Michael drew in a sharp breath.

'He would have walked away otherwise,' I said. 'Run out the clock, and we'd never have found him in time. It was the only way. It was almost like Shiro knew. Even back then.'

'God's blood, Harry,' Michael said. He pressed a hand to his stomach. 'I'm fairly sure that gambling is a sin. And even if it isn't, *this* probably should be.'

'I'm going to go get that little girl, Michael,' I said. 'Whatever it takes.'

He rose, frowning, and buckled his sword belt around his hips.

I held up my right hand. 'Are you with me?'

Michael's palm smacked solidly into mine, and he hauled me to my feet.

39

As war councils go, our meeting was fast and dirty. It had to be.

Afterward I tracked down Murphy. She'd gone back to Charity's sewing room to check on Kincaid.

I stood quietly in the door for a minute. There wasn't much room to be had in there. It was piled high with plastic storage boxes filled with fabric and craft materials. There was a sewing machine on a table, a chair, the bed, and just enough floor space to let you get to them. I'd been laid up in this room before. It was a comforting sort of place, awash in softness and color, and it smelled like detergent and fabric softener.

Kincaid looked like the Mummy's stunt double. He had an IV in his arm, and there was a unit of blood suspended from a small metal stand beside his bed – courtesy of Marcone's rogue medical facilities, I supposed.

Murphy sat beside the bed, looking worried. I'd seen the expression on her face before, when I'd been the one lying horizontal. I expected to feel a surge of jealousy, but it didn't happen. I just felt bad for Murph.

'How is he?' I asked her.

'This is his third unit of blood,' Murphy said. 'His color's better. His breathing is steadier. But he needs a doctor. Maybe we should call Butters.'

'If we do, he's just going to look at us, do his McCoy impersonation, and tell you, "Dammit, Murphy. I'm a medical examiner, not a pasta chef."'

Murphy choked out a little sound that was as much sob as chuckle.

I stepped forward and put a hand on her shoulder. 'Michael says he's going to make it.'

She sat stiffly underneath my hand. 'He isn't a doctor.'

'But he has very good contacts.'

Kincaid shuddered, and his breath rasped harshly for several seconds.

Murphy's shoulder went steely with tension.

The wounded man's breathing steadied again.

'Hey,' I said quietly. 'Easy.'

She shook her head. 'I hate this.'

'He's tougher than you or me,' I said quietly.

'That's not what I mean.'

I remained silent, waiting for her to speak.

'I hate *feeling* like this. I'm fucking terrified, and I *hate* it.' The muscles in her jaw tensed. 'This is why I don't want to get involved anymore. It hurts too much.'

I squeezed her shoulder gently. 'Involved, huh?'

'No,' she said. Then she shook her head. 'Yes. I don't know. It's complicated, Harry.'

'Caring about someone isn't complicated,' I said. 'It isn't *easy*. But it isn't complicated, either. Kinda like lifting the engine block out of a car.'

She gave me an oblique glance. 'Leave it to a man to describe intimate relationships in terms of automotive mechanics.'

'Yeah. I was kinda proud of that one, myself.'

She huffed out a quiet breath, squeezed her eyes shut, and leaned her cheek down onto my hand. 'The stupid part,' she said, 'is that he isn't interested in . . . in getting serious. We get along. We have fun together. For him, that's enough. And it's so *stupid* for me to get hung up on him.'

I didn't think it was all that stupid. Murph didn't want to get too close, let herself be too vulnerable. Kincaid didn't want that kind of relationship either – which made him safe. It made it all right for her to care.

It also explained why she and I had never gotten anywhere.

In the event that you haven't figured it out, I'm not the kind of person to be casually involved in much of anything.

I couldn't fit any of that into words, though. So I just leaned down and kissed the top of her head gently.

She shivered. Her tears made wet, cool spots on the back of my hand. I knelt. It put my head more or less on level with hers, where she sat beside the bed. I put an arm around her shoulders and pulled her against me. I still didn't say anything. For Murph, that would be too much like I was actually in the room, seeing her cry. So she pretended that she wasn't crying and I pretended that I didn't notice.

She didn't cry for long. A couple of minutes. Then her breathing steadied, and I could feel her asserting control again. A minute more and she sat up and away from me. I let her.

'They said you were under the influence,' she said, her tone calmer, more businesslike. 'That someone had done something to your head. Your apprentice said that. But Michael didn't want to say anything in front of the other wizard, I could tell. And no one wanted to say anything in front of me.'

'Secrets get to be a habit,' I said quietly. 'And Molly was right.'

Murphy nodded. 'She said that we should listen for the first words out of your mouth when you woke up. That if something had messed with your mind, your subconscious might be able to communicate that way, while you were on the edge of sleep. And you told us to listen to her.'

I thought about it and pursed my lips. 'Huh. I did. Guess I'm smarter than I thought.'

'They shouldn't have suspected you,' Murphy said. 'I'm a paranoid bitch, and I gave up suspecting you a long time ago.'

'They had a good reason,' I said. I took a slow breath. It was hard, but I forced the words out. 'Nicodemus threw one of those coins at Michael's kid. I grabbed it before the kid could. And I had a photocopy of a Fallen angel living in my head for several years, trying to talk me into picking up the coin and letting the rest of it into me.'

Murphy glanced obliquely at me. 'You mean . . . you could have become one of those things?'

'Yeah,' I said. 'Couple of times, it was close.'

'Is it still . . . Is that what . . . ?'

I shook my head. 'It's gone now. She's gone now. I guess the whole time she was trying to change me, I was trying to change her right back. And in the Raith Deeps last year, she took a psychic bullet for me – at the very end, after everyone else had gotten out.' I shrugged. 'I had . . . We'd sort of become friends, Murph. I'd gotten used to having her around.' I glanced at her and gave her a faint smile. 'Crazy, huh? Get all broken up over what was essentially my imaginary friend.'

Her fingers found my hand and squeezed tight once. 'We're all imaginary friends to one another, Harry.' She sat with me for a moment, and then gave me a shrewd glance. 'You never told Michael the details.'

I shook my head. 'I don't know why.'

'I do,' she said. 'You remember when Kravos stuck his fingers in my brain?'

I shuddered. He'd been impersonating me when he did it. 'Yeah.'

'You said it caused some kind of damage. What did you call it?'

'Psychic trauma,' I said. 'Same thing happens when a loved one dies, during big emotional tragedies, that kind of thing. Takes a while to get over it.'

'But you do get over it,' Murph said. 'Dresden, it seems to me that you'd lock yourself up pretty tight if someone took a regular bullet for you with a regular body. Much less if you were under psychic attack and this imaginary friend died right inside your own brain. Something like that happens, shouldn't you have expected to be a basket case, at least for a little while?'

I frowned, staring down at my hands. 'I never even considered that.'

She snorted gently. 'There's a surprise. Dresden forgets that he's not invincible.'

She had a point there.

'This plan of yours,' she said. 'Do you really think it's going to work?'

'I think I've got to try it.' I took a deep breath. 'I don't think you should be involved in this one, Murph. The Denarians have human followers. Fanatic ones.'

'You think we're going to have to kill some of them,' Murphy said.

'I think we probably won't have much choice,' I said. 'Besides that, I wouldn't put it past them to send someone here for spite, win or lose.'

Murphy glanced up at me rather sharply.

I shrugged. 'They know that Michael and Sanya and I are going to be out there. They'll know that there will be someone here, unprotected. Whether or not they get the coins, Nicodemus might send someone here to finish off the wounded.'

Murphy stared at me for a second, then looked back at Kincaid. 'You bastard,' she said without emphasis.

'I'm not playing big brother with you, Karrin,' I replied. 'But we are dealing with some very bad people. Molly's staying with Kincaid. I'm leaving Mouse here too. I'd appreciate it if someone with a little more experience was here to give the kid some direction, if it was needed.'

She scowled at Kincaid. Then she said, 'Trying to guilt me into playing worried girlfriend, domestic defender, and surrogate mother figure, eh?'

'I figured it would work better than telling you to shut up and get into the kitchen.'

She took a deep breath, studying the sleeping man. Then she reached out and touched his hand. She stood and faced me. 'No. I'm coming with you.'

I grunted, rising. 'You sure?'

'The girl is important to him,' Murphy said. 'More important to him than anything has been for a long time, Harry. He'd die to protect her. If he was conscious, he'd be demanding to go with you. But he can't do that. So I'll have to do it for him.'

'Could be real messy, Murph.'

She nodded. 'I'll worry about that after the girl is safe.'

There was a clock ticking quietly on the wall. 'The meeting's in an hour.'

Murphy nodded and reached for her coat. The tears were gone, and there was no evidence of them in the lines of her face. 'You'd better excuse me, then. If we're going to have an evening out, I need to change into something more comfortable.'

'I never tell a lady how to accessorize.'

Going forth to do battle with the forces of darkness is one thing. Doing it in a pair of borrowed sweatpants and an ill-fitting T-shirt is something else entirely. Fortunately, Molly had been thoughtful enough to drop my own clothes into the washer, bless her heart. I could forgive her for the pot roast.

In the laundry room I had skinned out of Michael's clothes and was in the act of pulling up my jeans when Luccio opened the door and leaned in, her expression excited. 'Dresden. I think I know wh— Oh.'

I jerked my jeans the rest of the way up and closed them as hurriedly as I could without causing any undue discomfort. 'Oh. Um. Excuse me,' I said.

Luccio smiled, the dimples in her cheeks making her look not much older than Molly. She didn't blush. Instead she folded her arms and leaned one shoulder on the door frame, her dark eyes taking me in with evident pleasure. 'Oh, not at all, Dresden. Not at all.'

I paused and returned her look for a moment. 'Aren't you supposed to be embarrassed, apologize, and quietly leave?'

Her smile widened lazily, and she shrugged a shoulder. 'When I was a girl, perhaps. But even then I had difficulty forcing myself to act awkward when looking at something that pleased me.' She tilted her head and moved toward me. She reached out and rested her fingertips very lightly against a scar on my upper arm. She traced its outline and glanced up at me, lifting an eyebrow.

'Bullet wound,' I said. 'FBI werewolves.'

She nodded. Then her fingers touched the hollow of my throat and slid slowly down over my chest and belly in a straight line. A shuddering sensation of heat fluttered through my skin in the wake of her fingertips. She looked up at me again.

'Hook knife,' I said. 'Sorcerer tried to filet me at the Field Museum.'

Her touch trailed down my bare arms, lingering on my fore-arms, near my wrists, avoiding the red, scalded skin around my left wrist.

'Thorn manacles,' I said. 'From when Madrigal Raith tried to sell me on eBay.'

She lifted my scarred left hand between hers, fingers stroking over the maimed flesh. These days I could move it pretty well, most of the time, and it didn't look like some kind of hideous, half-melted wax image of a hand anymore, but it still wasn't pretty. 'A scourge of Black Court vampires had a Renfield that got creative. Had a homemade flamethrower.'

She shook her head. 'I know men centuries older than you who have not collected so many scars.'

'Maybe they lived that long because they were smart enough not to get them,' I said.

She flashed me that grin again. At close range it was devas-tating, and her eyes looked even darker.

'Anastasia,' I said quietly, 'in a few minutes we're going to go do something that might get us killed.'

'Yes, Harry. We are,' she said.

I nodded. 'But that's not until a few minutes from now.'

Her eyes smoldered. 'No. No, it isn't.'

I lifted my still-tingling right hand to gently cup the line of her jaw, and leaned down to press my mouth to hers.

She let out a quiet, satisfied little moan and melted against me, her body pressing full-length to mine, returning the kiss with slow, sensuous intensity. I felt her slide the fingers of one hand into my hair, while the nails of the other wandered randomly over my chest and arm, barely touching. It left a trail of fire in my flesh, and I found myself sinking the fingers of my right hand into the soft curls of her hair, drawing her more deeply into the kiss.

I don't know how long that went on, but it wound down deliciously. By the time she drew her mouth away from mine, both of us were breathing harder, and my heart was pounding out a rapid beat against my chest. And against my jeans.

She didn't open her eyes for five or ten seconds, and when she did, they were absolutely huge and molten with desire. Anastasia leaned her head back and arched in a slow stretch, letting out a long, low, pleased sigh.

'You don't mind?' I asked her.

'Not at all.'

'Good. I just . . . wanted to see what that was like. It's been a long time since I kissed anyone. Almost forgot what it was like.'

'You have no idea,' she murmured, 'how long it has been since I've kissed a man. I wasn't sure I remembered *how*.'

I let out a quiet laugh.

Her dimples returned. 'Good,' she said, satisfaction in her tone. She looked me up and down, taking in the sights again. This time it didn't make me feel self-conscious. 'You have a good smile. You should show it more often.'

'Once we're done tonight,' I said, 'maybe we could talk about that. Over dinner.'

Her smile widened, and color touched her cheeks. 'That would please me.'

'Good,' I said. I arched an eyebrow at her. 'I'll put my shirt on now, if that's all right.'

Anastasia let out a merry laugh and stepped back from me, though she didn't lift her fingertips from my skin until the distance forced her to do it. 'Very well, Warden. As you were.'

'Why, thank you, Captain.' I tugged the rest of my clothes back on. 'What were you going to tell me?'

'Hmmm?' she said. 'Oh, ah, yes. Before I was so cleverly distracted. I think I know where the Denarians are holding the Archive.'

I blinked. 'You got through with a tracking spell?'

She shook her head. 'No, it failed miserably. So I was forced to resort to the use of my brain.' She opened a hard-sided leather case hanging from her sword belt. She withdrew a plastic tube from it, opened one end, and withdrew a roll of papers. She thumbed through them, found one, and put the rest back. She unfolded the paper into what looked like a map, and laid it out on the lid of the dryer.

I leaned over to look at it. It was indeed a map, but instead of being marked with state lines, highways, and towns, it was dominated by natural features – most prominent of which was the outlines of the Great Lakes. Rivers, forests, and swamps figured prominently as well. Furthermore, a webwork of inter-secting lines flowed over the map, marked in various colors of ink in several different thicknesses.

Footsteps approached and Molly appeared, carrying a plastic laundry basket full of children's clothing. She blinked when she saw us, but smiled and came over immediately. 'What's that?'

'It's a map,' I replied, like the knowledgeable mentor I was supposed to be.

She snorted. 'I can see that,' she said. 'But a map of what?'

Then I got it. 'Ley lines,' I said, looking up at Luccio. 'These are ley lines.'

Molly pursed her lips and studied the paper. 'Those are real?'

'Yeah, we just haven't covered them yet. They're . . . well, think of them as underground pipelines. Only instead of flowing with water, they flow with magic. They run all over the world, usually running between hot spots of supernatural energy.'

'Connect the dots with magic,' Molly said. 'Cool.'

'Exactly,' Luccio said. 'The only method that would have a chance of restraining the Archive's power would be the use of a greater circle – and one that uses an enormous amount of energy, at that.'

I grunted acknowledgment. 'It would have to be dead solid perfect, too, or she could break loose at the flaw.'

'Correct.'

'How much energy are we talking about?' I asked her.

'You might be able to empower such a circle for half an hour or an hour, Dresden. I couldn't have kept it up that long, even before my, ah' – she waved a hand down at herself – 'accident.'

'So it would take loads of power,' I mused. 'So how are they powering it?'

'That's the real question,' she said. 'After all, the Sign they raised at the Aquarium suggests that they have an ample supply.'

I shook my head. 'No,' I stated. 'That was Hellfire.'

Luccio pursed her lips. 'You seem fairly certain of that.'

'I seem completely certain of that,' I said. 'It's powerful as Hell, literally, but it isn't stable. It fluctuates and stutters. That's why they couldn't keep the Sign up any longer than they did.'

'To imprison the Archive, they would need a steady, flawless supply,' Luccio said. 'A supply that big would also be able to support a very complex veil – one that could shield them from any tracking spell. In fact, it's the *only* way they could establish a veil that impenetrable.'

'Ley lines,' I breathed.

'Ley lines,' she said with satisfaction.

'I know of a couple around town, but I didn't realize there were that *many* of the things,' I said.

'The Great Lakes region is rife with them,' Luccio said. 'It's an energy nexus.'

'So?' Molly asked. 'What does that mean?'

'Well, it's one reason why so much supernatural activity tends to happen in this area,' I said. 'Three times as many ships and planes have vanished in Lake Michigan as in the Bermuda Triangle.'

'Wow,' Molly said. 'Seriously?'

'Yeah.'

'Next summer I think I'll stick to the pool.'

Luccio started tracing various lines on the map with a fingertip. 'The colors denote what manner of energy seems to be most prevalent in the line. Defensive energy here. Disruptive force here, restorative lines here and here, and so on. The thickness of the line indicates its relative potency.'

'Right, right,' I said, growing excited. 'So we're looking for an energy source compatible with the use of a greater circle, and strong enough to keep a big one powered up and stable.'

'And there are four locations that I think are most likely,' Luccio said. She pointed up toward the north end of Lake Michigan. 'North and South Manitou islands both have heavy concentrations of dark energy running through them.'

'There's plenty of spook stories around them, too,' I said. 'But that's better than two hundred miles away. If I were Nicodemus, I wouldn't want to risk moving her that far.'

'Agreed. A third runs directly beneath the Field Museum.' She glanced up at me and arched an eyebrow as her voice turned dry. 'But I think you're already familiar with that one.'

'I was going to put the dinosaur back,' I said. 'But I was unconscious.'

'Which brings us to number four,' Luccio said. Her fingertip came to rest on a cluster of tiny islands out in the center of the lake, northeast of the city, and the heavy, dark purple line running through it. 'Here.'

Molly leaned across me and frowned down at the map. 'There aren't any islands in that part of Lake Michigan. It's all open water.'

'Listens-to-Wind gave this map to me, Miss Carpenter,' Luccio said seriously. 'He's spent several centuries living in this general region.'

I grunted. 'I hear a lot of things. I think that there are some islands out there. They were used as bases for wilderness fighters in several wars. Bootleggers used them as a transfer point for running booze in from Canada, back in the Prohibition days. But there were always stories around them.'

Molly frowned. 'What kind of stories?'

I shrugged. 'The usual scary stuff. Hauntings. People driven insane by unknown forces. People dragged into the water by creatures unknown, or found slaughtered by weaponry several centuries out-of-date.'

'Then why aren't they on the maps and stuff?' Molly asked.

'The islands are dangerous,' I said. 'Long way from any help, and the lake can be awfully mean in the winter. There are stone reefs out there, too, that could gut a boat that came too close. Maybe someone down at city hall figured that the islands would prove less of a temptation to people if everyone thought they were just stories, and invested some effort in removing them from the public record.'

'That wouldn't be possible,' Molly said.

'It might be,' Luccio responded. 'The energies concentrated around those islands would tend to make people unconsciously avoid them. If one did not have a firm destination fixed in mind, the vast majority of people in the area would swing around the islands without ever realizing what they were doing.'

I grunted. 'And if there's that much bad mojo spinning around out there, it would play merry hell with navigational gear. Twenty bucks says that the major flight lanes don't come within five miles of the place.' I thumped my finger on the spot and nodded. 'It feels right. She's there.'

'If she is,' Molly asked, 'then what do we do about it?'

Luccio tilted her head at me, frowning.

'Captain, I assume you already contacted the Council about getting reinforcements?'

'Yes,' she said. 'They'll be here as soon as possible – which is about nine hours from now.'

'Not fast enough,' I said, and narrowed my eyes in thought. 'So we call in some favors.'

'Favors?' Luccio asked.

'Yeah,' I said. 'I know a guy with a boat.'

40

I rushed around setting up details for the next half an hour. Everyone left to get into position except for me, Molly, and Kincaid. And Mouse.

My dog was clearly upset that I wasn't going to be bringing him along, and though he dutifully settled down on the floor near Molly's feet, he looked absolutely miserable.

'Sorry, boy,' I told him. 'I want you here to help Molly and warn her about any danger.'

He sighed.

'I got along just fine without you for quite a while,' I told him. 'Don't you worry about me.'

He rolled onto his back and gave me another pathetic look.

'Hah. Just trying to cadge a tummy rub. I knew it.' I leaned down and obliged him.

A minute later the back door opened, and Thomas came in. 'Finally,' he said. 'I've been sitting in my car so long, I think I left a dent in the seat.'

'Sorry.'

'I'll live. What can I do to help?'

'Get back in your car and give me a ride to my place.'

Thomas gave me a level look. Then he muttered something under his breath, pulled his keys out of his pocket, and stalked back out into the snow.

'You're horrible,' Molly said, grinning.

'What?' I said. 'I'm expressing my brotherly affection.' I shrugged into my coat and picked up my staff. 'Remember the plan?'

'Man the phone,' Molly said, ticking off each point on her fingers. 'Keep my eyes open. Make sure Mouse stays in the same room as me. Check on Kincaid every fifteen minutes.'

At one time she would have been sullen about the prospect of being forced to sit at home when something exciting was under way – but she had grown up enough to realize just how dangerous things could be out there, and to respect her own limitations. Molly was extraordinarily sensitive when it came to the various energies of magic. It was one of the things that made her so good at psychomancy and neuromancy. It also meant that when violent personal or supernatural events started happening, she experienced them in such agonizing clarity that it would often incapacitate her altogether, at least for a few minutes. Combat magic was never going to be her strong suit, and in a real conflict she could prove to be a lethal liability to her own allies.

But at least the kid knew it. She might not like it very much, but she'd applied herself diligently to finding other ways to help fight the good fight. I was proud of her.

'And don't forget your homework,' I said.

She frowned. 'I still don't understand why you want to know about our family tree.'

'Humor me, grasshopper. I'll buy you a snow cone.'

She glanced out the window at the world of white outside. 'Goody.' She looked back at me and gave me a small, worried smile. 'Be careful.'

'Hey, there were almost twenty of these losers at the Shedd. Now we're down to six.'

'The six smartest, strongest, and oldest,' Molly said. 'The ones who really matter.'

'Thank you for your optimism,' I said, and turned to go. 'Lock up behind me.'

Molly bit her lip. 'Harry?'

I paused.

Her voice was very small. 'Look out for my dad. Okay?'

I turned and met her eyes. I drew an X over my heart and nodded.

She blinked her eyes quickly several times and gave me another smile. 'All right.'

'Lock the door,' I told her again, and trudged out into the snow. The lock clicked shut behind me, and Molly watched me slog through the snow to the street. Thomas's military moving van came rumbling through the snow, tires crunching, and I got in.

He turned the heater up a little while I stomped snow off of my shoes.

'So,' he said, starting down the street. 'What's the plan?'

I told him.

'That is a bad plan,' he said.

'There wasn't time for a good one.'

He grunted. 'November is *not* a good time to be sailing on Lake Michigan, Harry.'

'The aftermath of a nuclear holocaust isn't a good time to be sailing there, either.'

Thomas frowned. 'You aren't just running your mouth, here, are you? You're serious?'

'It's a worst-case scenario,' I said. 'But Nicodemus could do it, so we've got to proceed under the presumption that his intentions are in that category. The Denarians want to disrupt civilization, and with the Archive under their control, they could do it. Maybe they'd use biological or chemical weapons instead. Maybe they'd crash the world economy. Maybe they'd turn every program on television into one of those reality shows.'

'That's mostly done already, Harry.'

'Oh. Well. I've got to believe that the world is worth saving anyway.' We traded forced grins. 'Regardless of what they do, the potential for Really Bad Things is just too damned high to ignore, and we need all the help we can get.'

'Even help from one of those dastardly White Court fiends?' Thomas asked.

'Exactly.'

'Good. I was getting tired of dodging Luccio. There's a limited amount of help I can give you if I have to stay out of sight all the time.'

'It's necessary. If the Council knew that you and I were related . . .'

'I know, I know,' Thomas said, scowling. 'Outcast leper unclean.'

I sighed and shook my head. Given that the White Court's modus operandi generally consisted of twisting people's minds around in one of several ways, I didn't dare let anyone on the Council know that Thomas was my friend, let alone my half brother. Everyone would immediately assume the worst – that the White Court had gotten to me and was controlling my head through Thomas. And even if I convinced them that it wasn't the case, it would look suspicious as hell. The Council would demand I demonstrate loyalty, attempt to use Thomas as a spy against the White Court, and in general behave like the pompous, overbearing assholes that they are.

It wasn't easy for either of us to live with – but it wasn't going to change, either.

We got to my apartment and I rushed inside. It was cold. The fire had burned down to nothing in the time I'd been gone. I lifted my hand and murmured under my breath, the spell lighting half a dozen candles at the same time. I grabbed everything I was going to need, waved the candles out again, and hurried back out to Thomas's car.

'You've got Mom's pentacle with you, right?' I asked him. I had a matching pendant on a silver chain around my own neck – which, other than Thomas, was my mother's only tangible legacy.

'Of course,' he said. 'I'll find you. Where now?'

'St. Mary's,' I said.

'Figured.'

Thomas started driving. I broke open my double-barreled shotgun, which I'd sawed down to an illegal length, and loaded two shells into it. Tessa the Mantis Girl had rudely neglected to return my .44 after the conclusion of hostilities at the Aquarium, and I have rarely regretted taking a gun with me into what could prove to be a hairy situation.

'Here,' I said when the truck got within a block or so of the church. 'Drop me off here.'

'Gotcha,' Thomas said. 'Hey, Harry.'

'Yeah?'

'What if they aren't keeping the little girl on the island?'

I shook my head. 'You'll just have to figure something out. I'm making this up as I go.'

He frowned and shook his head. 'What about those goons from Summer? What are you going to do if they show up again?'

'*If?* I should be so lucky.' I winked at him and got out of the Hummer. 'The real question is, what am I going to do if they *don't* show up, and at the worst possible time to boot? Die of shock, probably.'

'See you soon,' Thomas said.

I nodded to my brother, shut the door, and trudged across the street and into the parking lot of St. Mary of the Angels.

It's a big church. A really, *really* big church. It takes up a full city block, and is one of the town's more famous landmarks, Chicago's version of Notre Dame. The drive leading up to the delivery doors in the back of the church had been cleared, as had the little parking lot outside it. Michael's truck was there. The ambient glow of winter night showed me his form and Sanya's, standing outside the truck, both of them wearing long white cloaks emblazoned with scarlet crosses over similarly decorated white surcoats – the Sunday-go-to-meeting wear of the Knights of the Cross. They wore their swords at their hips. Michael wore an honest-to-God breastplate, while Sanya opted for more modern body armor. The big Russian, always the practical progressive, also carried a Kalashnikov assault rifle on a sling over his shoulder.

I wondered if Sanya realized that Michael's antiquated-looking breastplate was lined with Kevlar and ballistic strike plates. The Russian's gear wouldn't do diddly to stop swords or claws.

I'd made some modification to my own gear as well. The thong that usually secured my blasting rod, on the inside of my duster, now held up my shotgun. I'd tied a similar strip of

leather thong to either end of the simple wooden cane that held
Fidelacchius, and now carried the holy blade slung over my
shoulder.

Michael nodded to me and then glanced down at his watch.
'You're cutting it a little fine, aren't you?'

'Punctuality is for people with nothing better to do,' I said.

'Or for those who have already taken care of the other details,'
murmured a woman's voice.

She stepped out of the shadows across the street, a tall and
striking woman in motorcycle leathers. She had eyes that were
the warm brown shade of hot chocolate, and her hair was dark
and braided tightly against her head. She wore no makeup, but
even without it she was a knockout. It was the expression on
her face that tipped me off to who she was – sadness mingled
with regret and steely resolve.

'Rosanna,' I said quietly.

'Wizard.' She strode toward us, somehow arrogant and reserved
at the same time, her hips rolling as she walked. The jacket was
open almost all the way to her belly button, and there was
nothing but skin showing where it was parted. Her eyes, however,
remained on the Knights. 'These two were not a part of the
arrangements.'

'And it was supposed to be Nicodemus that met me,' I said.
'Not you.'

'Circumstances necessitated a change,' Rosanna replied.

I shrugged one shoulder – the one bearing *Fidelacchius*. 'Same
here.'

'What circumstances are those?' Rosanna demanded.

'The ones where I'm dealing with a pack of two-faced, backstabbing, treacherous, murderous lunatics whom I trust no farther
than I can kick.'

She regarded me with level, lovely eyes. 'And what is the
Knights' intended role?'

'They're here to build trust.'

'Trust?' she asked.

'Absolutely. I can kick you a lot farther when they're around.'

A very small smile touched her mouth. She inclined her head slightly to me. Then she turned to Sanya. 'Those colors hardly suit you, animal. Though it is more than agreeable to see you again.'

'I am not that man anymore, Rosanna,' Sanya replied. 'I have changed.'

'No, you haven't,' Rosanna said, those warm eyes locked onto Sanya's now. 'You still long for the fray. Still love the fight. Still revel in bloodshed. That was never Magog. That was always you, my beast.'

Sanya shook his head with a faint smile. 'I still enjoy a fight,' he said. 'I simply choose them a bit more carefully now.'

'It isn't too late, you know,' Rosanna said. 'Make a gift of that toy to my lord and my lady. They will accept you again with open arms.' She took a step toward him. 'You could be with me again, animal. You could have me again.'

Something very odd happened to her voice on the last couple of sentences. It became . . . thicker somehow, richer, more musical. The individual sounds seemed to have little to do with meaning — but the voice itself carried a honey-slow swirl of sensuality and desire that felt like it was going to glide into my ears and start glowing gently inside my brain. I was only on the fringe of it, too, and had gotten only a watered-down version of the promise contained in that voice. Sanya got it at full potency.

He threw his head back and laughed, a rich, booming, basso laugh that bounced back and forth from the icy stones of the church and the cold walls of the buildings around us.

Rosanna took a step back at that, her expression showing surprise.

'I told you, Rosanna,' he rumbled, laughter still bubbling in his tone. 'I have changed.' Then his expression sobered abruptly. 'You could change, too. I know how much some of the things you have done disturb you. I've been there when you had the nightmares. It doesn't have to be like that.'

She just stared at him.

Sanya spread his hands. 'Give up the coin, Rosanna. Please. Let me help you.'

Her eyelids lowered into slits. She shuddered once and looked down. Then she said, 'It is too late for me, Sanya. It has been too late for me for a long, long time.'

'It is never too late,' Sanya said earnestly. 'Not as long as you draw breath.'

Something like contempt touched Rosanna's features. 'What do you know, stupid child.' Her gaze swung back to me. 'Show me the Sword and the coins, wizard.'

I tapped the hilt of Shiro's Sword, hanging from its improvised strap over one shoulder. Then I drew the purple Crown Royal bag out of my pocket and held it up. I shook it. It jingled.

'Give the coins to me,' Rosanna said.

I folded my arms. 'No.'

Her eyes narrowed again. 'Our bargain—'

'You can see them after I've seen the girl,' I replied. 'Until then, you'll have to settle for some jingle.' I shook the bag again.

She glowered at me.

'Make up your mind,' I said. 'I haven't got all night. Do you want to explain to Nicodemus how you threw away his chance of destroying the Swords? Or do you want to get moving and take us to the kid?'

Her eyes flickered with something like anger, and warm brown became brilliant gold. But she only gave me a small, stiff nod of her head, and said, 'I will take you to her. This way. Please.'

41

The next few minutes were intense, and I didn't dare let it show. If I'd been completely wrong in my deductions — which was possible; God knew it had happened before — then Michael, Sanya, and I were about to walk into the lion's den together. Granted, that worked out for Daniel, but he was the exception to the rule. Most of the time it works out well only for the lions. That's why the Persians used it as a means of execution.

Granted, Michael was working for the same employer, and technically Sanya was too, even if he wasn't wholly decided on whether or not that was what he was doing. But me and the Almighty haven't ever really sat down for a chat. I'm not really sure where He stands on the Harry Dresden issue, and as a result my theological stance has been pretty simple: I try not to get noticed by anything Godly, godly, or god-ish. I think we're all happier that way.

All the same, given who I was up against, I didn't think it would be inappropriate if a couple of breaks came my way. Hopefully Michael had put in a good word for me.

Rosanna walked down the street and lifted a hand. A van cruised up out of the night. It was occupied by a single driver, a thick-necked, broken-nosed type whose eyes didn't look like he was all the way there. One of Nick's fanatics, probably. They had their tongues ritually removed as a point of honor and practicality — from Nicodemus's perspective, anyway. I supposed I could ask him to open up and confirm it, but it seemed a little gauche.

Michael stuck his head in the van and checked it out. Then he politely opened the passenger door for Rosanna. The Denarian stared levelly at him for a moment, and then nodded her head and slid into the van.

Sanya went in the van first, taking the rearmost seat. I went in after Michael. Rosanna muttered something to the driver, and the van took off.

I got nervous for a minute. The van headed west – in exactly the opposite direction from the lake. Then the driver turned north, and after a few minutes I realized that we were headed for one of the marinas at the north end of Lake Shore Drive. I forced myself to keep my breathing smooth and even. If the bad guys tumbled to the fact that we'd already guessed their location, the situation could devolve pretty quickly.

Michael sat calmly, his face imperturbable, his hands resting on the sheathed form of *Amoracchius*, the picture of saintly serenity. Sanya, behind us, let out a low, buzzing snore. It wasn't as saintly as Michael, but it conveyed just as much blithe confidence. I tried to match their calm, with mixed results. *Don't get jittery, Harry. Play it cool. Ice water in your veins.*

The van stopped at one of the marinas off Northerly Island. Rosanna got out without a word and we followed her. She stalked down to the shore, out onto the docks, and out to a modestly sized ski boat moored at the dock's end. Michael and I went aboard after her. Sanya untied the lines holding the boat to the dock, pushed it away from the pier, and casually hopped across the widening distance and into the vessel.

It took her a couple of minutes, but Rosanna coaxed the old boat's engines to life and turned us away from the lights of the city and out into the darkness of the great lake.

It was eerie how swiftly the world became pitch-black. That strange faerie-light of the night under a heavy snow vanished out on the waters of the lake, where the snow simply sank into the depths. The low overcast gave us a little light, for a time, reflecting the glow of the city, but as the boat continued skimming out into the center of the lake, even that faded away until I could barely distinguish the outline of the boat and its occupants against the water all around.

I wasn't sure how long we went on like that in the dark. It seemed like an hour, but it couldn't have been more than half that. The boat bounced across waves, *whump, whump, whump*, throwing up splashes of spray that coated the bow in a shining crust of ice. My stomach got a little queasy as I tried to anticipate the motion in the darkness and failed.

At length, the rumble of the boat's engine died away, and then stopped altogether. The silence was disorienting. I've lived my entire adult life in Chicago. I'm used to the city, to its rhythms, its music. The hum and hiss of traffic, the clatter of elevated trains, the blaring radios, the beeping horns, cell phones, sirens, music, animals, and people, people, people.

But out here, in the center of the vast, empty cold of the lake, there was nothing. No heartbeat of the city, no voices, no *nothing*, except the glug and slap of water hitting the hull of the boat.

I waited for a couple of minutes while the boat was rocked by the waves of the lake. Now that we weren't moving under power, I thought that they were rocking the boat to a really alarming degree, but I wasn't going to be the one to start whimpering.

'Well?' Sanya demanded, about five seconds before I would have cracked. 'What are we waiting for?'

'A signal,' Rosanna murmured. 'I would as soon not tear out the boat's bottom on rocks and drown us all, dear animal.'

I reached into my duster pocket and took out a chemical light. I tore it out of its package, snapped it, and shook it to life. Up sprang a greenish glow that lit up the immediate area well enough, considering how dark it had been for the past half an hour or so.

Rosanna turned to look at the light. Sometime during the trip her human form had changed, vanishing back into the shape of the scarlet-skinned, goat-legged, bat-winged demoness I had seen at the Aquarium. Her eyes, both the brown ones and the glowing green pair, focused on the chemical light, and she smiled, revealing white, delicately pointed fangs. 'No magic, wizard? Are you so fearful about husbanding your strength?'

Out this far from shore, floating over *this* much water, it
would have been difficult to put together a spell of any complexity
– but I was sure Rosanna knew that as well as I did, if the
flames I'd seen her tossing around back at the Shedd were any
indication. It *would* have been a waste of energy I might need
later. But I reminded myself about the ice water alleged to be
in my veins.

'Mostly I just think the glow lights are fun,' I said. 'Did you
know that they used these things for the blood of the Predator
in that movie with Arnold Schwarzenegger?'

The smile faltered. 'What are you talking about?'

'That's the problem with you nearly immortal types,' I said.
'You couldn't spot a pop culture reference if it skittered up and
implanted an embryo down your esophagus.'

At the back of the boat, Sanya started coughing.

Rosanna stared at him for a moment, her eyes unreadable.
Then the barest shadow of something mournful touched her
features, and she turned away from him. She walked to the front
of the boat and stood facing east into the darkness, her arms
folded across her body in a posture of tightly closed insecurity,
her wings wrapping around her like a blanket.

Sanya didn't miss it. He'd been forcing himself to conceal a
grin, but it faded into uneasy discomfort at Rosanna's reaction.
He looked like he was about to say something, then frowned
and shook his head. He turned his face to stare out over the
water. Large flakes of snow continued to drift down, flickers of
crystalline green in the glow light. Michael started humming
contentedly – 'Amazing Grace.' He must have learned the song
from some Baptists somewhere. He had a nice voice, rich and
steady.

I stepped up next to Rosanna and said in a quiet voice, 'Tell
me something. This maiden-of-sorrow thing you've got going
– how many Knights have you killed with it?'

Her eyes, both pairs, flicked aside to glance at me for a second,
then back out at the night. 'What do you mean?'

'You know. You've got that beautiful sad aura going. You

look mournful and tragic and pretty. Radiate that "save me, save me" vibe. Probably get all kinds of young men who want to carry you off on a white horse.'

'Is that what you think of me?' she asked.

'Lady,' I said, 'a year or three ago, I'd have been the first in line. Hell, if I thought you were serious about getting out, I'd probably still help you. But I don't think you want out. I think that if you were all that pathetic, you wouldn't be controlling your Fallen – it would be controlling you. I think you're Tessa's trusted lieutenant for a reason. Which means that either this tragic, trapped-lady routine is a bunch of crocodile tears, or else it's hypocrisy on such an epic scale that it probably qualifies as some kind of psychological dysfunction.'

She stared out into darkness and said nothing.

'You never did answer my question,' I said.

'Why not say it louder?' she asked me in a bitter undertone. 'If that is what you think of me, then your friends need to be forewarned of my treachery.'

'Right,' I said. 'I do that, and then your eyes well up with tears, and you turn away from me. You let them see one tear fall down your cheek, then turn your head enough to let the wind carry your hair over the rest. Maybe let your shoulders shake once. Then it's the big bad suspicious wizard, who doesn't forgive and doesn't understand, picking on the poor little girl who is trapped in her bad situation and really just wants to be loved. Give me some credit, Rosanna. I'm not going to *help* you set them up.'

The glowing green eyes turned to examine me, and Rosanna's mouth moved, speaking in an entirely different, feminine voice. 'Lasciel taught you something of us.'

'You might say that,' I replied.

Ahead of us and slightly to the right a light flared up in the darkness – a bonfire, I thought. I couldn't tell how far away it was, given the night and the falling snow.

'There,' Rosanna murmured. 'That way. If you would excuse me.'

As she walked back to the wheel of the boat, a breath of wind sighed over the lake. In itself that wasn't anything new. Wind had been blowing all the way through the snowstorm. Something about this breeze, though, caught my attention. It wasn't right.

It took me another three or four seconds to realize what was wrong.

This was a south wind. And it was warm.

'Uh-oh,' I said. I held up the chemical light and started scanning the waters all around us.

'Harry?' Michael said. 'What is it?'

'Feel that breeze?' I asked.

'*Da*,' Sanya said, confusion in his voice. 'Is warm. So?'

Michael caught on. 'Summer is on the way,' he said.

Rosanna shot a glance over her shoulder at us. 'What?'

'Get us to shore,' I told her. 'The things coming after me might not give a damn if they take you out along with me.'

She turned back to the wheel and turned the ignition. The boat's engine stuttered and wheezed and didn't turn over.

The breeze picked up. Instead of snowflakes, thick, slushy drops of half-frozen sleet began to fall. More ice began forming on the boat, thickening almost visibly in the green glow of my light. The waves began to grow steeper, rocking the boat more and more severely.

'Come on,' I heard myself saying. 'Come *on*.'

'Look there!' Sanya called, pointing a finger down at the water beside the boat.

Something long, brown, fibrous, and slimy lashed up out of the water and wrapped around the Russian knight's arm from wrist to elbow.

'*Bozhe moi!*'

Two more strands whipped up from different angles, one seizing Sanya's upper arm, one wrapping around his face and skull, and jerked him halfway from the boat in the time it took me to shift my weight and reach for him. I managed to grab one of his boots before he could be pulled all the way over the side into the water. I planted one foot on the wall of the boat and hauled on Sanya's leg for all I was worth. 'Michael!'

The boat's engine coughed, turned over, stuttered, and died.

'*In nomine Dei Patri!*' Michael roared as *Amoracchius* cleared its sheath. The broadsword flashed in a single sweeping slash, and severed the strands strangling Sanya. The edges of the slashed material burned away from the touch of *Amoracchius*'s steel like paper from an open flame.

I dragged Sanya back into the boat, and the big Russian whipped his saber from its sheath just in time to neatly sever another lashing brown tendril of animate fiber. 'What is it?'

'Kelpies,' I growled. If they tangled up the blades of the engine our boat wasn't going anywhere. I howled at Rosanna, 'Come *on!*'

The boat suddenly rocked violently to the other side. I twisted my head to look over my shoulder and saw kelpies coming up over the sides. They were slimy, nebulous things, only vaguely humanoid in shape, made up of masses of wet weeds with gaping mouths and pinpoints of glittering silver light for eyes.

I turned and swept my arm in a slewing arc, unleashing my will as I cried out, '*Forzare!*'

Invisible force ripped the kelpies from the sides of the boat, leaving long strands of wet plant matter clinging limply to the fiberglass hull. They let out gurgling screams as they flew back and splashed into the water.

The boat's engine caught and rose to a roar. The rear end of the boat sank, and its nose rose as it surged forward.

One of my feet flew out from underneath me. I went down, flailing my arms and legs, dimly aware that one of the kelpies had somehow gotten a limb tangled around my ankle. I got dragged to the back of the boat in a quick series of painful jerks and impacts, and had just enough time to realize that the boat was about to surge right out from under me, leaving me in the drink. Then it would just be a question of what killed me first – the icy water or the strangling embrace of the company within it.

Then there was a flash of scarlet and white, a whistle and a hissing sound, and a lance of fire on one of my feet. I went into free fall and bounced into the rear wall of the boat, then to the floor. Icy rain and freezing water splashed up against me, viciously cold. I looked down to find a strand of fibrous weed curling and blackening as it fell from my bleeding ankle. Sanya reached down and plucked the remains clear of my leg before tossing it over the rear of the boat and back into the water. My ankle was bleeding, my blood black in the green chemical light. More black stained the tip of *Esperacchius*.

I clutched at my ankle, hissing in pain. 'Dammit, Sanya!'

Sanya peered out at the darkness behind the boat and then down at my leg. 'Ah. Oops.'

Michael came back to kneel beside me and hunkered down over my foot. 'Harry, hold still.' He poked at my ankle, and it hurt enough to make me snarl something about his parentage. 'It isn't bad. Long but shallow.' He opened a leather case on his sword belt, opposite the sheath of *Amoracchius*, and withdrew a small medical kit. Sanya's sword had already slashed open my jeans, but Michael tore them a little more to get them out of the way of the cut. Then he cleaned the injury with some kind of disposable wipe, smeared it with something from a plastic tube, covered it with a thick white absorbent bandage, and wrapped it in tape. It took him all of two or three minutes, his hands quick and sure, which was just as well. By the time he was done the shock of the injury had worn off, and the hurt had started up.

'Not much to be done about the pain,' he said. 'Sorry, Harry.'

'Pain I can live with,' I said, wincing. 'Just give me a minute.'

'I am sorry, Dresden,' Sanya said.

'Yeah. Don't you dare save my life ever again,' I told him. Then I lifted my leg onto one of the benches in the back of the boat to elevate it, and closed my eyes. There were a lot of ways to manage pain besides drugs. Granted, most of them wouldn't help you much, unless you'd had several years of training in focus and concentration, but fortunately I had. Lasciel's shadow had shown me a mental technique for blocking pain so effective that it was a little scary – when I'd used it before, I'd pushed myself until my body had collapsed, because I hadn't been aware of exactly how bad my condition was. I could have died as a result.

Body or mind, heart or soul, we're all human, and we're supposed to feel pain. You cut yourself off from it at your own risk.

That said, given what was ahead of us and coming up behind us, I could hardly put myself in any *more* danger, relatively speaking, and I couldn't afford any distractions. So I closed my eyes, controlled my breathing, focused my mind, and began to methodically wall away the pain of my new injury, my broken nose, my aching body. It took me a couple of minutes, and by the time I was done the pitch of the boat's engine had changed, dropping from a roar to a lower growl.

I opened my eyes to find Sanya and Michael standing on either side of me, swords in hand, watching over me. Up at the front of the boat Rosanna cut the engine still more and turned her head to stare intently at me for a slow beat. The side of her mouth curved up in a slight, knowing smile. Then she turned to face front again, and I realized that there was light enough to see the outline of her delicately curling demon horns.

I rose and found myself staring at an island that rose from the increasingly turbulent waters of the lake. It was covered in the woods and brush of the midwestern United States – lots of trees less than a foot thick, with the space beneath them filled in with brush, thickets, and thorns to a depth of four or five feet. Snow lay over everything, and the light reflecting from it was what let me see Rosanna's profile.

The shoreline was covered in what looked like an old Western ghost town – only one that had been abandoned for so long that the trees had come back to reclaim the space. Most of the buildings had fallen down. Trees rose out of most of the ones that hadn't, and the sight reminded me, somehow, of an insect collection:

empty shells pinned to a card. A sign, weathered beyond reading, hung from its only remaining link of rusting chain. It swung in the wind, aged metal squeaking. There was the skeleton of an old dock down at the shoreline, all broken wooden columns, standing up out of the water like the stumps of rotten teeth.

Looking at the place filled me with a sense of awareness of the attention of an empty, sterile malevolence. This place did not like me. It did not want me there. It did not have the least regard for me, and the corpse of the little town ahead of me was a silent declaration that it had fought against folk like me before – and won.

'Gee,' I called to Rosanna. 'Are you sure this is the right place?'

She pointed silently up. I followed the direction of her finger, up the slope of the island, and spotted the light I'd seen from farther out in the lake – definitely a bonfire, I saw now, up on a hill above the town, at what looked like the highest point on the island. Something stood starkly against the sky there, the dark shape of a building or tower, though I couldn't make out any details.

Rosanna cut the engine completely, and the boat glided silently forward to the broken wooden post nearest the shore. She climbed into the front of the boat and was waiting with a rope when the prow of the vessel bumped the column. She tied the boat to the post, then hopped down into the water and waded the rest of the way ashore.

'Oh, good,' I muttered. 'More wet.'

From back behind us, the still-rising wind carried forward a gurgling, warbling cry. I'd been up north a few times, and it might have been the call of a loon – but all of us there knew better. Summer was still on our trail.

'We aren't going to make it any drier by waiting here,' Michael said quietly.

'There are men in those trees,' Sanya murmured, sheathing his sword and taking up the Kalashnikov again. 'Thirty yards up, there, and over there. Those are machine-gun positions.'

I grunted. 'Let's get moving. Before they get bored and decide to start making like this is Normandy.'

'God go with us,' Michael prayed quietly.

I unlimbered my shotgun and said, 'Amen.'

42

Michael had planned ahead. He had a dozen chemical heat bags with him, the kind made for hunters to slip inside the wristbands of their coats. He passed them around to us, and we put them inside our socks after we waded ashore. Otherwise I don't know if we would have made it through the snow up that hill, not with our pants soaked to the knees.

Rosanna, of course, wasn't having any issues with the weather. With her wings draped around her like a cloak, the demonic form she wore seemed inured to the cold, and her cloven hooves moved along the frozen, stony hillside as nimbly as a mountain goat's, her barb-tipped tail lashing back and forth dramatically as she went. Sanya walked along behind her, then me, and Michael brought up the rear. It wasn't a long walk, but it fit in a lot of unpleasantness into a little bit of time. The little town had been a company town, built up around what looked like an old cannery – a long building, falling to pieces now, at the very end of the ruined street.

Partway up the hill we ran across a trail that had obviously been in use over the past several days. Someone had kept it clear of snow, exposing a path that had been cut into the rock of the hillside, including stone stairs that led up to its summit. As we went up the stairs the shape at the top of the hill became clearer, as light from the large fire beside it revealed it more clearly.

'A lighthouse,' I murmured. 'Or what's left of one.'

It might have been a fifty-foot tower at one time, but it had been broken off perhaps twenty feet up as if snapped by a giant's hand. Beacon towers dotted the shorelines and islands of all of the Great Lakes, and like all such structures they had accumulated more than their due of strange stories. I hadn't heard any stories about this one – but staring up at the rough grey stones, I got the impression that it might have had something to do with the fact that in order for strange stories to spread, someone has to *survive* a dark encounter in order to start the tale.

This entire creepy place was giving me the idea that I wasn't merely walking on haunted ground – but that I was walking on major-league haunted ground, the kind of place that had never bowed its head to the advance of progress and civilization, to science and reason, that had no more regard for those children of human intellect than it did for their progenitors. The island seemed almost *alive*, aware of my presence in a sense that I couldn't really tangibly define – aware of it and sullenly, spitefully hostile to it.

But that wasn't the creepy part.

The creepy part was that it felt familiar.

Walking up those stone steps, my legs settled into a steady pattern of motion, as if they'd already walked up that path a thousand times. I swerved slightly on one step, for no reason that I could see, only to hear Michael, behind me, continue walking in a straight line and slip as the stone he stepped on shifted beneath his foot. I found myself counting silently to myself, backward, and when I hit zero we mounted the last step and reached the summit of the hill.

Somehow I knew, even before I saw it, that one side of the old lighthouse would be torn open to the sky, revealing an interior that was as hollowed-out and empty as the inside of a rifle barrel. I knew that the little stone cottage built against the base of the tower would still be reasonably intact, though about half of the slate-tile roof had collapsed inward and would need repairs. I knew that it had been made from the stones of the collapsed lighthouse. I knew that the front door rattled when you opened it, and that the back door, which wasn't in sight from here, would swell up during a rain and get stuck in its frame, much like the door at . . .

. . . at home.

I also knew that as freaking weird as all of that was, I couldn't afford to let any of it matter right now.

Nicodemus and company were waiting for us.

The sleeting rain was starting to cover everything in a thin layer of ice, but the bonfire laid on the ground before the opening in the wall of the tower was large enough to ignore it. The flames leapt ten or twelve feet in the air, and burned with an eerie, violet-tinged light, and the ice forming everywhere created the illusion of a purple haze that clung to anything inanimate.

Beside the bonfire stones had been piled up into something that resembled the throne of some ancient pagan king. Nicodemus sat atop them, of course. Tessa stood at his right hand, entirely in human form for the first time since I had seen her. She was a little slip of a girl who barely looked old enough to hold a driver's license, and was dressed in something black and skintight. Deirdre knelt at Nicodemus's feet, and with the three of them together like that, I could see the blending of the parents' features in their daughter. Especially around the eyes. Deirdre's showed a full measure of both Nicodemus's soulless calculation and Tessa's heartless selfishness.

Magog crouched at the base of the pile of stones, apelike and enormous, sullen eyes burning with bloodlust. The spined Denarian I had beaten down with the silver construct-hand lay reclining on the ground beside Magog, his face twisted with hate, one hand twisting and clenching – but his maimed body was otherwise motionless.

My heart sped up in sudden excitement. There were still six of them. They hadn't broken Ivy yet.

I held up a hand. We came to a stop, while Rosanna lightly mounted the steps to kneel down at Tessa's right hand.

'Wow,' I drawled. 'That isn't a contrived tableau or anything. Are you here to do business, or did you get lost on your way to auditions for *Family Feud*?'

'Gunman in the cottage,' Sanya murmured, very quietly.

'Beasts in the shadows behind the tower,' Michael whispered.

I kept myself from looking. If my friends said there were bad guys there, they were there, end of story.

'Good evening, Dresden,' Nicodemus said. 'Have you brought the merchandise?'

I jingled the Crown Royal bag and bumped the hilt of Shiro's sword, hanging over my shoulder, with the side of my head. 'Yep. But you knew that already, or Rosie, there, wouldn't have brought us this far. So let's skip the small talk. Show me the girl.'

'By all means,' Nicodemus said. He gestured with one hand, and the shadows – his shadow, I should say – suddenly fell away from the interior of the ruined lighthouse tower.

Red light filled that space, pouring up from the sigils and glyphs of the most elaborate greater circle I had ever seen – and I'd seen one made of silver, gold, and precious stones. This one incorporated all of those things plus art – grotesque pieces, mostly – sound, ringing forth in gentle, steady waves from upright tuning forks and tubular bells; and light, focused through prisms and crystals, refracted into dozens of colors that split and bent into perfectly geometric shapes in the air around the circle.

Ivy was trapped inside.

I've seen some fairly extreme abuse in my time, but it never gets easier to see more of it. Nick's people had gone with most of the classics for breaking someone down, and then added in a few twists that wouldn't be available to regular folks. They'd taken Ivy's clothes, for starters, which in this weather was sadistic on multiple levels. They'd shaved her hair away, leaving her bald, except for a couple of sad, ragged little tufts of gold. She was curled up into a fetal position, and she floated in the air, spinning slowly and apparently at random. Her eyes were tightly closed, her face pale with disorientation, terrified.

Outside the circle they had chained a number of those hideous hunting beasts, hairless creatures that resembled nothing in the animal kingdom but fell somewhere between a big panther and a wolf. The creatures looked hungry, and stared intently at the floating morsel. One of them snarled and threw itself to the end of its chain in an effort to snap its fanged maw closed upon the girl's vulnerable flesh. It couldn't reach her, but Ivy twitched and let out a thready whimper.

As she spun and twirled – a deliberate echo of what she'd done to Magog at the Aquarium, I felt certain – the motion revealed dozens of tiny scratches and bruises, evidence of a small legion of petty cruelties. They would, however, seem nightmarish enough to a child who had never experienced real pain of her own. All of this – the pain, the helplessness, the indignity, all of it – would be that much more horrific and terrifying to Ivy for its novelty. Say what I would about pain being a part of the human condition, when it comes to seeing it inflicted on children, I'm as hypocritical as the day is long.

Some things just shouldn't happen.

'There, you see?' the lord of the Denarians said. 'Safe and sound, as agreed.'

I turned my gaze back to Nicodemus, who was about ten seconds from an ass kicking—

—and caught a little glimmer of something approximating satisfaction in his eyes that made my combat-readying reflexes cool off almost instantly.

Ivy's treatment hadn't been only about putting her in the proper frame of mind to manipulate her.

It had also been about manipulating *me*. It wasn't even all that tough to understand why. After all, I'd been in a situation something like this before.

It wasn't enough for the Denarians to simply acquire the Sword. They couldn't break or smash or melt *Fidelacchius*, any more than the Church could smash or melt the thirty silver coins. The power of the Sword was more than merely physical, and as long as it was wielded by those of pure heart and intent, it would take more than mere physical means to undo it.

Of course, if you handed the Sword to, for example, a wizard who was known for playing it shady once in a while, and who was known for having a bad temper, and who was known for occasionally losing it, and maybe for burning down a building or two when he got angry, that could change the situation entirely. Put him in an intense situation, give him a really good reason to be angry, give him a mighty magical weapon near at hand, and he might well seize it and use it out of sheer outrage – despite the fact that he wouldn't exactly be acting from entirely pure motives by doing so. After all, I had come here, ostensibly in peace, to offer up the Sword as a sacrifice for the life of a child. If I then took up that same weapon and used it to strike at Nicodemus and company instead, I, its rightful bearer, would be employing *Fidelacchius*, the Sword of Faith, in an act of treachery.

Once I'd done that, then the Sword *would* just be a sword, an object of steel and wood. Once I'd done that, then Nicodemus and his insane little family could destroy the weapon. They *needed* someone to make that mistake, someone to make that choice, in order to unmake the weapon, just as any bearer of a coin had to make the choice to give it up to be free of the Fallen inside. They needed someone with a right to the Sword to choose to abuse that right.

I'd made that mistake once already, on a stormy night much like this one, when Michael had asked me to carry *Amoracchius* for him. I'd used the Sword of Love to try to save my ass from the consequences of my own bad decisions and nearly gotten it destroyed as a result. It would have been unmade, in fact, if not for the intervention of my brother – even if I hadn't known about our kinship at the time. Thomas had. He'd been looking out for his little brother even then.

Don't get me wrong: At times I can be a little thick – particularly when there's a woman involved. There's just no way I'm stupid enough to make a mistake quite *that* enormous twice.

But . . .

Nicodemus didn't know that I'd made it even *once*, now, did he?

Oh, he knew me pretty well. He knew how angry his actions had made me, how I would react to the sight of what they'd done to Ivy – and he was counting on me to react according to my nature, in order to help him unmake *Fidelacchius*.

This was going to be a dangerous game, going up against an opponent who had been around as long as Nick had, but I couldn't win if I didn't play – and I needed to buy a little more time and make sure that both of our prizes were on hand before we started the fireworks.

So I gave him what he wanted.

I slammed the end of my staff down onto the ground with my left hand, reached up to seize the hilt of *Fidelacchius* with my right, and snarled, 'Get her the hell out of that thing, Nicodemus. Right now.'

They laughed at me, all of them together, relaxed and insulting. It would have sounded rehearsed if it were any less well coordinated. Instead, it came off like something they'd done so often over the years that it simply came naturally now. 'Look at his face,' Tessa murmured, a little-girl giggle in her voice. 'It's all red.'

I clenched my jaw as hard as I could. It wasn't much of a stretch to keep pretending to be angry, but I tried to go all Method actor on them. *Eat your heart out, Sir Ian.* I jerked the Sword a couple of inches from its sheath. 'I'm warning you,' I said, trying to get a good look around. 'Let the girl go before this gets ugly.'

I must have been doing a pretty good job with the acting. Michael's voice, high-pitched with alarm, came from behind me. 'Harry,' he said, urgently, 'wait.'

I took two steps forward, ignoring Michael, and drew the Sword from its sheath. *Fidelacchius* was a classic, chisel-tipped katana, encased in what looked like an old wooden walking cane. I'd kept the blade clean and oiled while it was in my care. It came free of its casing without a sound and gleamed coldly in the violet light of the fire. 'I brought the Sword,' I told Nicodemus, throwing some taunt into my tone. 'See? You wanted this, right? In exchange for the girl?'

His eyes narrowed as he stared at the blade, and I noticed, for the first time, that he wore a sword of his own at his hip – as did Tessa, for that matter. Super. I made a mental note not to try fencing any of them. I'm tall and quick, and I've got a lunge that can hit from halfway across the county, but when it comes to deadly swordplay, I'm a piker compared to the serious swordsmen, like Michael – and Michael considered himself barely more than a mild challenge to Nicodemus.

'What on earth makes you think he's going to go through with the deal, wizard?' Tessa asked me, her voice a purr. 'Now that you're here, the Sword is here, the coins are here?'

'Maybe it escaped your notice, bitch,' I snarled, 'but the Sword *is* here. And the *other* two are as well. Maybe you want to think twice before making a fight of it.'

Thorned Namshiel let out a croaking laugh. 'You think six of us fear facing two Knights?'

'I think there's about five and a half of you, stumpy,' I shot back, taking another step toward them. I could see a little more of the tower's interior from there. 'And for all you know, you're facing three Knights.'

Nicodemus smiled, showing teeth. 'And for all Michael and Sanya know, Dresden, the two of them are facing seven Denarians, not six. You *did* lead them here, after all.'

'Harry,' Michael said again, his tone tense.

'Shut *up*!' I half screamed at Nicodemus, taking several steps closer. Almost.

Magog let out a snorting rumble and shuffled a yard closer to me, scraping at the ground with his feet and knuckles, shaking his shaggy, horned head threateningly.

I hefted the Sword and bared my teeth in a snarl. 'Oh, you want some of this, Magilla?' I taunted, taking two more steps forward. 'Come get some; I'll show you what keeps happening to Kong.'

There! At the base of the tower wall, a crumpled human form, bloodied, bruised, half-frozen, but alive. He lifted his face as I came into sight and I met the gaze of Gentleman Johnnie Marcone.

They'd tied him to the wall with ropes – something of a mercy, since metal chains would probably have killed him, given the weather over the past few days. One side of his face was puffy with bruises, but both eyes were open. He had a lot of blood on one side of his head. In fact . . .

Hell's bells. Something had ripped off the top half of his left ear. Not neatly, either. The flesh had been raggedly torn. The knuckles of his right hand were thickly crusted with blood. Marcone had torn them open on something before he'd been bound. He'd fought them.

I stopped talking trash and started backpedaling toward Michael and Sanya immediately.

Magog froze, his head tilted comically to one side, his expression confused.

Nicodemus sat up in place on the throne, sensing that the plan he'd thought was going along so swimmingly had begun to fall apart.

'Michael!' I said, and tossed *Fidelacchius* into the air behind me.

'Kill them!' Nicodemus snapped, his voice ringing over the hilltop. 'Kill them now!'

Tessa let out a scream that sounded almost orgasmic, and sections of scarlet-and-black chitin seemed to simply rip their way out of her flesh, her body stretching and distending into her mantis shape. Deirdre hissed and arched her back in a kinetic echo of her mother, her hair lengthening into steely blades, her skin darkening. Rosanna howled, and called fire – specifically Hellfire – into her spread hands, while Thorned Namshiel lifted his hand into the air and gathered flickers of green lightning between his fingertips.

Magog simply bellowed and charged, and with howls of hunger and rage a dozen hairless beasts bounded from the shadows all around us and flung themselves at us with bloodthirsty disregard for their own lives. And, as if all of that weren't enough, half a dozen points of brilliant red light, the emanations of laser sights of hidden gunmen, flashed at us through the mist and sleet.

Oh, yeah. Super plan, Harry.

I had them right where I wanted them.

43

I didn't stop to see what happened to the sword I'd just thrown toward Michael. I plunged my hand into my duster and came out with the sawed-off shotgun. I dropped my staff, lifted the gun in both hands, turned my face away, and shouted, 'Fire in the hole!' a second before I pulled the trigger.

Once upon a time I'd seen Kincaid use Dragon's Breath rounds against Red Court vampires in a fight at Wrigley Field. It had been impressive as hell watching those shotgun rounds belch out jets of flame forty feet long. Since then I'd done a bit of research on fun things you can fire out of a shotgun, and as it turns out, there's all *kinds* of interesting stuff you can shoot at people. It's astonishing, really, the creativity that goes into the design of all the different specialized ammunition available on the market today.

My personal favorite: a round known as the Fireball.

It fires out a spray of superheated particles of metal — tiny, tiny bits of metal blazing away at a temperature of over three thousand degrees. They spread out into an enormous cone of fire and light more than two hundred and fifty feet long, brighter and hotter than any fireworks you've ever seen. Forestry services use them to start backfires, and special weapons units use them to create enormous, eye-catching diversions.

I unleashed two Fireball rounds simultaneously, straight up into the air, and for an instant turned that weirdly firelit hilltop as bright as a midsummer noon.

Even with my eyes closed and my face turned away, the world turned bright pink through my eyelids. I heard gunfire from the direction of the cottage, and more from the tree line off to the left, but whatever gunmen Nicodemus had positioned there had been blinded by the flash, and it would take time for their night vision to recover.

That had been half the point of using the Fireball rounds, there in the dark. It wouldn't give us much time to act, no more than a handful of seconds – but a lot can happen in a handful of seconds, if you're willing to use them well.

I dropped the shotgun, grabbed my staff, and charged forward, screaming like a madman.

Michael and Sanya came hard on my heels. Michael bore *Amoracchius* in his right hand and *Fidelacchius* in his left, and as he ran both blades suddenly became limned in a low, flickering silver light. One of the beasts that had been lurking behind the tower had bounded forward at Nicodemus's command, even blinded by the flash, but it had the bad fortune to rush past me directly at Michael. The Knight of the Cross twisted his body left, then right, delivering a pair of slashes with each weapon. There were hiss-thumps of swift impact, a scream of pain from the beast, and Michael pounded on, barely even slowing his stride, leaving the still-twitching body of the beast on the ground behind him.

Then the air shook with the force of Magog's battle roar, and I jerked my gaze around to find the huge Denarian thundering directly toward me. I'd already tested my will against Magog's power, and I knew I could stop him if I had to do it. I also knew that it would take an enormous effort to manage it, and leave me vulnerable to one of his companions – so instead of trying to stop him, I called upon my will, and as the apelike creature bore down upon me, I swept my staff in an upcurving stroke, like the swing of a golf club, and cried, *'Forzare!'*

The unseen force of my will reached out, adding to the momentum of Magog's charge and lifting him from the ground. With a howl Magog went flying over our heads and arched out into the air and over the steep, rocky hillside we'd just climbed. The animalistic howl broke out into savage words in some ancient-sounding tongue, interspersed with screams of fury and grunts of pain as the huge Denarian bounced down the stony, frozen hillside. He sounded more angry than injured, and I knew that I'd taken him out of the equation for only a moment, at most.

Hopefully, that would be enough.

Deirdre came down from the mound of stones, using all four limbs and individual blade-strands of her hair interchangeably for locomotion, so that she looked like some kind of bizarre, enormous spider – until Sanya raised his Kalashnikov and began firing at her. None of that spray-and-pray automatic fire, either. The Russian skidded to a stop and took swift aim. He bounced one round off a rock an inch to Deirdre's left, put the second shot through her thigh, and raised a cloud of sparks from the steely blades of her hair near her skull with a third round. She let out a shriek of startled pain and fear, and scuttled sideways off into the shadows as swiftly as a roach caught out in the middle of the floor when the light comes on.

Gunfire came at us from both sides, still more or less blind and random, but no less lethal for that. Bullets are the damnedest things, going by. They aren't dramatic. By themselves they sound almost like big bugs, like something that might buzz by you real fast out in the country on a hot, muggy summer afternoon. It's almost hard to feel afraid of them, until it truly hits you exactly what they are. It's kind of handy, actually, that moment of disconnection between the time your senses tell you that death is flicking around randomly a couple of feet away, and the time your mind manages to make you understand that moving around in it is an awful idea. It gives you time to act before you get so scared that you just find a shady spot and stay there.

'Go, go, go!' I called, still charging forward. Our only chance was to keep moving ahead, to rattle Nicodemus and company into jumping out of the way, and to get into the only shelter on that hilltop.

'Kill them!' Nicodemus roared, his voice furious, and then there was the sound of rushing wind from overhead. He must have taken to the sky, flying upon that shadow of his as if upon enormous bat wings.

More of the beasts had closed on Michael, and both Swords were at work again, striking out, silver light gleaming more brightly now from their blades. Sanya let out a shout, and more light flooded the hilltop, casting my own shadow out darker in front of me as *Esperacchius* joined the battle, and more of the beasts' cries of pain shook the air.

In front of me Thorned Namshiel howled out in frustration and evident terror in some tongue I didn't know, and I saw that both Tessa and Hellmaid Rosanna had pulled a vanishing act. Namshiel, his arm outstretched in the general direction of the far side of the stone throne, added, despair in his voice, 'Come back!'

Then he turned toward me as he heard my feet churning through the wet snow. He still held a corona of green lightning in his spiny hand, and as his eyes focused on my general location he bared his teeth in a snarl of bitter hatred and flung out his hand, hurling a sphere of crackling emerald electricity at me.

My shield bracelet was ready to go, and I had terror and rage and determination in plenty to empower my defenses. I deflected the sphere at an angle and sent it rebounding harmlessly up into the sky.

'Amateur puppy,' Namshiel snarled, and began to gather more sickly green power at his fingertips. He made an odd little gesture and flicked his fingers, and suddenly five tiny threads of green light leapt toward me on five separate, spiraling paths.

I brought my shield around to intersect the new attack – and realized at the last second that each individual thread of energy was coming at me on a slightly different wavelength of the spectrum of magical energy, a variance of frequencies that my shield couldn't stretch to cover. Not all at the same time, anyway. I countered three of them and nearly got the fourth, but it slipped by me, and I never even touched the fifth strand.

Something that felt like cold, greasy piano wire wrapped around my throat, and I couldn't breathe.

'Insufferable, arrogant little monkey,' Namshiel hissed.

'Playing with the fires of creation. Binding your soul to it, as if you were one of *us*. How *dare* you so presume. How *dare* you wield soulfire against *me*. I, who was there when your pathetic kind was hewn from the muck.'

It wasn't so much being strangled to death that I objected to, or even the megalomaniacal monologue I was being subjected to in the process. I just wished that I knew what the hell he was talking about. Granted, I had busted him up pretty good with that silver hand thing, but he was taking it so freaking *personally*.

I lost track of what I'd been thinking. My head hurt. So did my neck. Thorned Namshiel was ranting about something. Practically foaming at the mouth, really – right up until *Amoracchius* flashed in a line of silver fire, and Thorned Namshiel's head hopped up off his shoulders, tumbled twice, and fell into the snow.

Suddenly I took a deep breath and the world started sorting itself out again.

Michael stepped forward, took one look at Namshiel's body, and hewed the right hand off at the wrist. He picked up the hand and dropped it into a pouch on his sword belt. Meanwhile, Sanya shouldered his rifle and dragged me to my feet.

'Go,' I choked out, barely able to get the words out through my half-crushed throat. I regained my own feet and waved Sanya off me, gesturing ahead. 'The lighthouse. Fast.'

Sanya looked from me to the hollow tower and promptly sheathed his Sword to take up his rifle again. The big Russian advanced on the tower, the Kalashnikov at his shoulder, and began putting precise shots through the heads of each of the beasts that had been chained to the walls inside to torment Ivy, who still floated bound within the greater circle.

I followed Sanya as quickly as I could, wheezing in breaths through my aching neck. By the time Michael and I had gotten into the shelter of the mostly closed ring of the tower's stones, the gunfire from around us had begun to close in on us again as the gunmen's night vision returned. The tiny window of opportunity the flash of the Fireball rounds had created had waned.

'How did you know?' Michael asked, panting. 'How did you know they would break if we charged them?'

'You don't survive two thousand years in a game like this one without predator reflexes,' I replied. 'Any predator in the world reacts the same way to a loud noise, a bright flash, and a noisy and unexpected charge. They get the hell out of the way. Can't really help themselves. Habit of a couple millennia is a bitch to break.'

Sanya calmly shot another beast.

I shrugged. 'Nicodemus and company thought that they knew how things were going to proceed, and when they didn't go the way they expected, they got flustered. So the Nickelheads got clear.' I pursed my lips. 'Of course, they're going to be back in a minute. And very upset. Hey, there, Marcone.'

'Dresden,' Marcone said, as if we'd passed each other outside the coffee shop. He sounded a little tired, but calm. All things considered, that was probably an indicator of exactly how much moxie the crime lord had. 'Can you help the child?'

Dammit. That's the thing I hate most about Marcone. Every once in a while he says or does something that makes it difficult to label him 'scum, criminal' and file him neatly away in a drawer somewhere. I glared at him. He returned the glare with a faint, knowing smile. I muttered under my breath and turned to study the elaborate circle, while Sanya finished the last of the beasts.

'I've never seen anything like this,' Michael said quietly, staring.

I didn't blame him. Even among professionals this circle was impressive. Lots of luminous, glowing lines and swirls involved, and that always looks fantastic, especially at night. The gold and silver and precious stones didn't hurt things, either. The light and music show being put on by the chimes and crystals added a wonderful little eerie edge to it all, especially given the grotesque art that framed the interior magical symbology. 'This is some upper-tier stuff,' I said quietly. 'It will be another century, maybe two, before I'm good enough to come close to this level of work. It's delicate. One single thing a fraction of an inch out of place and the whole thing goes kablooie. It's powerful. When you're putting this together, if any one of a couple of dozen of the power flows slips for even an instant, the whole thing goes out of balance and could go up with enough force to blow the top off of this whole hillside. It took a freaking *genius* to put this together, Michael.'

I hefted my staff.

'Fortunately,' I said, and took a two-handed swing at the nearest stand of slender, delicate crystal. It shattered with gratifying ease, and the encasing light around the greater circle began to waver and dissipate. 'It only takes a monkey with a big stick to take it apart.'

And I waded into the circle, smashing things with my staff. It was therapeutic. God knows how many times the bad guys had destroyed the careful work of lifetimes when they'd robbed people of homes, of loved ones, of life itself. It felt sort of nice to bring a little cup of Shiva D into *their* lives for a change. I shattered the crystals that bent light into a cage to hold the Archive prisoner. I bent and mashed the tuning forks that focused sound into chains. I crushed the depictions of bondage and imprisonment meant to restrain the very idea of freedom, and from there I went on to break ivory rune sticks, to crush glyph-scribed gems, to pound into illegibility golden plates inscribed with sigils of imprisonment.

I'm not sure at which point I started screaming in outrage. Somewhere along the line, though, it hit me that these people had taken magic, the power of life, of creation, a force meant to create and protect, to learn and preserve, and they had bent and twisted it into a blasphemy, an obscenity. They had used it to imprison and torment, to torture and maim, all in an attempt to enslave and destroy. Worse, they had turned magic against the Archive, against the safeguard of knowledge itself – and still worse, against a *child*.

I didn't stop until I had shattered their expensive, elaborate, elegant torture chamber, until I could deliberately drag my staff across the last, smooth golden circle at the innermost point of the design, marring it all the way across its surface, breaking the last remaining structure of the spell.

The energies of the prison let loose with an outraged howl, sailing straight up into the air overhead in a column of furious purple light. I thought I could see faces twisting and spinning inside it for a few seconds, but then the light faded, and Ivy fell limply to the cold ground, just a naked little girl, bruised and scratched and half-unconscious with cold.

Michael was at my side at once, removing his cloak. I took it and wrapped Ivy in it. She made whimpering sounds of protest, but she wasn't really conscious. I picked her up and held her close to me, getting as much of my own coat around her as I could.

I looked up and found Marcone watching me steadily. Sanya had cut him free from the wall and evidently given the crime lord the cloak off his back. Marcone now hunched against the sleet in the white cloak, holding one of the chemical warming packs between his hands. He stood just a bit over average height and was of medium build, so Sanya's cloak covered him like a blanket. 'Will she be all right?' Marcone asked.

'She will,' I said with determination. 'She damned well will.'

'Down!' barked Sanya.

Bullets raised sparks off the inside of the lighthouse and rattled wildly around its interior. Everyone got down. I made sure I had my body and my duster between Ivy and any incoming rounds. Sanya leaned out for a second and squeezed off a couple of shots, then hurriedly got back under cover again. The volume of fire from the outside grew.

'They're bringing up reinforcements from down the hill,' Sanya reported. 'Heavier weapons, too.'

Marcone glanced around the featureless interior of the ruined lighthouse. 'If any of them have grenades, this is going to be a relatively brief rescue operation.'

Sanya leaned out and snapped off another pair of shots, barely getting back before return fire started chewing at the stone where he'd been. He muttered under his breath and changed magazines on his rifle.

The enemy gunfire suddenly ceased. There was silence on the hilltop for twenty or thirty seconds. Then Nicodemus's voice, filled with anger, came through the air. 'Dresden!'

'What?' I called back.

'I'm going to give you one chance to survive this. Give me the girl. Give me the coins. Give me the sword. Do that, and I'll let you walk away alive.'

'Hah!' I said. It was possible that I didn't feel quite as confident as I sounded. 'Or maybe I'll just leave from here.'

'Cross into the Nevernever from where you're standing?' Nicodemus asked. 'You'd be better off asking the Russian to put a bullet through your head for you. I know what lives on the other side.'

Given that they'd chosen this location for the greater circle precisely because it was a source of intense dark energy, I had no trouble believing that it connected to some nasty portions of the Nevernever. There was every chance that Nicodemus was not bluffing.

'How do I know that you won't kill me the minute you get what you want?' I called back.

'Harry!' Michael hissed.

I shushed him.

'We both know what my word is worth,' Nicodemus said, his voice dry. 'Really, Dresden. If we can't trust each other, what's the point in talking at all?'

Heh. Gaining enough time to await the second half of what those Fireballs were supposed to accomplish, that's what.

The twin two-hundred-fifty-foot jets of fire had briefly blinded our enemies, true.

But they'd done something else, too.

Marcone tilted his head to one side for a moment and then murmured, 'Does anyone else hear . . . strings?'

'Ah,' I said, and pumped my fist in the air. 'Ah-hahahah! Have you ever heard anything so magnificently pompous and overblown in your *life?*'

Deep, ringing French horns joined the string sections, echoing over the hilltop.

'What is that?' Sanya murmured.

'That,' I crowed, 'is *Wagner*, baby!'

Never let it be said that a Chooser of the Slain can't make an entrance.

Miss Gard brought the reconditioned Huey up from the eastern side of the island, flying about a quarter of an inch over the treetops, blasting 'The Ride of the Valkyries' from loud-speakers mounted on the chopper's underside. Wind, sleet, and all, *still* she flew flawlessly through the night, having used the twin jets of the Fireball rounds, visible for miles over the pitch-black lake, to orient herself as to where to arrive. The Huey turned broadside as it rose over the hilltop, music blaring loud enough to shake snow from the treetops. The side door of the chopper was open, revealing Mister Hendricks manning a rotating-barreled minigun fixed to the deck of the helicopter – completely illegally, of course.

But then, I suppose that's really one major advantage to working with criminals. They just don't *care* about that sort of thing.

The barrels began to spin, and a tongue of flame licked out from the front of the gun. Snow and earth erupted into the air in a long trench in front of the cannon. I risked a peek and saw men clad in dark fatigues leaping for cover as a swath of devastation slewed back and forth across the open hilltop and pounded the mound of stones into a mound of gravel.

'There's our ride!' I said. 'Let's go!'

Sanya led the way, firing off more or less random shots at anyone who wasn't already lying flat in an effort to avoid fire from the gun on the helicopter. Some of Nicodemus's troops were crazier than others. Several of them jumped up and tried to come after us. That minigun had been designed to shoot down airplanes. What the rounds left of human bodies was barely recognizable as such.

There was no place for the chopper to land, but a line came down from the other side, lowered by a winch while the aircraft hovered above us. I looked up to see Luccio operating the winch, her face pale, but her eyes glittering with excitement. She was how Gard had been able to know where to look for the signal – I'd given Anastasia a couple of my hairs to use in a tracking spell, and she'd been following me ever since I left to meet Rosanna for the trade.

The line came down with a lift harness attached to it. 'Marcone,' I shouted over the sound of the rotors and the minigun – which is to say, I was more or less mouthing it exaggeratedly. 'You first. That was the deal.'

He shook his head and pointed his finger at Ivy.

I snarled and pushed the girl into his arms, then started slapping the harness over him. He got it after a second, and in a couple more we had him secured in the harness and holding the semiconscious Ivy tight against him. I gave Luccio the thumbs-up, and Marcone and Ivy went zipping gracefully up the line to the chopper, wrapped in the white cloak, the scarlet crosses on it standing out sharply in the winter light. Luccio helped haul them in, and a second later the empty harness came down again.

'Sanya!' I said.

The Russian passed me the Kalashnikov and slipped into the harness, then ascended to the helicopter. Again the empty harness came down – though now there were occasional bursts of heavier rounds coming from down the slope of the hillside, as evidenced by tracer fire that would sometimes go tumbling by in the night. It would be immediately answered by the far heavier fire of the minigun, but Gard couldn't possibly keep the chopper there for long.

'Harry!' Michael said, offering me the harness.

I was about to take it, but by chance I looked up and saw Gard looking down at us through the Plexiglas bubble around the pilot's seat – looking at Michael with an absolutely unnerving intensity that I had seen on her face once before, and my heart started hammering in terror.

The last time she'd looked like that, I'd been in an alley outside Bock Ordered Books back in Chicago, and a necromancer named Corpsetaker and a ghoul named Li Xian had been about to murder me. A few minutes later Gard had told Marcone that she had seen that it was my fate to die then and there. The only reason that I survived it was that Marcone had intervened.

But even if I'd never seen that look on her face before, I figured that anytime a Valkyrie hovering over a battlefield suddenly gets real interested in a particular warrior, it ain't good.

I'd made the grasshopper a promise. If things were about to get hairy for whoever was left on the ground, it wouldn't be Molly's dad that had to deal with it.

'You first,' I said.

He started to argue.

I shoved the harness into his chest. 'Dammit, Michael!'

He grimaced, shook his head at me, and then sheathed *Amoracchius*. Still holding *Fidelacchius* in his hand, he shrugged quickly into the harness. I gave Luccio the thumbs-up, and Michael began to rise. Gard frowned faintly, and some of my screaming tension started to ease.

Tessa and Rosanna came out from behind veils that were as good as anything Molly could have done, and I didn't have to be Sherlock to deduce who had done the lion's share of the work on the greater circle that had contained the Archive. I had half a second to act, but I got tangled in the strap of Sanya's gun, which he'd handed me so that I could defend myself in case I was suddenly attacked. Thank you, Sanya.

Tessa, her pretty human face showing, her eyes gleaming with manic glee, swept a mantis claw at my head, and I at least managed to interpose the rifle before she ripped my head off. Only instead of smashing the gun, as I'd expected, she ripped it out of my hand, just as easily as taking candy from a baby and spun away from me.

Then she winked at me, blew me a kiss, and opened fire on Michael with the Kalashnikov on full automatic from no more than ten feet away.

My friend didn't scream as bullets tore into him. He just jerked once in a spray of scarlet and went limp.

Fidelacchius tumbled from his fingers and fell to the ground.

Sparks flew from the Huey as the bullets tore into it, too, and a burst of flame and smoke poured from a vent on one side of its fuselage. It dipped sharply to one side, and for a second I thought it was simply going to roll over and into the ground – but then it recovered, drunkenly, gathering momentum like a car sliding down an icy hill, still dragging my friend's unmoving body on the trailing cable like a baited hook at the end of a fishing line, and vanished into the darkness.

44

Even as some part of me noted all of that happening, the rest of me started screaming in raw, red rage, in agony, in denial.

I was pretty sure I had worked out who had taken my blasting rod away. I was pretty sure I knew why they'd done it. I even thought that, looked at from a certain point of view, it might not have been an entirely stupid idea.

But as of now, I officially did not care.

I didn't have my blasting rod with me, and I was not sure that my raw power, no matter how furious, would be enough to hurt Tessa through the defenses the Fallen gave her. I had never been able to attain the kind of precision I would need without artificial aid.

As of right now, I officially did not care about that, either.

I focused my rage, focused my anger, focused my hate and my denial and my pain. I blocked away everything in the entire universe but the thought of my friend's bloody body hanging from that rope, and a spot two inches across in the center of Tessa's chest.

Then I drew in a breath, whirling a hand over my head and bellowed through my ragged throat, so loudly that it felt like something tore, 'Fuego, pyrofuego!' I stabbed the first two fingers of my right hand forward as I did, unleashing my fury and my will. 'Burn!'

A bar of blue-white fire so dense that it was nearly a solid object lashed across the distance from me to Tessa and slammed into her like an enormous spear.

The mantislike Denarian threw back her pretty face and screamed in agony as the shaft of fire bored cleanly through her, melting a wide hole that burned wider still before searing itself shut. She went down, howling and thrashing, burned by fire far deadlier and more destructive than any I had ever called before, with a blasting rod or without one.

I sensed something moving toward me from the side and rolled out of the way just as one of Rosanna's cloven hooves slashed through the air where my thigh had been an instant before. If she'd struck she would have opened the flesh to the bone. I whipped my staff at her face, forcing her to duck away, and followed with a surge of will and a shout of, '*Forzare!*' It wasn't my best kinetic strike, but it was a blow heavy enough to throw her a dozen feet through the air and into a tumble over the ground.

I seized the hilt of *Fidelacchius* from where the Sword had fallen. As my fingers closed around the weapon I realized several points of cold logic, as if having them explained to me by a calm, rational, wise old man who was utterly unperturbed by my rage.

First, I realized that I was now alone on an uncharted island in the middle of Lake Michigan, with nothing but madmen and fallen angels for company.

Second, that I still had the coins and the Sword that Nicodemus had been after – and that he was still going to be after them.

Third, that the Denarians were sure to be really ticked off, now that I'd taken their real prize from them.

Fourth . . .

The ground shook, as if with the impact of a heavy foot.

Fourth, that since I had confounded Summer's attempt to track me via use of the little oak leaf pin, Eldest Brother Gruff had probably been waiting for me to use fire magic in battle – the same magic that I had entwined with the power of the Summer Lady two years ago at Arctis Tor. It was the most probable reason why Mab, the most likely suspect for messing with my head, would have taken my blasting rod and my memories of how to use fire magic in battle – to prevent me from inadvertently revealing my position to Summer every time I got into a tussle.

Only now that I had, Eldest Gruff was probably on his way to visit.

And fifth, and last, I realized that I had no way to get off this stupid and creepily familiar island – unless I could get down to the docks and to the boat I'd come in on.

I still burned with the need to strike back at the people who had hurt my friend, but the fact of the matter was that I couldn't strike back at them and survive – and if they took me down, I'd only be handing them weapons to continue the war Michael had spent a lifetime fighting to end.

My only option was to run. Realistically, even escape wasn't looking likely – but it was my only chance.

So I slid the Sword back into its scabbard, oriented myself toward the run-down little town where we'd first come ashore, and ran. Fast.

Now, I'm not as strong as those really big guys, like Michael and Sanya. I don't do swordplay as well as folks like Nicodemus or Shiro. I don't yet have the magical experience and know-how to outfinesse the really experienced wizards and sorcerers who have been hanging around for centuries, like the Gatekeeper or Thorned Namshiel.

But I'll take any of those guys in a footrace. Guaranteed. I run – and not so that I'll be skinny and look good, either. I run so that when something that wants to kill me is chasing me, I'll be *good* at running. And when you've got legs as long as mine, you're skinny, and in good shape, you can really move. I hit the woods running like a deer, sticking to the path we'd broken on the way up. The snow made it easy to see the way, and though in another hour or two it would be a sheet of frozen ice, for the moment the footing was excellent.

I was benefiting from the chaos caused by Gard's entrance. I could hear all kinds of confusion as men shouted in the woods and tried to figure out what was going on, to get the wounded to help, and to follow what were probably conflicting orders thanks to holes ripped in their chain of command by Hendricks and his minigun. Radios clicked and voices buzzed over them, functioning unreliably, as they would in any area so rich with concentrated magical energy.

The fact that most of the men had had their tongues removed probably didn't help anything, either. Nick should have taken my advice and read that evil-overlord list. Seriously.

Someone a few yards off to my right shouted something at me. It came out as totally mangled gobbledygook. I shouted back at him in similar wordless garbage, pretending that I didn't have a tongue either, and added a rude gesture to the tirade. I don't know if it was the perfect charade, or if it just shocked him into stunned silence, but either way it got the same effect. I went on by him without garnering any further reaction whatsoever.

I thought I was home free as I reached the ruins of the little company town and its one main drag along the shoreline.

And then I heard Magog's bellow coming down the hill behind me – coming fast, too, easily making twice the speed I could manage. That was the damnedest thing about these demonic collaborator types. Even though they didn't work out and practice, they still got to run faster than we dedicated roadsters who actually sweated and strained for our ability to haul ass. Jerks.

It seemed clear that Magog was coming in pursuit of me, or at least that he was coming down the hill toward the dock and the boat off the island to cut off any chance of escape. I had little time to pick and choose where to go to avoid his notice, and wound up ducking into the long, heavily shadowed, cavernous length of the building that looked as if it had once been a cannery.

The roof had fallen through in several places, and snow covered perhaps a third of the floor, providing the only thing even vaguely like light. Most of the walls were still standing, but I had grave doubts about the floor. There wasn't space for much of a basement above the waterline, but there was plenty of room to break a leg if I fell through on a weak board. I would just have to stay close to the wall and hope for the best.

For once, enemy manpower was working in my favor. If

Nicodemus had brought only his fellow Denarians along, there would have been nothing but the footprints of cloven hooves and giant mantises and Grape Apes and whatnot in the snow of the island. But no, he'd had to bring along dozens and dozens of foot soldiers, too, and as a result there were regular old footprints everywhere. One more set, more or less, wasn't going to stand out. So all I had to do was get into the building, get out of sight, and lie low until Magog had gone past.

I had no sooner crouched down and begun my impersonation of a mouse than the ancient, half-rotted wood of the old cannery shuddered beneath me, a vibration that I felt in the soles of my feet. Then another, and another, rhythmic, like slow footsteps.

They were followed by the sound of Magog's approach, a heavy, leathery shuffling through the snow, accompanied by the steady heave of lungs like a blacksmith's bellows. Then I heard Magog slide to a sudden halt in the snow and snort in surprise – then let out an enormous roar of challenge.

And a voice, a very deep, resonant voice, said, 'Be thou gone from this place, creature. My quarrel is not with thee.'

Magog answered with a howl and spat out words in a language I did not understand.

'Be that as it may, Elder One,' the huge voice said, gently and with respect, 'I also have a duty from which I may not waver. We need not be at odds this night. Depart in peace, Elder One, with your beast of burden.'

Magog snarled again in that foreign tongue.

The deep voice hardened. 'I seek no quarrel with thee, Fallen One. I pray thee, do not mistake peaceable intention for weakness. I do not fear thee. Begone, or I will smite thee down.'

The gorillalike Denarian howled. I heard its claws dig and rip at the ground as it hurtled forward toward the source of the resonant voice.

Magog, it seemed, had a really limited vocabulary when it came to repartee.

I couldn't see what happened next. There was a flash of gold-green light, like sunlight reflected from fresh spring grass, and a detonation in the air, a sound that was not quite a crack of thunder, not quite an explosion of fire. It wasn't even *loud* so much as it was pervasive, something that I felt along the whole surface of my body as much as I did on my eardrums.

The wall of the cannery shattered inward, and Magog – what was *left* of Magog – came hurtling through it. It landed on the ground about twenty feet away from me. Enormous sections were missing from the front of the gorillalike body, including its thighs and most of the front half of its torso. It wasn't a messy wound, either. The empty chunks were limned with a gentle yellow-green glow that seemed to seal in any blood. Even as I watched, Magog quivered once, then went limp. Tiny sprouts of green flowered up from the fallen corpse over the course of a couple of seconds, leaves spreading, then budding out into wildflowers in a riot of colors.

The coating of flowering plants seemed to devour the body of the gorilla from around the mortal body beneath – that of a muscular young man, which gradually emerged, though was still modestly shrouded in a veil of flowers. He was thoroughly dead, his eyes glassy, empty, and there were flowers growing in a hole where his heart had been. He wore a leather collar, and hanging from it, in a little rubber frame like a dog tag, was another blackened denarius. He was a kid, Molly's age at the oldest.

From outside there was a deep, resonant sigh. Then another heavy, ground-shuddering thump. And another.

Coming closer.

My heart jumped right up into my teeth. Sure, I had no idea who that really was out there, but all those *thees* just screamed that it was one of the Sidhe. They really got into the archaic modes of speech – or maybe it was fairer to say that they never got *out* of them. Anyway, odds were running high that this was Eldest Brother Gruff come to settle up with Winter's champion in this affair, and given that he'd just swatted down one of the Denarians like he was an uppity pixie, it didn't bode real well for me.

I found myself taking a step back as that thumping sound came again, and the floorboard beneath my foot creaked precariously.

That gave me an idea. The bigger they are, et cetera. If Eldest Gruff was even bigger than the last one had been, maybe I could use the rickety flooring against him – long enough to get myself out to the boat and off the island, in any case. Open water was another fantastic neutralizer for the enormous size discrepancy. Setting realistic goals has always been the key to my success. I didn't have to win a fight with this thing. I just had to survive long enough to run away.

I took a chance, picked the most solid-looking floorboard I could see, and eased across the floor to the far side of the building, the one nearest the water, and turned to face the hole in the wall that Magog's body had smashed open on its way in.

Thump. Thump. Thump.

I readied my will and shook out my shield bracelet, in case I needed it. I lifted my staff and pointed it at where I thought Eldest Gruff's head might be when he came in, so he would know I was serious.

Thump. Thump. Thump.

I adjusted the aim on the staff a little higher.

Thump. Thump.

Sweat trickled off my brow.

Thump. Thump.

How far did this guy have to walk?

Thump. Thump.

This was just getting ridiculous, now.

Thump. Thump.

And Eldest Gruff appeared in the opening.

He was five feet tall. Five-two, tops.

He wore a robe with a cowl, pulled back so that I could

clearly see his curling ram's horns, the goatlike features, the long white beard, the yellow eyes with their hourglass pupils.

And in his right hand he carried a wooden staff carved with runes that looked almost precisely like my own.

He took a limping step forward, leaning on his staff, and when he planted the tool on the ground, it flickered with green light that then splashed out onto the earth beneath it, spreading outward in a resonating wave. *Thump.*

The floorboards creaked beneath him, and he came to a cautious stop and faced me quietly, both hands on his staff. His robe was belted with an old bit of simple rope. There were three stoles hanging through it – purple ones, faded and frayed with the passage of time.

Those were the mantles worn by members of the Senior Council, the leaders of the White Council of Wizards. They were, generally speaking, the oldest and strongest wizards on the planet.

And Eldest Brother Gruff had, evidently, killed three of them in duels.

'This,' I said, 'has really not been my day.'

The gruff regarded me solemnly. 'Hail, young wizard.' He had a deep, resonant voice, far too huge and rich for the frame it came from. 'Thou knowest why I have come.'

'To slay me, most likely,' I said.

'Aye,' said the gruff. 'By my Queen's command and in defense of Summer's honor.'

'Why?' I asked him. 'Why would Summer want Marcone taken by the Denarians? Why would Summer want the Archive under their control?'

The gruff only stared at me for a long moment, but when he spoke I could have sworn that his voice sounded pensive. Maybe even troubled. 'It is not my place to know such things – or to ask.'

'The gruffs are Summer's champion in this matter, aren't they?' I demanded. 'If not you, then who?'

'What of thee, wizard?' the gruff countered. 'Hast thou asked why the wicked Queen of Winter would wish thee to prevent Marcone from being taken by those servants of the darkest shadow? Why she who embodies destruction and death would wish to protect and preserve the Archive?'

'I have, actually,' I said.

'And what answers hast thou found?'

'Gruff,' I said, 'I find myself largely clueless about why *mortal* women do what they do. It will take a wiser man than me to understand what's in a fae woman's mind.'

Eldest Gruff stared at me blankly for a second. Then he threw back his head and made a sound that . . . well, more than anything it sounded like a donkey. *Hee-haw, hee-haw, hee-haw.*

He was laughing.

I laughed, too. I couldn't help it. The whole day had just been too much, and the laugh just felt too good. I laughed until my stomach hurt, and when the gruff saw me laughing, it only made him laugh harder – and more like a donkey – and that set *me* off in turn.

It was a good two or three minutes before we settled down.

'They tell children stories about you guys, you know,' I said.

'Still?' he said.

I nodded. 'Stories about clever little billy goats outsmarting big mean trolls until their bigger, stronger brothers come along and put the trolls in their place.'

The gruff grunted. He said, 'We hear tales of thee, young wizard.'

I blinked. 'You, uh?'

'We too like stories about . . .' His eyes searched his memory for a moment before he smiled, pleased. The gesture looked pleasantly nonviolent on his face. 'Underdogs.'

I snorted. 'Well. I guess this is another one.'

The gruff's smile faded. 'I dislike being cast as the troll.'

'So change the role,' I said.

The gruff shook his head. 'That I cannot do. I serve Summer. I serve my Queen.'

'But it's over,' I said. 'Marcone is already free. So's Ivy.'

'But thou art still here, upon the field of conflict,' the gruff said gently. 'As am I. And so the matter is not closed. And so I must fulfill my obligations – to my great regret, wizard. I have only admiration for thee, in a personal sense.'

I tilted my head and stared hard at him. 'You say that you serve Summer and the Queen. In that order?'

The gruff mirrored my gesture, his eyes questioning.

I fumbled in my pocket and came out with the other thing I had grabbed back at my apartment – the little silver oak leaf pin Mister had been batting all over Little Chicago. I'd figured that they'd stopped using it to chase me, once they'd gotten tired of Mister having his catnipped way with them.

The gruff's eyes widened. 'The confounding enchantment thou didst employ upon our tracking spell was most efficacious. I had hoped to ask thee how it was done.'

'Trade secret,' I said. 'But you know what came with this pin.'

'Indeed,' he said. 'You were made an Esquire of Summer, and granted a boon, but . . .' He shook his head. 'A boon can be a matter of importance, but not one this grave. Thou canst not ask me to yield to thee in a matter of conflict between the Courts themselves.'

'I won't,' I said. 'But just so we're clear. Once both of us have left this island, the matter is closed?'

'Once thou art safe again in Chicago, aye, it would be.'

'Then I ask for Summer to honor its pledge to me, and the debt it incurred to me when I struck at Winter's heart on its behalf.'

The gruff's ears stood up, facing me. 'Aye?'

'I want you,' I said, 'to get me a doughnut. A real, genuine, Chicago doughnut. Not some glamoured doughnut. An actual one. Freshly made.'

The gruff's teeth began to show as he smiled again.

'Of course,' I said, 'you could deny me the boon I rightfully earned in blood and fire and kill me instead, thus ensuring that Summer would renege on a debt and never be able to make good on it. But I don't think that would be very good for Summer and its honor. Do you?'

'Indeed not, wizard,' the gruff said. 'Indeed it would not be.' He bowed his head to me. 'Likest thou jelly within thy doughnut?'

'Nay, but prithee, with sprinkles 'pon it instead,' I said solemnly, 'and frosting of white.'

'It could take some time to locate such a pastry,' the gruff said seriously.

I bowed my head to him. 'I trust in the honor of Summer's champions that it will arrive in good time.'

He bowed his head in reply. 'Understand, young wizard, I may not aid thee further.'

'You're pushing the rules enough already,' I said dryly. 'Believe me. I know how that is.'

Eldest Gruff's golden eyes glittered. Then he lifted the staff and thumped it quietly onto the floorboards. Once again there was a pulse of green light and a surge of gentle thunder – and he was simply gone.

So was the silver oak leaf pin. Just gone from my fingers, and I hadn't felt a thing. Give it up for the fae; they can do disappearing like nobody's business.

Maybe I should have taken some lessons. It might have helped me get out of this mess alive.

I made my way carefully back across the creaking floor to the body of the young man. He looked relaxed in death, peaceful. I had the impression that whatever Eldest Gruff had done to him, it had been painless. It seemed like the sort of thing the old faerie would do. I reached down with my gloved left hand and grasped the tag containing the blackened denarius of Magog. I jerked it sharply, pulling it off the collar, and pocketed it, careful not to let it touch skin. I was getting to be kind of blasé about handling these coins, but it was difficult to keep getting terrified over and over again, especially given the circumstances. The risk of once more exposing my immortal soul to a fiendish presence seemed only a moderate danger, compared to what still stalked the night outside the old building.

Speaking of which . . . I took a deep breath and made my way quietly back out to the street. I could still hear shouting from farther up the hillside. I heard the sound of a boat's engine on the far side of the island. There must have been other vessels docked elsewhere along the shore.

Well, I'd known about only the one, and it was close. I slipped back out of the cannery and hurried down the street as quickly and quietly as I could.

Down past the bottom of the rough stone staircase the boat still floated, tied beside the broken stump of an old wooden column. I restrained the urge to let out a whoop, and settled for hustling down the frozen stones as fast as I could without breaking my neck. The water was viciously cold, but I still wasn't feeling it – which probably wasn't a good thing. There was going to be hell to pay in afterthought pain when this was over. But compared to the other problems I'd had recently, that one was a joy to think about.

I got to the boat, tossed my staff in, and clambered aboard. I heard a shout up the hillside and froze. A flashlight swept back and forth up in the trees, but then moved off in another direction. I hadn't been seen. I grinned like a fool and crept up to the driver's seat. Once I got the engine started it would attract attention, but all I had to do was drive west as fast as I could until I hit ground. The whole western shoreline hereabouts was heavily occupied, and it should be no problem to get to a spot public enough to avoid any further molestation.

I eased into the driver's seat and reached for the ignition key.

But it was gone.

I felt around for it. Rosanna had left it in the ignition. I specifically remembered that she had done so.

The shadows rippled away from the passenger seat opposite the driver's seat, revealing Nicodemus. He sat calmly in his black silk shirt and dark trousers, the grey noose worn like a tie around his throat, a naked sword across his lap, his left elbow resting on his left knee. In the fingertips of his left hand he held a key ring, dangling the grease-smeared ignition key of the boat.

'Good evening, Dresden,' he said. 'Looking for this?'

45

The sleet had stopped coming down in favor of large, wet flakes of snow again. The boat rocked gently on the troubled waters of the lake. Water slapped against the sides and gurgled around the curve of the hull. Ice had begun to form all along the sides and front of the boat. I think there are boat words for all the pieces that were being covered, like *prow* and *gunwale*, but I'm only vaguely aware of them.

'Harry Dresden speechless,' Nicodemus said. 'I can't imagine this happens every day.'

I just stared at him.

'In the event that you hadn't worked it out for yourself yet,' Nicodemus said, 'this is endgame, Dresden.' The fingers of his right hand stroked the hilt of his sword. 'Can you puzzle out the next part, or must I explain it to you?'

'You want the coins, the sword, the girl, the money, and the keys to the Monte Carlo,' I said. 'Or you shoot me and drop me over the side.'

'Something like that,' he said. 'The coins, Dresden.'

I reached into the pocket of my duster and . . .

'What the hell,' I said.

The Crown Royal bag was gone.

I checked my other pockets, careful of the coin I'd taken from Magog – and careful not to reveal its presence to Nicodemus. No bag. 'It's gone.'

'Dresden, don't even try such a pathetic lie on m—'

'It's *gone*!' I told him with considerable heat, none of it feigned. Eleven coins. Eleven freaking cursed coins. The last time I remembered definitely having them had been up at the tower, when I'd jingled them for Nicodemus.

He stared at me for a moment, his eyes searching, and then murmured something under his breath. Whispers rolled from the shadows around him. I didn't recognize the language, but I did recognize the tone. I wondered if the angelic tongue had swear words, or if they just said nice words backward or something. *Doog! Teews doog!*

Nicodemus's sword came up as swiftly as a flickering snake's tongue and came to rest against my throat. I didn't have time to flinch; it was that fast. I sucked in a quick breath and held very, very still.

'These marks,' he murmured. 'Thorned Namshiel's strangler spell.' His eyes drew a line from the last apparent mark on my neck down to the duster pocket that the bag of coins had been in. 'Ah. The strangulation was the distraction. He picked your pocket with one of the other wires before he was incapacitated. He did that to Saint . . . someone-or-other, in Glasgow in the thirteenth century.'

There's nothing like getting taken with an old trick, I guess. But that meant that Namshiel had been working together with someone else – someone else who had to have been hanging around to collect the coins after he'd taken them from my pocket and tossed them off to the side in the confusion. Someone who hadn't been pulling a fade after all.

'Tessa and Rosanna,' I said quietly. 'They got their collection of thugs back. They bailed at just the right moment to ruin your plan, too.'

'Deceitful bitches,' Nicodemus murmured. 'One of them is our own Judas; I was sure of it.'

I lifted my eyebrows. 'What?'

'That's why I let them handle the more, shall we say, memorable aspects of the Archive's initiation to our world,' Nicodemus said. 'I suppose now that the child is free, she'll have some rather unpleasant associations with those two.'

'And you're telling me this why?'

He shrugged a shoulder. 'It's somewhat ironic, Dresden, that I *can* talk to you about this particular aspect of family business.

You're the only one that I'm sure hasn't gone over to this new force — this Black Council of yours.'

'How can you be so sure about me?' I asked him.

'Please. No one so obstreperous has been corrupted by anything but his own pure muleheadedness.' Nicodemus shook his head, never taking his eyes off me. 'Still. My time here has not been wasted. The Knights carried away Namshiel's coin, so Tessa has lost her sorcery teacher. I heard Magog's bellow end quite abruptly a few moments ago, just before you walked out of the same building, so with any luck Tessa's heaviest bruiser is out of the game for a time as well, eh?' Nicodemus smiled cheerily at me. 'Perhaps his collar is in one of your pockets. And I have *Fidelacchius*. Removal of one of the Three is profit enough for one operation, even if I did lose this chance at gaining control of the Archive.'

'What makes you think,' I said, 'that you have *Fidelacchius*?'

'I told you,' Nicodemus said. 'This is endgame. No more playing.' The pitch and intonation of his voice changed, and though he still spoke in my direction, it was clear that he was no longer speaking to *me*. 'Shadow, if you would, disable Dresden. We'll talk some sense into him later, in a quieter setting.'

He was talking to Lasciel's shadow.

Hell, wizards didn't have a monopoly on arrogance.

Neither did the Knights of the Cross.

I stiffened in place, my mouth half-open. Then I fell over sideways, body resting against the boat's steering wheel, my spine ramrod straight. I didn't move, not one little twitch.

Nicodemus sighed and shook his head. 'Dresden, I truly regret this necessity, but time is growing short. I must act, and your talents could prove useful. You'll see. Once we've cleared some of these well-intentioned idiots out of our way . . .' He reached for *Fidelacchius*.

And I punched him in the neck.

Then I seized the noose and jerked it tight. I hung on, pulling it tighter. The noose, another leftover from Judas's field, made Nicodemus more or less invulnerable to harm — from everything but itself. Nicodemus had worn the thing for centuries. As far as I knew, I was the only one who had worked out how to hurt him. I was the only one who had truly terrified him.

He met my eyes for a panicked second.

'Lasciel's shadow,' I told him, 'doesn't live here anymore. The Fallen have no power over me. And neither do you.'

I jerked the noose a little tighter.

Nicodemus would have screamed if he could have. He thrashed uselessly, feeling for his sword. I kicked it out of reach. He lunged up and raked at my eyes, but I hunched my head down and hung on, and his motions were more panicked than practiced. His shadow rose up in a wave of darkness and fury – but as it plunged down to engulf me, white light shone forth from the slits in the wooden cane sheath of the holy sword on my back, and the shadow itself let out a hissing, leathery scream, flinching away from the light.

I was no Knight, but the sword did for me what it had always done for them – it leveled the field, stripping away all the supernatural trappings and leaving only a struggle of mind versus mind and will versus will, one man against another. Nicodemus and I fought for the sword and our lives.

He threw savage kicks into my wounded leg, and even through the blocks Lash had taught me to build, I felt them. I had a great handle on his neck, so in reply I slammed my forehead against Nicodemus's nose. It broke with really satisfying crunching sounds. He hammered punches into my short ribs, and he knew how to make them hurt.

Unfortunately for him, I knew how to *be* hurt. I knew how to be hurt with the best of them. It was going to take a whole hell of a lot more pain than this loser could dish out in the time he had left to put me down, and I knew it. I *knew* it. I tightened my grip on that ancient rope and I hung on.

I took more blows to the body as his face turned red. He got one of my knees with a vicious kick as his face turned purple. I was screaming with the pain of it when the purple started looking more like black – and he collapsed, body loosening and then going completely limp.

A lot of people let up when that happens, when their opponent drops unconscious. But it could have been a trick.

Even if it hadn't been I'd been planning to hang on.

I'm *not* a Knight.

In fact, I squeezed harder.

I wasn't sure how much longer I'd had him down. Might have been thirty seconds. Might have been a minute and a half. But I saw a flash of furious green light and looked up to see Deirdre coming down the hillside toward me on her hair and three limbs, one leg bound up in white bandages. She had twenty or thirty tongueless soldier types with her, and her glowing eyes burned with verdant fury, like a pair of spotlights. She focused on me for half a second, hissed like a furious alley cat, and screamed, 'Father!'

Crap.

I grabbed Nicodemus by the shirt and pitched him over the side, into the black waters of the lake. He went down with hardly a splash, his dark clothing making him all but invisible an instant after he hit the water.

I scanned the bottom of the boat frantically. There, the key. I scooped it up and jammed it into the ignition.

'Don't shoot!' Deirdre screamed. 'You might hit my father!' She bounded into the air, all that writhing hair folding back into a single, sharklike swimming tail as she dove, and hit the water with barely a splash.

I turned the key. The old boat's engine coughed and wheezed.

'Come on,' I breathed. 'Come on.'

If I didn't get this boat moving before Deirdre found her daddy, game over. She'd order her soldiers to open fire. I'd have to raise a shield to stop the bullets, and once I did that the already wonky engine would sure as hell never get moving. I'd be stuck, and it would only be a matter of time before a combination of weariness, mounting pain, number of attackers, and wrathful daughter took me down.

Deirdre surfaced, cast a glance around to orient herself, and dove into the featureless darkness again.

The engine caught, and then turned over drunkenly.

'Boo-ya!' I screamed.

Then I remembered that I hadn't untied the boat.

I lunged awkwardly up to the front and untied the rope, very much aware of all the guns pointing at me. The boat came free. I pushed off the pole, and the vessel began to sluggishly turn. I hobbled back to the steering wheel, cranked it around, and gave the engine some power. The boat throbbed and then roared and began to gather speed.

Deirdre surfaced maybe twenty feet in front of me, carrying her father. Before she even looked around she screamed, 'Kill him, shoot him, shoot him!'

Cheerfully, I swerved the boat right at her. Something thumped hard against the hull. I hoped for some kind of lawn mower–like sound from the propellers, but I didn't get one.

Gunfire erupted from the shore, meanwhile, and it wasn't blinded by bright lights or hurried or panicked. It started ripping the boat to splinters all around me. I started shouting curse words and crouched down. Bullets hit my duster. For several seconds the range was pretty close, at least for the military-grade weapons they were using, and while the duster was up to the chore of stopping those rounds, it wasn't any *fun* to experience. My back got hit with half a dozen major-league fastballs over the next few seconds.

And cold water washed over my feet.

And, half a minute later, over my ankles.

Double crap.

The engines were making really odd noises too. My back protested when I turned to look. It was damned dark out here on the lake, as I got farther and farther from shore, but the disappearing form of the island was being blotted by a lot of black smoke coming out of the boat's engines.

The pain blocks were falling now. I was hurting a lot. The water in the bottom of the boat was up to the bottom of my calves now, and . . .

And there were three searchlights coming toward me from the direction of the island.

They'd sent out pursuit boats.

'This just isn't fair,' I muttered to myself. I gave the engine all the power I could, but from the way it was rattling around that was more or less a formality. It wasn't going to last long, and it was sinking in any case.

I knew that if I went into the water I'd have about four or five minutes to live, given the temperature. I also knew that I had to get past the stone reefs around the islands, the ones Rosanna had needed the beacon light to navigate through.

Nothing for it but to keep going.

I was struck by a sudden thought: Bob the skull was going to be crushed that he missed this one, a genuine pirate adventure. I started singing, 'Blow the Man Down' at the top of my lungs.

Then there was a horrible noise, and the boat just *stopped*. The steering wheel hit me in the chest pretty hard, and then I bounced back into the driver's seat.

Water started pouring in thick and fast and dark.

'Ahoy!' I slurred drunkenly. 'Reef!'

I made sure I still had the coin and the sword. I grabbed up my staff and got out the pentacle amulet from around my neck. The lights of the pursuing boats were getting nearer by the moment. This was going to be a close one.

The old ski boat was literally breaking apart around me, its prow shattered on a thick spike of stone that had penetrated it just left of its center, up by the front of the boat. The old stone ridge that rose up through the waters of the lake came to within a couple of feet of the surface here. It would give me a place to do something besides instantly immerse myself in cold water and go into hypothermia.

And it would give me solid rock on which to plant my feet, and through which to draw power. The water of the lake would wash some of it away – not as much as free-running water, but some – but I would still be able to do *something* to defend myself.

So before the boat could capsize and dump me into the water, I gritted my teeth and jumped in.

My body immediately informed me that I had made an insane decision.

You have no idea what the depths of cold can be until you have jumped into near-freezing water.

I screamed my way into it, finding places to stand with my frozen feet, being careful of the leg that Nicodemus had rendered gimpy for me. Then I held up my mother's amulet in my right hand and focused on it, forcing energy into it carefully and slowly. It happened sluggishly, the way everything was happening in the mounting cold, but I was able to draw power up through the stone beneath my feet, and to call silver-blue wizard light from the amulet – brighter and brighter, light that spread out over the waters in a literal beacon that read, clear as day, *Here I am.*

'T-T-Thomas,' I muttered to myself, shivering so hard I could barely stand. 'Y-y-you'd b-better b-be c-c-close.'

Because Deirdre's men were.

The searchlights oriented on me instantly, and the boats – rubber raft things that would skim right over the reefs – came bouncing toward me over the waves.

It wouldn't have been impossible to sink one of the rafts. But it would have killed every man inside. And those weren't people collaborating with demons for their own dark gain. They were just people, most of whom had been brought up from childhood to serve Nicodemus and company, and who probably thought that they were genuinely doing the right thing. I could kill someone like Nicodemus and sleep peacefully afterward. But I wasn't sure I could live with myself if I sent those rafts down into the lake and condemned the men in them to die. That isn't what magic is for.

More to the point, killing them wouldn't save me. Even if I managed to sink every other raft out there, send every man in them into the water, it wouldn't stop me from freezing to death and drowning. It would just mean that I had a lot of company.

I'm not a Knight. But that doesn't mean I don't draw the line somewhere.

They started shooting from about a hundred yards away, and I raised a shield. It was hard to do in the icy waters, but I raised it and held it, a shimmering quarter-dome of silver light. Bullets smashed against it and skipped off it, sending out little concentric rings of spreading energy as their force was distributed over the shield. Most of the shots never really came anywhere close. Shooting from a moving rubber raft at a hundred yards isn't exactly a recipe for precision marksmanship.

They got closer, and I got colder.

I held the light and the shield.

Please, brother. Don't let me down.

I never heard anything until a wave of cold water hit my shoulder blades and all but knocked me over. Then the heavy *chug-chug-chug* of the *Water Beetle*'s engines shook the water around me as my brother's battered old ship bellied up dangerously close to the reef, and I turned to find the ship wallowing broadside behind me.

I liked to give Thomas a hard time about the *Water Beetle*, teasing him that he'd stolen it from the prop room of *Jaws*. But the fact of the matter was that I didn't know a damned thing about boats, and that I was secretly impressed that he could sail the thing around the lake so blithely.

'Harry!' Murphy called. She came hurrying down the frozen deck, slipping here and there on patches of ice as she did. She slapped a line attached to a harness she wore to the ship's safety railing, and threw the other end of the line to me. 'Come on!'

'It's about time you got outside the reef,' Thomas complained from the top of the wheelhouse. As I watched, he drew his heavy Desert Eagle from his side, aimed, and loosed a round. A dark form on one of the oncoming rafts let out a cry and fell into the water with a splash.

I scowled at Thomas. He doesn't even practice.

I stumbled forward and grabbed the line, wrapping it around my right arm. That was pretty much all I had enough energy left to do. Murphy began hauling it in, and started yelling for Thomas to help her.

'Cover me!' Thomas yelled.

He came down from the wheelhouse pirate style, just jumping down, all graceful and stylish despite the roll of the ship, despite the ice and the cold. Murphy, her feet planted, secured to the railing, shifted her grip and produced the little assault weapon she'd had on a strap around her back – the P-90 Kincaid had given her as a gift. She raised it to her shoulder, sighted through the scope at one of the oncoming rafts, and started calmly squeezing out rounds, one and two at a time. *Fam. Famfam. Fam. Famfam. Fam. Fam.*

One of the rafts foundered. Maybe she'd struck whoever was steering it and caused him to misguide it. Maybe the lake had simply swamped it. I don't know. But a second raft immediately turned to start picking up men who had spilled into the water from the first. Murphy turned her gun onto the remaining raft.

Thomas started hauling me out of the water by the line around my arm, just pulling me up arm over arm as if I'd been a child and not an adult a hundred pounds heavier than he was. He doesn't even work out.

I was tired enough that I just let him do it. As a result I had enough spare attention to notice when my feet cleared the water, and Deirdre surged out of the blackness and seized my ankles.

'Kill you!' she snarled. 'Kill you for what you did to him!'

'Holy crap!' Thomas yelled.

'Ack!' I agreed.

Most of those deadly strands of her hair were thrust into the stone reef below, holding her down, but a few that were free whipped wildly at Thomas. He ducked aside with a yell, barely managing to hold on to the line.

It felt like she was going to pull my legs off at the ankles. I screamed and kicked at her as best I could, but my legs were so numb that I could barely move them, much less shake her off. Thomas had all that he could do to simply hold on to the line and prevent those bladed strands from severing it.

'Karrin!' he screamed.

Murphy swung her legs up over the railing of the ship, still attached to it by the line fastened to her harness. Then she swung herself out into empty air above the water until she hung alongside me.

Then she aimed the P-90 down at Deirdre and flicked the selector to full automatic.

But before she could pull the trigger, Deirdre hissed, and a flickering blade swept up and struck Murphy across the face. She screamed and recoiled as the blade continued, an S-shaped cut that missed Murphy's throat by a finger's breadth and sliced through the strap that held the P-90 on her body. The weapon tumbled into the water.

'Bitch!' Murphy snarled, one side of her face a sheet of blood. She tried to reach for her pistol – in its shoulder holster, beneath her harness, beneath her coat. It might as well have been on the surface of the moon.

'Murph!' I said. I twisted my shoulders and thrust the end of *Fidelacchius* to within reach of her hand.

Murphy's fingers closed on the hilt of the holy blade.

She drew it maybe an inch from the scabbard.

White light blinded me. Blinded Deirdre. Blinded Murphy. Blinded Thomas. Blinded everyone.

'No!' Deirdre screamed, utter despair and terror in her voice. 'No, no, no!'

The pressure on my ankles vanished, and I heard the Denarian splash into the water.

Murphy released the hilt of the sword. The light died. It took maybe half a minute before I could see anything else. Thomas recovered faster, of course, and by that time he had us both back onto the deck of the *Water Beetle*. There was no evidence of Deirdre anywhere, and the two boatloads of soldier boys were hightailing it away as fast as they could go.

Murphy, bleeding from a cut running parallel to her right eyebrow all the way into her hairline, was staring in shock at me and at the sword. 'What the fuck was that?'

I slipped the sword off my shoulder. I felt really tired. I hurt everywhere. 'Offhand,' I mumbled, 'I'd say it was a job offer.'

'We've got to move before we get carried onto the reef,' Thomas muttered. He hurried off, pirate style. He looked good doing it. Of course. He doesn't even moisturize.

Murphy stared at the sword for a second more. Then she looked at me, and her bloody face went tight with concern. 'Jesus, Harry.' She moved to the side of my wounded leg and helped support my weight as I hobbled into the ship's cabin. 'Come on. Let's get you warmed up.'

'Well?' I asked her as she helped me. 'How 'bout it? I got this sword that needs somebody to use it.'

She sat me down on one of the bench seats in the ship's cabin. She looked at the sword for a moment, seriously. Then she shook her head and said quietly, 'I've got a job.'

I smiled faintly and closed my eyes. 'I thought you'd say that.'

'Shut up, Harry.'

'Okay,' I said.

And I did. For hours. It was glorious.

46

I woke up covered in a couple of heavy down comforters and innumerable blankets, and it was morning. The bench seat on the *Water Beetle* had been folded out into a reasonably comfortable cot. A kerosene heater was burning on the other side of the cabin. It wasn't exactly toasty, but it made the cabin warm enough to steam up the windows.

I came to slowly, aching in every joint, muscle and limb. The after-action hangover was every bit as bad as I had anticipated. I tried to remind myself that this was a deliriously joyous problem to deal with, all things considered. I wasn't being a very good sport about it, though. I growled and complained bitterly, and eventually worked up enough nerve to sit up and get out from under the covers. I went to the tiny bathroom – though on a boat, I guess it's called a 'head' for some stupid reason – and by the time I zombie-shuffled out, Thomas had come down from the deck and slipped inside. He was putting a cell phone back into his jacket pocket, and his expression was serious.

'Harry,' he said. 'How you doing?'

I suggested what he could do with his reproductive organs.

He arched an eyebrow at me. 'Better than I'd expected.'

I grunted. Then I added, 'Thank you.'

He snorted. That was all. 'Come on. I've got coffee for you in the car.'

'I'm leaving everything to you in my will,' I said.

'Cool. Next time I'll leave you in the water.'

I pulled my coat on with a groan. 'Almost wish you had. Coin? Sword?'

'Safe, stowed below. You want them?'

I shook my head. 'Keep them here for now.'

I followed him out to the truck, gimping on my bad knee. I noted that someone had, at some point in the evening, cleaned me up a bit and put new bandages on my leg, and on a number of scrapes and contusions I didn't even remember getting. I was wearing fresh clothing, too. Thomas. He didn't say anything about it, and neither did I. It's a brother thing.

We got into the battered Hummer, and I seized a paper cup of coffee waiting for me next to a brown paper bag. I grabbed the coffee, dumped in a lot of sugar and creamer, stirred it for about a quarter turn of the stick, and started sipping. Then I checked out the bag. Doughnut. I assaulted it.

Thomas began to start the car but froze in place and blinked at the doughnut. 'Hey,' he said. 'Where the hell did that come from?'

I took another bite. Cake doughnut. White frosting. Sprinkles. Still warm. And I had hot coffee to go with it. Pure heaven. I gave my brother a cryptic look and just took another bite.

'Christ,' he muttered, starting the truck. 'You don't even explain the little things, do you?'

'It's like a drug,' I said, through a mouthful of fattening goodness.

I enjoyed the doughnut while I could, letting it fully occupy all my senses. After I'd finished it, and the coffee started kicking in, I realized why I'd indulged myself so completely: It was likely to be the last bit of pleasure I was going to feel for a while.

Thomas hadn't said a damned thing about where we were going – or how anyone was doing after the events of the night before.

The Stroger building, the new hospital that has replaced the old Cook County complex as Chicago's nerve center of medicine, is only a few yards away from the old clump of buildings. It looks kind of like a castle. If you scrunch up your eyes a little, you can almost imagine its features as medieval ramparts and towers and crenellation, standing like some ancient mountain bastion, determined to defend the citizens of Chicago against the plagues and evils of the world.

Provided they have enough medical coverage, of course.

I finished the coffee and thought to myself that I might have been feeling a little pessimistic.

Thomas led me up to intensive care. He stopped in the hallway outside. 'Luccio's coordinating the information, so I don't have many details. But Molly's in there. She'll have the rest of them for you.'

'What do you know?' I asked him.

'Michael's in bad shape,' he said. 'Still in surgery, last I heard. They're waiting for him up here. I guess the bullets all came up from underneath him, and that armor he was wearing actually kept one of them in. Bounced around inside him like a BB inside a tin can.'

I winced.

'They said he only got hit by two or three rounds,' Thomas continued. 'But that it was more or less a miracle that he survived it at all. They don't know if he's going to make it. Sanya didn't go into anything more specific than that.'

I closed my eyes.

'Look,' Thomas said. 'I'm not exactly welcome around here right now. But I'll stay if you need me to.'

Thomas wasn't telling me the whole truth. My brother wasn't comfortable in hospitals, and I was pretty sure I'd figured out why: They were full of the sick, the injured, and the elderly – i.e., the kind of herd animals that predators' instincts told them were weakest, and the easiest targets. My brother didn't like being reminded about that part of his nature. He might hate that it happened, but his instincts would react regardless of what he wanted or didn't want. It would be torture for him to hang around here.

'No,' I said. 'I'll be fine.'

He frowned at me. 'All right,' he said after a moment. 'You've got my number. Call me; I'll give you a ride home.'

'Thanks.'

He put a hand on my arm for a second, then turned, hunched his shoulders, bowed his head so that his hair fell to hide most of his face, and walked quickly away.

I went on into the intensive care ward and found the waiting area.

Molly was sitting inside, next to Charity. Mother and daughter sat side by side, holding hands. They looked strained and weary. Charity was wearing jeans and one of Michael's flannel shirts. Her hair was pulled back into a ponytail, and she didn't have any makeup on. She'd been pulled from her bed in the middle of the night to rush to the hospital. Her eyes were focused into the distance and blank.

Small wonder. This was her greatest nightmare come to life.

They looked up as I came in, and their expressions were exactly the same: neutral, distant, numb.

'Harry,' Molly said, her voice hollow, ghostly.

'Hey, kid,' I said.

It took Charity a moment to react to my arrival. She focused her eyes on the far wall, blinked them a couple of times, and then focused them on me. She nodded and didn't speak.

'I, uh,' I said quietly.

Molly raised her hand to stop me from speaking. I shut up.

'Okay,' she said. 'Uh, let me think.' She closed her eyes, frowning in concentration, and started ticking off one finger with each sentence. 'Luccio says that the Archive is stable but unconscious. She's at Murphy's house and needs to talk to you. Murphy says to tell you her face will be fine. Sanya says that he needs to talk to you alone, and as soon as possible, at St. Mary's.'

I waved a hand at all of that. 'I'll take care of it later. How's your dad?'

'Severe trauma to his liver,' Charity said, her voice toneless. 'One of his kidneys was damaged too badly to be saved. One of his lungs collapsed. There's damage to his spine. One of his ribs was fractured into multiple pieces. His pelvis was broken in two places. His jaw was shattered. Subdural hematoma. There was trauma all through one ocular cavity. They aren't sure if he'll lose the eye or not. There might also be brain damage. They don't know yet.' Her eyes overflowed and focused into the distance again. 'There was trauma to his heart. Fragments of broken bone in it. From his ribs.' She shuddered and closed her eyes. 'His heart. They hurt his heart.'

Molly sat back down beside her mother and put her arm around Charity's shoulders. Charity leaned against her, eyes still spilling tears, but she never made a sound.

I'm not a Knight.

I'm not a hero, either.

Heroes keep their promises.

'Molly,' I said quietly. 'I'm sorry.'

She looked up at me, and her lip started quivering. She shook her head and said, 'Oh, Harry.'

'I'll go,' I said.

Charity's face snapped up and she said, her voice suddenly very clear and distinct, 'No.'

Molly blinked at her mother.

Charity stood up, her face blotched with tears, creased with strain, her eyes sunken with fatigue and worry. She stared at me for a long moment and then said, 'Families stay, Harry.' She lifted her chin, sudden and fierce pride briefly driving out the grief in her eyes. 'He would stay for you.'

My vision got a little blurry, and I sat down in the nearest chair. Probably just a reaction to all the strain of the past couple of days.

'Yeah,' I said, my throat thick. 'He would.'

I called everyone on the list Molly had quoted me and told them they could wait to see me until we knew about Michael. Except for Murph, they all got upset about that. I told them they could go to hell and hung up on them.

Then I settled in with Molly and Charity and waited.

Hospital waits are bad ones. The fact that they happen to pretty much all of us, sooner or later, doesn't make them any less hideous. They're always just a little bit too cold. It always smells just a little bit too sharp and clean. It's always quiet, so quiet that you can hear the fluorescent lights – another constant, those lights – humming. Pretty much everyone else there is in the same bad predicament you are, and there isn't much in the way of cheerful conversation.

And there's always a clock in sight. The clock has super-powers. It always seems to move too slowly. Look up at it and it will tell you the time. Look up an hour and a half later, and it will tell you two minutes have gone by. Yet it somehow simultaneously has the ability to remind you of how short life is, to make you acutely aware of how little time someone you love might have remaining to them.

The day crawled by. A doctor came to see Charity twice, to tell her that things were still bad, and that they were still working. The second visit came around suppertime, and the doc suggested that she get some food if she could, that they should know something more definite after the next procedure, in three or four hours.

He asked if Charity knew whether or not Michael had agreed to be an organ donor. Just in case, he said. They hadn't been able to find his driver's license. I could tell that Charity wanted to tell the doctor where he could shove his question and just how far it could go, but she told him what Michael would have told him – yes, of course he had. The doctor thanked her and left.

I walked down the cafeteria with Charity and Molly, but I didn't feel like eating or having food urged upon me. I figured that Charity probably had a critical back pressure of mothering built up after this much time away from her kids. On the way, I claimed that I needed to stretch my legs, which was the truth. Sometimes when there's too much going on in my head, it helps to walk around a bit.

So I walked down hallways, going nowhere in particular, just being careful not to pass too near any equipment that might be busy keeping someone alive at the moment.

I wound up sitting down in the hospital chapel.

It was the usual for such a place; quiet, subdued colors and lights, bench seating with an aisle in the middle, and a podium up at the front – the standard layout for the services of any number of faiths. Maybe it leaned a little harder toward Catholicism than most, but that might have been only natural. The Jesuits actually had a chaplaincy in residence, and held Mass there regularly.

It was quiet, which was the important thing. I sank onto a pew, aching, and closed my eyes.

Lots of details chased their way around my head. Michael had come in with gunshot wounds. The cops were going to ask lots of questions about that. Depending on the circumstances of the helicopter's return to Chicago, that could get really complicated, really fast. On the other hand, given the depth of Marcone's involvement, the problems might just vanish. He had his fingers in so many pies in Chicago's city government that he could probably have any inquiry quashed if he really wanted it done.

Given what he'd been saved from, it would be consistent with his character for Marcone to repay the people who bailed him out with whatever aid he could render in turn. It irked me that Marcone could ever be in a position to offer significant aid to Michael, regardless of the circumstances.

Of course, for that to happen, Michael would first need to survive.

My thoughts kept coming full circle back to that.

Would he be in danger right now if I hadn't insisted that he put on that harness? If I hadn't shoved him onto that rope ahead of me, would he still be up there under the knife, dying? Could I really have been that arrogant to assume, based on one glance at Gard's face, that I not only knew the future, but had the wisdom and the right to decide what that future should be?

Maybe it should be me up there. I didn't have a wife and a family waiting for me to come home.

I'd expected Charity to scream and throw things at me. Maybe

I'd even wanted that. Because while I intellectually understood that I'd had no way of knowing what was going to happen, and that I'd only been trying to protect my friend, a big part of me couldn't help but feel that I deserved Charity's fury. After all, it reasoned, I had gotten her husband killed as surely as if I'd murdered him myself.

Except that he wasn't dead yet – and thinking like that was too much like giving up on him. I couldn't do that.

I looked up at the podium, where Whoever would presumably be when someone was there delivering a sermon.

'I know that we don't talk much,' I said, speaking out loud to the empty room. 'And I'm not looking for a pen pal. But I thought You should know that Michael makes You look pretty good. And if after all he's done, it ends like this for him, I'd think less of You. He deserves better. I think You should make sure he gets it. If You want to bill it to me, I'm fine with that. It's no problem.'

Nobody said anything back.

'And while we're on the subject,' I said, 'I think the rules You've got set up suck. You don't get involved as much as You used to, apparently. And Your angels aren't allowed to stick their toes in unless the bad guys do it first. But I've been running some figures in my head, and when the Denarians pulled up those huge Signs, they had to have a lot of power to do it. A *lot* of power. More than I could ever have had, even with Lasciel. Archangel power. And I can only think of one of those guys who would have been helping that crew.'

I stood up and jabbed a finger at the podium, suddenly furious, and screamed, 'The Prince of fucking Darkness gets to cheat and unload his power on the earth – twice! – and You just *sit* there being holy while my friend, who has fought for You his whole life, is *dying*! What the hell is *wrong* with You?'

'I guess this is a bad time,' said a voice from behind me.

I turned around and found a little old guy in a dark blue coverall whose stenciled name tag read, Jake. He was pulling behind him a janitor's cart with a trash bin and the usual assortment of brooms and mops and cleaning products. He had a round belly and short, curling silver hair that matched his beard, both cropped close to his dark skin. 'Sorry. I'll come back later.'

I felt like an idiot. I shook my head at him. 'No, no. I'm not doing anything. I mean, you're not keeping me from anything. I'll get out of your way.'

'You ain't in my way, young man,' said Jake. 'Not at all. You ain't the first one I ever seen upset in a hospital chapel. Won't be the last, either. You sure you don't mind?'

'No,' I said. 'Come on in.'

He did, hauling the cart with him, and went over to the trash can in the corner. He took out the old liner. 'You got a friend here, huh?'

'Yeah,' I said, sitting down again.

'It's okay to be mad at God about it, son. It ain't His fault, what happened, but He understands.'

'Maybe He does,' I said with a shrug. 'But He doesn't care. I don't know why everyone thinks He does. Why would He?'

Jake paused and looked at me.

'I mean, this whole universe, right? All those stars and all those worlds,' I continued, maybe sounding more bitter than I had intended. 'Probably so many different kinds of people out there that we couldn't count them all. How could God really care about what's happening to one little person on one little planet among a practically infinite number of them?'

Jake tied off the trash bag and tossed it in the bin. He replaced the liner with a thoughtful look on his face. 'Well,' he said, 'I never been to much school, you understand. But seems to me that you assuming something you shouldn't assume.'

'What's that?' I asked.

'That God sees the world like you do. One thing at a time. From just one spot. Seems to me that He is supposed to be everywhere, know everything.' He put the lid back on the trash can. 'Think about that. He knows what you're feeling, how you're hurting. Feels my pain, your pain, like it was His own.' Jake shook his head. 'Hell, son. Question isn't how could God care about just one person. Question is, how could He *not*.'

I snorted and shook my head.

'More optimism than you want to hear right now,' Jake said. 'I hear you, son.' He turned and started pushing the cart out the door. 'Oh,' he said. 'Can an old man offer you one more thought?'

'Sure,' I said, without turning around.

'You gotta think that maybe there's a matter of balance, here,' he said. 'Maybe one archangel invested his strength in this situation overtly and immediately. Maybe another one was just quieter about it. Thinking long-term. Maybe he already gave you a hand.'

My right hand erupted into pins and needles again.

I sucked in a swift breath and rose, spinning around.

Jake was gone.

The janitor's cart was still there. A rag hanging off the back was still swinging back and forth slightly. A folded paperback book was shoved between the body of the cart and the handle. I went over to the cart and looked up and down the hall.

There was no one in sight, and nowhere they could have conveniently disappeared to.

I picked up the book. It was a battered old copy of *The Two Towers*. One page was dog-eared, and a bit of dialogue underlined in pencil.

' "The burned hand teaches best," ' I read aloud. I made my way back to my seat and shook my head. 'What the hell is that supposed to mean?'

Grimalkin mewled from the pew beside me, 'That your experience with resisting the shadow of the Fallen One has garnered the respect of the Watchman, my Emissary.'

I twitched violently enough that I came up off my seat an inch or two, and came back down with a grunt. I slid down as far as I could to the end of the pew. It wasn't far. I bought myself only another inch or three before I turned to face Mab.

She sat calmly, dressed in a casual business suit of dark blue, wearing plenty of elegant little diamonds. Her white hair was bound up into a braided bun, held in place with ivory sticks decorated with lapis. She held Grimalkin on her lap like a favorite pet, though only a lunatic would have mistaken the malk for a domestic cat. It was the first time I'd seen Grimalkin in clear light. He was unusually large and muscular, even for a malk – and they tended to make your average lynx look a little bit scrawny. Grimalkin must have weighed sixty or seventy pounds, all of it muscle and bone. His fur was dark grey, patterned with rippling black fur almost like a subtle watermark. His eyes were yellow-green, very large, and far too intelligent for any animal.

'The Watchman?' I stammered.

Mab's head moved slightly with the words, but it was Grimalkin's mewling voice that actually spoke. 'The Prince of the Host is all pomp and ceremony, and when he moves it is with the thunder of the wings of an army of seraphim, the crash of drums, and the clamor of horns. The Trumpeter never walks quietly when he can appear in a chorus of light. The Demon Binder takes tasks upon his own shoulders and solves his problems with his own hands. But the Watchman . . .' Mab smiled. 'Of the archangels, I like him the most. He is the quiet one. The subtle one. The one least known. And by far the most dangerous.'

I sorted through what knowledge I had of the archangels. It was meager enough, but I knew *that* much, at least. 'Uriel,' I said quietly.

Mab lifted a finger and continued speaking through the malk. 'Caution is called for, Emissary mine. Were I in your position, I would speak his name sparingly, if ever.'

'What has he done to me?' I asked her.

Mab stared at me with iridescent eyes. 'That is a question

only you can answer. But I can say this much: He has given you the potential to be more of what you are.'

'Huh?'

She smiled, reached to the bench on the other side of her body, and produced my blasting rod. 'The return of your property,' the malk said. 'The need to keep it from you has passed.'

'Then I was right,' I said, accepting it. 'You took it. And you took the memory of it happening.'

'Yes.'

'Why?'

'Because I deemed it proper,' she replied, as if speaking to a rather slow-witted child. 'You would have risked your own life – and my purpose – to protect your precious mortals had I not taken your fire from you. Summer would have tracked and killed you two days ago.'

'Not having it could have gotten me killed, too,' I said. 'And then you'd have wasted all that time you've put in trying to recruit me to be the next Winter Knight.'

'Nonsense,' Mab said. 'If you died, I would simply recruit your brother. He would be well motivated to seek revenge upon your killers.'

A little cold feeling shot through me. I hadn't realized that Mab knew who he was. But I guess it made sense. My godmother, the Leanansidhe, had been tight with my mother, one way or another. If Lea had known, then it might make sense that Mab did, too. 'He isn't a mortal,' I said quietly. 'I thought the Knights had to be mortals.'

'He is in love,' Grimalkin mrowled for Mab. 'That is more than mortal enough for me.' She tilted her head. 'Though I suppose I might make him an offer, while you yet live. He would give much to hold his love again, would he not?'

I fixed her with a hard gaze and said, 'You will stay away from him.'

'I will do as I please,' she said. 'With him – and with you.'

I scowled at her. 'You will not. I do not belong to y—'

The next thing I knew I was on my knees in the center aisle, and Mab was walking away from me, toward the door. 'Oh, but you do, mortal. Until you have worked off your debt to me you are mine. You owe one favor more.'

I tried to get up, and I couldn't. My knees just wouldn't move. My heart beat far too hard, and I hated how frightened I felt.

'Why?' I demanded. 'Why did you want the Denarians stopped? Why send the hobs to kill the Archive? Why recruit me to save the Archive and Marcone in the event that the hobs failed?'

Mab paused, turned, casually showing off the gorgeous curves of her calves, and tilted her head at me. 'Nicodemus and his ilk were clearly in violation of my Accords, and obviously planning to abuse them to further his ambition. That was reason enough to see his designs disrupted. And among the Fallen was one with much to answer for to me, personally, for its attack upon my home.'

'The Black Council attack on Arctis Tor,' I said. 'One of them used Hellfire.'

Mab showed me her snow-white teeth. 'The Watchman and I,' Grimalkin mewled for her, 'had a common enemy this day. The enemy could not be allowed to gain the power represented by the child Archive.'

I frowned and thought of the silver hand that had batted the fallen angel and his master sorceries around as if he'd been a stuffed practice dummy. 'Thorned Namshiel.'

Mab's eyes flashed with sudden, cold fury and frost *literally* formed over every surface of the chapel, including upon my own eyelashes.

'There are others yet who will pay for what they have done,' Mab snarled in her own voice. It sounded hideous – not unmelodious, because it was as rich and full and musical as it ever had been. But it was filled with such rage, such fury, such pain and such hate that every vowel clawed at my skin, and every consonant felt like someone taking a staple gun to my ears.

'I am Sidhe,' she hissed. 'I am the Queen of Air and Darkness. I am Mab.' Her chin lifted, her eyes wide and white around the rippling colors of her irises – utterly insane. 'And I repay my debts, mortal. All of them.'

There was an enormous crack, a sound like thick ice shattering on the surface of a lake, and Mab and her translator were gone.

I knelt there, shaking in the wake of hearing her voice. I realized a minute later that I had a nosebleed. A minute after that, I realized that there was a trickle of blood coming out of my ears, too. My eyes ached with strain, as if I'd been outdoors in bright sunlight for too many hours.

It took me still another minute to get my legs to start moving again. After that I staggered to the nearest bathroom and cleaned up. I spent a little while poking at my memory and trying to see if there were any holes in it that hadn't been there before. Then I spent a while more wondering if I'd be able to tell if she *had* taken something else.

'Jesus Christ,' I breathed, shivering.

Because though I hadn't been in on the original attack on Mab's tower, and when I *did* attack it I had been unwittingly serving Mab's interests, the fact remained that I had indeed offered her the same insult as Thorned Namshiel. The lacerating fury that turned her voice into razor blades could very well be directed at me in the near future.

I hurried out of the chapel and went down to the cafeteria.

Being bullied into eating dinner sounded a lot more pleasant than it had a few minutes ago.

The doctor came into the waiting room at ten seventeen that night.

Charity came to her feet. She'd spent much of the day with her head bowed, praying quietly. She was beyond tears, at least for the moment, and she put a sheltering arm around her daughter, pulling Molly in close to her side.

'He's in recovery,' the doctor said. 'The procedures went . . .' The doctor sighed. He looked at least as tired as either of the Carpenter women. 'As well as could be expected. Better, really. I hesitate to make any claims at this point, but he seems to be stable, and assuming there are no complications in the next hour or two, I think he'll pull through.'

Charity bit her lip hard. Molly threw her arms around her mother.

'Thank you, Doctor,' Charity whispered.

The doctor smiled wearily. 'You should realize that . . . the injuries were quite extensive. It's unlikely that he'll be able to fully recover from them. Brain damage is a possibility – we won't know until he wakes up. Even if that isn't an issue, the other trauma was severe. He may need assistance, possibly for the rest of his life.'

Charity nodded calmly. 'He'll have it.'

'That's right,' Molly said.

'When can I see him?' Charity asked.

'We'll bring him up in an hour or two,' the doctor said.

I cleared my throat. 'Excuse me, Doc. Is he going to be on a respirator?'

'For the time being,' the doctor said. 'Yes.'

I nodded. 'Thank you.'

The doctor nodded to us, and Charity thanked him again. He left.

'Okay, grasshopper,' I said. 'Time for us to clear out.'

'But they're going to bring hi— Oh,' Molly said, crestfallen. 'The respirator.'

'Better not to take any chances, huh?' I asked her.

'It's all right, baby,' Charity said quietly. 'I'll call home as soon as he wakes up.'

They hugged tightly. Molly and I started walking out.

'Oh,' Molly said, her voice very tired. 'I did that homework.'

I felt pretty tired, too. 'Yeah?'

She nodded and smiled wearily up at me. 'Charlemagne.'

*   *   *

I called Thomas, and he gave me and Molly a ride to Murphy's place.

The night was clear. The cloud cover had blown off, and the moon and the stars got together with the snow to turn Chicago into a winter wonderland months ahead of schedule. The snow had stopped falling, though. I suppose that meant Mab had turned her attention elsewhere. Thomas dropped me off a short distance away, and then left to drive the grasshopper back to her home. I covered the last hundred yards or so on foot.

Murphy lives in a teeny little house that belonged to her grandmother. It was just a single story, with two bedrooms, a living room, and a little kitchen. It was meant for one person to live in, or possibly a couple with a single child. It was certainly overloaded by the mob of Wardens who had descended on the place. Luccio's reinforcements had arrived.

There were four Wardens in the little living room, all of them grizzled veterans, two young members in the kitchen, and I was sure that there were at least two more outside, standing watch behind veils. I was challenged for a password in an amused tone by one of the young Wardens when I came in the kitchen door. I told him to do something impolite, please, and asked him where Luccio might be.

'That's anatomically unlikely,' the young man replied in a British accent. He poured a second cup of steaming tea and said, 'Drink up. I'll let her know you're here.'

'Thanks.'

I was sipping tea and sitting at Murphy's table when Luccio came in a few minutes later. 'Give us the room, please, Chandler, Kostikos.'

The younger men cleared out to the living room – a polite illusion, really. The house was too small to provide much in the way of privacy.

Luccio poured herself a cup of tea and sat down across from me.

I felt my shoulders tense up a little. I forced myself to remain quiet, and sipped more tea.

'I'm concerned,' Luccio said quietly, 'about the Archive.'

'Her name is Ivy,' I said.

She frowned. 'That's . . . part of my concern, Harry. Your personal closeness with her. It's dangerous.'

I lifted my eyebrows. 'Dangerous? I'm in danger because I'm treating her like a real person?'

Luccio grimaced as if tasting something bitter. 'Frankly? Yes.'

I thought about being diplomatic and polite. Honest, I really did. But while I was thinking about it, I accidentally bumped the button that puts my mouth on autopilot, because it said, 'That's a load of crap, Captain, and you know it.'

Her expression went still as the whole of her attention focused on me. 'Is it?'

'Yes. She's a kid. She's alone. She's not some computer data-base, and it's inhuman to treat her like one.'

'Yes,' Luccio said bluntly. 'It is. And it's also the safest way to deal with her.'

'Safest for who?' I demanded.

Luccio took a sip of tea. 'For everyone.'

I frowned down at my cup. 'Tell me.'

She nodded. 'The Archive . . . has been around for a long time. Always passed down in a family line, mother to daughter. Usually the Archive is inherited by a woman when she's in her early to mid-thirties, when her mother dies, and after she's given birth to her own daughter. Accidents are rare. Part of the Archive's nature is a drive to protect itself, a need to avoid exposing the person hosting it to risk. And given the extensive knowledge available to it, the Archive is very good at avoiding risky situations in the first place. And, should they arise, the power available to the Archive generally ensures its survival. It is extremely rare for the host of an Archive to die young.'

I grunted. 'Go on.'

'When the Archive is passed . . . Harry, try to imagine living your life, with all of its triumphs and tragedies – and suddenly you find yourself with a second set of memories, every bit as real to you as your own. A second set of heartaches, loves, triumphs, losses. All of them just as real – and then a third. And a fourth. And a fifth. And more and more and more. The perfect memory, the absolute recall of every Archive that came before you. Five thousand years of them.'

I blinked at that. 'Hell's bells. That would . . .'

'Drive one insane,' Luccio said. 'Yes. And it generally does. There is a reason that the historical record for many soothsayers and oracles presents them as being madwomen. The Pythia, and many, many others, were simply the Archive, using her vast knowledge of the past to build models to predict the most probable future. She was a madwoman – but she was also the Archive.

'As a defense, the Archives began to distance themselves from other human beings, emotionally. They reasoned that if they could stop adding the weight of continuing lifetimes of experience and grief to the already immense burden of carrying so much knowledge, it might better enable them to function. And it did. The Archive keeps its host emotionally remote for a reason – because otherwise the passions and prejudices and hatreds and jealousies of thousands of lifetimes have the potential to distill themselves into a single being.

'Normally, an Archive would have her own lifetime of experience to insulate her against all these other emotions and memories, a baseline to contrast against them.'

I suddenly got it. 'But Ivy doesn't.'

'Ivy doesn't,' Luccio agreed. 'Her grandmother was killed in a freak accident, an automobile crash, I believe. Her mother was a seventeen-year-old girl who was in love, and pregnant. She hated her mother for dying and cursing her to carry the Archive when she wanted to have her own life – and she hated the child for having a lifetime of freedom ahead of her. Ivy's mother killed herself rather than carry the Archive.'

I started feeling a little sick. 'And Ivy knows it.'

'She does. Knows it, feels it. She was born knowing exactly what her mother thought and felt about her.'

'How could you know this about her . . .' I frowned, thinking. Then said, 'Kincaid. The girl was in love with Kincaid.'

'No,' Luccio said. 'But Kincaid was working for Ivy's grandmother at the time, and the girl confided in him.'

'Man, that's screwed up,' I said.

'Ivy has remained distant her whole life,' Luccio said. 'If she begins to involve her own emotions in her duties as the Archive, or in her life generally, she runs the serious risk of being overwhelmed with emotions and passions which she simply is not – and cannot be – psychologically equipped to handle.'

'You're afraid that she could go out of control.'

'The Archive was created to be a neutral force. A repository of knowledge. But what if Ivy's unique circumstance allowed her to ignore those limitations? Imagine the results of the anger and bitterness and desire for revenge of all those lifetimes, combined with the power of the Archive and the restraint of a twelve-year-old child.'

'I'd rather not,' I said quietly.

'Nor would I,' Luccio said. 'That could be a true nightmare. All that knowledge, without conscience to direct it. The necromancer Kemmler had such a spirit in his service, a sort of miniature version of the Archive. Nowhere near as powerful, but it had been studying and learning beside wizards for generations, and the things it was capable of were appalling.' She shook her head.

I took a sip of tea, because otherwise the gulp would have been suspicious. She was talking about Bob. And she was right about what Bob was capable of doing. When I'd unlocked the personality he'd taken on under some of his former owners, he'd nearly killed me.

'The Wardens destroyed it, of course,' she said.

No, they hadn't. Justin DuMorne, former Warden, hadn't destroyed the skull. He'd smuggled it from Kemmler's lab and kept it in his own – until I'd burned him to death, and taken it from him in turn.

'It was just too much power under too little restraint. And it's entirely possible that the Archive could become a similar threat on a far larger scale. I know you care about the child, Harry. But you had to be warned. You might not be doing her any favors by acting like her friend.'

'Who's acting?' I said. 'Where is she?'

'We've been keeping her asleep,' Luccio said, 'until you or Kincaid got here.'

'I get it,' I said. 'You don't think I should get close to her. Unless you're worried about what's going to happen when you wake her up and she's really scared and confused.'

Luccio's cheeks flushed and she looked away. 'I don't have all the answers, Dresden. I just have concerns.'

I sighed.

'Whatever,' I said. 'Let me see her.'

Luccio led me into Murph's guest bedroom. Ivy looked very tiny in the double bed. I sat down beside her, and Luccio leaned over to gently rest her hand on Ivy's head. She murmured something and drew her hand away.

Ivy let out a small whimper and then blinked her eyes open, suddenly hyperventilating. She looked around wildly, her eyes wide, and let out a small cry.

'Easy, easy,' I said gently. 'Ivy, it's all right. You're safe.'

She sobbed and flung herself tight against me.

I hugged her. I just rocked her gently and hugged her while she cried and cried.

Luccio watched me, her eyes compassionate and sad.

After a long while Ivy whispered, 'I got your letter. Thank you.'

I squeezed a little.

'They did things to me,' she said.

'I know,' I said quietly. 'Been there. But I was all right after a while. You're going to be all right. It's over.'

She hugged me some more, and cried herself back to sleep.

I looked up at Luccio and said, 'You still want me to push her away? You want her baseline to be what she shared with those animals?'

Luccio frowned. 'The Senior Council—'

'Couldn't find its heart if it had a copy of *Grey's Anatomy*, X-ray vision, and a stethoscope,' I said. 'No. They can lay down the law about magic. But they aren't telling me who I'm allowed to befriend.'

She looked at me for a long moment, and then a slow smile curled up one side of her mouth. 'Morgan told them you'd say that. So did McCoy and Listens-to-Wind. The Merlin wouldn't hear it.'

'The Merlin doesn't like to hear anything that doesn't fit into his view of the world,' I said. 'Japanese.'

'Excuse me?'

'Japanese. There's a Japanese steakhouse I go to sometimes to celebrate. Surviving this mess qualifies. Come with me, dinner tomorrow. The teriyaki is to die for.'

She smiled more broadly and inclined her head once.

The door opened, and Murphy and Kincaid arrived. Kincaid was moving under his own power, though very gingerly, and with the aid of a walking stick. I got out of the way, and he came over to settle down next to Ivy. She woke up enough to murmur something about cookies and a Happy Meal. He settled down on the bed beside her, and she pressed up against his arm before settling down to rest again. Kincaid, evidently exhausted himself, drew a gun, took the safety off, placed it on his chest, and went to sleep too.

'It's cute,' I whispered to Murphy. 'He has a teddy Glock.'

She was looking at Kincaid and Ivy with a decidedly odd expression. She shook her head a little, blinked up at me, and said, 'Hmm. Oh, hah, very funny. I had your car dug out of the snow, by the way.'

I blinked at her. 'Thank you.'

'Got your keys?'

'Yeah.'

'Give you a ride to it,' she said.

'Groovy.'

We took off.

Once we were in the car and moving, Murphy said, 'I like Luccio.'

'Yeah?'

'But she's all wrong for you.'

'Uh-huh,' I said.

'You come from different worlds. And she's your boss. There are secrets you have to keep from her. That's going to make things difficult. And there are other issues that could come up.'

'Wait,' I said. I mimed cleaning out my ears. 'Okay, go ahead. Because for a second there, it sounded like you were giving me relationship advice.'

Murphy gave me a narrow, oblique look. 'No offense, Dresden. But if you want to compare total hours of good relationships and bad, I leave you in the dust in both categories.'

'Touché,' I said. Sourly. 'Kincaid was looking awfully paternal in there, wasn't he?'

'Oh, bite me,' Murphy said, scowling. 'How's Michael?'

'Gonna make it,' I said. 'Hurt bad, though. Don't know how mobile he's going to be after this.'

Murphy fretted her lower lip. 'What happens if he can't . . . keep on with the Knight business?'

I shook my head. 'I have no idea.'

'I just . . . I didn't think that taking up one of the swords was the sort of job offer you could turn down.'

I blinked at Murphy. 'No, Murph. There's no mandatory martyrdom involved. You've got a choice. You've always got a choice. That's . . . sort of the whole point of faith, the way I understand it.'

She digested that in silence for a time. Then she said, 'It isn't because I don't believe.'

'I know that,' I said.

She nodded. 'It isn't for me, though, Harry. I've already chosen my ground. I've taken an oath. It meant more to me than accepting a job.'

'I know,' I said. 'If you weren't the way you are, Murph, the Sword of Faith wouldn't have reacted to you as strongly as it did. If someone as thick as me understands it, I figure the Almighty probably gets it too.'

She snorted and gave me a faint smile, and drove the rest of the way to my car in silence.

When we got there she parked next to the Blue Beetle. 'Harry,' she said, 'do you ever feel like we're going to wind up old and alone? That we're . . . I don't know . . . doomed never to have anyone? Anything that lasts?'

I flexed the fingers of my still-scarred left hand and my mildly tingling right hand. 'I'm more worried about all the things I'll never be rid of.' I eyed her. 'What brings on this cheerful topic?'

She gave me a faint smile. 'It's just . . . the center cannot hold, Harry. I think things are starting to fall apart. I can't see it, and I can't prove it, but I *know* it.' She shook her head. 'Maybe I'm just losing my mind.'

I looked intently at her, frowning. 'No, Murph. You aren't.'

'There are bad things happening,' she said.

'Yeah. And I haven't been able to put many pieces together. Yet. But we shut down some of the bad guys last night. They were using the Denarians to get to the Archive.'

'What do they want?'

'Don't know,' I said. 'But it's going to be big and bad.'

'I want in on this fight, Harry,' she said.

'Okay.'

'All the way. Promise me.'

'Done.' I offered her my hand.

She took it.

Father Forthill was already asleep, but Sanya answered the door when I dropped by St. Mary's. He was rumpled and looked tired, but was smiling. 'Michael woke and was talking.'

'That's great,' I said, grinning. 'What did he say?'

'Wanted to know if you made it out all right. Then he went back to sleep.'

I laughed, and Sanya and I traded a hug, a manly hug with a lot of back thumping, which he then ruined with one of those Russian kisses on both cheeks.

'Come in, come in,' he said. 'I apologize for trying to rush you earlier. We wanted to be sure to collect the coins and get them safely stored as soon as possible.'

I exhaled. 'I don't have them.'

His smile vanished. 'What?'

I told him about Thorned Namshiel.

Sanya swore and rubbed at his face. Then he said, 'Come.'

I followed him through the halls in the back of the enormous church until we got to the staff's kitchen. He went to the fridge, opened it, and came out with a bottle of bourbon. He poured some into a coffee cup, drank it down, and poured some more. He offered me the bottle.

'No, thanks. Aren't you supposed to drink vodka?'

'Aren't you supposed to wear pointy hat and ride on flying broomstick?'

'Touché,' I said.

Sanya shook his head and flexed the fingers of his right hand. 'Eleven. Plus six. Seventeen. It could be worse.'

'But we nailed Thorned Namshiel,' I said. 'And Eldest Gruff laid out Magog like a sack of potatoes. I'll get you his coin tomorrow.'

A flicker of satisfaction went through Sanya's eyes. 'Magog? Good. But Namshiel, no.'

'What do you mean, no? I saw Michael cut his hand off and drop it into his pouch.'

'*Da*,' Sanya said, 'and the coin was under the skin of his right hand. But it was not in his pouch when he went to the hospital.'

'What?'

Sanya nodded. 'We took off his armor and gear in helicopter, to stop the bleeding. Maybe it fell out into the lake.'

I snorted.

He grimaced and nodded. '*Da*, I know. That did not happen.'

I sighed. 'Marcone. I'll look into it.'

'Are you sure?'

'Yeah. I know those people. I'll go see them right now. Though I was looking forward to going home for a while.' I pushed my hips up off the counter they leaned on. 'Well, what's one more thing, right?'

'Two more things,' Sanya said. He vanished and returned a moment later.

He was carrying *Amoracchius* in its scabbard. He offered it to me.

I lifted both eyebrows.

'Instructions,' Sanya said. 'I'm to give it to you and you will kn—'

'Know who to give it to,' I muttered. I eyed the ceiling. 'Someone is having a huge laugh right now at my expense.' I raised my voice a little. 'I don't *have* to do this, You know! I have free will! I could tell You to go jump in a lake!'

Sanya stood there, offering me the sword.

I snatched it out of his hands, grumbling under my breath, and stalked out to my Volkswagen. I threw the sword into the back. 'As if I didn't have enough problems,' I muttered, slamming the passenger door and stalking around to the driver-side door. 'No. I gotta be carrying around freaking Excalibur now, too. Unless it isn't, who knows.' I slammed the driver-side door, and the old paperback copy of *The Two Towers* Uriel had left me, and which I'd dropped into the pocket of my duster, dug into my side.

I frowned and pulled it out. It fell open to the inside front cover, where there was writing in a flowing hand: *The reward for work well-done is more work.*

'Ain't that the truth,' I muttered. I stuffed the book back in my pocket and hit the road again.

It took a phone call and an hour to set it up, but Marcone met me at his office on the floor over Executive Priority. I walked in carrying the sword to find Marcone and Hendricks in his office — a plain and rather Spartan place for the time being. He had only recently moved in, and it looked more like the office of an active college professor, functional and put together primarily from expediency, than that of a criminal mastermind.

I cut right to the chase. 'Someone is backstabbing the people who saved your life, and I won't have it.'

Marcone raised his eyebrows. 'Please explain.'

I told him about Thorned Namshiel and the coin.

'I don't have it,' Marcone said.

'Do any of your people?' I asked.

He frowned at that question. Then he leaned back in his chair and put his elbows on the arms of it, resting the fingertips of his hands together.

'Where is Gard?' I asked.

'Reporting to her home office,' he murmured. 'I will make inquiries.'

I wondered if Marcone was lying to me. It wasn't a habit of his, but that only meant that when he did tell a lie, it was all the more effective. I wondered if he was telling the truth. If so, then maybe Monoc Securities had just acquired their own Fallen angel and expert in magic and magical theory.

'The child,' Marcone said. 'Is she well?'

'She's safe,' I said. 'She's with people who care about her.'

He nodded. 'Good. Was there anything else?'

'No,' I said.

'Then you should get some rest,' Marcone said. 'You look' — his mouth twitched up at the corners — 'like a raccoon. Who has been run over by a locomotive.'

'Next time I leave your wise ass on the island,' I said, scowling, and stalked out.

I was on the way out of the building when I decided to make one more stop.

Madam Demeter was in her office, dressed as stylishly as ever.

'Hello, Mister Dresden,' she said as she put several files away, neatly, precisely ordering them. 'I'm quite busy. I hope this won't take too long.'

'No,' I said. 'I just wanted to share a theory with you.'

'Theory?'

'Yeah. See, in all the excitement and explosions and demonic brouhaha, everyone's forgotten a small detail.'

Her fingers stopped moving.

'Someone gave the Denarians the location of Marcone's panic room. Someone close to him. Someone who would know many of his secrets. Someone who would have a good reason to want to hurt him.'

Demeter turned just her head to face me, eyes narrowed.

'A lot of men talk to the women they sleep with,' I said. 'That's always been true. And it would give you a really good reason to get close to him.'

'He's like a lot of men,' Demeter said quietly.

'I know you've got a gun in that drawer,' I told her. 'Don't try it.'

'Why shouldn't I?' she said.

'Because I'm not going to give you to Marcone.'

'What do you want from me?' she asked.

I shrugged. 'I might ask you for information sometimes. If you could help me without endangering yourself, I'd appreciate it. Either way, it doesn't affect whether or not I talk to Marcone.'

Her eyes narrowed. 'Why not?'

'Maybe I want to see him go down someday,' I said. 'But mostly because it's none of my damned business. I just wanted you to know that I'd seen you. This time maybe he won't put it all together. He's got more likely suspects than you inside his organization – and I'd be shocked if you hadn't already realized what a great patsy Torelli is going to make.'

Demeter gave me a wintry smile.

'But don't get overconfident. If you make another move that obvious, he'll figure it out. And you'll disappear.'

Demeter let out a bare laugh and shut the filing cabinet. 'I disappeared years ago.' She gave me a steady look. 'Are you here to do business, Mister Dresden?'

Granted, there was a building full of very . . . fit girls who would be happy to, ah, work on my tone. And my tone was letting me know that it would be happy to be worked on. The rest of my body, however, thought that a big meal and about two weeks of sleep was a much better idea. And once you got up to my neck, the rest of me thought that this whole place was looking prettier and hollower every time I visited.

'It's done,' I said, and left.

At home, I couldn't sleep.

Finally I had enough spare time to worry about what the hell was wrong with my right hand.

I wound up in my lab, dangling the packet of stale catnip for Mister and filling Bob in on the events of the past few days.

'Wow,' Bob said. 'Soulfire. Are you sure he said soulfire?'

'Yeah,' I said wearily. 'Why?'

'Well,' the skull said. 'Soulfire is . . . well. It's Hellfire, essentially. Only from the other place.'

'Heavenfire?'

'Well . . .' Bob said, 'yes. And no. Hellfire is something you use to destroy things. Soulfire is used the opposite way – to create stuff. Look, basically what you do is, you take a portion of your soul and you use it as a matrix for your magic.'

I blinked. 'What?'

'It's sort of like using rebar inside concrete,' Bob said. 'You put a matrix of rebar in, then pour concrete around it, and the strength of the entire thing together is a great deal higher than either one would be separately. You could do things that way that you could never do with either the rebar or the concrete alone.'

'But I'm doing that with my *soul*?' I demanded.

'Oh, come *on*, Harry. All you mortals get all hung up over your precious *souls*. You've never seen your soul, never touched it, never done anything with it. What's all the to-do?'

'So what you're saying is that this hand construct was made out of my soul,' I said.

'Your soul and your magic fused together, yeah,' Bob said. 'Your soul converted into energy. Soulfire. In this case, the spirit energy drawn from your aura right around your right hand, because it fit the construct so well, it being a big version of your right hand and all. Your standard force-projection spell formed around the matrix of soulfire, and what had been an instantaneous exertion of force became a long-term entity capable of manipulation and exertion to the same degree. Not really more powerful than just the force spell, as much as it was *more* than simply the force spell.'

I wiggled my tingling fingers. 'Oh. But my soul's going to get better, right?'

'Oh, sure,' Bob said. 'Few days, a week or two at most, it'll grow back in. Go out and have a good time, enjoy yourself, do some things that uplift the human spirit or whatever, and it'll come back even faster.'

I grunted. 'So what you're saying is that soulfire doesn't let me do anything new. It just makes me more of what I already am.'

'A *lot* more,' Bob said, nodding cheerfully from his shelf. 'It's how angels do all of their stuff. Though admittedly, they've got a lot more in the way of soul to draw upon than you do.'

'I thought angels didn't have souls,' I said.

'Like I said, people get all excited and twitchy when that word gets used,' Bob said. 'Angels don't have anything *else*.'

'Oh. What happens if I, uh, you know. Use too much of it?'

'What's five minus five, Harry?'

'Zero.'

'Right. Think about that for a minute. I'm sure you'll come to the right conclusion.'

'It's bad?'

'See? You're not totally hopeless,' Bob said. 'And hey, you got a new magic sword to custodianize, too? Merlin, eat your heart out; he only got to look after one! And working a case with Uriel! You're hitting the big-time, Harry!'

'I haven't really heard much about Uriel,' I said. 'I mean I know he's an archangel, but . . .'

'He's . . . sort of Old Testament,' Bob said. 'You know the guy who killed the firstborn children of Egypt? Him. Other than that, well. There's only suspicions. And he isn't the sort to brag. It's always the quiet ones, you know?'

'Heaven has a spook,' I said. 'And Mab likes his style.'

'And he did you a *favor*!' Bob said brightly. 'You just know that can't be good!'

I put my head down on the table and sighed.

But after that I was able to go upstairs and get some real sleep.

I always like the onion-volcano thing they do at the Japanese steak houses. Me and the other seven-year-olds at the table. I got to catch the shrimp in my mouth, too, when the chef flicked them up into a high arc with his knife. I did so well he hit me with two, one from a knife in either hand, and I got them both, to a round of applause from the table, and a genuine laugh from Anastasia.

We had a delicious meal, and the two of us lingered after everyone else at our little table-grill had left.

'Can I get your take on something?' I asked her.

'Certainly.'

I told her about my experience on the island, and the eerie sense of familiarity that had come with it.

'Oh, that,' Anastasia said. 'Your Sight's coming in. That's all.'

I blinked at her. 'Uh. What?'

'The Sight,' she replied calmly. 'Every wizard develops some measure of precognizance as he matures. It sounds to me as if yours has begun to stir, and has recognized a place that may be of significance to you in the future.'

'This happens to *everyone*?' I said, incredulous.

'To every wizard,' she said, smiling. 'Yes.'

'Then why have I never *heard* about it?' I demanded.

'Because young wizards who are anticipating the arrival of their Sight have an appalling tendency to ignore uncomfortable truths by labeling more appealing fantasies revelations of their

Sight. Everything they care about turns into a prophecy. It's vastly irritating, and the best way to avoid it is to keep it quiet until a young wizard finds out about it for himself.'

I mulled over that idea for a few moments. 'Significant to my future, eh?'

'Potentially,' she replied quietly, nodding. 'One must proceed with extreme caution when acting upon any kind of precognizant information, of course – but in this case, it seems clear that there is more to that island than meets the eye. If it were me, I'd look into it – cautiously.'

'Thank you,' I told her seriously. 'For the advice, I mean.'

'It cost me little enough,' she said, smiling. 'May I get your take on something?'

'Seems only fair.'

'I'm surprised at you, Harry. I always thought that you had an interest in Karrin.'

I shrugged my shoulders. 'Timing, maybe. It's never seemed to be the right time for us.'

'But you do care for her,' she said.

'Of course,' I said. 'She's gone with me into too many bad places for anything else.'

'That,' Anastasia said, her eyes steady, 'I can understand.'

I tilted my head and studied her face. 'Why ask about another woman?'

She smiled. 'I wanted to understand why you were here.'

I leaned over to her, touching her chin lightly with the fingertips of my right hand, and kissed her very gently. She returned it, slowly, savoring the touch of my mouth on hers.

I broke off the kiss several moments after it had become inappropriate for a public venue and said, 'Because it's good for the soul.'

'An excellent answer,' she murmured, her dark eyes huge. 'One that should, perhaps, be further explored.'

I rose and held out her chair for her, and helped her into her coat.

As it turned out, the rest of the night was good for the soul, too.